I0590951

Novichok

A novel by

Terry Stanton

Novichok

All Rights Reserved

Copyright © 2024 Terry Stanton

Reproduction in any manner, in whole or in part,
in English or any other language, or otherwise,
without the written permission of the copyright holder is
prohibited

This is a work of fiction.
All characters portrayed in the book are fictional.
Any resemblance to real persons is purely coincidental.

For information address
tez_stanton@hotmail.com

First Printing 2024

ISBN: 978-0-6459672-9-6

Other works by Terry Stanton

Deliver Me From Evil

No Mayday! No Mayday!

Prologue

London, November 2015

"Enter!" Colin Lacey went straight into the Commander's large, expensively carpeted and furnished office, and sat in one of the gentleman's club style leather armchairs. He had a good idea what was coming. Even so, he was relaxed; casual even. After all, he and the Commander were on very friendly terms, but not so that discipline was prejudiced.

Elbows on his oak desk, fingers in their characteristic resemblance to a church steeple, the Commander began. "You're finished here at SO15, Lacey. I hate to tell you that, but making yourself known to the public is absolutely verboten, just as it was in the old Special Branch."

"This is about the missing plane, SEA439, isn't it, sir?"

"It most certainly is. The press conference made sure every journalist in the country - in fact pretty well every journalist in every country – knows exactly who you are, what you look like, and that you work for us. Half the population knows it too. And of course, so do all the foreign intelligence services."

"So I have no cover left at all. But you knew that; I cleared it with you first."

"Not so. I agree you told me about it beforehand, but did I say 'OK, go ahead'?"

Colin took a moment and a deep breath, adjusting one carefully pressed trouser-leg over the other. "No, you didn't. You said, 'I can see why you want to make the murder of Lynn Gallagher, the deaths of all passengers, and the identity of the perpetrators public.'"

"You helped her TV company broadcast it. You gave them the best possible free advertising with your press conference."

"Sir, you know as well as I do, it was about all we could do. Those murdering CIA bastards - pardon my French - were never going to be arrested, tried, convicted, or anything else."

"Yes, Colin, we discussed that, and I agreed with you." The Commander paused, smoothing his black hair with its parting on the left. "But you really pissed the Prime Minister and – well, the whole bloody Cabinet actually – right off. They want you out of here fast."

"So I'm being fired. No pension. No unfair dismissal. So much for SO15's alleged independence"

The Commander smiled: "Don't jump the gun, Colin. You're too good a cop for that. Everyone knows that - even Number 10. I had a word with the Commissioner of the Met. If you agree, you're to be moved sideways into the CID or counter terrorism and promoted to Detective Chief Inspector from your present rank. More pay, and no loss of anything."

The Commander raised both hands in a suggestion of an offering. "We felt you needed some sort of compensation for being moved compulsorily, and a reward for what you did to get those bastards named, if nothing else."

Lacey nodded. "What will I do there?"

"Not for me to say, but I shouldn't be surprised if you were put in charge of some murder investigation or other. Maybe more sensitive ones, perhaps like the Lynn Gallagher case, but perhaps not. Who knows?" The Commander paused. "So, do you agree, or will you walk the plank?"

It was Colin's turn to smile. "I always wanted to be a detective, so I'm not going along a plank to chuck my career down the drain. Sorry. Mixed metaphor: chuck it down Davy Jones's locker. I accept. When do I go to Scotland Yard?"

"You can clear your desk tonight and tomorrow and go there Monday. I've already spoken to Chapman. I think he'll make a good fist of taking on your cases. Please cooperate with him."

Both men stood. Each being five feet eleven inches tall, they looked each other straight in the eye. The Commander looked like the former Cambridge Blue Rugby player he had been. Lacey's frame was slighter, but very fit. He had a pleasant smiling face, but an expression which announced openly that he could be very dangerous if need be.

"I always cooperate, sir. I may not be much of a team player, but I always cooperate." Lacey hesitated briefly. "May I ask a favour, sir? Peter Shuttleworth worked well with me on the Gallagher case. Is it possible I can take him with me?"

"What rank is he, Colin?"

"Detective Constable."

"Well, if he wishes to accompany you, he may. Is he worth promoting to Sergeant?"

"I believe so, sir."

"Very well. I'll see what we can do."

The Commander held out his hand, and Lacey took it; they shook with genuine friendship. "You know, sir, when I came in, you called me Lacey for the first time for years. I thought: 'Well, I've really blown it this time!'"

"You know me. I'm just too formal too much of the time. I'm sorry you've got to go, Colin. You are one of the best men we've ever had in SO15. Monday fortnight I'll take you to lunch at my Club and you can fill me in on the secret life of the Metropolitan Police."

Chapter 1

West Sussex, Saturday, 23rd April, 2016

Chichester on a beautiful late spring day. Sussex is wonderful from one end to the other. Sprinkled with venerable buildings and historic villages running from East to West either side of the South Downs right through the county, its crowning glory is the ancient and formerly Roman city of Noviomagus, or Chichester as it is now known, though the people of Arundel or Lewes might dispute the crown and the glory. The local residents, planners and the Chichester District Council have resisted all attempts by developers to allow any high-rise buildings to obstruct any view, from any rural direction, of the spire of the Cathedral dominating its surroundings.

Mr Angus Spencer, six foot one, athletic, with dark wavy hair, senior orthopaedic surgeon at St Richard's Hospital, and at the neighbouring private Nuffield Hospital, had no view of the Cathedral as he walked home from the public hospital at 5.20pm. It was hidden from him by the twelve foot high Roman Wall on his left in New Park Road.

Samantha Curtis, fairly badly overweight, and only slightly shorter than Angus, the anaesthetist with whom he often worked, puffed along at his side; both were tired after four tricky operations since 8.00 am. Sam had a longer walk to her house far down West Street than Angus had to his in North Pallant.

"I'll be glad to get home, sit down with a scotch, and then eat the excellent dinner Anne always dishes up."

Sam chuckled. "I'll be glad to get home to the meal Jim'll have prepared for me, to be eaten after a G & T."

Neither Angus nor Sam was troubled by working on an occasional Saturday, even if that were rare for NHS consultants. Dedication to needy patients was their credo.

"You're lucky Jim's a good house-husband, Sam, and so good and patient with the kids. He ...." Angus stopped, took Sam's arm, and pointed at a couple of men sitting, or rather slumped, on a bench at the side of the footpath they were following through the garden lining the street at the side of the old wall. "What do you make of that? What on earth's wrong with them?"

"Blimey! Looks like they're stinking drunk, or far gone on drugs. Maybe even anaesthetised." She stepped closer. "Well, they don't smell of drink. Hang on a mo', though. The older bloke's started twitching."

"That's more than a twitch, Sam. It looks more like a seizure, or epileptic fit. He's going rigid." Angus knelt on his left knee, took the man's wrist, and compared what he found with his watch. "His pulse is very slow and irregular. His breathing is very shallow, laboured, like he's struggling. There's something odd about this. Rings a bell somewhere, but I'm damned if I recognise it. Something I've read sometime." He looked at the younger man on the bench. "His breathing's similar but not quite so strained."

Letting go of the second man's wrist Sam said, "Right. His pulse is slow too."

Spencer looked up, about to ask Sam to phone 999 and call an ambulance. He saw she already had her phone in hand, making the call. When she'd given all necessary details and ended the conversation she said, "There was an ambulance and crew just standing by, so they'll be here in a minute or two."

"Thank God we're only about half a mile from accident and emergency."

Sam smiled: "Didn't know you believed in God, Angus."

An ambulance siren could be heard approaching fast.

"Indeed I do. I have no illusions that I know everything. You know the old joke. 'What's the difference between God and a doctor? God doesn't think he's a doctor!' I guess some of our brethren would think me odd, but I utter a silent prayer for guidance every time I pick up my scalpel or other implement. Seen me through a few near misses."

"Well, you certainly have the best outcomes record for miles around."

At that moment an ambulance ground to a rapid halt at the kerbside, and two paramedics, a short stocky man and a tall, willowy blond woman, leapt out, running across the grass to the bench.

The woman spoke: "Hello, Dr Curtis. Hey, Mr Spencer, didn't expect to see you here."

"No, I didn't mention that when I phoned, did I?" Sam indicated the two men collapsed on the bench.

Jack, the male paramedic asked, "So what we got here? Two drunks, druggies?"

Angus shook his head. "That's what we thought at first, Glen, but then we saw the man was shaking in a most unusual manner, almost having some sort of a seizure. Look at him now. I think they may have been poisoned. Can't tell you what did it, but I think it's very nasty."

By this time the ambulance crew had oxygen masks and bottles on the couple. "Well, no smell of booze, that's for sure." The woman looked up at Sam. "Any idea who they are, Doctor Curtis?"

"Not yet, Gloria. Haven't looked for I.D. Looking at the grey-headed chap, I guess he's about sixty-five? What do you reckon about the other one? Late thirties?"

"Maybe, or early forties. Both nicely dressed, aren't they? There's something a bit foreign looking about the younger bloke's clothes, maybe that one's face too. His suit looks like it cost a packet. Best English tailoring too, I'd say."

By this time the older man was on a stretcher and being carried to the ambulance, and the two crew ran back to repeat the procedure with the younger one. Angus Spencer had been observing the two patients with care as all this was going on. The elder was of medium height and well-built as well as expensively dressed, probably around five foot nine, and as Dr Curtis said, in his sixties. Now he thought about it, the ambulance woman was right; there was something slightly foreign looking about him. Come to think of it, there was a resemblance in the men's faces, but the older fellow's hair was short, white and wavy, whereas the younger man's was dark brown and straight, like an early Beatles cut. He was two or three inches taller, but equally well built.

Gloria got in the back of the ambulance to keep an eye on the patients and administer oxygen if needed. As he mounted the driver's seat Glen turned to Angus. "You two going to follow us back to the hospital, Mr Spencer?"

"What do you think, Sam? You might go back. A good anaesthetist might shed some light on what may have knocked them out, but this isn't a case for a scalpel or orthopaedist. More like a poisons specialist."

Sam asked, "Is there room for me, Glen?"

Reaching across the driver pushed open the passenger door and Sam jumped in as Angus said, "You'd better phone Jim and tell him you'll be late for dinner."

"Good idea." She pulled out her mobile.

Angus shouted as the ambulance pulled away: "I'm going home to do some research. See if I can work out what's bugging me about these two." He broke into a run, glad that he went out jogging two mornings a week and played a bit of tennis most weekends. It wasn't far from where he'd spotted the sick couple to his home in North Pallant.

A few minutes later Angus opened his front door. Anne came out of the kitchen at the end of the hallway. He did what he always did when he got home; threw his arms around her buxom figure, kissed her apple cheeks fondly, and told her he loved her.

"Dinner will be at 6.30."

"Thanks, Anne. I must look something up beforehand," and he told her what he'd seen on the way home. "Trouble is I'm not sure what it is I want to look up, nor where to find it!"

"What was it you said? Something about drugs or poison, and the symptoms these two people were showing reminded you of something you read once, not long ago?"

"That's about it."

Anne twiddled her hair as she usually did when lost in thought. Suddenly she poked him in the chest with her index finger. "What about that book you bought in the Charity Shop a few months ago?"

Angus laughed. "Which Charity Shop?"

"Don't you make fun of me, Angus Spencer. It's not the Charity Shop you're worried about, or have you lost the plot? Wasn't that about drugs and poisons and ..."

"Hey! I do believe you might be right. Where is it, that book?"

"By my side of the bed, darling. I'm still reading it. So far, it's one of the most frightening books I've ever read! And it's not even a horror story."

He was off up the stairs two at a time at once. Picking up the book, he sat down on the bed and leafed through it. It was one of the most terrifying reads he had ever had as well: Robert Harris and Jeremy Paxman's "A Higher Form of Killing." What had been particularly horrifying about it was that his own profession, and so many scientists from other disciplines, had been prepared to work on chemical and biological weapons to cause multiple deaths and dreadful suffering, many with diseases capable of wiping out whole populations or even the human race. The other vile aspect was the lies and deceit practised by all sides of politics in every major country to keep from the public and the voters any knowledge of what these people were up to, allegedly to protect those same people.

Angus found what he was looking for on the first page of Chapter 3; the tale of Dr Gerhard Schrader.

Following the use on both sides in the First World War of poison gases like mustard, phosgene and chlorine chemical weapons, a Convention was held in Geneva in 1925 effectively condemning the use of chemical weapons. It added restraints to the use of bacteriological terrors too. It was signed by all the major parties to WW1 except the USSR, which had not attended.

Curiously this Convention did not stop these weapons but acted as an incentive to their research and development. As one Japanese Army officer apparently expressed it, if these things should be banned, they must be weapons worth having, so almost everyone was making and stockpiling them. That was where Dr Schrader came in. He was a German research chemist. He had been working on a huge variety of organic phosphorous mixtures. Insecticides made of some of these things had been known since the last decades of the 19th century and known to be dangerous to humans since the early decades of the 20th.

He found a new mixture which he used on thousands of a type of lice and killed them all very quickly. He hadn't even used a strong solution. He was astounded by the power of this stuff. Then he found out it wasn't good for him either. If he breathed any of it in, or got a minute splash on his skin he couldn't see properly, couldn't read by a lamp, and couldn't drive home in the dark. More frighteningly, he could hardly breathe.

This discovery or invention was the forerunner of the dreadful gases used by the Nazis in their concentration camps on the multitude of unfortunate Jews and other people they classed as 'undesirable'.

This was what Angus had been unable to put his finger on when he saw the couple on the bench, particularly the way the man was twitching. "It was like the death spasms of someone dying of Zyklon B in a gas chamber," he said out loud to himself. "I've got to tell A & E!" he muttered as he ran back down the stairs.

Anne emerged from the dining room where she was laying the table. "What was that, Angus?"

"I'll tell you later love. I've got to make some calls as soon as possible, or those two people may die. They'll probably die anyway, but at least they may stand a ghost of a chance." He rushed past her to the phone in his study.

****

Sam Curtis was standing beside Mr Aloysius Abbott, one of the Accident and Emergency consultants at St Richards. They were looking at the body of the young man from the bench in New Park Road. The body of the older man had already been thoroughly examined; both were naked and still breathing through oxygen masks.

"At least they're still breathing," Abbott said. "Doubt they've been taking any ordinary drugs. The effect on the breathing and blood pressure makes me think along the lines of Fentanyl. I've given them some antidotes for that, which shouldn't do any harm even if it's something else. Got to keep their blood pressure level and their breathing going – I hope!"

"You sure it's Fentanyl? The opioid that's much stronger than morphine?"

"Most certainly it is. Up to 100 times more powerful; but no, I'm not positive that's what we have here. Properly used medically it's a painkiller, but some idiots use it recreationally. That's mainly in the USA. It killed over 1,700 people with overdoses in 2015. Some mix it with other drugs like heroin. Most of it is made illegally or smuggled in from China. They've no idea what they're doing! I read that it was so worrying even some major drug dealers stopped selling it on the dark web and their other outlets. Despite that some pop singer killed himself doing this last year."

Sam nodded. She knew pop music. "It was Prince. Other musicians've done it too."

Abbott snorted contemptuously. "Suppose it's a matter of opinion whether they're really musicians. Ashkenazy or Perlman for me."

It was Sam's turn to snort, just as dismissively. "They only play all that old violin stuff. Boring!" Sam hesitated, looking around at several nurses scurrying about in a disciplined fashion with drips, stands, and medical supplies. A good bit taller than Abbott, she addressed the top of his balding head. "We're off the point here. What'll you do for these two now?"

"You heard me a minute ago, ordering two beds in ICU to be made ready as soon as possible. I'm going to get them down there immediately where we can attach all the monitors, drips, and anything else we need. I've already taken blood and urine samples and sent them to the path lab for tests. Trouble is this is such a rare drug for an overdose here in the UK. In the US or Canada, they see it a lot. In British Columbia, two people a day on average die of an overdose of it. Just two milligrammes of this stuff is a lethal dose for almost everyone. A proper medical dose is only a hundred microgrammes. It's a class A drug. I'll have to see if I can find any articles about it."

"I can do that. Where's your computer?"

"Thanks. The one on the office desk outside is closer. Use that." He turned and looked at her sharply, speaking with contempt. "And Ashkenazy is a pianist and conductor, not a violinist."

Sam Curtis tossed her brown ponytail and poked her tongue out at him in fun. At that moment, four male ward orderlies came through the door with two trolleys and began to move the patients carefully on to them.

Sam's phone started ringing in her pocket, so she slipped outside the door. "Curtis."

"Sam, this is Angus. Look, what's A & E think is wrong with our couple?"

"Opioid overdose is what Abbott says. Probably Fentanyl. We've also been thinking about an insecticide problem, since it can give similar symptoms to opioids, like pin-prick pupils and twitching, and breathing problems."

"Well, it could be, but I think it's some very nasty organophosphate poisoning. I've been reading up on it a bit. He should be looking at that too. It's those spasm-like twitches. They were too violent. I'm going to ring someone I know. I'll get back to you as soon as I can. Tell Abbott now."

Sam started to speak but Angus had already cut the call. The doors opened again, and the two trolleys started off very fast down the corridor, heading for the lift. Mr Abbott was helping an orderly push a stand with the two oxygen bottles attached to it, keeping them connected to the patients. Sam caught him up.

"That was Angus Spencer. He says to look at organophosphate poisoning."

"Shit!" Swear words from Abbott, such a straight-laced individual, always in a formal suit, collar and tie, were quite shocking. "This just gets worse and worse. If it's not a deadly drug we know little about, it's an even more dangerous chemical we know even less about."

"He's looked it up and is phoning someone. He'll phone again."

"I just hope someone can tell me what the hell to do!"

By now Angus Spencer was on the phone to the Queen's Square Hospital for Nervous Diseases in London.

"Good evening. Norma speaking, Hospital for ..."

"This is Angus Spencer, consultant at St Richard's Chichester. I need to speak to Professor Geoffrey Alleyn at once. We have two patients about to die and I think he can help me."

"Well, it's Saturday, Mr Spencer. I'll see if I can get him at home."

The phone went dead. Then some Vivaldi started up. Drumming his fingers on his desk frantically, he waited no more than ten seconds.

"This is Norma again. I've given the Professor your number and he'll ring you now."

A minute later the phone rang. Spencer picked it up on the first tinkle. "Angus, you old villain? Haven't seen you since medical school. How are you doing?"

"OK, Geoffrey, thanks. Look, this is urgent, as I think we've got two people about to die down here in Chichester.

Found them on a park bench in the city. Out cold. First glance looked like drug overdoses, but then I thought it might be some nerve agent, Zyklon B type of thing. Do you know ...?"

"Christ! That's wicked. I've never come across it. As you know, my field is diseases of the nervous system, not the poisoning of it, but I've read a lot about this sort of thing. The latest version is called Novichok, from Russia. A big businessman and his girlfriend were said to have been murdered with it by another oligarch a few years ago over there. He may not have done it. May have been a KGB-style cover-up. I'll tell you what to do."

"OK. I've got a pen and paper."

"Get on to the Counter-terrorism force in London, and Porton Down. I think Porton may have some of this killer stuff, so they'd be able to help analyse it, and may even know a bit about how to treat it."

"Fine. I'll do that immediately. Before you go, if you've ever got to stay in Chichester, come to me and Anne – my wife – we've got years of talking to do."

Both men rang off. Angus picked up the phone again, dialling. "Sam?"

"Is that you, Angus?"

"Right. Listen. I found what I was looking for. You need to tell Abbott to look for a nerve agent, like the sort the Nazis used in the concentration camps."

"Fuck! Are you sure?"

"Not at all, but if I'm right and we get it wrong they'll be as dead as doornails in no time. What have you done so far?"

"They're intubated because of their breathing problems, and we've administered Naxolone, as we thought it was an opioid overdose."

"If it's a nerve agent I doubt that'll do much good. I've got other calls to make to find out more." He replaced the receiver, and picked it up at once, and dialled.

A voice said "Operator."

"Hello. I want the Counter Terrorism Unit of the police in London. It's life or death."

"That's a restricted number, sir."

"I dare say, but I'm a surgeon with two dying patients on my hands as a result of what may be a terrorist incident. Your job may be on the line. Just get the number and dial it. You don't have to tell me what it is. Just put me through."

"OK, sir, keep your hair on."

Angus heard the phone ringing. As it was answered and before anyone could say a word, he told them who he was, that he might have two Novichok or similar victims down in St Richards, and it was possibly a terrorist incident.

"Thank you, sir. I'll put you through to the senior duty officer, Detective Chief Inspector Lacey."

A pause of thirty seconds. "Lacey speaking."

Angus Spencer repeated what he had told the telephonist. Lacey asked, "Where did you say this was?"

"Chichester. We found them on a park bench in New Park Road."

"Who's 'we'?"

"Me and Sam Curtis. She's an anaesthetist. I'm an orthopaedic surgeon."

"Thank you, Mr Spencer. What makes you think it might be Novichok?"

"The old boy was shaking in a way that made me think it wasn't drugs. He was getting really stiffened up, as though he was cramped all over. I thought he might be going into a paralytic seizure, so I looked up nerve agents in a book at home, and then I phoned Professor Geoff Alleyn at ..."

"I know who he is. What did he say?"

"He put me on to the idea of Novichok. I'd never heard of it. He told me to phone your office, and also to get onto Porton Down as they know all about this poison."

"Good thinking." Lacey dictated the Porton number, then he asked, "Any idea who these people are?"

"Never gave it a thought, except Sam and I thought they might be foreign. Some ID may have been found by the hospital by now."

"I want you to contact the Chichester nick and get them to send some people to meet you by that bench at once. It has to be isolated. If it's got any of that stuff on it, it could kill you and other people. Don't touch it and don't let anyone else do so. Then phone Porton and tell them what you told me. I'm going to get a Police Helicopter and fly down now. I'll go straight to the hospital. Thanks for the call."

"There's a landing pad right by the A & E entrance." They rang off.

Angus phoned Chichester Police. He knew the number by heart. He asked the clerk who answered to be put through to the senior duty officer, who turned out to be the Station Sergeant he knew well from the tennis club.

"Hello, Angus," said the Sergeant. "What's up?"

Angus repeated all he'd said to Lacey, told him about that call too, and what Lacey had said, and that he had to call Porton Down.

Having listened in somewhat stunned silence, Sergeant Davies said, "Bloody hell. Don't recall anything like that here before. I'll get a posse down there straight away. I think one of our blokes has been on training for this sort of thing. They'll need protective suits, boots, masks, gloves, all that, won't they?"

"I'd say so, Sean. From what I've read you can be killed by a drop of these nerve agents on the skin."

"I'd better get a couple of officers up to the hospital. Once the news gets out, you'll have all sorts turning up, and the press won't leave you lot alone. In any other nick, I'd be afraid someone'll get fifty quid or more for phoning the media."

"Good, but you'd better tell your lot that SO15 and Counter Terrorism are already involved, this may be top secret, and any leaks will cost them their job and pension and going to clink for years. That's not all. If someone tried to kill these men, they may have another go when they learn where they are. I'm at home. I've got to get back to New Park Road to meet your officers and show them which bench it is."

"You stay right where you are Angus. I'll send a fast driver to North Pallant to pick you up; get you there sooner that way. The rest must get their protective gear on. They'll be a few more minutes. I'll get a couple of uniforms to go there straight away to keep the public away from the bench."

As the phones went down Angus hung out of the study door. "Anne, I'll have to skip dinner, I'm afraid. Got to go out. This thing is worse than I thought."

Anne came out of the kitchen quickly, rushed up to Angus, kissed him on the forehead. He was looking at the phone and clicking the numbers already, and said, "OK, darling" she said. "See you later. Tell me all about it when you get back." She returned to the kitchen, looking at him over her shoulder as she went.

"Hello is that Porton Down? No, I don't have a password. Just listen, will you? I've just finished speaking to Detective Chief Inspector Lacey at the Counter Terrorism Unit. He told me to phone you. Look, don't interrupt again, OK? He and I think there may have been a terrorist attack in Chichester with a nerve agent called Novichok. I think two people are about to die..... That's better. Yes, put me through as fast as you can."

There were a couple of clicks on the line and a very authoritative voice said, "Desmond Horne-Bassett here. What's all this about Novichok? I didn't wait to be told the rest, so please fill me in as quickly as you can. You know this stuff is deadly?"

"Too right. That's why I'm phoning you. Detective Chief Inspector Lacey of Counter Terrorism told me to phone you; he's getting a helicopter to Chichester as we speak." Angus Spencer then told Horne-Bassett all he knew about the incident. As he was doing so a Police siren was right outside the front door. Angus apologised, and said he had to go, and gave him Sam Curtis's number.

Horne-Bassett announced he'd helicopter a specialist doctor down at once, and advised that anyone dealing with the patients at the hospital must wear safety clothing. Angus thanked him and rushed out, shouting goodbye to Anne as he went.

As soon as he was in the passenger seat the car shot a few yards towards East Street, reversed fast into the short turning on the other side almost opposite the Spencer's house, and roared off through the Pallants on the way to the park bench.

****

While that was going on, Sam Curtis went back into the ICU to tell Abbott there was no point in researching Fentanyl. Her phone rang again. "It's Angus. Listen, this Novichok stuff's so bloody dangerous you, Abbot, everybody, has to wear safety gear, head to foot."

She immediately ordered up the suits, masks, footwear, and breathing equipment from the stores, and she, Abbott, and the two nurses helping them, put them on.

****

Ten minutes later Angus watched as a team of Police Officers, clad in all sorts of safety gear from thick, virtually untearable polythene suits with hoods pulled up over face masks, to rubber boots fastened tightly round the calves over the suit legs, and polythene gloves, covered the park bench with polythene sheeting and a kind of small green tent. The face masks had breathing equipment attached. Two other uniformed officers were hammering metal stakes into the turf surmounted by notices in bright red with yellow backgrounds: "Do not touch this seat: Danger of Death." A third was erecting a similar coloured poster announcing: "If

You Have SAT ON or TOUCHED THIS BENCH in the last two hours go to Accident and Emergency immediately."

Spencer took out his phone and made another call to Dr Curtis: "Is that you, Sam? Angus here. Detective Chief Inspector Lacey from Counter Terrorism is on his way by helicopter. I'm also expecting some help from Porton Down. Their expert should be able to advise on the treatment and will tell us whether it really is a nerve agent. It's probably something deadly called Novichok."

Sam Curtis gasped: "Blimey, Angus, you've been a busy boy!"

"We don't want these two dying on us, do we? By the way, found out who they are yet?"

"Not yet. They're still not talking. You don't when you're in a coma."

"Well, get someone to turn their pockets out; look in their man-bags if they've got them. But they must use surgical gloves. What's Abbott doing with them now?"

"They're in an ICU room. We're ventilating them. The major risk, if it's Fentanyl or some other opioid, is they'll stop breathing. As you know, both of them have had a tracheotomy, and have been intubated. Even if Fentanyl isn't the problem, keeping them breathing won't do any harm. We've given them doses of Naxolone like I told you, but it doesn't seem to be doing much good, if any."

"Probably won't if it's a nerve agent like Novichok. Check out what treatment for that may be. I'm going to go home again, grab some dinner, and look it up myself. With a bit of luck, someone from Porton will be with you soon."

He ended the call, He noticed a reporter from the Chichester Observer whom he knew slightly walking up to the roped-off area, and taking photos from different angles. As he turned to leave, he heard the reporter thank a male by-stander for giving him the nod, and pass him what looked like a bank-note.

The man replied: "They'll all be here soon. I let the nationals know too."

Angus thought: '*I bet Lacey will just love that! Good job Sean's sending some bobbies up to the hospital.*'

Sam's phone rang again as soon as Angus ended the call. "Sam Curtis."

"Dr Curtis, this is Captain Jordan from Porton Down. I shall be in a helicopter on the way to you in a minute or so. You have two patients who may have Novichok poisoning, I understand."

"Right. We're keeping them breathing with intubation. We thought it was opioid poisoning, but I've just been told it's possibly this Novichok stuff. I'd never heard of it."

"You wouldn't. It's almost a secret unless you're into CBRN."

"Never heard of that either."

"Chemical Biological Radiation and Nuclear Weapons training. Look, no time to waste. Do you have Atropine there?"

Sam thought a moment: "Yes."

"The other thing you need is Pralidoxime. What about that?"

"I doubt it; never heard of it."

"OK. Give them doses of Atropine. I'll bring some of the other stuff with me. These are the main treatment agents." There was a pause. "Oh yes; I was told the man was twitching badly. That may be a precursor to convulsions.

Give them both some diazepam; should head that off. I'll be with you in an hour, maybe less. And if you're not wearing safety gear, you should be."

The Army Officer rang off before Sam could respond. Immediately she told Aloysius Abbott what Jordan had said, and then phoned down to the chemists' dispensary for some Atropine and diazepam to be sent up at once. The pharmacist confirmed they had no Pralidoxime; he hadn't heard of it either.

Forty-five minutes later Abbott said, "I can hear a helicopter; it's landing."

Five minutes after that a tall, slim, athletic man, with thick sandy hair and a very well-cut blue chalk stripe suit, knocked at the door of the ICU. He was accompanied by a shorter, younger man in a brown tweed sports jacket and smartly creased grey trousers, yellow shirt and green tie. Abbott came out to speak to the older man: "And you are?"

Holding out his warrant card, the man said, "Lacey. Detective Chief Inspector, Counter Terrorism." He indicated the man in the sports jacket. "And this is Detective Constable Shuttleworth. I gather you may have a Novichok incident on your hands. That sort of thing is usually terrorist related. That's why I'm here."

"Well, you can't go in there. The ICU has to be uncontaminated as far as possible. You couldn't talk to the victims anyway. They're completely unconscious, and likely to be so for days."

At that point a helicopter could be heard taking off. Almost at once another could be heard landing. Abbott said, "That could be a chap from Porton Down. We need help. I've never dealt with this before. Nor has Dr Curtis, who's working in there with me and a couple of nurses." He paused: "I'm Dr Abbott, by the way; Aloysius Abbott. Better not shake hands. These surgical gloves could have the poison on."

Lacey nodded: "You'd better get in there at once and get some safety stuff sent up for me and Shuttleworth here, and we'll put it on straight away."

Abbott turned and went through the door back into the ICU. As the door closed a very fit looking mid-thirties brown-haired woman in an Army Officer's uniform walked into the corridor carrying a complete outfit of protective clothing, accompanied by a nurse, who said, "This is the ICU, Captain. This is Detective Chief Inspector Lacey. I brought him up here a few minutes ago."

Extending his right hand to grasp the Captain's, Lacey introduced himself and Shuttleworth; Jodie Jordan did the same. She was about four inches shorter than he was, and about the same height as the constable. Turning to the nurse, and gesturing with the safety clothing, Jordan said, "I need to get this lot on."

"Use that office over there, ma'am, unless you'd rather go to the cloakroom."

"No. I need to be quick." With that she crossed the corridor as the nurse opened the door of the office for her. "Who's the doctor in the ICU?"

"Dr Abbott and Doctor Sam Curtis. He's an A&E consultant, and she's an anaesthetist."

"OK. Get one of them to come in here and tell me what's been going on." The nurse went into the office first and picked up the phone. She asked Dr Curtis to come into the office.

Lacey spoke up. "Can we join you to hear what's said?"

"Certainly, but don't ask any questions. I need to get this straight as fast as possible." Lacey admired her no-nonsense demeanour, which was rather like his own, but he hoped he was not as curt. He and Shuttleworth followed her into the office.

The nurse went out and as she did a male orderly with a pile of personal protective clothing arrived. Captain Jordan told him to put it in the office, and as the man left, Sam came out of the ICU in her safety suit and entered the room. Lacey, Shuttleworth and Jordan were dressing in their own safety outfits whilst Jordan questioned Sam Curtis.

"What's been going on?"

"They were found on a park bench near here. I was one of the people who found them. I was with Angus Spencer. He's an orthopod. At first, we thought it was an opioid overdose, but Angus was suspicious, so he went home to do some research. Going on opioid poisoning we'd intubated each patient with a tracheotomy and gave them Naxolone. It seems to be having no effect at all."

Jordan nodded and smiled understandingly. "Then what's making them ill is not an opiate."

"After that Angus phoned and said he thought it was a nerve agent. Then we were told it might be Novichok. We gave them some Atropine, like you told me, and we've been waiting for you to bring the other stuff."

"Pralidoxime. It's in my case. OK. I'd better get in there and give the victims some."

Full of questions he could not ask, Lacey asked just one. "Dr Curtis, did you find any ID on the victims?"

"Yes, we did." She reached into the pocket of the white coat she'd discarded and produced a driving licence and passport. Captain Jordan checked Lacey had donned the suit and surgical gloves before taking up the articles Sam Curtis was holding out to him. She held them until he had the gloves on. Handing them to Lacey with a set of keys, Sam said, "These may be their door keys. I found them in the old chap's pocket." She and Jordan left the room. Lacey looked at the documents. To say he got a shock put it mildly.

Chapter 2

Russia, 1999

Igor Vasilyevich Schaplinov was given to
contemplating his life and family history. He wanted to do
something very important to him, which arose out of that
personal background. He was born in 1970 in a small village
near Belokurikha in Southern Siberia. He was the
illegitimate son of an officer high in the Army Corps of the
USSR, a brigadier general. He did not bear his father's
surname, which was Gordanov: Oleg Petrovich Gordanov.
His mother gave Igor her own father's name, but the general
was proud he had a son. He was unmarried and had no other
offspring, and visited the girl who had for a time been his
mistress - one of many - quite often, and continued to make
love to her when he did so. She had not fallen out of love for
this tall, fit gentleman with the short military cut to his
brown hair, distinguished grey around his ears, who treated
her so politely. Besides, such a significant and well-
remunerated man of influence more or less guaranteed her
and Igor a comfortable existence.

The father was forty when Igor drew his first breath. His
mother was twenty. She met Oleg when he was in

Belokurikha for a vacation, the town being a holiday resort in summer and a skiing area in winter. Irina Schaplinova was a bright and beautiful girl, but had not had a terribly good education. She worked as a waitress in one of the better restaurants. It was there that her thick straight black hair, shapely figure, and striking blue eyes in a face that had much of the Asiatic about it, attracted the army officer's attention. He studied her frankly and openly, but without prurient interest, as she took his order, and watched her walk away to the kitchens.

When she returned with his first course, a caviar dish, Oleg spoke: "You have an intriguing face, with Asiatic or Oriental shaped eyes which are blue, where normally they would be brown. Is one of your parents Russian and the other from Mongolia or the Chitinskaya Oblast, or around Chita?"

Irina was blushing furiously. "I do not know, comrade. I have no idea about those places. I've never heard of them."

"Please sit. Stay and talk."

Irina looked round with a terrified expression. "I must not. The Head Waiter or the manager would be furious. We are not allowed to socialise with the customers." She rushed away. Oleg could have spoken to the manager; his standing as a senior officer in uniform always overcame any problem with the rules of a restaurant, or almost any other place. Still, he was too taken with this girl to risk getting her into any trouble. He did not want his rank to influence her attitude towards him. He made no other attempt at conversation, but spoke his thanks politely each time she returned with another course, or poured more wine. When she brought his bill, he gave her a good but not excessive tip.

Strolling back to his hotel, one of the best in Belokurikha, he speculated that the blue eyes were probably a genetic throwback to the Rus Vikings who had invaded what is now known as Ukraine and the west of what became Russia, giving it their name. They were very tough, violent men, heavily armed, with red hair and blue eyes. They needed to be tough to repel the native population which dared to oppose them. As traders and adventurers, they travelled and spread across the land in smaller versions of the sea-going long-ships with which they had sailed to the British Isles, Western Europe and the Mediterranean, and east from Scandinavia along the Baltic, dropping down the Oder, the Neva, the Dnieper, and the other great rivers of the region. A crew could carry their small boat from one river to another because they were lighter than the larger versions.

A few days later he went to the restaurant again, having reserved the same table as it was clearly in the part of the restaurant under the young woman Irina's care. He was dressed in a very good pale grey suit he had bought off the peg at Harrods on one of his assignments in England, with a crisp white shirt and a subdued red tie with small white spots. He wanted to create a more relaxed but nevertheless impressive appearance.

Irina smiled as she approached his table, and blushed again. Oleg smiled back, and asked how she was before placing his order.

She stammered her reply. "Well, thank you."

Having placed his order, he said, "I must apologise for speaking to you as I did last week. It was ill-mannered."

Irina shook her head. "No sir. I was taken aback. No-one as important as you has ever shown any interest in me before. I was tongue tied. I'm sorry."

Oleg almost laughed at her charming naivety. He had had many attractive women, but none like this young woman. He was pierced by her innocence. At the end of his meal, he asked her to let him take her to lunch on her day off. He was delighted when she agreed. Two days after that he took her to dinner elsewhere, and she went back to his hotel with him. The following year, after two more holidays in Belokurikha, and many more walks together back to his hotel, Irina was pregnant with Oleg's only child. She was terrified at the idea of telling Oleg this. Would he abandon her, or tell her to get an abortion, or refuse to help or support her or the baby? He did none of those things. He was kind, gentle, and did all he could to help her.

Oleg Gordanov moved the mother and child to a flat in the much bigger town of Barnaul before the child was born. Once Igor entered the world, Oleg made sure the boy had a good education. Discreetly he called in favours which got the boy into a Russian Chemical and Biological Weapons research establishment when he had graduated well in Maths and Chemistry and gained a highly valued Chemistry PhD from the University in Novosibirsk at 22 years of age. During research for his PhD thesis, Igor had the opportunity to visit the Moscow Institute of Physics and Technology (known as Phystech) and MICP, or Moscow Institute of Chemical Physics.

Phystech is and was located in the Dolgoprudny suburb of northern Moscow, and the MICP in the town of Chernogolovsk, thirty or so miles from Red Square. Igor found the visit very inspiring when he learned that the college was more or less founded in 1956 by another chemist, Nobel Prize Winner Nikolai Semyonov. Much of Semyonov's success in establishing this faculty was due to his ability to impress both Joseph Stalin, and his replacement, Nikita Khrushchev, and stay on his good side. Igor Schaplinov's visits to Moscow, despite its magnificent Tsarist architecture and its huge and unbeatable cultural environment, convinced him he would not want to live there. He wanted a quieter existence.

In 1988, Oleg Gordanov moved Irina from Barnaul to a spacious well-furnished apartment in Novosibirsk when Igor went to study there. She found a good job in another restaurant and after a year or two became the head waitress, in charge of a dozen waiters of both sexes. It was a good restaurant, some said the best in the city, which was the third largest in the Asian part of Russia. Because many high government and Army personnel ate there, its menu was as gourmet as could be found anywhere in the USSR.

No-one who was likely to say anything detrimental of an officer of Oleg's rank was involved in these moves, and none knew the details. So far as anyone else was concerned Oleg was trying to help the orphaned son of a fellow soldier killed in action in Afghanistan. No-one at the University or the Chemical and Biological Weapons place had any idea whose son Igor really was. His excellent qualifications would probably have got him the job in any case.

At school Igor had studied English conscientiously and had continued with it in addition to chemistry at Novosibirsk University. There he became friendly with an English chemistry lecturer, Simon Grant, who spoke excellent

Russian, and was on an exchange programme from Southampton University. Simon was from an aristocratic family, and had been to Harrow and Cambridge, with an accent to match. Occasionally the pair went for a drink or to the cinema together, sometimes speaking English, sometimes Russian.

One evening, over a drink in a bar, Igor asked the somewhat older, dark haired, bearded Simon: "Could you teach me to talk with a proper English accent, do you think?"

The lecturer's amusement showed: "You'd like to talk like me, then?"

"Yes, that is what I mean."

For the rest of his time in Russia, Simon gave him elocution lessons. In return Igor helped Simon with Russian grammar and colloquial speech. By the end of Simon's stay in Novosibirsk, Igor spoke English pretty much like a toff himself. Simon joked that if he got fed up with doing science in Russia he could get a job at the BBC, certainly on the World Service, where his Russian and perfect English would be invaluable.

There were a few English exchange students too, and Igor found their company amenable. He went on an exchange himself, to Cambridge, where he stayed at weekends and during the vacations with the family of a former Repton pupil, Alan Carpenter, also studying chemistry. Alan, who was a county team cricketer, tall, slim, with fair hair in a long public school cut, came back to his mother's home in Novosibirsk. Igor realized that Simon and Alan had the same sort of accent. It was called 'upper class', and he now understood what Simon had meant by a job at the BBC. Igor also felt rather conscious, if not exactly embarrassed, by the difference between the modesty of his mother's two-bedroom flat, which formerly he had thought magnificent, where he and Alan had to share his bedroom, and the luxury of the Carpenter's extensive accommodation, five bedrooms and three bathrooms, at Alan's father's mid-nineteenth century rectory. Despite that, he was soon put at his ease by the family, who were extremely amicable, and admired his faultless English. He revelled in the walks around the country surrounding the house in Long Buckby, Northants. Alan borrowed his father's Triumph Stag and took Igor to Great Brington and Althorp, home of the Spencers, to Castle Ashby, and Naseby Field, site of the battle which brought Cromwell to fame and set Charles 1st on the road to the block.

Igor began to recognise regional accents from London, Sheffield, Manchester, and elsewhere. In Novosibirsk he dated a couple of English girls, too, and one from Canada. With the English girls he was just a friend, but he found the Canadian extremely sexy and attractive. The feeling was mutual. Igor was not widely sexually experienced. He'd had a few encounters with local girls around Barnaul, but they were brief and the love-making unskilful. He learned little.

The Canadian, Caroline Trondsen, was different. She knew it all and took great pleasure in teaching him. She was in turn excited by his rapid adoption of the techniques, and the embellishments he invented for himself. By the time he left University it would have taken Professor Henry Higgins to detect he wasn't English; he knew a lot of colloquial expressions and habits of speech, including the Canadian ones Caroline had taught him in bed. Perhaps only Mae West or Mata Hari could have taught him more about sex.

By now Igor was beginning to look much like his father: tall, fit, with a military bearing, and his thick dark hair cut in a similar military style. Admiring Oleg greatly, he wanted to emulate him as far as possible.

He found the work at the Weapons establishment exciting because of the science, and rather disgusting because of its purpose. What really drove home the abominable nature of his work was something he learned during a training session about previous experiments. One of the departmental managers, a man in his late fifties, told the staff: "In 1979 some of my predecessors were experimenting with anthrax, using it on a herd of a few hundred or so reindeer. There was an accidental dispersal of the spores of the disease to some neighbouring villages in an area of Siberia near Sverdlovsk. Almost a hundred villagers had contracted the disease, and more than sixty of them died."

A woman sitting near Igor asked, "Were the villagers told what happened?"

"Of course not! Naturally, they were told something else, since the true source of the outbreak was top secret, but it was leaked in 1993. Some of you may then have seen it in Samizdat newspapers."

Igor had no recollection of having heard about it at all. Once he knew of it, he would have found some excuse to leave for another job, had that been easy to do. However, in Russia, when he had been engaged in such a secret enterprise, it was almost impossible to quit, let alone find other employment. He thought about it a lot, but could not make a decision.

Three years later he was saved from making the effort to do this. At lunch one day in 1996 in the restaurant at the weapons facility he mentioned the worry about the work extremely vaguely and cautiously to a senior, middle-aged colleague, Basil Klavinov. More positively he related the anthrax episode.

"You don't need to worry about that sort of thing," the man responded. "Everyone's doing it. D'you know, in the Great Patriotic War - World War 1 - the British military evacuated a small island, called Guinard I think, off the coast of Scotland, tethered six hundred sheep on it, and blasted them with anthrax from some small explosive devices. Naturally, or should I say unnaturally, they all died pretty quickly. Then the scientists dynamited an area to bury the corpses of the sheep near a beach. By extreme bad luck, one of these deadly animals was exhumed by a very high tide, and carried out into the channel between the island and the mainland, and washed ashore. Some of the spores spread to the local village and about 60 people were very ill and one or two may have died."

"How do you know this?"

His grey-haired companion tapped the side of his rather large nose with a straight index finger. "Trust me. The British government never told the truth about it. Russia has secret spy networks everywhere. So do all the other major countries. Very few things are completely secret. People sell information for money, for sex, for drugs. Some even do it out of high principles. At least that's what we say if they are giving the facts to us. If they're giving our secrets to other nations they're just traitors; filthy, despicable traitors."

Klavinov looked casually around the room and whispered: "This sort of thing is just international hypocrisy."

"So one country's traitor is another country's hero." Igor looked down at his plate, and then back at his companion. "Anyway, how do you know about that?"

"Like I said, trust me. I have many sources."

"Fine. I trust you. If you trust me, tell me: how do you 'have many sources'"?

"It's not difficult if you marry the daughter of a senior KGB official."

That took Igor's breath away. Had he gone too far, talking to this man about his worries about the kind of work they were doing? He did his utmost to control his facial expression. As far as he could tell Basil had noticed nothing unusual. Mind racing, he decided to change the subject.

"What about that island? Gurnard, did you call it?"

"Guinard. It was fenced off, declared a danger zone, notices all over it warning the public to stay away. All that happened in about 1917. As far as I know it is still a prohibited place, over seventy years later. Always will be unless the British remove or decontaminate the soil somehow. Mind you, we've done something similar ourselves, but we don't use sheep."

"You're kidding me!"

Basil Klavinov smiled, shook his head, and said, "There's an island called Vozrozhdeniya in the Aral Sea. We tie monkeys to stakes driven into the ground and fire any chemical or biological weapon we need to test into the air above the creatures so the fall-out drops all over them. Then we keep them under observation and record the results."

Loyalty to Russia and this conversation convinced Igor he should stay where he was. If the enemy did these awful things too, what difference did it make if he was a part of it? He decided the CBRN establishment where he now worked near Pochep in the Bryanskaya Oblast was not such a bad place after all. It was only four hundred kilometres from Moscow, on a main road and a direct railway line. He liked to go to the ballet, the opera, and classical music concerts. The architecture of some of the older buildings in Pochep impressed him, but not the utilitarian monstrosities built under Stalin and since. Sometimes he went with Basil Klavinov to see the town, and they discussed the architecture. They found their tastes were very similar.

When they visited the town's white Resurrection Church, Igor told Basil: "I'm not sure I believe in God, or a god, but I can't help loving the appearance of this. Do you like it??"

"Yes, I do. The fenestrated dome topped off by what looks like a small sugar shaker, and its soaring tower at the other end are really striking. I even attend services here on rare occasions."

Igor stared at his friend. "Well, that's a surprise. I have too. I find the calm atmosphere reassuring, and the chanting of the priests and congregation hypnotic."

"Right. Must be something to do with it being a two hundred and seventy-five year old building. The music's even older, of course."

Another time they toured a very striking old monastery, covered in pink plaster, with a dome and tower similar to those of the Church.

During visits to the municipal library Igor learned that for just over two years of the Second World War, from August 1941, Pochep was occupied by the Wehrmacht. According to the Soviet records he found there, 1,875 Jewish men, women, and children were murdered during the Holocaust. Most of them were shot by the Germans in a massacre in March 1942. He also saw a collection of photographs of the fighting which went on in and around the town as the Werhmacht invaded it, and again when they were forced to abandon it.

The drawback of Pochep was being over one thousand kilometres from his mother. Igor could not afford to move her there from Novosibirsk. He could not rely on his father to do it either; Oleg Gordanov had been executed for treason at the Lefortovo prison the year before the conversation with Basil. Whether he believed in God or not, Igor could not help thanking Him that no-one in Pochep knew whose son he was. A traitor's offspring would not keep a job in a defence establishment and might be singled out for extreme measures.

That thought brought him back to where his thinking started. He wanted to avenge his father. The problem was how to accomplish it.

Chapter 3

Chichester, 23rd April, 2016

Colin Lacey was finding it hard to believe what he was looking at. He showed the documents to Shuttleworth.

He was tired of calling the men in comas 'the older and the younger man'. He now thought of them as Boris for the old one and Yevgeny for the young one. The driving licence for Boris Mamontov was a standard photo version from the DVLA in Cardiff. The name was Russian, by the look of it. The passport, which had the younger man's photo, was also Russian; he was Yevgeny Pedchenko. Some family connection? There seemed to be some facial resemblance. Maybe he was a friend visiting from Russia? Yevgeny had clearly arrived at Heathrow a couple of years ago. Colin's normally nimble mind was paralysed by the implications of the documents. It took a few moments for the fog to clear.

When added to the use of Novichok, the fact that these people were Russian made it more likely that terrorism, or even a political assassination attempt, had occurred. He knew that years ago, a couple of citizens of Iron Curtain countries had been assassinated by the KGB in countries outside the Soviet Bloc. One of them was murdered in

England, on Waterloo Bridge when he'd been pricked in the leg by a poisoned umbrella.

More recently another Russian had been killed with an injection of polonium by Russian agents, dying a horrid lingering death, and that was since glasnost. There was something familiar about the names of these victims, or one of them anyway. Lacey could not place it; he'd have to look it up or make enquiries. He turned to Peter Shuttleworth and pointed at the driving licence. "Get onto Carl Boyce. Tell him to do a search and find out as much as he can about these fellows."

The constable nodded and called the office on his mobile. "Listen, Carl, the guv'nor wants you to get on the internet and go down to archives and find out all you can about a couple of Russians called Boris Mamontov and Yevgeny Pedchenko." He spelt out the names, continuing in his South London accent. "They may be related, the guv' thinks. See if Boris has a son or nephew called Yevgeny, and dig out everythin' on 'im too, if there is anythin'. Email it all to me as fast as you can."

As he was doing this the door opened and Abbott walked in wearing only his shirt and trousers. He was rather put out. "I've just been made to shed my clothes and have a shower. I've been told there's some safety suit I'm supposed to put on in here. Is that alright with you?"

"Indeed. Can I ask you some questions while you're getting ready?"

"Fire away."

"Thanks. How are the victims?"

"Not good, I fear. They have had tubes stuck into their windpipes so they can be 'pumped' for want of a better non-technical expression, with oxygen. The nerve agent sort of paralyses all the muscles because it stops certain enzymes from doing their job. There's one sort which fires electrical impulses across the joints – or synapses – of the nervous system to make muscles do things, and there's another which stops the impulses when the muscle is doing as it was told by the first one."

"Why do these impulses have to be stopped?"

Abbott gave a strange mysterious smile. "Because if the first lot of impulses continue, the muscles contract more and more strongly and the victim goes into a paralytic sort of seizure. They can even break bones, it can be so violent. What Novichok does, apparently, is to stop the second enzyme from halting the impulses from the first one. If the dose is direct and strong enough death can result in minutes. The lungs won't work because the diaphragm and other muscles controlling breathing cease to work. You've heard of Zyklon B in the Holocaust gas chambers?" Colin Lacey nodded. "Well, Novichok does the same job but is more powerful. That soldier, Captain Jordan, was just explaining it to me, but she used more jargon."

Lacey laughed. "Well, I thank you for sparing me!" He paused. "Next question, if you don't mind."

"Not at all, I'm still struggling into this bloody plastic suit as you can see. Never done this before. Still, it's for my own good, I daresay. Jordan says one can get very ill from touching these people or inhaling vapour from what hit them."

Lacey took Vladimir's driving licence from Shuttleworth and glanced at it again. He asked Abbott, "Do you know where Alexandra Road might be?"

"Certainly. It's on the other side of Spitalfield Lane; that's the road that runs in front of this hospital. You've heard these two were found on a park bench?"

"Yes. In New Park Road, wasn't it?"

"Right. Well opposite the bench there's a terrace of – oh, I don't know – late Victorian or Edwardian houses. At the end of that there's a big field. Used for football, I think. Marvellous horse-chestnut trees, if you play conkers. Alexandra Road is on the other side of that."

"Peter, we must go. Let's get these togs off." Handing the licence back to his constable, Lacey told him to put them in an evidence bag. Then they both stripped off the safety outfits.

Lacey made for the door, addressing Abbott simultaneously. "I've got to go." Then he spoke to the constable. "The address on the licence, that's where the old man lived - he's Boris, and the other one - Yevgeny - was probably staying with him. The house will have to be cordoned off and inspected. It may be the crime scene. Come on." And they went.

The Police driver was waiting for them.

"Take us to the bench in New Park Road, then Alexandra Road."

"Yes sir. But from the bench you can run across the park quicker than I can get you there."

"I shan't be getting out. I just want to give the team isolating the bench an order. Get a move on."

The Police car roared away. It screeched up to the bench where the victims were found. Lacey was considerably put out to see a TV van already there, and several reporters who were shouting questions at the police. Lacey wound down his window and shouted for the leader of the team, "Who's in charge?" An officer in a space suit approached as Lacey said, "The crime scene may be over there – Alexandra Road. I need someone fully kitted out in safety gear over there at once."

"OK sir, but he can't come with you. Can't risk his clothing having been contaminated working on this bench. He – well, it might be a she – might come into contact with you."

"Fine. We'll be waiting outside the house. I've got the keys. Get them there as fast as possible, please." Lacey's manner was invariably polite, but there was something about him that meant disobedience was not an option.

Just minutes later, another Police vehicle drew up behind Lacey's outside the stuccoed cottage, painted yellow with a burgundy-coloured door. An officer got out, withdrew a set of protective clothing with mask and breathing apparatus from the back seat, and came to Lacey's passenger window.

"I'll just get into this lot, sir. Then I'll go in. I was told this may be the crime scene for the two in hospital."

"Yes. I want you to look for any sign they may have been poisoned here. If you find anything let me know at once. Have you done this before?"

"Not exactly this, but I was in the Army before the Police, and I went on a CBRN course. I should be OK."

"Great. Let's hope so. Get your kit on, and then I'll give you the keys. What's your name, sergeant?"

"Hopkins, sir."

Shortly, Hopkins in his space suit went into the terraced cottage. He seemed to be gone an age, but when he emerged

Lacey saw from the car clock that he'd only been gone twenty-five minutes. He spoke through the car window again. "Find anything?"

Hopkins kept his distance. "Nothing obvious, sir. No bottle with Novichok labels on. Looks like they had a hand delivered package recently; maybe it came today."

"What makes you think it was hand-delivered?"

"No address on it, sir, and no stamps. It was an A4 sized envelope, with a name in Russian on the outside, and it looks like it had had a newspaper inside it. I couldn't make anything out of it; it was all in Russian. Nothing else. It was spread out on the kitchen table with the envelope. I didn't touch it. Left it for Scene of Crime."

"Right. We'll have to get them in there fast. They'll need to be kitted out, too. Not just the stuff they usually wear to prevent contaminating the scene."

"Spot on, sir. We don't know how much of this stuff the victims handled. Anyone touching anything which had a good smothering of a strong nerve agent on it could be dead pretty quick. Might be best to get the Army in. Shall I keep the keys?"

"Do that. And phone the station and get SOCO to join you immediately. I'll get back to the hospital. I can contact the Army from there. Lacey turned to his driver. "You heard that? Back to the hospital."

A couple of minutes later as the car turned right out of Victoria Road into Spitalfield Road, lights flashing and siren blaring, Lacey asked the driver: "Are there CCTV cameras in New Park Road, constable?"

"I believe so, sir. When I've dropped you off, shall I get the recordings for you?"

"Exactly."

****

Lacey went straight to the ICU, was pleased to see a police officer outside, and another near the lift and stairs. He asked a nurse to get Captain Jordan to come out and talk to him. After a short wait she emerged. "What can I do for you, Inspector?"

"Sorry to drag you away. Dr Curtis gave me the keys to the victims' house. It's possibly the crime scene where they were poisoned. There's a suspicious package, and there may be other things. I've got to get scene of crime officers in there. They'll need safety gear, of course, but the cop who went in just now has been in the Army and on CBRN training. He thinks SOCO - scene of crime officers - should have some army people with them."

Jordan agreed. "It'll be better if I ask for them to be sent here. Leave that to me. I'll get onto it."

"Thank you, Captain. Look, this might not be strictly relevant to my investigation, but I'd like to understand a bit more of what you are doing for these two people. Could you spare a few minutes to go through that with me?"

"Certainly, but let me phone for some Army back-up first." Jordan smiled. "I need to get something to eat soon. Give me your mobile number and I'll call you when I head off to the canteen or wherever."

They exchanged numbers, and the Captain went back into ICU, having told Lacey there was no change in the Russians' condition, and made her phone call to the Army. The patients were still in a coma, and would have to be kept that way for a few days at least, especially the older man, as he seemed to be the worst affected.

Colin Lacey then phoned Chichester Police to find out what progress they were making. He was put through to Sergeant Sean Davies, who told him he'd taken the first call about the incident from Angus Spencer, the Surgeon who'd found the couple on the bench. In reply to Colin's questions, he said that the Scenes of Crime team had identified what they believed to be samples of the poison on the front door handle, and the letter box. The package with the newspaper had been taken away for forensic analysis, and was believed to be pretty well saturated in the poison, but there was no smell. However, Sergeant Hopkins, the officer who had found it, despite his protective outfit and a mask, somehow seemed to have come into contact with the stuff, was feeling rather unwell, and had been taken to the hospital.

****

An hour or so later Lacey met Captain Jordan in the canteen. He was surprised to see how long her wavy brown hair was now it was freed from her officer's cap and piled on top of her head in a bun. He ordered a coffee and a tinned salmon and cucumber sandwich. She asked for a peppermint tea with no sugar, and the same sort of sandwich. Lacey paid.

Colin Lacey felt he needed to understand this case better. When they had found a table, he asked Jordan: "Can you help me with this poisoning? Dr Abbott gave me a layman's rundown of what he'd got from you in more technical terms, but I'd be grateful if you could go into some detail."

"I'll do my best and try to keep it fairly simple."

"Yes, please."

"OK. Well, organophosphate compounds were discovered in the 1880s or thereabouts. They were used a lot as insecticides on farms in the USA but were found to make people ill. They still get used for sheep dip in some countries, and still make people ill. In India, for example they are used extensively, so doctors and hospitals are more familiar with them and the diseases they cause. If you get enough of it, it will kill you."

"Abbott said it has some effect on enzymes."

"Correct. The two relevant ones are Acetylcholine (Enzyme A) and Cholinesterase (Enzyme C). I'll call them A and C. So what they do is this ...."

Colin held up a hand and interrupted. "Let's see if I understood what Mr Abbott told me, please. When you want to do something, A makes the muscle start to do it, and then C comes in and stops A so your muscles don't go on and on tightening up or whatever is wanted. Without C to halt A your muscles would go into spasm and might kill you."

"That's pretty good. What these organophosphate insecticides do is prevent C coming on, and that's when the spasms occur. They actually destroy C, so they are called Anticholinesterase Agents. They're about the most poisonous insect killers you can get, but they'll finish us off too. You may absorb them through your skin, or breathe them in, or swallow it."

"So what's special about Novichok, Captain?"

"Do you want me to go on calling you Inspector? I'm happy for you to call me Jodie. Saves a lot of time. We may be discussing this quite a bit as I work on the patients, and you investigate what happened."

"That's fine with me. It's Colin. So, what's special about Novichok, Jodie?"

"As far as we know it's the deadliest chemical weapon in the world, invented by the Russians in the 1970s, and there have been several different types, but they all have the effect of making the muscles seize up until the breathing and then the heart cease to function."

"And you die." Colin paused. "How can you treat it?"

"If you get the patient – victim – in time you give them a combination of Atropine (which is fairly common in hospitals), and Pralidoxime, which is not. I had to bring some with me from PD."

"Porton Down?" When Jordan nodded, Lacey went on: "How is it administered?"

"Intravenously. The mixture is the same as soldiers in the field have in an epipen, which is about the size of a proper fountain pen. Usually, epipens with insulin are used for diabetes or other chemicals for people who may get anaphylactic shocks from eating nuts or something else they're allergic to. In action we often carry them because of the risk these nerve agent poisons may be used in gases or sprays against our troops. When we treat victims, we have to wear protective clothing and a mask. As you know, Mr Abbott, Dr Curtis and I had to wear this gear when we were in the ICU with the Russians. Bearing in mind they and Mr Taylor had handled them here and on the bench, and so had the paramedics, before they knew they needed the safety clothing, it's lucky they haven't shown any symptoms, yet, which I think they would have done if they'd touched much of the Novichok. It doesn't take much. I'll keep an eye on them."

"How do you know it's Novichok, Jodie?"

"We have a device which is a bedside medical diagnosis tool. In a way it works like a breathalyser. It takes a sample of any substance off the skin, or in the breath, or blood, and analyses it. I brought some with me. I used a couple on Abbott and Curtis. Other samples from the patients have been sent to PD to check."

Colin Lacey pondered that for a moment and finished the last of his coffee. "Tell me; if this stuff was a Russian secret, how can you know what it is? How can anyone make a device to analyse it?"

"Interesting question. At various times samples have found their way to the West. After Glasnost and Perestroika, and the collapse of the USSR, Red Army people started stealing things and selling them abroad. You probably know there were always fears that nuclear weapons would come on the black market. Other weapons did so. It's not at all well-known that these poisons did too."

"What happened?"

"Well, first, it stopped being a complete secret in 1992, when two of their scientists, Mirzayanov and Fyodorov, published a piece in a Russian magazine in 1992. They said Russia had been making these poisons since the 70s. They were unlucky to let the secret out of the bag at that time, since Russia was just about to join up to the Chemical Weapons Convention. It seems Mirzayanov was acting out of altruistic environmental motives, as he found that the Novichok versions were stronger than the maximum safety margin for previous organophosphate poisons by a factor of eighty. He should know. He was a counter-intelligence expert in charge of testing whether what was going on in the manufacturing plant could be detected from outside by spies from other countries."

Lacey shook his head in disbelief. "He took a huge risk."

"And it didn't pay off. He was arrested for treason in 1992, and was held in prison, but his trial failed as he'd named none of the sites where testing took place and most of the rest of his magazine article was already in Soviet media. He was released. The reason he'd been targeted was for revealing that Red Generals had been telling porkies to the world and to their own people, denying they were making the poisons. That was the real crime."

"But that doesn't tell me how you can verify it's Novichok."

"I'm coming to that, Colin. In the early 90s a Russian agent sold a sample of Novichok to the German Secret Service, the BND. I understand it was then separated into its ingredients, maybe in Sweden, and the formula was then passed on to all the members of NATO. Once you know the formula you can work with it. We and the Americans used this to find out what would be suitable defensive clothing, and so on, and to try to develop cures."

Lacey smiled rather cynically. "So PD made some."

"I'm not supposed to answer that." Jodie Jordan smiled too. It made her look extremely attractive.

"I'll have to look into it, then. After all, this is an attempted murder case, and if one of them dies ..."

"Then it's murder. In either case the easy way out for the British Government is to accuse the Russians."

"I dare say, Jodie, but it's my job to discover what really happened, whether it's them or someone else. In any case, was I meant to hear what you just said?"

Abruptly Jordan stood up, frowning. "Let's leave it there. I must get back to the patients." She marched away. Colin Lacey could not imagine her walking in any other fashion.

****

Lacey muttered to himself as he and Shuttleworth walked into the hospital canteen for breakfast the next day. Lacey thought he still needed more information about what Novichok was all about, how this sort of thing was treated in the ICU, and especially whether Porton Down really had any of it. Luckily, he saw Sam Curtis, the anaesthetist, sitting at a small table on her own. He asked whether he and the constable might join her and she agreed. Having ordered himself and Shuttleworth some bacon and eggs and cups of tea, he carried his meal back to the table and sat opposite her bowl of cornflakes. "How's it going, Dr Curtis?"

"Well, OK, but I'd rather have muesli."

Shuttleworth laughed. Lacey smiled. "I meant the patients."

"Sorry, got to have a bit of a joke sometimes. No change, really. They're both still comatose. Not likely to wake up for quite a while. May be better if they stay asleep for a good few days, or even weeks, so their bodies can get to grips with the poison and the treatment. Captain Jordan says in this type of case a by-product of the poison is that the victims worry and panic if they wake too soon. That just makes them worse, so it's better to sedate them if they're coming to the surface."

"Are you sedating them now?"

"No need. They're still out for the count."

"What else do you have to do for them?"

"Quite a bit, Inspector. I think you heard yesterday that they've been intubated. What that means is a pipe is stuck into your windpipe. It helps keep your breathing going. Sometimes we put the pipe up a nostril or into the mouth and throat. In a case like this where muscles may seize up, we make a hole in the throat through into the windpipe - what we call the trachea. It may also keep saliva or muck from their noses going down into their lungs. We can't rely on their diaphragm muscles working when they've had this nerve agent used on them ...."

"Because that's what it's supposed to do: stop them breathing."

"You've got it. So we connect the tube to a ventilator which does the breathing for the victim. The Russians are being ventilated now, and ever since we got them here. They get a regulated amount of oxygen pumped in at regular intervals per minute. Their pulse, blood pressure, and the quantity of oxygen in their blood are monitored all the time."

Shuttleworth put down his fork. "A bit strange isn't it, treating someone who can't tell you anything?"

Sam giggled a little. "Not in A & E it isn't. Patients can be out cold with drink, drugs, a good punch to the head, or completely unconscious from a bad road accident. Normally we have to get a patient's consent to treatment, but in emergencies like this we just have to get on with it. These people can't even tell us what drugs and medicines they may be allergic to, so we're not sure whether we're doing them good or harm some of the time."

Colin shook his head in wonder. "That must be nerve-racking."

"It's no fun, but mostly experts like Abbott take it all in their stride."

"So, if they've got this tube in their throat they can't eat or drink."

Sam Curtis giggled again. "That's where catheters come in. Most people think they are just for weeing through, but we stick one in the vein in an arm, and supply liquids and liquid nourishment that way. We can feed them through a tube in the throat, but not when they can't breathe, for obvious reasons. That is why force-feeding the Suffragettes was so painful and controversial. They got the grub in bulk through a thick rubber tube and a funnel."

Lacey asked, "What happens now, Doctor?"

"We're waiting to see what effect the drugs Captain Jordan administered will have. I'm told it can take ages with nerve agent poisoning. Meanwhile at least one nurse is with them all the time, keeping an eye on the monitors."

Shuttleworth's phone vibrated in his pocket. "Yes Carl."

"I've just sent Lacey an email with what you wanted, Pete. Get to a proper terminal. You and the guv won't want to read all this on a phone screen unless going blind or stark staring bonkers is your idea of fun."

Shuttleworth gave Lacey this news. He was already rising from the table leaving half an egg and one rasher on his plate. "Sorry, Doctor Curtis, got to go. Some new information to study. Can I use the computer in the office we were in yesterday?"

"OK. No problem: it's been thoroughly cleaned," she mumbled through a mouthful of cornflakes.

Despite running being banned in the hospital, Colin sprinted back through the labyrinth to the office near the ICU. He logged on to his email address, noting that the hospital internet was a secure site. He did not want just anyone seeing what he was up to. Carl had copied him into an obscure Dark Web entry, not for porn, child abuse or S & M, but for defence and secret service 'secrets' obtained by rogue reporters, dedicated pacifists, and even whistleblowers chancing their luck. Was there anything on the internet Carl didn't know how to find?

Boris Mamontov is the alias provided by the British Government to Vladimir Pedchenko, a former high-ranking member of the Russian secret service, the KGB (or Committee for State Security), now called the FSB. He was born in Karkov in 1950. He was employed as a diplomatic attaché in various Russian Embassies and Consulates from 1974 until 2009, when he was arrested in Moscow. He pleaded guilty to numerous charges of betraying secrets vital to the USSR and subsequently the Russian Federation. Some counts alleged he had sold plans of new weaponry to the United Kingdom, and others that he had betrayed to the British, the identities of secret agents working for Russia, some of whom were Russians or from other Iron Curtain countries, working or living in Britain and elsewhere. Other victims, whose sympathies lay with Russia and communism, or were simply taking Russian bribes, were British citizens or those of other NATO countries.

Pedchenko had acquired this information through his important connections in the KGB and its successors and his easy access to KGB records and archives. The Russians had no idea of his treachery at the time. They learned of it when an FSB contact in the UK Secret Intelligence Service gave information which, whilst not identifying Pedchenko by name, was sufficient to enable them to work out who the traitor was.

He was sentenced to twelve years in prison. He could have been sentenced for life or even executed, but received this much lighter sentence because he had cooperated with the investigation and the prosecutors, who thereby acquired much useful data on how British and NATO forces and governments worked, particularly in clandestine fields.

In 2011 a complex deal was negotiated between the Russian Federation and certain NATO powers, including Britain, for the exchange of spies and informers. Six NATO spies and agents imprisoned in Russia were swapped for nine Russian agents held by NATO. Three of the former went to France, two to the USA, and one, Pedchenko, to Britain. It was at that time that he was provided with the alias Boris Mamontov. The swap took place in the airport at Vienna, in a secure facility from which the press and public were excluded. However, a UK Foreign Office press release about it was later published, which had been agreed with its French and American counterparts, who released it to all the prominent media outlets in both of those nations too.

Vladimir Pedchenko (Mamontov) was taken to an unknown destination believed by some to have been in a non-descript part of Hounslow, for a form of interrogation known as 'debriefing'. It lasted three months. What he revealed has never been made public.

Media interest in Pedchenko has never gone away since his trial. It appears that in 1979 when he was sent as military attaché to a Russian Embassy in Cuba, he had been involved in what appeared to be a honey-trap with a very beautiful Jamaican girl of African ancestry. She worked as a waitress for a catering company which provided refreshments and meals for British High Commission functions in the West Indies. They were followed covertly after Pedchenko was observed taking a rather keen interest in her at one of those functions. The young woman had no intention of acting as a femme fatal; indeed, she did not have a clue that she was one, nor that MI6 were using her as though she were one. Their liaison was discovered by the British Secret Service, when they were observed twice in the same restaurant. The apartment they used for their affair was fitted secretly with cameras and microphones. Pedchenko was then blackmailed by MI6 into treachery towards his homeland, or heroism towards his British paymasters, depending on one's point of view. He was rewarded fairly handsomely for his cooperation. His UK handler had some photos of them together taken secretly. According to a leak to 'The Times' he gave Pedchenko copies of some to remind him that revealing his treachery to the USSR would be simple.

It is believed that, in addition to military secrets, his revelations about Russian secret agents and spies resulted in about sixty of them being required by the UK government to be sent home at various times from supposedly diplomatic posts from Britain to Russia or other countries allied to them. Of these, some dozen were prosecuted, allegedly for acting as double agents against the USSR. Five of those, according to Russian media sources, pleaded not guilty, but were convicted and condemned to death. Four pleaded guilty and were executed too. There had been a slackening of the use of show trials under the Federation. As a result, of the other three, one was acquitted, one was pardoned, and one was sentenced to imprisonment. That one was Vladimir Pedchenko.

After his debriefing in Hounslow was concluded, he continued to be retained by the UK Secret Intelligence Service, or SIS, usually called MI6. He even had the occasional use of an office in the Wizard of Oz-like SIS building on Albert Embankment, on the south side of the Thames. He was sent by MI6 under the name Mamontov as a consultant to foreign countries, alerting them to Russian spy networks, and teaching at confidential seminars on ways to recognise spying and other secret activities which might be cloaked by Embassy or Consulate activities, and by business demonstrations at Expos. During his time with the Russian Foreign Ministry as a diplomatic attaché he had taken part in and organised such operations with regard to the USSR's enemies, so he knew what he was talking about.

In this capacity he visited French speaking countries in Africa, including Senegal and the Congo, and Finland where he spoke English. Many Finns speak Russian, but as a former foreign colony of the Russians, that language was not popular in Helsinki. In WW2 there was a frightful struggle for mastery of Finland when the USSR took advantage of the Peace Treaty between Hitler and Stalin to invade. The Finns kept the Russians at bay.

Personal Life.

Vladimir Pedchenko has a brother, Yevgeny, and was educated at Leningrad University on an Army scholarship after joining the forces at eighteen years of age. He obtained an Honours degree in French with English, and a PhD in English Literature. These skills resulted in his being used abroad as an attaché.

In 1973 he married Martina Gornikova, by whom he has a daughter Katerina, born in 1976. Martina unfortunately died in childbirth three years later and two years after Vladimir started spying for British Intelligence. The baby was stillborn. Vladimir has not remarried. Katerina is unmarried as far as can be ascertained, and has no partner, and lives in St Petersburg. Yevgeny Pedchenko has a son of the same name.

Two years ago, Yevgeny Pedchenko Junior was given permission to leave Russia to join his uncle. He then arrived in the UK. The whereabouts and home address of Mamontov/Pedchenko are not known, but rumour places him in West Sussex. The nephew, Yevgeny, gives Russian conversation lessons at Chichester and Portsmouth Universities. It was this fact that enabled an enterprising journalist from the Daily Mirror to track the former spy down to a house in the city of Chichester in 2014. By contrast, in the case of the former spy Oleg Gordievsky, whose escape from Moscow just before he was due to be arrested by the KGB in 1985 was engineered by SIS, his alias and exact whereabouts have remained a secret.

There followed a long list of official and media references. Carl's email said that he had been unable to find any Russian articles or reports about the nephew. There were links to newspaper articles and TV broadcasts from 2001 about Pedchenko, and a few about sightings of him in some of his foreign postings, both earlier material when he was a military attaché abroad for Russia, and later pieces from his travels for SIS. There were copies of newspaper articles about the assassination attempt on Litvinenko, and one about an alleged attempt on Gordievsky in November 2008. It seemed a Russian attack on Pedchenko was a definite possibility.

Colin Lacey decided he would have to make enquiries about Vladimir, if the secret service would tell him anything. No wonder he had thought the man's name was familiar. It had been in all the newspapers in 2009. He decided he would study all that later. Someone would now have to update the Dark Web entry to deal with the attempted assassination of Pedchenko and his nephew. Or murder if one or both of them died. There was bound to be something of this in Wikipedia soon.

One way or another Weapons of Mass Destruction were bad news for everyone. You could die making them, or using them, or being the victim of such use by the other side. Like thousands of Iraqi civilians, you might be killed because a couple of nutty rulers like Prime Minister Blair and President Bush think your country has them when it isn't true, or that your President, like Saddam Hussein, should not be allowed to govern, even if you like him. And you might kill yourself or be murdered, like Dr David Kelly, because you got sucked into a row about whether WMD could reach Britain from Iraq in forty-five minutes or not, and who said so.

Chapter 4

London, December, 1995

In 1982, Oleg Gordanov had been serving as a military attaché in the USSR embassy in Havana, Cuba. The fact that he was a Brigadier General in the Russian Army was, of course, not public knowledge, but it was known to the SIS. His behaviour and morals were always impeccable when abroad, whatever his predilection for amours might be when he was at home in Russia. Nothing he did in foreign countries (apart from the highly covert spying he was there for) gave any foreign secret service any grounds to hope he might be turned to help them. He was so successful in covering his spying tracks that those did not come to foreign notice either, even though they were on the look-out for and suspected it. All attempts by foreigners to suborn and recruit him were doomed to fail and did.

In Cuba Gordanov met a diplomat whose name, he learned, was Vladimir Pedchenko. After that the two men's paths often crossed in various foreign postings.

Vladimir was about twenty years younger than Oleg. Despite the age difference, they got on well together, although the elder found it necessary to warn the younger man that the attention he paid to the opposite sex might get him into trouble. Vladimir hid his resentment of the warning, and took no notice of it, apart from trying to be a little more discreet. He concealed the fact that he was KGB too. They continued to meet over the next couple of years for a drink or a meal occasionally, and regularly attended meetings of mutual interest at the Embassy, and outside functions.

By this time Vladimir had been providing secrets to the British for several years. He had told his handlers at MI6 about a KGB spy based in the Russian Embassy in Rome who had ingratiated himself with an Italian Air Force commander, bribing him to sell NATO secrets. MI6 passed the details to their Italian counterparts. The unfortunate Italian went to prison. The spy, Andrei Koudriavtov, was sent home to Leningrad. In revenge an Italian diplomat was expelled from Moscow.

With Pedchenko's information, MI6 was able to arrest a Russian agent who worked as a businessman living in Manchester while spying in the course of his travels as a shipping forwarder. He visited all the ports around the UK, genuinely making contact with shipping companies, and doing some genuine business, but at the same time cultivating informers, some unwitting, others receptive to bribery, in nearby Naval installations. His reports of what he found, and the documents he was sometimes given, were sent via the Russian Embassy in Kensington Palace Gardens, not even a mile from Kensington Palace, by diplomatic bag, to KGB headquarters, the Lubyanka Building in Moscow. The Russian agent, Sergei Belyavsky, went to Wakefield Prison for eight years.

Up to this point Pedchenko considered his greatest coup, even though he was simultaneously ashamed of it, was the betrayal of Amelia Olivier. This event occurred after the USSR had been dissolved in the early 90s and the KGB had been renamed and nominally reformed as the FSB. He had become aware during his visits to the Soviet Embassy in London that a number of British paid agents based in and spying against Russia there, in other Iron Curtain satellite states, and in different foreign countries, were being recalled at the request or insistence of the Russians. There seemed to be too many of these occurrences. Being a senior KGB officer himself, he made discrete enquiries and found that all the evidence pointed to Amelia, whose real name was Olga Opadnova, who was passing details of these agents to the KGB. He gained access to her files. She worked as a confidential secretary with high security clearance for a high-ranking civil servant in the Foreign Office. This officer's function was to liaise with MI6 about placements for SIS personnel in British Embassies abroad, deal with any claims they were spies, and help repatriate them should their recall be demanded by a foreign – and particularly a Russian - government.

Pedchenko gave all this information to MI6, including the fact that she was really Russian with a genuine but fraudulently acquired British passport and British citizenship. Pedchenko conferred with his MI6 handler about this in a shadowy booth in a restaurant. What did they want him to do? He was told to do nothing; they would attend to it, and tell him the outcome later. Before squirming along the seating to leave, the handler passed Vladimir an envelope. When he returned to his hotel, he found it contained five thousand pounds.

He was doing well, but realised he must not spend the cash ostentatiously. Olga was not shipped back to Moscow, nor eliminated by other means. It suited the UK to leave her in place but promote her and move her to another position where she could be surreptitiously fed true but useless information mixed with totally false 'intelligence'. In this way she was of little value but considerable concealed risk to the KGB, and of substantial importance to MI6. Vladimir was not told this.

A month later the handler, whose contact name was Archie, called for another meeting, this time in Hyde Park, by the Serpentine. It was spring 1994. They arrived ten minutes apart to sit on the same park bench, at opposite ends. They started an apparently random conversation about the weather, followed by a discussion about the sports story on the back of the 'Daily Mail' the Englishman took out of his briefcase. Once satisfied no-one was in earshot, Vladimir asked; "What happened to Olga?"

The Archie said, "We have neutralised her. You needn't concern yourself with the details. Better if you don't know." Apart from anything else, spies being notoriously fickle, MI6 was alert to the possibility the FSB could turn Pedchenko into a double agent and tell them about Olga's new duties. That was the moment at which Pedchenko felt shame for the first time; he had never betrayed a woman before. Whilst he did not know her new function, if the KGB discovered that she was now being exploited by the British, she might be recalled to Moscow and executed. Whenever he remembered Olga afterwards and wondered what had happened to her, he cheered himself up by contemplating the money he was making.

He thought the interview with his handler was at an end, and began to stand. Looking around casually to check they were still unobserved, the handler, still seated, reached out to put a hand on his arm and told him quietly to sit down again. They sat making more small talk about films it was worth going to see, as a young couple with a pram approached pushing a stroller with twins in it. Vladimir made a remark about how pretty the babies were, everyone smiled, and the family went its way. The two men continued their desultory conversation until the couple were over two hundred yards away and clearly paying them no attention.

The handler once again looked all around. No-one else was anywhere near. "There is a very effective Russian Army Officer who comes to your Embassy from time to time. When he is abroad, he is a spy for Russia; of that I am sure, but we cannot pin anything on him. He is incorruptible. His name is Oleg Gordanov."

Vladimir nodded. "I know him. We served together in our Embassy in Cuba a few years ago. I've met him in other places too. I know he is – how do you say? – straight as a die? He's at the Embassy for a few weeks right now."

"We know that, Vladimir, and we want to get rid of him." The MI6 man put his newspaper down on the bench.

Vladimir said, "Why don't you just get him sent home as persona non grata?"

"Two reasons. One, doing that will only result in a tit-for-tat exchange of diplomatic personnel. We don't want that. Two, it suits us to stir up some trouble with the KGB.

After all, your lot have caused us enough trouble over the years, what with Burgess and Maclean, Philby and others."

Vladimir scratched his left ear. "So why are you telling me all this?"

Archie gestured at the Daily Mail. "Inside this you'll find copies of some top-secret papers from your Defence Ministry relating some recent 'secrets' they know about MI5. We got them from a mole we have in that Ministry. These papers are harmless to us, now we know Russia has them, but your people do not know we know, as far as we can tell. They are in a plastic gusset. Whatever you do, do not touch them or the plastic with your fingers or hold them in your hand without wearing the surgical gloves you will also discover. These gloves are free from powder, smell or anything else which could leave traces on the paper."

"What do you expect me to do with them?"

"Put them in Gordanov's briefcase when he goes to a meeting with a British Colonel we have fixed up for two weeks' time. These two know each other from places they have served abroad, and this Colonel Webster has invited Gordanov to lunch at his Army and Navy Club in the West End. It was our suggestion."

"How the hell do you expect me to get the papers into his case?"

"You will tell your bosses that you have reason to suspect him, and to have some agents outside the club as Gordanov arrives. They will confront him, and stop him entering the club, and seize his briefcase. You will stride up to this little gathering. Do not wear the gloves for this encounter. I repeat, do not wear the gloves! Take the case, inspect it, turn your back on Gordanov, and let the papers slip out of the plastic folder into the case. The two men must hold him to prevent him interfering with you. Turn back and face him. Tell him to pull the documents out of the case, and to tell you what they are. His fingerprints will then be on them. Show them to the other men, but do not let them touch the documents. They can tell him he is under arrest and will be flown home."

"How do you know he'll carry a briefcase?"

"Because he and the Colonel are interested in military history and have agreed to swap some magazines about it."

"What use will Russian military magazines be to the Colonel, Archie? He won't understand them, will he?"

"We're not that stupid, Vladimir. Webster studied Russian at Durham University before going to Sandhurst. In any case, if this goes as planned, he'll never get to see them."

"Suppose Gordanov doesn't turn up?"

"We'll have to arrange something else."

"What happens if he starts a fight, or the Police intervene?"

The handler laughed. "We've got that covered too. He must be tranquilised. The Police will be there, at both ends of Pall Mall where the Club is, and ...."

"Fuck; then they're bound to step in, aren't they?"

"These coppers will be from Special Branch, dressed like ordinary constables, and fully briefed to take no notice, but to make sure no-one else horns in on the action."

"OK Archie, so what about the Colonel? What if he turns up at the same time?"

"Very unlikely. He's told Gordanov to be at the Club at 1.00 but the Colonel will get there before noon, so he'll be in the Club in case anything goes wrong and Gordanov gets in."

"So if anything does go wrong it'll almost certainly be our fault."

"Right on the button, laddie, so you'd better not bugger it up, had you?"

"What's in it for me then?"

"Well, apart from the fact that it will continue delaying us showing the films of your lusty meetings with the Jamaican lady, there's three thousand quid in large notes tucked into the newspaper, and there'll be another seven grand to come if you pull it off. Goodbye."

The handler casually moved off, leaving the newspaper on the seat. Vladimir shouted after him: "You've left your paper behind!"

"That's OK. I've finished with it. You keep it if you like."

Worried as he was about this forthcoming assignment, Pedchenko was delighted with his own quick wit in covering the acquisition of the paper.

Two weeks later, the seizure of Oleg Gordanov was accomplished without a hitch. He was drugged again, his face bandaged like the victim of a serious head injury, and taken on the next Aeroflot flight back to Moscow.

Eighteen months later news of Oleg's execution for treason against the Soviet Union was reported in Izvestia and repeated in the western media. Oleg Gordanov was doubly unlucky. First, his defence that he had never seen the documents until he was told to remove them from his briefcase, was rejected by the Court. If he were not a traitor, why had he been walking into an ultra upper-class London

Club to meet a British Army Colonel? When his lawyer asked the prosecution witnesses how they knew he was meeting the Colonel, no satisfactory answer was forthcoming. The Court ignored that because the prosecutor said it was up to Vladimir to explain why he was meeting the Colonel with his briefcase full of secret papers. Secondly, it was 1995. If it had been twelve months later, he would not have died according to law, as President Yeltsin put a moratorium on the death penalty. On the other hand, Oleg might have been done away with in secret after that cessation by less traditional methods, and very much more painfully, had the FSB decided he was too dangerous to live, and that a less than subtle message needed to be sent to other military and diplomatic officers who might think of betraying Mother Russia.

When Igor read of his father's death in Izvestia in December 1995 his pain, fury and desire for revenge knew no bounds. But revenge on whom? However, he was too intelligent to act rashly or in anger. He vowed to plan carefully and bide his time.

He had admired his father as a patriotic officer, and a man of loyalty and honour for the Motherland. Igor simply could not believe Oleg was a villain and a traitor. True, he lived well, and had money, but that was because of his rank. No-one of significance in the military was poor.

Father and son both liked walking, and when they could, they made their way into the countryside to walk, admire the scenery, and watch the animal and bird-life. During one such trek, while relating their different walking experiences, Oleg told Igor how he had fallen once, when posted in Britain, on a walking holiday in North Wales, cut his leg very nastily, had to go to a hospital in Caernarvon for treatment, and had lost a lot of blood.

One of the memories Igor had cherished with pride was what Oleg had told him one evening during a dinner in a very good restaurant in Novosibirsk when he had visited his son at the University. They had been walking for most of a blustery day. Their meetings were infrequent, irregular in timing, and always in different places: cafes, parks, restaurants, concerts, and on the face of it, always casual or by chance. This particular dining experience was not in the restaurant Igor's mother Irina ran. They never were, as any potential embarrassment by recognition of the family together had to be avoided. For the same reason, the two men called each other by their forenames, not Dad or Father, and not Son. This restaurant was in a converted theatre from the end of the Romanov era, on Ulitsa Sovetskaya. It was a magnificent setting, with old chandeliers, upmarket but classic wall-coverings, beautiful wooden furniture and luxurious cloths, napkins, and cutlery.

Igor asked his father what it was like to work for the government, and particularly the Armed Services.

Oleg pondered, for a moment. "Well, Igor, it's a lot better than it used to be. Under the old regime, before Gorbachev especially, it was easy to get into serious trouble. The KGB had its nose in everything and tabs on almost everyone. If you were pretty high up you were not harassed or bullied so much, but if they had it in for you, or you had done something they didn't like – trivial even – you had further to fall and could end up in the worst parts of Siberia."

"But as a general you must be high up. You've never been in trouble, have you." It was a statement of belief.

"No, but I could have been. When I was abroad as a military attaché, I was approached a couple of times by NATO people to spy for them. Once it was by the CIA in the Caribbean, and once by the British in Canada. I just brushed it off, and reported it to the Army and the KGB, but nothing happened as it was on foreign soil. But there was a third time."

Igor was excited. "What happened?"

"I was at a reception at the British Embassy in Moscow, right near the Kremlin. I was there as an Army Officer, not in a diplomatic role. The British Military attaché, a man I knew slightly - his name was Mark Bailey - gave me a second glass of scotch, took me by the elbow and guided me unobtrusively into an alcove off the hall where the gathering was assembled."

"And?" Igor was getting impatient.

"I'm fairly good at keeping emotions and surprised expressions in check, but this almost took my breath away. Bailey just told me that they'd like me to be a spy and let them have defence secrets. They recognised my rank, and it would be worth a lot of money to me, and they'd get me out if it ever leaked out. He must have been told to do this, but I think he'd been at the bottle. I'd never heard anything so crude in my life."

"So what did you do? I can't imagine you'd have accepted."

"Not, as our English friends would say, for all the tea in China, Igor. No. I went to the KGB and reported Mr Bailey to them. In no time at all he was relieved of his post and sent back to the UK. He's not been allowed back here since."

This conversation was important in Igor's mind for confirming his Dad's honourable, loyal status. How could a man like him have been found guilty of treason and executed? It made no sense. When his lawyer had raised this very point at the trial, it had been swept aside as of no significance in view of his having had the treacherous documents in his possession when arrested. That made no sense to Igor either.

Maybe he'd endeavour to find the lawyer one day. He'd have to go to Moscow.

Chapter 5

Chichester, 24th April, 2016

Colin Lacey knew he was not going to get much information from Captain Jodie Jordan in a formal location such as the hospital, or even in its canteen. Getting her to come to the Police Station would be worse, even though he now had more adequate space there. The day before, Lacey had had time to obtain some additional accommodation. He had spoken to the Chief Super at the nick, who had this morning given him another room, much larger, in addition to his small office. The new room was set up as an incident room, with three phones so officers could receive phone calls from anyone with information, and three computer terminals linked to the Station network, the Police National Computer system, and all its sources of information. The Chief had also found Lacey two constables, P.C. Sharon Jones, and Detective Constable Harry Morton, both from Chichester Nick. Lacey had the Counter Terrorism Unit send him a Sergeant, a young woman of Indian parentage called Kiara Charcko who had joined the Unit from the Met a few months ago. He now felt much better equipped to investigate the two attempted murders.

He needed to engineer an informal meeting with Jordan in truly neutral territory. As it happened they were both staying at The Harbour Hotel in North Street. He resolved to try to meet her accidentally on purpose in the dining room at breakfast or dinner. He would make the attempt that evening.

However, the day was not wasted in waiting. During the morning and early afternoon he and Shuttleworth interviewed members of the public who had seen what they thought was something relevant to the Police investigation. They questioned these people in the office Lacey had been allocated on the first floor of Chichester nick. Most of it was of no assistance, but one middle-aged woman had phoned in saying she had a clear and detailed recollection of seeing a man of about fifty turning the corner out of Priory Road. She related her account to Detective Constable Shuttleworth, who went to her home in Donnington. The 1960s house was in Selsey Road, two storey, and, in keeping with the period of its construction, in pale brick, with some wooden cladding on the first floor. Inside the furniture was also from the 60s, and the place was comfortable, spotless and well-maintained, rather like Mrs Mason herself. She said she had lived there from the time of her marriage, staying on since her husband died five years before.

In answer to Shuttleworth's question she told him:

"He had a swarthy complexion and very dark hair, as if he came from the east somewhere, but he had rather bright blue eyes. He was a bit taller than you, Sergeant; yes, maybe a bit taller, but looked more academic, like a lecturer or teacher."

"You got a good look at him, Mrs Mason."

"Well, I try to be observant. I like writing and belong to a local scribblers group. If I see someone or something unusual I like to memorise it so I can use it in the little stories I write."

"Perhaps I'd better let you write your own statement. I don't suppose you'd care for the way coppers put witness statements on paper."

Mrs Mason laughed. "Maybe not. They never walk or drive anywhere, do they? They always 'proceed'."

Peter laughed too, politely but briefly. "Do you mind telling me what you were doing in New Park Road?"

"Not at all, officer. My friend Betty lives in the workers' cottages opposite the car park where the Festival Theatre is. You know the ones I mean? Well, perhaps not, you not being local. They're all gentrified now, of course. The cottages, I mean. I'd gone in on the bus to join her for afternoon tea."

"What do you remember about the afternoon?"

"Oh, the boiled cake! Lovely old wartime recipe; lots of sultanas and bits of date." Mrs Mason smiled at the thought of her wickedness. "I had two pieces."

Shuttleworth hoped his frustration was not too evident: "And what happened when you left Betty."

"I was walking back to the bus station - I like a bit of a walk, you see. I'd got to within a few yards of the turning into Priory Road when this man came round the corner towards me."

"And?"

"There was something different about him, so I took a few more steps and turned to watch him. That's how I knew he went up towards the bench where those poor people were discovered."

"Why did you come forward with this?"

"Well, I knew it was about a poisoning at the bench up near the roundabout. When this chap turned the corner he went right up New Park Road in the direction of that bench. He was carrying a black leather handbag, like some men use, on a strap over his shoulder. I thought it could have something in it. I don't know if it helps. I just saw the news when they asked people to come in with information. So I phoned the Police Station."

"You did the right thing. It may be nothing, Mrs Mason, but it might help us identify the man responsible."

"If it was a man. Women can do some dreadful things too, you know." She rubbed her chin. "The Prime Minister is already saying this was a Russian assassination attempt."

Shuttleworth looked serious. "So he is, but our job - mine and Inspector Lacey's - is to find out who really did it, without speculating and making accusations before we know." A pause. "Did you notice what he was wearing?"

"I did, actually. He had a light coloured jacket, fawn or creamy, with black trousers, a black shirt, and a panama hat." She clapped her hands together. "That's it, of course it is. Not really an academic; more like a vicar or a minister of religion might wear in the summer, because he had one of those white clerical collars through the shirt. Well, it was a lovely warm spring day, wasn't it? Oh, yes! He was probably two or three inches taller than you."

"Great." Shuttleworth made another jotting in his note-book. "Let's go back a bit. Did you see the people on the bench? Were they there when you walked past?"

"Well, I can't say it was the people who were attacked, but two men were sitting there. I thought they looked rather alike. They were talking a bit, but I couldn't understand what they said. It was all foreign. They looked like they might fall asleep."

"And what time was this?"

"Let's see." She paused for thought, and twiddled her fingers. "I left Betty's just after five, so it would have been about five past, I suppose. I must have seen the vicar a few minutes after that; maybe around ten past."

He took her to the Police Station where she could write out her statement in the presence of a uniformed officer, who then took her home to Donnington. Then Peter joined Lacey in the office he was using.

Lacey agreed with Shuttleworth that this was the only potentially helpful account they, Charcko, Morton and Jones, had had all day, despite having spoken with seventeen witnesses between them, most in the station, four in their homes or work places.

At lunchtime the forensic reports came in about the park bench, the Pedchenko's house, and the clothes the two victims were wearing at the time Spencer and Curtis found them. They left the canteen and went back to the office.

"So what do the reports say, Peter? What's the gist? I'll read them carefully later."

"Well, guv, the paper from the package Pedchenko got that day was coated pretty thoroughly with Novichok. It seems only his nephew's fingerprints were on the paper, so presumably he opened the packet. Some of this poisonous chemical was found on the front door. He had traces of the stuff on his hands."

"What about Vladimir?"

"That's the really interesting part. He had a lot of it in his hair, on his scalp, and on the back of his neck. Forensics scientists say it looks like he was sprayed with it from behind. They say it might explain why he is so much worse than his nephew Yevgeny. He also had this muck on his hands."

"When could that have happened?"

"What, guv?" Shuttleworth brushed a lock of black hair off his forehead.

Lacey sounded impatient. "When could someone have sprayed this stuff on him?"

"It looks like forensics found the answer to that. Scenes of Crime took a sample off the back of the bench. So it might have happened when they were sittin' there. It was on the top part of the back of his jacket up by the shoulders. If any of the spray went past 'is head he might have breathed it in when it came round near 'is face. Seems unlikely, but maybe that vicar Mrs Mason saw did it."

Lacey laughed. "Seems a bit like Cluedo, Peter, You know. Reverend Green in the ballroom with the rope?

Both men contemplated that for a minute. Lacey got up and strolled about before stopping in front of Shuttleworth and saying: "Let's think about that."

Before they could, Colin's phone vibrated in his pocket. "Lacey speaking."

"Hello, Inspector. This is Sergeant Davies. I was told you wanted to see all the CCTV footage from New Park Road for the day the two Russians were found. It's all set up for you in the viewing room."

"Thank you Sergeant. We'll be there as fast as we can." He put his phone away. "The CCTV stuff is ready for us." He smoothed his hair. "Where were we, Peter?"

"Wonderin' how the two men got dosed with nerve agent, sir."

Lacey agreed. "Yevgeny gets his dose from the papers in the package. Vladimir gets his from touching his hand on the front door, probably as they went out. They've got it on their skin, so it doesn't work as fast as if it had been injected or breathed in then. They walk across the football field, and by the time they've crossed New Park Road they're feeling unwell, so they sit on the bench ..."

"And someone walks behind 'em and sprays the poison over Vlad's head, and then it can seep into the skin on his neck and scalp, plus he can inhale it."

"He's either already so ill he doesn't notice, or can't get up to do anything about it. Maybe Yevgeny didn't notice it happening for the same reason."

Peter nodded, and then jerked upright. "But why didn't the perp spray Yevgeny's head thoroughly too?"

Lacey shrugged. "I don't know. All this is guesswork, of course, but maybe the assassin didn't need to kill him. Maybe his uncle was the target. After all, Yevgeny didn't catch much of the spray, apparently. In view of Vladimir's record of betraying Russian secrets to us, an attempt to murder him alone is fairly consistent with the PM blaming the Russians, or one of their special ops units."

"You going to suggest we just drop it, guv? I mean, if it was them, we're never goin' to prove it, are we? And Putin's hardly likely to come clean about it, is he?"

"Dropping it, as you put it, Peter, is not my style. We're going to pursue this as far as we can. If the Prime Minister is right, I'd like to provide him with the evidence to prove it. If he's wrong, we'll find out who did do it."

Shuttleworth put his hands in his pockets and stood up. "The PM'll think you're the awkward squad if you prove him wrong."

"I believe he already knows I'm the awkward squad. I'll tell you the story one day." Lacey brushed hair back from his forehead. "By the way, how do you think you got on with the sergeant's exams before we were called down here?"

"Pretty well, I think, sir. Should get the results soon."

****

Twenty minutes later they were sitting in the video room at Chichester Police Station with Sergeant Sean Davies, who introduced himself to Shuttleworth as the Station Sergeant. The video operator was also present. Much of what they watched looked irrelevant, but at the time signal of 17.00 things looked up. A camera opposite the junction of Priory Road and New Park showed the vicar type coming round the outside of the railings surrounding the park towards New Park Road, make a left, and walk up the road towards the crime scene bench. As he did that, Mrs Mason hove into view walking towards him. He took no notice of her, and as he passed she turned to watch him, as she had told Shuttleworth, who commented: "Her recollection's pretty accurate, isn't it sir?"

"It is, and he could be the one with the spray gun, aerosol, or whatever."

Sergeant Davies chimed in with: "No camera with a view of the bench, sir."

"That's a bugger, sir." Peter went on: "His panama hat mostly hid his face, too, didn't it?"

"Yes. He kept his head down as he walked towards the other camera, so the brim covered all but his chin, and when he went round the corner the CCTV was almost over his head." Lacey turned to Sergeant Davies: "See if you can round up all the other CCTV films in the town centre, and any others you can find. Get a couple of people to watch them all, looking out for this vicar bloke, and anyone who looks like they might be Russian. I've no idea how the Prime Minister got the idea it was them."

Davies laughed. "It's like Tony Blair telling us about Saddam's Weapons of Mass Destruction, sir."

"WMD?"

"No evidence of them either, sir."

****

That evening Lacey told Shuttleworth to go out and relax. He knew Jordan would leave the hospital at about 5.30pm and return to the hotel. Five minutes before that he stood on the other side of North Street, outside a big flint faced 18th Century house occupied by a clothing chain as a shop. He had a clear view of the hotel as long as nothing large parked in the road in front of it.

Twenty-five minutes later Jodie Jordan walked up the steps into the hotel. He ran across the road and entered the building in time to see her retrieve her room key from reception and make for the stairs. He went to the bar and asked for a tonic water with ice and lemon, after which he returned to reception, and stood idly reading The Times newspaper, and chatting, equally idly, to the young man behind the desk. Then he found a seat and sat looking at the paper, where he could see the stairs, and waited.

Just before 6.20pm Lacey saw Captain Jordan emerge from the lift. He continued to pretend to be reading the news on the inside pages. She no longer looked like an army officer. Gone was the uniform. In its place she wore an elegant red dress, black patent leather shoes with a modest heel, and tights of a very pale honey colour. Her hair was no longer in the bun, which had been replaced by a smart French pleat. In fact, a sophisticated Parisienne was just what she looked like. As she entered the dining room, on the face of it not having noticed Colin Lacey, he put down the paper and strode after her. As he walked in the Head Waiter was showing Jodie Jordan to a table near the windows.

Uninvited, Lacey followed the Captain and waiter to the window table. As the waiter held her chair and Jodie sat, Colin put his hand on the back of the chair opposite hers and asked if he might join her. She looked up and smiled. "This is getting to be a habit. First the canteen, now the restaurant."

"May I? I saw you come down the stairs and thought you might be able to continue my education on the mysteries of Chemical Weapons."

"Fancy that!" An impish grin curled her lips up at the corners. "There was I thinking you were sitting patiently hiding behind a newspaper in the foyer waiting for me to appear just so you could have dinner with me. Instead I find you are not bowled over by my beauty. It's my mind you're after."

"I see that my amateurish subterfuge was pointless. In any case, beauty and brains is an irresistible combination."

"Touché, Inspector." She laughed. "Sorry! We're Colin and Jodie, aren't we?"

"We can go back to being more formal if you wish. I shouldn't want you to think that because you're looking rather lovely this evening I have something other than Chemical Weapons on my mind."

Was it Lacey's hopeful imagination or did a hint of disappointment flicker over her face? It lasted a nanosecond if it was there at all, and Jodie smiled again: "Well whatever it is, you can't stand there all night, so yes, please do join me, Colin."

He sat, and the head waiter came back with menus and a wine list. They chose their meals in silence until the waiter returned to take their order. Colin asked Jodie if she wished to choose the wine, and she selected St Emilion, which suited him very well. He offered to pay, and she accepted. He was not displeased that the wine, whilst a good year, was not an extra-expensive vintage.

Wishing to avoid launching straight into his investigation again, he asked her where she came from. "I was born in a village near Lincoln. Dad was an engineer and we moved about the country to where he was needed. His expertise was in water purification machinery and its repair and replacement. We ended up in Kent and Surrey for most of my primary education and secondary school. That's where some of the major water works in England are, serving London."

"Why the Army?"

"I joined the Army Reserve - it was known as the Territorial Army then - when I was doing my A levels. We went on exercises on public commons round London, firing blanks, and to camps in tough country; Welsh Mountains, Cairngorms, the Lake District. I just loved it, the rifle range and other shooting experiences. I got three 'A's in Maths, Physics, and History. Then I joined up to train as an officer."

"That means going to Sandhurst, doesn't it?"

"Indeed it does. Us girls" (she giggled) "have been allowed there since 1992. Before that there was a place at Bagshot just for women. Yes, I had two spells at the Royal Military Academy Sandhurst. A couple of weeks at the start, and then back there for the third module. I'm not going to be shy and pretend to be modest, but I was runner up for one of the swords of honour."

"Your parents must have been proud." Colin sat back. "But you're a doctor."

"Yes, they were, and yes, I am. The Army sent me to medical school in Manchester. Now I have two simultaneous careers I really love. And I can go on being a doctor when I leave the Service, if I want to."

"So what about this chemical weapons stuff?"

"I did that - CBRN training – er – Chemical Biological Radiological and Nuclear - as part of the third module, but after qualifying as a medico, I was posted to the CBRN training centre at Winterbourne Gunner in Wiltshire for an intensive course. From there I was sent to Porton Down. I also went to the US's CBRN training centre at Fort Leonard Wood. That was part of an exchange programme for the Allied medical teams to share knowledge, treatment etc. That's why I'm based at Porton, and why they sent me here." Her face took on a different look from the one when she was talking about herself. "That's enough of me. What about you?"

"Me? I was born in a Council House in a less than salubrious part of Epsom. My father was a gardener in the municipal parks. I went to local state schools, but somehow managed always to be in the top set. I went to work for a Bank and then a Council, but neither job lasted very long as I couldn't stand the sort of atmosphere where no-one dared query what the man above you said. So I joined the Met. I found the hierarchy attitude similar but the Police work much more interesting. I got into the CID, got on well, so they sent me to London University where I got an Upper Second in law. Then I transferred into Special Branch – SO15, it's called now."

"But you're in Counter-Terrorism, aren't you? Why?"

"Do you recall the disappearing aeroplane, SEA439 – vanished into the Southern Indian Ocean, so we were led to believe? Well ...."

"There was a TV programme about it which showed that it was hijacked by the CIA, though."

"Indeed. Well, I was the SO15 officer responsible for helping that programme to go out. My Special Branch cover and anonymity were completely blown, so I was moved sideways and promoted."

"Heavens above! So you're what some would call a right shit stirrer, then. A bit like Inspector Frost or George Gently." Jodie was not smiling. Colin was surprised by her earthy phraseology. It might go with the uniform, but not with the red dress.

"I should be so lucky! And I didn't say you're not supposed to query what the boss says in the Police Force. Most officers wouldn't dare. Is that it then? Should the shit stirrer leave the table now?"

She was still staring at him with what seemed to be marked disapproval. Then she grinned. "Well, not yet. But I can see I'm going to have to be very careful what I tell you."

Before Colin could say anything else another waiter brought her trout and his lamb shank. He was slightly surprised she would drink a red such as St Emilion with trout, but recognised that he could be said to be unnecessarily fussy about that. Or did she choose it to go with his red meat? He decided not to flatter himself. The waiter topped up their glasses. For the most part they were quiet as they ate, but made small talk while waiting for the desserts they ordered.

Having finished their delicious blackberry and apple pie with ice-cream, Colin sat back. "Let's not beat about the bush any longer. What can you tell me about Porton Down?"

Jodie laughed and wagged a finger at him. "Nothing secret, but even so, there's a lot I can tell you. For a start, it's huge. It covers 7,000 acres of prime land about 6 miles from Salisbury."

"Sounds more like the estate of a Scottish Duke."

She made a dismissive gesture. "I suppose it does, but they mostly go back centuries. This one was only set up in 1912. The scientists spend their day analysing chemical and biological weapon samples we get from other nations, especially those we regard as potential enemies ...."

"Such as Russia, China, Iran?"

"Yes, and North Korea. And of course in Saddam Hussein's day, Iraq too, though after we invaded them in 2003 it turned out they had destroyed them all by 1991. I remember an MP called George Galloway telling us that was so, long before we invaded, but as he had been friendly with Hussein everyone said he was a liar."

Lacey shook his head. "Terrible. At least a hundred thousand people died. And then Blair and Bush made out the war was all about regime change to topple Saddam. I'm afraid all the secrecy, lying, and cover-ups make me very cynical."

"I'd noticed. The boffins also experiment with the foreign stuff, and their own chemicals and bacteria to see how new weapons might be made, and how they might be used. Then they use the results to work out how to protect people, and particularly troops, against their use."

"So did they make some Novichok? Is that how you knew what it was on these two people?"

Now Jordan shook her head. "I shouldn't tell you that even if I knew. All I know is that the epipen I told you about says it's Novichok Treatment, and the boffins at PD confirmed it from the samples sent to them to be analysed."

"OK. So what is your role?"

"I help monitor the effects on those who test the weapons, or the substances, and treat anyone who becomes ill."

"Becomes ill? That's ominous. There are laws and international agreements against that, aren't there?"

Jordan shrugged and said, "OK, I'll go as far as I can. The Geneva Protocol was signed by the UK in 1930. That came about because of all the mustard and chlorine gas used in World War 1. The aim was to stop their use. The UK accepted the Chemical Weapons Convention in 1993 and ratified it in May 1996. Even so we've tested loads of chemical weapons constantly since 1930. There were some trials in Rawalpindi. Mustard gas was used on a few hundred Indian soldiers. The idea was to work out how much gas to use in an actual battle. A lot of these men were badly burnt by the gas."

The waiter returned. Having ordered coffee for two, a brandy for Jordan, and a Laphroaig for himself, Lacey leaned his elbows on the table. "But that was *after* the Protocol!"

"It was. Large numbers of former Servicemen complained about mental and physical health problems, many lasting years, after being subjected to nerve agent and other tests. Usually they say that they were not told what was really being done to them, nor of the dangers they might be running. Some were told they were helping to cure the common cold. That was in breach of the Nuremberg Code of 1947. These 'abuses'" (she made a quotation marks gesture as she said this) "and the use of volunteers to test chemical weapons and defences against them at Porton Down were investigated by the Police. The investigation was called Operation Antler, and looked at many allegations from 1939 up to 1989."

Lacey nodded. "I read about that."

"Ronald Maddison died in 1953 because Sarin was used on him. He didn't know what it was. An inquest was opened in May 2004 into his death and lasted until November that year. A confidential MoD inquest had said it was just 'misadventure', but in 2002 the High Court overturned that finding. Then there was a proper Coronial Inquest. The Coroner's jury found that Maddison died from 'application of a nerve agent in a non-therapeutic experiment'. In other words it was not done for his health or his benefit."

Lacey groaned. "That's the understatement of the year, I should think. So he was just a guinea-pig."

"After the Inquest the files on several men were sent to the Crown Prosecution Service. They decided some people should be charged with crimes, but that decision was reviewed, and in the end no-one was prosecuted."

Lacey shook his head in disgust. "I can guess why. Politicians wouldn't want to run the risk they knew or ordered what was going on. Nor would they want the secrets about it all to come out as it might endanger National Security."

He uttered the last four words with complete contempt, and almost glared at Jordan as he did so. "How do these people think they're doing anything to defend us? It could have been my Dad, or yours."

Jodie looked at him even more seriously than she had been throughout this conversation. "You don't expect me to respond to that, do you? Has it occurred to you I'm one of 'these people'?" She sounded exasperated. They were statements, not questions. Lacey felt he was getting nowhere. Despite getting Jodie Jordan away from the hospital and its environment of official control, he was failing to get her to go far on just how much PD knew about Novichok, and whether they had any. He would have to go there. Arranging that might prove difficult, but he felt that being an officious policemen would get him nowhere with her.

They finished the meal in virtual silence and a poor atmosphere. Lacey thought she disliked him.

Chapter 6

Porton Down, Wiltshire, Monday, 25th April, 2016

Peter Shuttleworth drove Lacey to Porton Down in an unmarked police BMW. He drove fast and well, and other road users were not inconvenienced or intimidated by the blue flashing lights and the siren, as he did not use them. Lacey had an appointment to see the man he had spoken to on the phone yesterday when the appointment was made. He had left the Indian sergeant in charge of the incident room, and sent the two constables out on more door to door enquires in the neighbourhood of the crime scene and the victims' home.

Dressed in his blue suit, with a white shirt but a different tie, he again made a contrast with Peter's sports jacket and grey slacks. Fairly tall as Lacey was, and fairly stocky as his side-kick was, neither of them measured up to the PD executive who invited them into his office.

Mr Cyrus Horne-Bassett was a big man. Some two or three inches over six feet was Lacey's guess when he walked into the executive's large office. He was also broad and heavy, but not athletic or fit looking, and clearly seemed to think he was a big man in the sense of importance and status.

It showed in his expensive Prince of Wales check grey suit, gold watch chain across the belly of his waistcoat, bold blue striped shirt, and Royal Artillery tie.

After shaking hands with Lacey, he sat behind his mahogany desk in a leather swivel chair costing an average man's wages for a couple of months, and waived Colin to a lower and not quite so costly leather armchair opposite. The psychology was too obvious. "You, my visitor, are beneath me." Their preamble was brief as Colin had told him on the phone who he was and why he was coming. Colin thanked him for granting an appointment.

The civil servant acknowledged this with a slight inclination of the head, leaning forward with his hands clasped on the desk. "So how can I help you, Chief Inspector?"

"I need to know more about what goes on here. How did you know that what was – is - wrong with the Pedchenkos is due to Novichok? How were you able to make an authoritative analysis if you do not have any and have never made any? Has this stuff been used in Russia, where it's supposed to come from?"

Horne-Bassett smiled indulgently. "Hmm. Three in one. Let's look at the last one first. Has this stuff been used in Russia? Well, yes, and it has definitely come from there. Sometimes its use has been accidental rather than deliberate. We know, for example, that some of their scientists became very ill or died from working on its development. One was Andrei Zheleznyakov. What happened to him was an accident, but it was ultimately fatal for him. By mischance he came into contact with a small amount of Novichok when he was helping develop a variety of it. It was May 1987 in

Moscow. His injuries were severe and he was unconscious for about ten days. As the product was a secret operation, he was secretly treated in a special clinic in Leningrad. He could not walk, his arms were extremely weak, he got hepatitis poisoning, as a result of which he developed liver cirrhosis, as if he were a heavy drinker. One might think that was bad enough, but he became epileptic, had periods of chronic depression, was unable to read or concentrate. He was totally disabled, and work was out of the question. After five years of this torment, he passed away in 1992."

Colin Lacey was stunned and managed to utter: "So you'd be better off being killed by an adequate dose; at least, I think I would."

Horne-Bassett nodded his agreement: "Quite. Stories like that made me think, in light of what you told me, that Novichok was more than likely the cause in the case you have now." He continued: "Then it was used in Russia by one of their so-called businessmen to murder another a few years ago." The word 'businessmen' was emphasised with contempt. "The victims were Ivan Kivelidid and Zara Ismailova.

Lacey indicated that he knew of that case. "Yes, it was in 1995 and Vladimir Khutsishvili was convicted of the murders at a secret trial in 2006."

"Indeed. There was fairly authoritative speculation that he was framed by the Secret service on the say-so of a top-level member of the Russian government, and that the FSB had supplied the Novichok. But what shows that this ghastly weapon was available illegally from time to time was that in 1994 a GosNIIOKhT employee – one of the departments dealing with these things - Leonid Rink, was sentenced for selling it to some Chechens."

Colin was struck by this point, since it showed that the assassination attempt on Pedchenko did not have to be an official Russian action. It could have been a personal or private enterprise venture. What could the motive have been? He had to drag himself back to what the Porton Down man was saying.

"So far as deliberate deployment of this sort of weapon is concerned, there was, of course the hostage crisis at the crowded Dubrovka Theatre in Moscow. In October 2002 forty or fifty Chechen rebels ..."

"Or freedom fighters."

Now Horne-Bassett's smile was not so indulgent. "Seized more than eight hundred hostages in an attempt to force the Russian government to give Chechnya its independence. It is a mainly Muslim country and doesn't fit too well in a Greek Orthodox Christian or left wing atheist society. The rebels, whose leader was Movsar Barayev, said they belonged to an Islamist freedom group. They wanted Russian forces removed from Chechnya to end the Second Chechen War. The siege ended with the death of at least 170 people."

Lacey uncrossed his left leg from his right and crossed them the other way. "I remember that."

"I'd be surprised if any reasonably well-informed person could forget it."

Lacey grinned cynically. "If you were in my business, trying to gather evidence, you'd be even more surprised at the things people can forget, or pretend to."

Horne-Bassett did not grin back. "The design of the theatre meant that Special Forces had one hundred feet of passageways to fight along, then attack up a well-defended staircase before they could reach the auditorium in which the hostages were held. The attackers had numerous explosives, with the biggest in the middle of the building. On the third day, two female hostages were murdered, so to avoid the inevitable gun-fight, Spetznaz men from the FSB, supported by a special unit from the Ministry of Internal Affairs, pumped an unnamed gas through the theatre's air vents prior to rescuing the hostages."

"And 170 people died."

Horne-Bassett nodded. "As I said, all the rebels were killed, and well over a hundred innocent civilians died from exposure to the gas. Nine were from other countries. The two female hostages who were murdered beforehand were the only ones, amongst those who died, who were not killed by the gas."

Lacey's reaction was grim. "The Special Forces, or those who authorised the use of the gas, must have known it wouldn't just eliminate the rebels, so in effect it was state murder of the hostages who died."

Horne-Bassett nodded again. "I think we can safely say that." He paused. "The nature of the gas was never disclosed by the Russians, but some think it was a fentanyl derivative. So do we here at PD."

"How could you find that out if you didn't have a sample of what was used?"

The indulgent smile returned to Horne-Bassett's face. "We had a stroke of luck. It seems the Russian government refused to tell the doctors what type of gas it was, so their efforts to treat victims were frustrated. In the records of the official investigation, the nerve agent is referred to as a 'gaseous substance'. In other cases, it is referred to as an 'unidentified chemical substance'.

"The Russian Federation is a member of the Chemical Weapons Convention. They undertook 'never and under no circumstances' to develop, accumulate, stockpile or use chemical weapons that can cause death, temporary incapacitation, or permanent harm to humans or animals. The Convention States have to comply with requirements to prevent or minimise the injuries and seriousness of the use of toxic chemicals. It permits the use of some chemical agents like tear gas for law enforcement and riot control, but the effects of riot control agents must fade completely soon after the gassing ceases."

Lacey thought this was becoming an endless lecture. "So how did you discover what the Russians used?"

"Yes, that's the question, isn't it?" Lacey decided that pomposity would usually annoy people about Horne-Bassett. "Three British hostages who survived brought samples with them unwittingly when they were flown home. We were able to extract samples of the stuff from the clothes of two of them, and from the urine of the third, to analyse it. Our chemical and biological weapons scientists did it here in the laboratories. This showed that a couple of fentanyl substances were used. The Russian Health Ministry did not specify which."

Peter glanced at Lacey for permission to ask a question and received a slight nod of assent. "Sorry, but I'm a bit lost. What's this got to do with Novichok, sir?"

The Porton Down man gave him a withering look. "I'm coming to that, young man. I'm telling you this Chechen story to indicate that the Russians are quite capable of using very dangerous chemical weapons, even on their own people. Novichok and these two Russian victims in Chichester, the Pedchenkos, were the subject of your first question. As with the samples from the Dubrovka theatre, we were able to analyse the samples recovered from these two Chichester victims. It was on the paper which had been delivered to them, but not on the packaging. Also, it was in the dried liquid which had been sprayed or wiped on the doors. The traces which were on young Pedchenko's hands must have come from there. However, the largest and best analysis was from the extraordinary amount found on the hair and scalp of the older man. There was a small amount of it on the shoulder of the younger chap's jacket, suggesting he caught the edge of the spray when it was aimed at the Uncle."

Lacey could see that this interview was going to get few results unless he could pull a rabbit out of the hat. Perhaps the executive's pomposity and evident vanity was the key. "Well, it's clear you have a very efficient and expert establishment here, and it's no doubt due to the quality of men like you overseeing it all."

Horne-Bassett gave another of his mock-modest bows of the head in acknowledgement. "I do what I can, Mr Lacey."

"Evidently. So were your people able to make a comparison?"

"Indeed they were. You heard that a corrupt Russian sold some to the Germans?"

"I did. And it was analysed by the Swedes, I think, who promulgated the formula?"

"Correct, Chief Inspector. We obtained a small sample, as did the Americans and other NATO Allies. With the benefit of the formula and the use of the sample, we were able to manufacture a quantity ourselves."

Lacey reflected briefly and then said, "I suppose that was just to check how it was done, and the accuracy of the formula the Swedes had made known, and then the amount PD had made was destroyed."

"Not as far as I know, no, it wasn't."

Lacey felt an urge to give a triumphant yell and thrust a fist into the air, hoping his gleeful emotion was not noticeably inscribed on his face. Simultaneously he realised gloomily that life would be so much easier for him in this investigation if the evidence showed that the poison could only have come from Russia. Now he had multiple potential sources of the poison to deal with, if most of NATO had samples. He hoped the gloom did not show either. "Can I see the stores and the personnel who run them?"

If Horne-Bassett realised he'd been flattered into revealing what must be classified information he gave no sign of it. "Today? I'll phone down and authorise it, then. Someone will come over to fetch you. It's a bit of a walk, and we don't want you getting lost." He guffawed: "Or experimented on!"

"Thank you; that's most helpful." Lacey could not help being pleased that he had obtained these details without getting Jodie Jordan to put herself in the firing line. Why did she come to mind so often?

Chapter 7

Russia, 2010

In the late summer Igor took two weeks holiday. He went to Novosibirsk by train and stayed with his mother for almost a week. He took her to a pop concert by Nyusha, a group she liked. The lead girl and her backing singers and dancers were very attractive and sexy, and he liked that, but he could not stand the music. He did not understand how his Mum, at getting on for seventy, could like what he saw as rubbish, but she was rocking along to it, just like the youngsters in the audience.

She provided him with a couple of excellent meals in her restaurant, and after saying a fond farewell to her on the platform at the railway station, he travelled to Moscow in bright sunshine to find his father's lawyer. The lovely countryside journey lasted three days and nights in a sleeping compartment. Igor knew from the old newspaper articles that the advocate's name was Grigory Korshunev, and had found his office in the Lefortovo district by searching on the internet.

Having booked himself into a cheap hotel a mile from there, he phoned the office, and the receptionist gave him an appointment for the following afternoon. He then went to an internet cafe and searched for further details on Mr Korshunev. The lawyer had qualified and been admitted to the Bar in 1980 and had done little but criminal defence ever since. His record of success was poor until President Gorbachev was well established and reforms were making justice easier to obtain. By 1995, when Oleg Gordanov came to trial, the criminal courts were much fairer, and slightly less likely to convict to please the government. In this changed atmosphere it seemed that Korshunev's practice grew and his reputation soared. His website showed evidence of this, but Igor did not rely on that alone. He went to a library and researched back numbers of newspapers for reports of cases handled by the lawyer. Korshunev's success was making him a legend in his own lifetime.

His photo showed a slim chap of medium height with black hair parted at the left side and a small, pointed beard and moustache. Igor thought he looked like Trotsky.

When he turned up in the rain for the appointment at very well appointed but not excessively ostentatious offices, the smart receptionist who had fixed the meeting for him asked him to wait on a Romanov style 19th Century sofa. She went down a corridor, knocked on a very solid wooden door, and announced Mr Schaplinov. She then came back and told Igor: "Mr Korshunev will see you at once." She took him to the door and closed it behind him.

The lawyer was standing behind his large desk. It was the same age and style as the sofa, and so were the four chairs in the room, including Korshunev's. He came round the desk to shake hands. In the flesh he looked even more like Trotsky, with a pair of half-moon glasses on a thin gold chain round his neck.

"How can I help you, Mr Schaplinov?"

"Well, it may seem a bit odd, but I do not have a case and I'm not in any trouble. I need some help about a case you dealt with about twelve years ago. No, actually thirteen."

"So, we're looking at 1995?"

"Right."

"Do sit down. Would you like some tea? My receptionist keeps the samovar going all day."

"Yes, please. That is very kind."

Grigory went to the door. "Natasha, please bring in two cups of tea." He came back smiling. "I don't charge for the tea, but you should understand that my charges are usually 25,000 roubles an hour."

Igor was taken aback at that, but this was the only lawyer who could tell him about his father's case. "That's fine."

"And I cannot breach my duty of confidentiality to a client."

"But this client is dead. He won't care what you tell me now, surely. I want you to tell me about Oleg Petrovich Gordanov."

Surprise was evident on Korshunev's face, which had gone rather pale as he went back to his chair and sat down. He took a clean handkerchief from the breast pocket of his pinstriped charcoal grey suit. He wiped his glasses with care. Eventually he looked up. "You were rather young when that case came to Court. Why is it of interest to you?"

"I'm his son; his only child."

Grigory rubbed his forehead with the handkerchief before returning it to the top pocket. "He told me he had no children and had not been married."

"He wasn't married to my mother, either. I'm illegitimate. As you know, he was a high-ranking army officer. We all kept the relationship secret for the sake of his reputation and career."

"Forgive me if this sounds offensive, but why should I believe that?"

"He saw me through school in Barnaul, and University in Novosibirsk. He was my mother's lover until he was arrested. He told me about British and CIA attempts to recruit him as a spy."

Grigory shook his head in a kindly way: "You could have read that in the newspapers."

"True, but they did not say that the MI6 agent who tried to bribe him was Mark Bailey, did they? My father told me that." As the secretary brought in two cups of tea Igor pulled an envelope out of his inside coat pocket. He waited until she left the room. "And here's a letter he wrote me when I was at University. If you've got his writing on file, you can compare it."

Korshunev left his desk and sat in the chair next to Igor's. He took the letter with his left hand, glanced at it, and put his right hand on Igor's shoulder. "OK. I recognise the writing. I shall never forget him. He certainly shouldn't have been convicted or hanged. I still wake up in a sweat some nights trying to understand why he died; or why and how I lost the case."

"I don't understand it either, but the newspaper accounts made me think the judge was biased. You made some very good points, but according to the newspapers they seemed to have been just forgotten or ignored by the judge."

"Yes. The judge had a certain old-fashioned attitude that the state was never wrong. He's gone now, thank heavens." He paused. "By the way, there will be no charge for this. I am so sorry for you, as I was for your father. He was an honourable chap, and I believed him innocent. I don't often feel that way. So, what do you want to know?"

"I'd like to read a transcript of the trial, if there is one. Do you have one?"

"I believe I do. I was able to obtain one even though the trial was in secret, as your father wanted my advice on an appeal. There were no grounds. Just because we thought the judge was biased, that did not mean it could be shown from the transcript, and the fact that he decided not to take account of the Mark Bailey story…"

"Which was not reported in the press."

"Correct, and the fact that the judge disbelieved General Gordanov on the question of whether he'd ever seen the documents before meant little. The judge was entitled to believe what he liked as long as there was evidence to support his conclusion. I'm so sorry, Igor."

Grigory picked up his phone and called his secretary. "Raisa, please look up the Gordanov file from 1995, or it might be under 1996. When you've got the number, go to the store and fetch it for me." Replacing the phone, he looked at Igor. "It'll take her a little while to find the file and make a copy of the whole thing for you, not just the transcript. Why not wait outside and have another tea? Or go out for a walk for half an hour or so. It should all be ready then."

Igor got up. "Thanks, but no more tea. I'll go for a stroll." They shook hands.

Grigory said, "I'll see you later." He put both hands on Igor's shoulders. "I am so pleased to have met you. And when you've read the file, let me know if you want any more information."

****

When he got back to his hotel Igor started reading the file. The transcript was not as long as he had expected, which made him think the biased judge had kept a very tight rein on the length of the proceedings, which may have made it even more difficult for Korshunev to get his points across more effectively. The rest of the lever arch file was a bulging mass of paper. There was no way he could read it all there and then. He would have to take it back to Pochep and be very careful that no-one else at the weapons base got a look at it. The last thing he needed now was to be identified as the son of a man held to be a traitor.

He went out to dinner, and on his return read the transcript in bed. He noted the names of all the witnesses who gave evidence against his father. He badly wanted to know who had betrayed him. One witness was not named in the Court record, which showed that the prosecutor had requested, and the Judge had ordered, that this person's name not be mentioned. He would have to ask Korshunev about that, but he wanted to read the rest of the file first, as it might tell him the name anyway, and there might be much more to discuss.

The next day Igor read more of the file, making notes and comparing parts with the transcript. In the evening, he went to the opera to see Tchaikovsky's *'Eugene Onegin'*.

He'd have to go back to work, reread the transcript, and study the whole file thoroughly. It would be no hardship to return to see Korshunev in Moscow in a few weeks. He could take in another concert or opera. He went back to Pochep on the train.

****

Over the next few weeks Igor pored over the file at every opportunity. He was not foolish about it. He took time during his weekends and other rest periods to meet some of his colleagues for a drink, or go to a club in Pochep where he might get to dance or go home with a woman. He kept up his twice weekly running. It had been his best sport at school and college; he'd even made it into the athletics team. He liked to keep fit and spent one evening a week at a gym. He didn't want the authorities at the establishment or the manager of the apartment block where he lived to wonder why he was always buried away in his room.

His method of keeping the file and transcript away from prying eyes was simple. His wardrobe was old, wooden, and rather heavy. At the bottom it was the shape of an upside-down rectangular box. He contemplated removing the floor of this piece of furniture so that he could replace it after stowing the papers in it. That was not such a good idea. If anyone searched his room, they would almost certainly test whether the bottom floor of the wardrobe was loose and they could lift it. To create a hidey-hole, he carefully detached one end of the rectangle; with a couple of ball-bearing sprung catches which he bought in a hardware shop fitted to the inside of the box and the inner edge of the piece he had taken out, this end could be removed and replaced very swiftly indeed.

If a searcher could not remove the floor of the wardrobe they would be unlikely to try to lift the whole thing or start demolishing it, unless their search were more than just cursory or routine. It would have to be a very thorough inspection.

The tenants of the block were expected to keep their own apartments clean, and Igor did so scrupulously, so that when the monthly check by the manager occurred, he would have no reason to do more than take a swift glance through the door. Igor had to avoid an enthusiastic cleaner smacking the side of the wardrobe with a vacuum cleaner and knocking off the end of the concealed space.

He acquired an account book ruled into columns. In the first he wrote the date of a document, interrogation, court appearance, or other incident; in the second the names of the persons involved; in the third the facts or points he considered important, and in the fourth, a cross-reference to any related information. He had a laptop which he used for emails and other purposes, but he did not want anyone to be able to hack into any record he might make on it about this investigation of his father's case. He bought a top of the range Lexilogos tablet with a keyboard in Cyrillic and English script.

He did not connect it to the internet or any social media sites. He did not understand why governments and global corporations had all their information on computers linked to satellites and internet systems. In some instances, these had even been hacked by teenagers, never mind spies, and on occasion secret information had even been released to outside agencies by accident.

Every few days he took a break from the file and the transcript to enter onto the memory the growing store of facts and what he hoped were clues about the unjust verdict on his father. It was not safe to spend more than an hour or two a day on the papers and the tablet, and sometimes no time at all, so it was a slow and long-drawn-out process. He kept the new laptop under the wardrobe with the file and the account book.

It was in the sixth week of this labour that he found what he believed to be what he was looking for. He took another week to recheck all his facts against the documents. He knew he had to go back to see the lawyer to confirm his suspicions.

****

Two months later, he asked for permission to go to Moscow to meet his mother for her birthday. It was granted. He bought tickets for the Tarja concert at the B1 Maximum Club in the city, another band his Mum liked but he did not. He had saved up for this treat and sent her the money for a train from Novosibirsk. They spent three days together; Igor showed her the Kremlin and the theatres and concert halls he had been to.

On the second day they went by train to Tsaritsyno Station, which takes its name from the nearby Palace of that name, built for Catherine the Great. She did not like the first one which was completed in 1786, so had it completely demolished. Only the foundations could now be seen. A second palace, designed by a different architect in the New Gothic style was started, but was unfinished when Catherine died in 1796. Subsequent Tsars showed no interest in it; it was abandoned for two hundred years. Irina Schaplinova had seen on television that the Palace had been finished and completely restored and decorated in 2006. Igor took her there on the day of her birthday. She had all she really needed to be comfortable, and this kind of outing with her son was, she thought, so much better than a present she might or might not want, let alone need.

Igor found the visit as rewarding as Irina did. Like her, he was proud that the new Russia could put to use the artistic works of the past. It was so sad that revolutions in some countries resulted in contempt for the achievements and beautiful creations of previous regimes, and their destruction. The Communists had rarely done that, except to some churches, and now that the country was open for business, those beauties were available for Russians and foreign tourists alike.

They spent the third day walking around the city and through the parks and along the banks of the Moskva. The following morning Igor put Irina on the inter-city train back to Novosibirsk. He made his way by local train to the office of lawyer Korshunev in Lefortovo district.

****

"I have an appointment to see Mr Korshunev at noon." The receptionist checked the diary. "Yes, Mr Schaplinov. I'll tell him you're here."

A few minutes later Grigory Korshunev invited Igor into his office. "How can I help you this time?"

"I've brought my copy of your file. I want you to look at some of the documents in it. I've been studying them carefully and drawn up a kind of schedule comparing the transcript of the trial with the other papers. This is it." Igor put his notebook on the desk in front of the lawyer and came round to his side of the desk. Resting his right hand on the green leather surface he pointed with his left to some entries in two columns. Then he turned over the pages of the file until he came to a witness statement. "This statement is about the arrest of Oleg, my father. But it has no name on it."

Grigory's index finger landed on a black oblong at the top of the statement. "This shows that the name was edited out. We were not supposed to know who the witness was, and during the trial he gave evidence from behind a screen so that only the judge and the lawyers could see him."

Igor nodded. "Yes, I worked that out, so I went through the transcript to see what this person said in the witness box. He was introduced to the Court as witness X."

"Correct."

Igor reached down and took the transcript out of his briefcase. "On page fifty-eight, as the man is about to start his evidence, the Judge says that his name is not to be recorded, and if it is mentioned, it must be struck from the record."

"Yes, I recall that. And when it happened a couple of times, he told the stenographer to strike it out."

Igor was quite excited by this time. "I saw that, but on page sixty-three, something odd happens. Look." He turned to that page. "See here, line 1, page fourteen, the judge himself talks to someone and uses his name. See that?"

"He seems to be talking to the witness."

"And he doesn't tell anyone to strike it, does he?"

"No. It must have been overlooked at the time, or forgotten when the transcript was typed. Maybe the judge didn't realize he'd spoken the name himself. As far as I know no-one except you has ever noticed that. Even I missed it, but it made no difference to the outcome; it would not have been grounds for an appeal."

"That's what I thought. Now, if we compare the statement with what that witness said in Court, it must be the same man, mustn't it?"

Korshunev picked up the six-page statement and scanned it quickly. "Ah yes, I remember all this now." He replaced it in the file and turned to the transcript, flicking back to page fifty-eight and then reading through the oral evidence until he came to the name. He looked up, took off his glasses, and faced Igor. "Vladimir Pedchenko. That's the name of the man who was in charge of the arrest of Oleg Gordanov. He helped betray him, and according to your father, framed him by planting the incriminating documents in his briefcase."

Igor's feeling of triumph was so strong he threw his arms around the shoulders of the undemonstrative Grigory, gave him a hug and planted kisses on both cheeks. Then he apologised, but Grigory was smiling. "I'm glad you are so happy and have what you wanted after battling through these old papers. We must celebrate. Let me take you to lunch before you have to make your way back to Pochep."

Over lunch in a cafe a stone's throw away, Korshunev asked, "And what will you do with the information you have uncovered?"

Igor smiled. "That is a secret, a real secret. You're a lawyer. You must know you should never tell anyone a secret."

Chapter 8

England, Monday, 25th April, 2016

"I'm going to turn off the Police radio for a while, Peter. I need to think, and we need to talk. Well, what did you think of what we saw in the stores?" The BMW was doing eighty-five miles an hour along the M4, heading to the A34 which would take them south to the M27 and then Chichester.

"First, sir, I was surprised we got in there."

Lacey grinned. "Frankly, so was I. Couldn't make up my mind whether Horne-thingy had forgotten what he was doing, or genuinely wanted to help."

"Can't tell you that, sir. Mind readin's more your game. So secondly, what did I notice? Clearly, they've got all these substances in bigger or smaller quantities which are supposed to be illegal under these conventions and stuff. But then according to Captain Jordan and all the internet research we've been doin', it seems that all the other major countries and some smaller ones have these biological and chemical weapons."

"Correct. What about the Novichok?"

"Part of the store was used for nothing else. In a room on its own. And when you asked him, the storeman – er - Mr Middleton, 'e said some of it was manufactured there at PD. I was surprised he said anythin'. There seemed to be three main types, stored in three separate containers, all thick glass. The labels stated what types they were, and one of 'em was the sort that forensics and those experts at PD say was used on the Pedchenkos."

"Yes. Any other thoughts?"

Before Peter could reply, the car phone rang. He accepted the call and answered it. On speaker was Sergeant Davies at the nick. He said, "Tell Lacey old man Pedchenko died a little while ago."

Colin said, "Thanks, Sergeant. I'm right here. We'll be back as soon as we can." Peter ended the call. Both men sat in a stunned silence for a few minutes. Peter put his foot down.

Within minutes a Police siren was suddenly coming loudly from behind them. Shuttleworth said, "Shit!" He pulled over on to the hard shoulder. The police car tucked in behind them.

Lacey unfastened his seatbelt as the BMW came to a stop. "Stay there. I'll see to this."

He left the car, and the driver of the chasing car approached. He was heavy set, with a country accent, possibly from the Bath area. "Going a bit quick there, weren't we, sir? Ninety mph in a seventy area? Any case, it's the driver I have to talk to. Not going to pretend you were driving, were you?"

"No, constable, I wasn't, and he hasn't been drinking, but you're welcome to breathalyse both of us, if you wish."

Lacey took his hand out of his pocket. "You might like to look at that, too." He held out his warrant card.

The traffic cop smiled dismissively, as though he thought he was being offered a bribe to forget all about it. He took the card, took his eyes off Lacey's face, and looked at the card. His smile vanished and he looked very miserable. "Bloody hell! Sorry sir, and sorry for swearing."

"That's alright, constable. You were doing your job. We were doing ours, but forgot to put our blue lights on. You've delayed us a little, but we shouldn't have been speeding."

"Sorry again, sir. What were you doing, if I might ask?"

"Have you heard about the attempted assassination of the two Russians in Chichester?"

Looking down at the warrant card still in his hand the man said, "Bugger; no wonder I thought I knew the name on here", and handed the warrant card back to Lacey. "Yes, sir, some sort of poisoning."

"Well, we're heading that investigation, as you've realised. We're just returning from Porton Down where we've been asking about the poison, and going to Chichester where the victims are in hospital, to check on their progress."

The officer's face went from misery to serious worry about disciplinary proceedings on the horizon. "Sir, it was just on the Police radio that the old man died an hour ago, but the other one looks like he'll regain consciousness soon. You didn't know?"

Lacey winced. "I'm afraid we only heard on the car phone ten minutes ago. That's why we were exceeding the speed limit. It's now an assassination, not an attempt."

"You're dead right there, sir, if you'll forgive the pun." He paused a moment, then brightened considerably and stood taller. "Tell you what, sir, my partner'll radio in, say there's an emergency and we're helping out, and we'll escort you to Chichester as fast as we can. We'll have our lights flashing and use the siren when necessary. You got flashing lights in that car, sir?"

"Yes, and we're going down the A34 and on to the M27."

"No go that way, sir. Massive accident just outside Havant, we heard. Somehow two articulated lorries crashed and jack-knifed, blocking both carriageways, and a coach and eight cars smashed into the pile-up. There's a four-mile tail back in both directions. It'll take hours to clear. Much faster to go via Petersfield and the A272, with us leading the way. You just follow me, sir, with the lights going. But ..."

"Don't get too close at speed, eh?"

"That's it, sir."

"Just escort us to the outskirts of the city, and we'll be OK from there."

"Right you are, sir. Let's go.

From then on much of the journey was done at ninety-five, even on the country roads. Shuttleworth was in his element using his advanced police driver training. Lacey decided it was prudent to wait until they arrived to get an answer to his last question about Peter's thoughts on the poisons.

****

In the hospital corridor Lacey asked his question again: "So what else did you think or notice about the store?"

Peter Shuttleworth swept his hair off his forehead and scratched his left ear. "Well, sir, the storeman, Middleton, told us we could see the records of amounts of poisons and nerve agents. He also showed us that the ingredients for Novichok were kept in separate bottles."

"Because?"

"Because that way they were less volatile and much less dangerous. That made them safer to handle and you just mix them carefully when you want to use them. They can last quite a long time when mixed, but even longer when they stay separate."

"Is that it, Peter?"

"Just something odd. I don't know if they have more records they didn't show us, but the ones we saw didn't mention the separate bottles of ingredients, only the three lots where mixing had already been done."

"So ....." At that moment Lacey saw Jordan emerge from the ICU suite. She nodded to him. No smile. *Boy is she tough,* he thought, before saying, "Have you got a minute? I want to ask you how Vladimir Pedchenko died."

"How did you find out?"

"It was on Police radio and a traffic cop told us on the way back from Porton."

Jordan shook her head derisively, looking from Lacey to Shuttleworth and back. "Being naughty boys, then, were we?"

Peter bridled: "Is that all you're interested in? Er - Captain."

Lacey repeated: "How did the victim die?"

Jodie Jordan was clearly affronted by Peter's rebuke. She paused to regain control of her anger. "It was about two-and-a-half hours ago. His breathing suddenly choked off despite the ventilator. Then his heart stopped. We tried the defibrillator but he'd gone. We couldn't bring him back."

"Any idea why his system packed up?"

"Not really. The post-mortem may tell us. My guess is that he had had more of the Novichok than we realised, and somehow it just overwhelmed him, despite our drugs and treatment. He was in a very bad way before we were able to start caring for him, and the hours when the thinking was it was Fentanyl or some other opioid did him – and us – no favours at all." Jodie started to turn away, then turned back. "Yevgeny Pedchenko is improving. He may wake up tomorrow, but he won't be fit to interview straight away."

"I see. Can you let me know when I can see him? Thanks," he said as she nodded. He turned to Shuttleworth. "Come on, Peter. We have some serious thinking to do." Colin put his hand on the Sergeant's shoulder to start moving him down the corridor.

Jodie spoke from behind them in a manner Colin could not interpret accurately. "I won't find you lurking and waiting for me at dinner tonight then?" He asked himself whether she was joking or issuing a strange sort of invitation.

Over his shoulder Colin answered: "No, not tonight. Maybe another time." They exited the corridor at the far end, and as the door shut behind them Shuttleworth said, "Blimey, sir! Are you dating her?"

"What?"

"Well, she's pretty tasty, isn't she?"

"Let's keep our minds on the job, Shuttleworth."

Peter smirked. "On the job is what I thought you were ...." Then he blushed. "Sorry sir, never mind that. I was telling you about the separate bottles and the absence of any mention of them in the records we saw."

"Yes, you were. So what did you think about it?"

"Well, first I must admit that it would be pretty difficult for anyone to nick any of the stuff."

"It would. Security is very tight there. I don't think a stranger could do it."

"No, sir. As you said in the car, we were bloody lucky to be shown the store at all. Even then we were under Middleton's eye all the time. I suppose one of us could have distracted him for a while, but it would be really tricky to do that, get out a bottle or other container, fill it, and not be seen."

"And we don't know how this stuff has to be handled, and we don't have the safety gear."

"But we were given some to wear, and masks, because we were there officially. Someone unofficial would have to get inside the place to start with. And then be able to find and get dressed in those things and know what he was doing. Or she."

Colin nodded in agreement. "So the conclusion is that *if* the stuff was taken – stolen – to commit this murder, it must be an inside job."

"That's what I was comin' to, sir. But you'd got there anyway." Shuttleworth paused a second or two. "Middleton could only get into the store because his eyes match what the controllers have recorded on an eye recognition system. If eyes are unique, like fingerprints and DNA, then we or other strangers could never get in there.

Lacey smiled at him. "Peter, two heads *are* better than one." He sighed: "But we have to keep other scenarios in mind, like the two Russians. When we were moved out of SO15, I asked our old commander if he could fix your promotion to Sergeant. I heard yesterday that it came through as soon as you passed the sergeant's examination. You deserve it. We'll have a drink later to celebrate."

Shuttleworth blushed, and they shook hands.

Chapter 9

Russia, Spring 2011

The Communist era decoration of Moscow Underground Railway stations always astounded Igor. Their representations of the heroic, proud and happy proletariat workers creating bewilderingly brilliant buildings, or manufacturing miracles of mechanical engineering, were so dramatic. He was making his way across Moscow from the Central Railway Station to an office of the FSB his friend Basil Klavinov – he of the many sources – had told him about. It was in the Yazenevo District of Moscow.

Following the collapse of the USSR in December 1991, the KGB was dissolved after aiding an attempted coup against Soviet President Mikhail Gorbachev. It was divided into the Foreign Intelligence Service (SVR) and the Federal Security Service (FSB). Its sister organisation, the GRU, continued as an important part of Russia's intelligence services, and was never split up, unlike the KGB. In 2006, brand-new Headquarters for the GRU were opened at Khoroshovskoye Shosse at a cost of nine and a half billion roubles.

In 2006 President Putin gave the FSB the legal power to murder terrorism suspects overseas if he ordered it. Perhaps assassination of other enemies of Russia came into a similar category. This is by no means a unique power. The CIA does it for the USA, and Mossad for Israel. Obviously that legal authority, even if granted by Putin, by the American or Israeli governments, would not protect the murderers from the force of law in the country where such atrocities were committed, should they be apprehended.

The FSB building Igor headed for was in Ulitsa Katerina, and the nearest station was almost a mile from it. Emerging from the station onto the street he turned left and walked for ten minutes along to a road junction. Here he turned right and after two hundred and fifty yards or so, entered an old doorway which gave onto a poorly painted stairwell and staircase. Six flights of steps led to the third floor. There were no notices or signs indicating who or what might operate within these dingy premises. He knocked at the dark brown door which looked as though it had last been painted in Lenin's day.

After thirty seconds a shadow blocked the peep-hole glass in the door as someone looked through it at him, studying him for at least a minute. Igor heard the sound of bolts being retracted, the door opened, but no-one stood there. He hesitated, but nothing happened, so he stepped through the doorway. The door slammed behind him, a muscular arm propelled him into the hallway, and the bolts slid home to secure the place again.

The strong-man remained behind him, and as Igor looked round to see him properly, another man came out of a room down the corridor in front of him.

"You're Igor Schaplinov, then." He addressed the minder. "Give me the photo." It was handed to him. "This is the picture you sent us. We like to know who we're expecting." There was no smile, no handshake. "Come in here." The man stepped aside, gestured for Igor to pass through the door before him, followed him into the room, and closed the door. "I am Nikita Rostow. I am a Captain in the FSB. If you muck us about, I'm telling you now, you will suffer badly. So will your mother. We checked her out and know where to find her in Novosibirsk." He paused for effect, and then said, very loudly and in a threatening manner. "Do you understand that?"

Igor was somewhat shaken. He had been apprehensive about this meeting but now he was almost afraid. He felt threatened by Rostow's fit looking six-foot physique, the staring black eyes, and the cropped iron-grey hair. The thought of the strong-arm thug the other side of the door did not help. "Yes, sir, I am Igor Schaplinov. I have absolutely no intention of mucking you about."

Rostow nodded his acceptance of this statement and sat behind his desk. "You may sit over there." He pointed to an old upright ladder-back chair with worn carpet-like upholstery matching the grey commercial cord carpeting on the floor. The whole room was stark and devoid of ornament. "Now, when you phoned three weeks ago you said you had something very important to tell us. We asked you for a photo and some information, and so you are here." Again he paused. "You work at the Pochep CBRN place, you told us, and we checked that out." Another pause as he continued to stare intently and fairly menacingly at Igor. "So what is this momentous news you have for us? Have you identified a traitor at work?"

Igor took a deep breath. "I've nothing of that sort for you. I've come here to tell you I want to defect to Britain."

Rostow bellowed an extremely unpleasant laugh. "That's a new one, even on me! I thought I'd heard it all." He smacked the palms of both hands down on the desk. He was angry at the apparent waste of his time. "You've come here to tell *me* you want to defect? Have you just left an asylum, young feller?"

"No, sir, I know exactly what I'm doing."

"Don't you know that defectors defect in secret?"

"I am aware of that, sir, but I want you to help me defect."

Rostow laughed once more, but not so loudly this time. "What? Do you want both of us to go to prison, or be eliminated for good?"

"No sir, I am very serious. As you know, I work at Pochep. I speak English with what they call an upper-class accent, I am told, and I can pass for an Englishman easily, if I want to. I can get a job there."

Rostow was incredulous as he interrupted. "You want me to help you leave Russia and go to work in England. What the hell makes you think I would do that? You're out of your mind."

"But the job I want is at Porton Down. You know about that place, sir?"

"You cheeky little bastard. Of course I fucking well know about it. So what?"

"If I get a job there, I can get all sorts of information for you. What chemical or biological weapons they have, what stocks they've got, what new ideas they're working on. Then after a year or two I'll go on holiday somewhere, like Portugal, or Cyprus, places the English visit a lot, and you can snatch me back here."

"You've seen too many James Bond films, you idiot. Anyway, what makes you think you'd be given a job there?"

"It all depends on how it's done, and what help you give me. But you've got my file there." Igor pointed at it. "Did you read it all?"

"Of course I did."

"Then you know I've got a degree and a PhD in chemical engineering, and I spent a year on an exchange in Cambridge when I was at University in Novosibirsk. The sort of work and research we do at Pochep is the same kind of thing the British do at Porton Down."

"You think speaking English like an aristocrat and pretending to be English will help you?"

"I didn't say I would pretend to be English. I said I can pass for English if I wish. I want to show up in the UK as a defecting Russian scientist. Their SIS people probably know I was in Cambridge as a student."

Rostow leaned back in his chair and clasped his long fingers together on the desk. He looked and sounded sceptical, but he was also becoming interested. "So what would you want us to do?"

"Help me plan my defection. Make sure I've got genuine records of my work which I can secrete in my case or clothes or somewhere. Bring my genuine Russian passport up to date. Get me a false passport in some other name, an alias, and, later, a holiday visa in that name. I'll let you know when. The visa must be for some European Union country where I can easily go to the British Embassy, tell them I'm defecting and get them to take me to England. You make a fuss in official circles, so it gets back to the UK that I have defected. Don't do it in the papers, on TV and so on about my treacherous defection. You will only 'become aware' of it after the horse has bolted. If you do it the other way, publicly through the media, the British may smell a rat, since they know defectors are not something Russia is proud of."

"Is that all, Schaplinov?"

"No, sir. You have to make sure that all proper checks on me and my alias's passport are made at Moscow Airport or wherever I am to fly from, but that nothing much happens to stop me leaving Russia. My passage through the check-in desk and all the rest must go pretty smoothly so as to arouse no foreign suspicion."

Rostow nodded. "In other words, we make sure all the checks are properly carried out by someone who knows exactly what's what, so it all looks routine and above-board and no-one here spots you're not who the false identity and documents say you are." After a few seconds thought, Rostow said, "It would be better still if the 'false' passports were actually genuine, and only the names were fakes. We can do that here easily. The passport people do exactly as we tell them."

"Very well." Igor hesitated. "But that's not all. To make my flight and defection look genuine, I need some perfectly plausible papers from Pochep or other CBRN places here to give the British. Some of them have to relate to things MI6 and MI5 probably don't know, but low-level stuff so we're not giving away anything vital. That'll help show I'm the genuine article. Others will be about stuff you're certain they know anyway. Finally, you can include, if you want to, disinformation to mislead ...."

"You don't need to tell me what disinformation is. This directorate invented the idea." He picked up a pen and began tapping the desk rhythmically. "You realise you would have no diplomatic immunity if you were caught, don't you?"

"I do, sir. I should be what's known as 'an illegal'. Legal spies are the ones in Embassies and consulates. I should be an illegal spy, and liable to go to prison for years."

"Not only that. It is extremely unlikely that we should ever take steps to bring you back here. If we tried to arrange an exchange, it would be to admit that we had helped to deceive the British government and prove that you had not really defected in the first place. You might end up even worse off."

Schaplinov said he knew the consequences, but he wanted to go ahead. "However, I said that I'd go on a holiday to Cyprus or somewhere, and you could snatch me – a pretend kidnap, if you like – but if I have to get out in a hurry, a second genuine passport in another alias would be very useful."

Rostow nodded slowly, contemplatively, and stood. As he strolled round his desk to Igor, he said, "This will have to go to the First Directorate of the GRU, as they are more experienced in working abroad. To a large extent, they will be doing what they can to look after you." He stopped and put his hand on Igor's shoulder in a surprisingly sympathetic manner. "This adventure may also have to be approved up the line. It may even go to President Putin, so you may not hear anything for quite a while. Go back to work and say nothing to anyone. As you know, I thought you were a nutcase to start with, but it is a very interesting idea. Let's see how it develops."

Rostow escorted Igor out of the building and shook hands with him as they parted. He watched him walk away and chuckled to himself at his pretence of sympathy. If Schaplinov's little game paid off, it should be a feather in Rostow's cap as he had fostered it. If it failed, this foolish chap would have been the author of his own misfortunes. On the other hand, the GRU and SVR had been running illegal spies in foreign countries for years. The FSB, GRU, and SVR were well funded, reported direct to President Putin now, and had few restraints on what they were allowed to do. They were rather good at their work, though they had had some bad experiences when traitors like Gordievsky had defected to Britain after giving away secrets for many years. They had also inflicted similar losses on Western powers when important British SIS officials such as Burgess, Maclean, Philby, and Blunt, had spied for the USSR.

But the American CIA and FBI had suffered just as badly when Aldrich Ames and Robert Hanssen sold US secrets (and some British ones) for years to the KGB for millions of dollars. It took the CIA thirteen years to trace Ames. As a result of his activities, twelve Russians - CIA diplomatic and illegal spies working against the USSR - were rounded up there in a fairly short space of time, and another two fled abroad to safety in the USA and the UK.

Rostow knew that series of arrests were authorised by Mikhail Gorbachev against the advice of his experts. They feared that so many spies vanishing more or less simultaneously would alert the CIA to the fact that they had a traitor in their midst. Surely the CIA would realise that only a senior operative officer could have access to so much information? In fact, the CIA completely misread the signs, targeted the wrong man for a while, and then for a whole year followed a false trail laid by the Russians to suggest the traitor was in a CIA facility at Warrenton, Virginia. Meanwhile Ames went on spying and was largely brought down by ostentatiously living beyond the means of an officer even of his exalted salary. Only his Russian pay enabled him to do this. He went to prison in the US for life.

So did Hanssen. He worked as a spy on and off for twenty-one years, and although he received less money from the Russians than Ames, the damage he inflicted on his nation dwarfed the other man's efforts. Until Hanssen, Ames had been the worst spy the USA had suffered. His identity was never known to his paymasters, originally the KGB in the USSR, nor the secret services which replaced the KGB. Some of the product of Hanssen's spying had occasionally passed over Rostow's desk. Once the Communist regime collapsed Hanssen dropped out of sight to avoid detection, but after a short intermission, anonymously offered his services to the new Russian Federation once he thought it safe to do so.

Occasionally, when he thought about it, Rostow wondered just how valuable secrecy and spying were. It was almost impossible to keep a secret, as spies and defectors on both sides made a mockery of efforts to do so. He thought that everyone in the secrecy game should know the old Greek fable of the King, who, put under a spell, grew donkey's ears. He grew his hair long to hide them and had anyone who had seen his ears executed; with one exception. He spared his barber and swore him to secrecy.

After some years the barber could no longer tolerate the weight of this secret hanging over his head like the Sword of Damocles. He had to share it. He took a walk in the countryside and walked into a wheat field when no-one was about and no houses were nearby. He whispered to the growing crop: "His Majesty has the ears of a donkey" and walked home.

Some weeks later the King went out with a troop of his guards. They went past the field. A breeze stirred the wheat, and it whispered: "His Majesty has the ears of a donkey." The barber was never heard of again. As the fable writer put it, "A secret should never be told to anyone."

Rostow hoped that the secret of Igor could be kept. Should Schaplinov be in Porton Down for only a short while before being exposed or apprehended, it would be worth it to Russia if he had sent back useful information. If that happened and he was put in prison or even killed, it would still be worth it. No-one is indispensable; nobody knows that better than a spymaster.

Chapter 10

London, Tuesday, 26th April, 2016

Colin Lacey and Peter Shuttleworth waited in the foyer of the Wizard of Oz building on the South Bank of the Thames. They had an appointment to see Charles Peregrine Sawyer, the head of MI6. Unlike so many of his predecessors, Sawyer was not an old Etonian or Harrovian, nor a Wykehamist or from any of the other half-dozen top public schools, nor even a minor one. He was an old boy of a State Comprehensive School in Nottingham who had won a scholarship to Hertford College Oxford, where he gained First Class Honours in Law. He then took 'the hardest exam in the world' and passed it to study at All Souls College Oxford. His special subjects were law and history, and for the latter he specialised in Machiavelli, the Italian master of the hidden aspects of politics and government. He won his scholarship, placing him amongst many former illustrious fellows of All Souls, including the philosopher Sir Isaiah Berlin, former Lord Chancellor Quentin Hogg, and the warrior and writer, T.E.Lawrence of Arabia.

He continued to study there with the benefit of the two-year stipend, but abandoned academe when his brilliance came to the notice of SIS, and he was recruited into the intelligence services. He was in his last year of study at the college in 1980 when he met and married Margaret Stanfield. Women had not been admitted to All Souls during its four hundred year history until 1979, and Margaret was one of the first. Slim, beautiful, fiercely intellectual, five foot ten, and with a large quantity of russet auburn hair, she was the most gorgeous thing Charles had ever set eyes on. She was also the daughter of a member of the House of Lords, but Charles did not know that at the time.

She, on the other hand, was not at all taken with the appearance of this young Notts man, who talked about the local football team a bit to cover his shyness. He was a mere five foot eight, so with high heels she towered over him at the party in a pub in the High Street adjoining the college. His face was unremarkable apart from yellow eyes like a cat, and thick brown hair brushed straight back from his forehead. He was fit and strong, having twice been in the Oxford Rowing Team for The Boat Race from Putney to Mortlake. It was when she tried to poke a little gentle fun at him over their beers that she encountered the fierceness of Charles's brain, at least the equal of her own, and his gentle wit. Charles had little small talk, nor any evident and vain desire to impress by proclaiming his intelligence from the roof-tops, as did so many of the inadequate men who tried to date her.

His customary tactic, particularly where girls were concerned, was to ask them about themselves. He asked Margaret.

"I come from a small village in Wiltshire." She spoke in a beautifully modulated voice, which made her even more desirable to Charles. "It's very rural, so I was sent to boarding school; Bedales in Hampshire."

"What does your Dad do?"

"Boring. ...."

He gave a frosty smile. "Sorry, I'll try a more interesting question."

Shocked at the wit and sarcasm of his reply, Margaret replied: "Oh gosh, I didn't mean that. I meant what my father does. He's a Minister of State in the Home Office."

"Really? So he's either Augustus Dunnett MP, or Lord Stanfield."

"My goodness, you are well informed. The latter, actually."

"Well, I try. Let me guess. You live in a 17th Century manor house. And Dad – sorry, your father – is Lord of the Manor." Margaret was struck by Charles's matter-of-fact acceptance of what was clearly a considerable chasm of class and wealth between them. He was neither cowed nor resentful.

"Yes, he is, but the house is 16th Century."

"It sounds picturesque."

"Absolutely, but cold and inconvenient. Must be better in a lot of Council Houses."

Charles slipped easily into the local Notts dialect he was striving to discard. "Don't you believe it, m'duck. Certainly not t'one Mum 'n' I live in. The coal fire fills t'place wi' smoke and the Council has only just tacked a proper bathroom onto the 'ouse, so Dad lost 'alf his vegetable plot."

Margaret smiled, mimicking: "So you're working class, m'duck!"

Charles gave a slight bow. "Correct, Madam. Working made me top of my class and got me the highest First Class Honours." Somehow he managed to say that without boasting; just another set of facts.

When Margaret stopped laughing and recovered her composure she asked him about his parents. He told her his father was a skilled engineer and foreman of a machine shop, while his Mum was a nurse. Margaret slipped into the conversation that she had a First in her studies of human biology: "But I was not top scholar. I came a miserable third."

"That's not miserable, Margaret. That's fantastic."

From that moment they were inseparable and married three months later, despite Lord Stanfield's objections.

Once in the SIS, Sawyer's astuteness and grasp of the craft of intelligence gathering and spying, his ability to apply the devious teachings of Machiavelli, and above all his talent for joining the dots so that apparently unrelated items from different sources revealed the secret behaviour of foreign powers hostile to Britain, ensured his rise to the top was rapid. Charles would be the first to admit, if asked, that having a politically active peer in the family might have had something to do with it too, but that was only in his mind. It had nothing to do with his ascension at all. But the substantial moral and intellectual support he got from Margaret did.

When Lacey was waiting to see him, Charles Sawyer had been in the top job for five years. He was sixty-one, his hair was still abundant, and there were silver-grey flashes in the brown at his temples. His immaculately tailored suit came, unbeknown to Lacey, from the same Saville Row outfitters Lacey used. Most interesting from the detective's point of view was that Sawyer had been there in MI6 when Pedchenko defected.

When they were shown into this important man's office, they saw it was well and comfortably furnished, but with no ostentation, no personal photographs, and only a portrait of the Queen on the wall to the side of the large oak desk. Colin and Peter were invited to sit, and offered coffee which they accepted.

With only the slightest trace of his old Nottinghamshire accent and never again a 'm'duck', Sawyer said, "So you want me to tell you about Vladimir Pedchenko." He paused. "What, precisely would you like to know?"

"Frankly you have me there, sir. Precise I cannot be. I just want to know as much as possible about him. It's the way we coppers usually proceed when there is a serious crime ...."

Sawyer held up an index finger. ".... because more often than not, the victim's history and personality provide a motive."

Lacey replied, "Exactly, and finding a motive may pave the way to the killer."

Again, Charles Sawyer paused. "But the Russians did it, didn't they?"

"Forgive my bluntness, sir, but it's highly convenient for the PM and SIS to make that assumption, but where is the evidence to support it?"

Sawyer's smile reappeared. "Oh, I'm in no doubt you'll find the evidence eventually, Inspector."

Lacey smiled too, despite the fact he felt there was something sinister in that reply. The Director General's attempt to change the subject subtly had not escaped him either. "And your help with as much information about Pedchenko as possible will be of great assistance in doing that. Or perhaps I should say it will help us find out who the real killers may be, whether Russian or otherwise. I like to look for all the evidence, not just the bits which will convict a pre-selected suspect. sir."

"Of course, Inspector. I stand corrected."

After a soft knock on the door a female clerk with a tray of coffee cups, a silver coffee pot, cream jug, and sugar bowl came in, deposited the refreshments, and silently departed with a quiet "Thank you" from Sawyer.

Lacey decided to go back to a previous point from another angle. "I have to confess I struggle with the idea it was an official – even if secret – Russian attempt to kill the man. Two reasons. First, why should they bother?"

"Because he was a traitor, of course."

"Yes, sir, but he was well past his sell-by date. He was taken out of circulation when he was arrested in Moscow in 2009. I don't suppose the FSB or GRU left him any opportunity to acquire new Russian secrets while he was in custody being interrogated, and then in prison after his trial. He came here in 2011. He hasn't been back to Russia since, and, once again, I doubt that Russian diplomats and spies in the countries he's visited for you since then have been falling over themselves to load him with secret documents and data. They could have bumped him off on any of those trips. He's been out of the loop for seven years."

With a poker face, all Sawyer did was murmur, "Hmmm." And then, "The second reason?"

"They didn't have to kill him here. As I said just now, they could have killed him years ago in any of the countries SIS used him in. Why didn't they?"

"As I don't know everything the Russians think or do, I'm afraid I can't tell you, Inspector."

Shuttleworth laughed and said, "Or won't?"

Lacey gave him a stern glance and Charles Sawyer responded with, "Let's say 'might not', shall we?" He smiled again.

"You see, sir, if he'd been killed in Finland or Nigeria, say, years ago," Lacey continued, "suspicion could fall on all sorts of people, but the Russians would be the prime target, because they'd clearly have a lot more to gain when he might still have useful information to tell you. His murder or assassination in England eight or nine years after his arrest means that the chances are even greater it was someone else."

"Such as?"

"I think I might discuss that with you when you've told me all about Pedchenko."

Was it Lacey's imagination, or was the old spymaster rattled by his analysis?

Sawyer used both hands to smooth his silver-edged hair back and said, "Supposing you tell me what you know first. Then I'll try to fill in the gaps."

"Very well, sir." Colin Lacey told the mandarin all he had gleaned from Wikipedia and the huge stack of newspaper and other media sources Carl Boyce had discovered for him. He continued, "So what are the gaps?"

"Well, as you've gathered, Pedchenko worked for us, selling us information on his Russian colleagues who were spying on us, and on the USA and other allies. Normally these people who were the subject of our complaints were shipped back to Russia. Some – the illegals - were arrested by us, tried and went to prison. Sometimes, using the information Vladimir gave us - or sold us, I should say – we arranged some sort of sting so that the Russians pulled an operative out in disgrace. In fact you could say they were 'arrested' by the KGB or FSB on our soil, and flown home to Moscow without extradition proceedings."

"What would have happened to them?" Lacey contrived a disinterested tone for that question.

Sawyer shook his head. "Some may have gone to prison, some executed summarily by the KGB. Since the wall came down and Gorbachev, things have eased up a bit in the Federation, so there is usually a trial, and until a decade or so ago, they could be hanged. As you know from your reading, Pedchenko was lucky. Yeltsin had done away with capital punishment, so he went to prison for spying for us until we got him out in an exchange of spies - or traitors - depending on your point of view."

"So they could easily have had him bumped off when he was in prison in Russia. Why wait years and then kill him in Britain. Does that make any sense?" Lacey paused a second. He could see Sawyer was rather more agitated, "Do you know of any people who were sent back to Russia or executed there? Or Allied personnel who were punished in the West after being targeted by Pedchenko?"

"Of course. One man springs to mind. Andrei Koudriavtov was a KGB man posing as Russian Air Force attaché at the Russian Embassy in Rome. He compromised a senior Italian Air Force officer with a homosexual honey trap with a gay prostitute he introduced him to. The Italian, who was Nicolo Saltiero, then took Russian bribes to sell NATO secrets. Pedchenko was based in Rome then, told us about it (for cash, naturally), and we passed the details to our Italian counterparts. They arrested their Airman, who went to prison for fifteen years. Andrei was declared *persona non grata* by the Italian government, went home to Leningrad, and was treated as a hero."

Sawyer broke off for a moment, drumming his fingers on the arm of his chair. He rose and began to pour coffee for them, and as he handed it round, he spoke again. "There was a woman called Amelia Olivier he told us about. She worked for us, here in MI6. How she had managed to get a job here we do not know, some sort of slip-up somewhere, but she was half English, with a Russian father so she was bi-lingual. Her real name was Olga Opadnova. She had excellent forged documents based on a little girl of six called Amelia who'd died in Pembrokeshire in 1965. The Russians had her birth certificate, little Amelia's, that is. They probably put the information together to get it from the General Register Office by taking details from her gravestone and the parish register where she was christened. Several of our agents and 'blacks' - agents with no diplomatic cover - had disappeared, and she was responsible. Pedchenko got all the details when he was at the Russian Embassy here in London, and with the information he gave us we were able to identify Olga."

Lacey asked, "Was she sent home?"

"No. We promoted her to a useless position where we could feed her false leads to mislead her paymasters, while letting her nowhere near anything important." In a genuinely modest tone, he added: "Rather clever, I thought."

Lacey hesitated, and then, "So there would have been lots of others in prison or sent home; but who was executed?"

"Yes, Inspector, quite a number of others in prison or deported. And yes, a few of those were executed. That was mainly under the USSR. Since then, we think that the FSB may have murdered a small number secretly by their usual method: a bullet in the back to the head. All we know is that they disappeared and have never been heard of again."

"And that didn't happen to Pedchenko, or you wouldn't have been able to bring him out in the spy swap."

"Indeed. He told us he was treated leniently, mercifully if you like, because he made a full confession, and gave away more British secrets."

Peter Shuttleworth asked, "So what were the names of the people who were executed?"

Lacey smiled at his Sergeant for picking up on the unanswered question, but Sawyer sat silent for a couple of minutes.

Eventually the spy chief shook his head. "Look, you know I cannot tell you anything which might divulge, or enable you or someone with access to your files to work out, exactly how we learn things, or from whom."

"Sir, it embarrasses me a little to say this, but it may embarrass you a lot more if you don't. In November 2007, there was allegedly an attempt on the life of Oleg Gordievsky, another of your most important spies in the

KGB. The Police and Special Branch started an investigation, but SIS ordered it to cease. That order leaked out, and there was an outcry in the press. I hope I don't need to remind you that ...."

"Our Director at MI6, after being approached on Gordievsky's behalf by Eliza Manningham-Buller, a former head of MI5, insisted the inquiry proceed in 2008. But you see, in that case no poison was in Gordievsky and no-one was accused." After a pause Sawyer continued. "Of course, in that case the attack, if it was one, was twenty-three years after we had got him back here, which tends to undermine your thesis that Pedchenko had been here so long it wasn't worth the Russians' while to bother to kill him. It wasn't even ten years since his arrest in Moscow and he'd only been here five years."

Lacey leaned forward. "You said *if* it was an attack. In this case we know the poison and we know someone must have administered it somehow."

"Very well. Where does that get you?"

"To this point, sir. If you refuse to help us, things being what they are, there may be another leak to the media."

For the first time Charles Sawyer allowed a thread of emotion to break cover. "Are you threatening me, Detective?"

"Far from it. But you know as well as I do that no branch of the Police is immune from leaks and leaky officers. Do you – does MI6 – need another leak of orders not to investigate crime properly and conscientiously? And you're only telling me and Sergeant Shuttleworth here about people who have died or gone to prison years ago. Nobody will gain much from that."

Sawyer raised his forearms with palms out in a small signal of surrender. "Very well, Inspector. One who was executed before the Wall came down was Slava Lugovoi. Mikhail Stanislavski was another." He paused and sounded sad or regretful when he spoke again. "The third I can recall off the top of my head was Gordanov, Oleg Petrovich Gordanov."

Lacey picked up on this. "You don't seem to be terribly keen or triumphant about getting rid of the last one."

"I'm not proud of it. It wasn't one of my cases. It was a sting. Gordanov was a very successful spy, we're sure of that, but we could never catch him at it. He'd resisted several attempts to recruit him to spy for us against his Motherland and the KGB he worked for. No matter how good he was at deceiving us, he was too upright and honest for that. We had to get rid of him. Getting him sent home as *persona non grata* would have been insufficient. After a year or two back in Moscow he'd have been sent to spy somewhere other than England. We used Pedchenko to plant secret Russian documents on Oleg Gordanov when he was going to meet a senior British Army Officer. It looked as though he'd copied these in the Embassy and was about to hand them to the Army Officer, a colonel, for us. The KGB did not know we already had them. We'd got them from another source, so Gordanov did not know about them either. Pedchenko and some KGB thugs turned up, snatched Oleg off the street, and smuggled him back to Russia."

"Did you want him murdered?"

Sawyer shook his head again. "I don't think anyone here expected that. We knew he'd go to prison, but not to his grave."

"Mr Sawyer, were all of these people betrayed by Pedchenko?"

"All those I've told you about? Yes."

Lacey let that sink in. "So if they had family or friends, Pedchenko would have a lot of enemies."

Charles Peregrine Sawyer made no comment. Lacey asked, "Could you give me the name and address or a contact number for the Colonel you mentioned?"

Sawyer screwed the cap off his very expensive looking fountain pen, scribbled on a notepad, tore off the sheet and handed it to the detective. Lacey was surprised that Sawyer knew these details by heart from so long ago.

Chapter 11

Russia, May 2011

Igor had only been working back at Pochep for a month after his visit to meet Rostow when his supervisor told him there was a message for him in the Director's office. He was to report at once. In a few minutes he stood before the Director's desk. This officer handed him a note in a sealed envelope from the Defence Ministry. It was clearly marked "Secret – addressee only."

The Director said, in a tone which invited a breach of confidence: "I shall not ask you what that is about."

Igor held up the envelope, pointing at the legend on it: "And I shall not tell you, you will be glad to know." He went to the toilet, locked himself in a cubicle, took down his trousers and pants to make it look as though he was there for the right purpose, in case a snooper tried to look over or under the door or the walls of the cubicle. He sat down, and opened the envelope. The letter was on Ministry paper and asked, or rather ordered him, to telephone a landline number in the body of the letter and ask for Alexeii.

After work, he went to a phone box to make the call. When the phone was answered the voice just said, "Hello." Igor asked if he could speak to Alexeii.

"This is he." Igor recognised Nikita Rostow's voice, but decided to be cautious. "Hello, Alexeii. I received your letter. How can I help?"

"Following upon what happened a month ago I want you to meet me at the entrance to St Basil's Cathedral. I shall take you to meet some friends of mine who are interested in your project."

"Very well. When?"

"Ten days from now. It's a Monday. 3.00 pm. Your Director will receive a phone call soon telling him you have to report to the Ministry then, and you are to have four days off with pay. I shall send you a travel warrant for the train." The line went dead.

Two days later Igor was summoned to the Director's office again. The man was cross and worried. "What is all this, Schaplinov? Are you in trouble, or are you trying to get me in the shit?"

"There's no trouble, sir, for either of us so far as I know." Igor was silent for a while, awaiting a reaction, but the Director said nothing; he was visibly trembling. "What makes you think there might be?"

"This is still Russia, you idiot, even if it's not the USSR and the KGB have gone. We're still watched, 'specially in a place like this, where it's all secrets. The Ministry phoned to tell me to let you go to Moscow and to give you three days off with pay. They say next week I'll get a letter authorising this."

"Well, I'm not going to worry myself about it," said Igor. "If you're in trouble they just send some heavies to pick you up without warning, don't they? If they ask about you, I shall tell them how well, from my humble perspective, you run this establishment. As it happens, I still don't know what they want."

"So what was that letter about you had the other day? What do the Ministry want with the likes of you?"

"It just asked me to phone. Then when I did, they told me to go to see them."

"I don't like it."

"Look sir, I've done nothing wrong or you'd be the one to report me, wouldn't you? So unless you've done something, I don't see why you should worry."

"I've told you before you're an impertinent bastard! Don't you take the piss out of me."

"No sir. Can I go now?"

"Just bugger off."

"Before I do, sir, are you sure it was only three days off? They told me it would be four with pay."

A vivid crimson hue spread all over the Director's face as he realised his little scheme to pocket a day of Igor's pay had just vanished. He nodded. "Of course it was. Got muddled up. Off you go." He essayed a smile. He'd have been in real trouble if he'd taken the money and Igor queried it at the Ministry. In any case, the Ministry would want to know why Igor thought he had to leave a day early.

****

On the Monday designated by Rostow, Igor arrived in Moscow by train. Afternoon sunshine was wonderful, but it was still cool. He made his way to St Basil's Cathedral near the Kremlin. It was seething with people. Igor thought if Rostow wanted their meeting to go unobserved, he could hardly pick a better venue. They would be just two men amongst hundreds, if not thousands.

At 3.00 pm, Igor was strolling about in the main porch of the Cathedral looking at a guidebook. A party of about twenty French tourists walked past him with a guide. It was the fourth or fifth such group he had seen, of many nationalities. As the French went past, a man at the back in shorts with dark glasses, hiking boots, a T-shirt emblazoned with "J'aime Paris" on the front and "Pour L'Amour" on the back, and apparently not looking where he was going, bumped in to him and said, very quietly: "Join the back of the next group. I'll find you inside." And then loudly: "Je vous prie me pardonner M'sieur", before hurrying off to rejoin the group. Like two or three others he wore a French beret. It was Rostow.

Within two minutes a group of Siberian tourists came into the entry, and Igor casually tacked himself to them. They had gone about fifty feet into the cathedral and had stopped a couple of times for short lectures by their guide when the man with dark glasses and beret stood at his side.

"I'm going out now," he said. "Look around for another minute and then come out to the Square. A car will pull up for both of us."

Igor did as he was told. Rostow was standing outside the gates of the Kremlin, and at that moment a large black Mercedes with blacked out windows came to a rapid but noiseless halt in front of them. A rear door swung open, and Rostow jumped in, ordering Igor to do likewise. The luxurious vehicle sped away, but not far. Igor saw they were approaching the Lubyanka. He was, at last, rather fearful. Did Rostow want to talk to him, or torture him?

There could hardly be a Russian who did not know what the Lubyanka stood for. Even so, Igor had done some reading about it. Some years before the 1917 Revolution it had been built in a Baroque style for the All-Russia Insurance Company. After the Revolution it became the home of the Secret Police, then the KGB, and ultimately the FSB, the Foreign Intelligence Division of the Russian Federation. Igor understood the basement was still the workshop of sadistic interrogators. The building was known to the people who worked there as "The Monastery," presumably because all visitors to the basement finished up praying - for release from pain.

As they drove into the vehicular entrance to this dreaded structure, Rostow was saying, "Maybe you found our meeting arrangements strange. I didn't want to risk anyone knowing you were with me. We want to keep you clear of any link with us, if you still want to go to the UK and do what you told me previously."

They drove into a covered entrance where they could not be observed and entered the building by a rear door after Rostow identified himself to an armed guard.

Igor was shown into a bleak waiting room on the fourth floor and told to wait. After fifteen minutes, Rostow reappeared, dressed in the uniform of a Captain of the FSB.

"Come with me, Schaplinov."

They walked down the corridor to a lift and got out on the next floor up. A guard outside a double wooden door opened it for them and Rostow led Igor into a vast, bare, and intimidating room. He saluted. "Gentlemen, this is Igor

Schaplinov, the man from Pochep experimental station I told you about." He then pointed out to Igor the three men seated behind the long table. "Major-General Melekhov on the left, Colonel Sholokev on the right, and General Dennisev in the centre." He turned to Igor. "Sit there."

There was a solitary chair placed in the centre of the room about ten feet from the table. Igor sat on it. Rostow went to sit at the side of the table on the left. Igor thought that putting him at his ease was not what this was all about. He was very surprised when the full General leaned forward on his elbows, smiled, and said, "We've heard a lot about you, Igor."

Igor said nothing. General Dennisev continued. "Like me, Major-General Melekhov is with FSB, but Colonel Sholokov is with the GRU. We consider this idea of yours to be very interesting but risky for all of us in Russia for various reasons, so we have consulted with our colleagues in other departments of State Security." Again, Igor said nothing, but inclined his head in acknowledgement.

"Don't be afraid. There is nothing to be afraid of. You came to my colleague Captain Rostow with this very intriguing idea, and we want to explore it with you."

So Igor repeated what he'd told Rostow over three weeks before about fleeing with a false passport to a European Country - he suggested France, for example - then producing his genuine Igor Schaplinov passport in the British Embassy, asking for asylum in Britain, and aiming for a job at Porton Down with a view to spying for Russia, and supplying the British with false leads, misleading documents and a few titbits of good but not vital data.

"But why do you want to go under your own name to the SIS?"

"Because I want them to believe I am genuine. That is why the passport I leave Russia with must be the false one. I could wear green contact lenses to defeat any photo identification equipment in other countries. A story that I had to leave here for fear of something will then seem to have more merit than otherwise."

The General nodded. "That is what we hoped you would say." Then he whispered something to Melekhov, and turned to Sholokev. "Colonel?"

"Why do you want to do this? You know it will be extremely dangerous."

Igor indicated Nikita Rostow and said, "Indeed Colonel. The Captain explained it very forcefully."

"And the answer to my question is?"

"Sir, I am a patriotic Russian. I have no idea who my father was, and my mother has struggled to make a good living and bring me up well. But our Motherland gave her the chance to succeed and educated me to the highest degree. In addition to all that, I now have a good job. I want to do something more challenging to repay my debt to Russia than working day after day in peace and quiet in a laboratory. I want to make a real difference." The statement about his father was, he knew, a lie, and if they had any inkling his father was Oleg Gordanov he could be dead in minutes. He had to take a chance they knew nothing.

All three men smiled at him. Relief flooded his brain. He hoped it didn't show.

They continued to question him: about his education, his friendship with Simon Grant, his time at Cambridge and the return visit by Alan Carpenter; about his work; and what sort of papers he expected them to give him, or allow him to take from Pochep to hand over to SIS. The meeting adjourned and they told Rostow to take Igor out to dinner, put him in a good hotel for the night, and to bring him back in the morning.

****

At 9.00 am the next day, Igor Schaplinov was back in the solitary chair facing the three senior officers behind their long table, but this time Nikita Rostow sat behind him near the door. The two of them had had a very pleasant evening in a good restaurant off the beaten track, and the conversation had been anodyne but interesting. They largely talked about their careers to date, and Rostow spoke of his wife and children. Despite that camaraderie, Igor felt threatened by the presence behind him at this second meeting. The Soviet and the Federation secret services had a reputation for putting bullets in the back of the head.

His fears were soon allayed when General Dennisev, in dress uniform with the left side of his chest almost covered in medal ribbons, rose and came round the table to shake hands with him.

"We discussed your project for much of the evening, Mr Schaplinov, and we have decided to back it. As these two important State Security departments have agreed on it, we have not had to go higher for approval. And I can assure you that harmony in the intelligence community is not guaranteed!"

Igor saw Colonel Sholokov laugh, and Major-General Melekhov smile, and heard a chuckle from behind him.

"But," Dennisev continued, "there are some important preliminaries. First, you must be trained as an illegal, what our 'friends' in the UK and US would call 'black' agents. This is for your protection and ours. You do not want to be caught and end up dead in some bungled arrest, or in prison for years if successfully arrested and convicted. Spying being the game it is, to be frank it matters little to us if you are killed, because then you cannot talk. We do not want you caught and able to talk and tell all you know about us, do we?"

He paused and held his hands out, index fingers pointing upward in a confidential gesture. "You think that cold and brutal? Well, you're right, and I make no bones about it. Spying is a cold and brutal business."

"What is this training, sir, and where is it done? By the way, I thank you for telling me the exact truth about this. I guess a black or illegal agent has little or no hope of rescue, and would be lucky to be included in an exchange of spies internationally."

As General Dennisev returned to his seat Melekhov leaned forward. "Correct. We would do what we could, but exchanges are hard to arrange, and the British or Americans would want somebody important of theirs we were holding for it to be worth their while. That is how MI6 got Gordievsky back. We received several of our spies in the swap. He was one of the worst traitors we have ever had. In another case you may have heard of we swapped our excellent illegal Vilyam Fisher for Gary Powers, the American U2 spy plane pilot. They were desperate to get him back, but he'd told us all he knew before we released him. He'd been quite cooperative."

Dennisev took over. "To answer your question, Igor, you will be sent for six months to the Academy of Foreign Intelligence. It's in the forests north of Moscow. There are two campuses, one at Yurlovo, but you will go to the main one at Chelebityevo. The instruction will include avoiding and losing surveillance to which you may be subjected; we call that *proverka*. Then there'll be the use of chalk marks to warn a contact of information drops or the need for meetings, and you'll be taught how to disguise yourself. We shall give you a tiny camera to photograph documents, and lessons on how to turn them into microdots. You'll be taught the workings of codes and ciphers."

"Forgive me, sir, for asking, but do I really need all that? After all, I shall, if we get lucky, be working in one secret location. I shan't be roving all over the place making contact with lots of English people to dig up secrets from lots of different places. All I need is one contact to whom I can deliver the secret stuff."

All three men at the table stiffened. They were unaccustomed to being asked questions which doubted their judgement. Then Dennisev sighed, relaxing with a smile as he reflected that Schaplinov was no soldier subjected to rigid disciple. "I hope you may be right, but as I said, this is for your good. Spies never know when the sky may fall in. You need to be fully prepared for the worst that may, we hope, never happen. In any case, the course you will do is comparatively short. That reduces the risk that MI6 or the CIA may spot you on it somehow. Normally it lasts for a few years. We shall not even put your presence there in any records. Your instructors will just be told to teach you, and we shall give you a false name for use with them and your fellow students."

Igor indicated his acquiescence. "I understand, sir. May I make a suggestion?"

The General nodded.

"I'm not going to be producing huge amounts of information on a daily or even weekly basis, so I don't need a complex system of contacts. Maybe one or two, just to receive any urgent messages about problems. I might never need them. What would be useful would be a regular place I could visit. Britain is very cosmopolitan, or multicultural as they call it these days. If you set up or bought a restaurant in Salisbury, say, where lots of tourists and foreigners go, and the population is pretty well off, I could dine there often, but not on a regular basis."

"What would be the purpose of that?"

Igor took a deep breath, wondering whether he was about to make a complete fool of himself. "I could leave documents or messages there, and the owner could get them to the Embassy without suspicion falling on me. The owner would know I was there, so I could slip the documents into the menu folder while I examine it. It is not as though I should be likely to be submitting huge masses of stuff as Penkovsky and Gordievsky did. I could also go to the toilet and stick the papers behind the cistern. You remember how the gun was left in the toilet for Michael in 'The Godfather'?" All of the officers smiled and indicated agreement. "Well, one visit I could do the menu trick, and the next I could go to the toilet. If I am only ever served and waited on by the owner who reports to you, and if he is otherwise completely clean, why should my meals attract attention?"

"What do you mean by 'completely clean'?"

Igor extended a hand palm up, as if offering them the explanation. "Just that he should be told to run a good business, pay his taxes, trade honestly, and not have any other spies or agents of yours to handle. If he falls under suspicion, it may lead SIS to me."

"You have spent a lot of time thinking about this, haven't you," Colonel Sholokov stated rather than asked this.

"I have, sir. You may all be able to think of other ways in which the restaurant can be used for messages."

The Colonel again. "How would the restaurateur know you were there?"

"I should always ring and book a table. I would book a table in every restaurant I went to in Salisbury, so it would not be suspicious. If I were on my own, it would be a menu drop. If it were a day when I had a friend with me - a man or a woman - it would be the toilet. And if I went with two or three or more friends, there would be no drop at all."

"But a new boy at Porton would be suspect if he were Russian, in any case." Melekhov that time.

Igor was prompt. "I entirely agree, sir. That is why the restaurant should be in existence for a good while before I get there. Like the owner, the restaurant must be squeaky clean. I shall visit it a number of times with or without friends, some of whom I hope will be from the Weapons place - people I work with. I shall be unable to give you anything much for several months. With luck by that time if I'm being spied on they'll be fed up with finding me doing nothing. They'd look at my other activities which will be completely innocent."

General Dennisev slapped a hand softly on the table-top. "I dislike the idea of the owner going direct to the Embassy. He should give or send the material to another clean person who could go to the Embassy or meet one of our agents from it."

"Yes, sir, that's why I said, 'get them to the Embassy', not 'take' them. Once the papers and messages are with the owner it would be up to you to set up how they get back to you." Igor paused. "One small detail, if I may sir?"

The General agreed.

"The cafe should have several toilet cubicles so if I'm followed by any chance, the surveillance won't know which one I went in, and the owner should follow me in as soon as I come out. Also, the cisterns should be the old sort, high up on the wall with a chain to pull, so that no-one can see the drop casually. They'd have to be looking for it."

The General chuckled. "But such old-fashioned toilets would look out of place in a modern restaurant."

"That, sir, is why the whole premises should have an Edwardian or Victorian theme, or an early twentieth century Russian appearance; pre-revolutionary sort of decor. Or Middle Eastern. Of course, you would have to find a way to make sure the owner was clean, and unconnected with FSB, GRU, or any other Russian or Soviet State Security organ."

The General leaned forward again, with a smile - something rare in the FSB when delivering a reprimand: "My dear Igor, we ....", he included his colleagues with a sweeping hand movement, "we are full of admiration for the way you have thought this whole thing through, but you must credit us with a little knowledge of our own business."

"Of course, sir; I apologise." Igor recognised the smile was like that of a hungry crocodile. It simply obscured the threat slightly.

"Very well. Wait outside for a moment, Captain Rostow."

Rostow shot to his feet, saluted, and remained at attention. "Yes, General."

"Escort Mr Schaplinov to another room and bring him back as soon as the bell rings."

"Yes sir." He saluted again, took Igor by the elbow and marched him out of the room to an antechamber. They both paced the floor without a word. Both reflected on their fate. Igor was worried that he might not get to do what he wanted. Rostow was petrified that if the panel of senior officers blamed him for bringing a worthless proposal to them, his career might end there and then.

After three or four minutes the bell rang and Rostow took Igor back to the room of the long table. The scientist took the chair and Rostow stood to attention behind him.

The General stood, and Igor followed suit. "We have decided to adopt your project, Igor Schaplinov. In a short time you will be sent to the Academy, as I said earlier. Now you must return to Pochep. You may tell them that you may be sent away on a tour of all the other experimental stations around the country, as you are to be prepared for promotion if you are found to be satisfactory. You know no more than that, should anyone ask. In the meantime, we shall be preparing a complete cover story for you. We shall be considering your idea of a 'safe restaurant' as opposed to a safe house. You may leave that to us. Believe me, we know what we're doing."

All three officers walked round to Igor's side of the table and shook hands with him. Then Dennisev turned to Rostow. "Captain." Rostow saluted again, remaining at attention. "You did well to bring this man to us. It required courage to do so, as on the face of it, the idea might seem extreme or even foolish." He looked at his colleagues, who looked approvingly at the Captain. "We have decided to recommend you for promotion, Captain Rostow. You are now a Major"

The Major saluted once more. The General told them to depart.

Chapter 12

London, Wednesday, 27th April, 2016

The train from Chichester got into Victoria at 10.40 am, and Lacey and Shuttleworth stepped out of the First Class carriage near the barrier. Colin wanted some peace so he could think carefully how he would approach Colonel Webster. A Christian name (Lacey could not get accustomed to the idea that calling a first name a Christian name was politically incorrect) like Ramsey suggested someone from the upper or upper middle classes. Instant camaraderie was unlikely, so he resolved to be a combination of respectful and authoritative. He hoped the retired army officer would greet a senior police officer from Counter-terrorism with some measure of equality.

Lacey had left Detective Sergeant Kiara Charcko setting up white boards, making notes on them with felt tip of everything they thought relevant, or pasting and pinning all the photos of the victims, the crime scene, and Pedchenko's house on display boards. The two constables, Morton and Jones, were continuing door-to-door enquiries, widening the net in Chichester. So far no-one (apart from the Prime Minister) had any idea who might have spread the poison;

the nearest thing they had to a sighting so far was the statement from Mrs Mason about the vicar, or more accurately, the man dressed like a vicar.

Webster had invited Colin to meet him at the Army and Navy Club. The two police officers took a taxi to Pall Mall and alighted outside the Club.

"Blimey, sir," said Shuttleworth, pointing in amazement at the statue in a glass cage outside the 1960s building. "Got his bollocks on display, so he's a bloke alright. Bit daft, going into battle like that, I'd say." He pointed again, this time at the face. "Seems to be an awfully feminine kind of warrior, doesn't he? Or is it meant to show it's the women who really have balls?"

Lacey smiled. "These days women are every bit as good as men at being warriors. Always have been, actually. Look at Boudicca."

"Who's Boudicca?"

"How about Boadicea?"

"I get it now. The ancient Briton who fought the Romans. She's got a huge bronze statue of herself and her daughters on a chariot. On the other side of Westminster Bridge from Parliament."

"Yes, Queen of the Iceni, when we were still tribal people." Lacey stepped smartly away. "Come on lad. We're meeting the Colonel at eleven. We've got two minutes."

Inside the double doors an important looking member of Club staff who might have been a butler approached them from behind a desk, but before he reached them a strong, deep and well-spoken voice issued from the bottom of the stairs. "That's fine Barton. My guests. Leave 'em to me."

With a slight inclination of the head and a "Very well, Colonel," the man withdrew to his desk. Colonel Ramsey Webster was about seventy, tall and slim, fit and tanned, with a silver pencil moustache to match his thick silver short back and sides, brushed straight back from his forehead 1940s style. He wore a red, brown and green striped Regimental tie with a mid-grey three-piece suit, and perfectly polished but clearly ancient brown brogues, judging from the crazed cracking of the leather.

He held out his hand. "Chief Inspector Lacey, I take it."

Lacey shook the hand. "Yes, Colonel, and this is my Sergeant, Peter Shuttleworth."

Webster smiled and shook his hand too. "Welcome, Sergeant. Come on, let's have coffee, and if there's time, we'll have lunch. In a hurry, are you?" He led them to a very comfortable lounge and ordered a pot for three.

Colin was surprised when Webster asked him about his background. Laughing a little he said, "I thought I'd come here to ask the questions, sir."

"Drop the sir. I'm retired now; don't like all the pulling rank stuff. Call me Ramsey." He gestured at Shuttleworth. "You're Peter, right? The one who phoned me up?"

"Yes, sir."

"Got it. Always care to know my men, y'see. Not familiar, but sympathetic. Do anything for a caring officer, most will. D'you agree?"

Colin looked at Shuttleworth. "What say you, Peter?"

Looking at the Colonel, Peter replied with a wag of the head towards Colin: "That's what he's like too, sir."

"Ramsey, Peter. So, Colin, we've got similar backgrounds. Asked around about you. Both old grammar school boys, but I got into Sandhurst. Brushed up the old accent to sound like the Public School fellers. Elocution lessons from an actress. Rather beautiful, she was." He winked. "Taught me a few other useful things too." He halted and indicated his tie. "Royal Tank Regiment. Tried never to lose the common touch with my men."

"Lacey grinned. "I recognised the tie, sir. My father was a sergeant in the 55th."

"Well, what d'you know, eh! So what can I help you with?"

"Is it OK if Peter takes notes? Not against club rules is it?"

"Not as far as I know. Fire away. About something happened here at the Club a few years ago, you said on the phone."

"Do you remember the name Oleg Gordanov?"

"Christ! Will I ever forget it? I didn't know it at the time, but I believe that was the most shameful thing I've ever done."

"What happened?"

"Awful. Bloody awful. See, I knew Oleg. Met him abroad a couple of times, and here in London at Embassy and other functions where military attaches and so on were allowed. Thought him a damned decent chap for a Russian. Knew he was suspected of being a spy, but he never tried any old malarkey with me. Never told him anything he couldn't have read in the News of the World or any other rag. Not that I read 'em, you understand. I read the Telegraph and The Guardian; try to get a balance." A pause. "Never tried to get me to tell him anything, either. Played golf with him a couple of times. He was hopeless. So then we went clay pigeon shooting. He was bloody good at that, I tell you."

"So what happened?"

"Sorry, gone off at a tangent. Happens at my age. Well, I was still in the regiment then. I got an order to arrange to meet Oleg at my club. Knew he was interested in military history. He was going to give me some Russian historical magazines or books about the Napoleonic Wars from the Tsar's perspective, and I was going to give him stuff about Wellington's campaigns."

Peter spoke, sounding surprised. "Do you speak Russian, then sir?"

"Peter, it's Ramsey. Yes. Studied it at Durham. Got an Upper Second."

"Sorry, Ramsey. It's just you look like someone who I ought to call 'sir'."

Webster and Lacey laughed. Webster continued. "I was told to be at the Club at noon, but to get Oleg to turn up at one. I waited, but no sign of him."

"And then?"

"I asked Barton, the man you saw in the lobby. In fact, come to think of it, Barton came to me in the restaurant. He's been here forever. He said there had been an extraordinary incident on the steps outside. A man was just entering the Club when he was stopped by three or four others. After some business with a brief case, he was carted off. Barton said it looked as though the man had been arrested, maybe drugged, but there were no police if it was an arrest, and he was put in an ordinary Rover."

"Who was it?"

"Barton described him to me, and it was Oleg Gordanov. I was both upset and furious at the same time. Went straight back to the barracks, phoned the chap who'd got me to arrange the meeting. He was someone in the regiment. He knew nothing except he gathered his orders had come down from SIS somehow."

"What did you do then?"

"Managed to get onto MI6. Waste of bloody time. 'You're not entitled to know anything, sir'. Hate that, don't you? They call you 'sir' while they treat you like some sort of worm. 'But he's a friend of mine'. 'Then you should choose your friends more carefully, sir.' Nearly had apoplexy. Then this civil service twit – even if she was MI6 – said, 'Keep your eye on the papers, sir. It'll all be in there soon.' And it was. Then I heard on the grapevine that MI6 had framed Oleg and he'd been smuggled back to Moscow and executed not long after."

Lacey saw the old gentleman was disturbed and gave him a minute. "Do you think he had any enemies here?"

"Might have. After all, the Russian who helped nab him was brought over here in a spy swap, wasn't he?"

"Yes, Ramsey, he was. He's the chap, Pedchenko, whose murder we're investigating now."

"Just shows, doesn't it. All this spying, all the money it costs, we spy on them, they spy on us, and eventually we end up back where we started." He took out his handkerchief and blew his nose. His eyes glistened but he did not wipe them. "Y'know, I didn't like the idea of Oleg being a spy, but I've killed bunches of men with shells from tanks, machine gunned them, thrown grenades. Might have been women and kids in some of the houses we smashed. Who am I to judge people? Getting rid of him like that was plain dirty." Then the Colonel blew his nose again and laughed in a sad fashion. "D'you know, I've never told anyone but my wife all that before. Must be getting soft." He slapped the arms of his club chair and stood up. "Come on, lunch is on me. Cheer me up. We'll have a good bottle of wine. Fantastic cellars here."

Neither Colin nor Peter objected that they were on duty. And it was a good bottle of a vintage Chambertin.

Over lunch Webster reminisced about his Army career, places he'd served, and told anecdotes. Colin swapped with anonymous Special Branch stories, including his involvement with the disappearing plane, which needed no editing as it had been all over the newspapers and TV. Now Peter knew that story too. He could contribute little, but said he played golf, and asked, "Where did you and Gordanov play?"

"Oh, nowhere very special. One course near Cowdray Park and another rather hilly one somewhere out behind Southampton."

"D'you mean the one off the road to Romsey? I've played that. It's really hilly. I've played the other one too."

Webster smiled. "Talking of hills reminds me that was Oleg's choice. He liked hills. We even went walking in North Wales once over a long weekend. Snowdonia. Then he slipped on some shale and gashed his leg badly. I had to half carry him back to our car and drove him to hospital in Bangor. I think it was the year before he was kidnapped right outside this Club."

Chapter 13

Pochep, Russia, June 2012

One early evening, exactly a month to the day after his last occupation of the solitary chair before General Dennisov and the other two officers, Igor was surprised by a knock at the door of his small apartment in Pochep. He was even more surprised, but simultaneously pleased on opening it, to find Captain Rostow standing on the threshold wearing a rather creased grey suit and a tie. For a month he felt he had been in a state of suspended animation waiting for his orders to go to the Academy. Now he would hear the news.

They smiled at each other and Igor stood aside to let the officer pass, and was about to greet him with "Welcome, Captain Rostow," when the latter put his finger across his lips, and quietly and authoritatively whispered "Say nothing."

In silence Igor shut the door. Rostow said, "A walk on a lovely evening like this would be best, don't you think?"

"Yes, of course. I'll just put my shoes on. Shall we go for a beer?"

"Excellent idea, Igor."

Five minutes later they emerged onto the street and started off in the direction of the town. As they passed a rather dirty old red Lada 1500, Rostow pointed it out and said, "I took that out of the car pool to be inconspicuous."

"Is that why you're not in uniform?"

"Certainly. That's why I'm shabby and stopped you saying 'Hello Rostow,' or calling me Captain or something of the kind. You know how thin the walls are in those old flats. The place might be bugged, too; probably is. Your mission is, as the General told you, a real solid platinum secret. Be no use if we let the cat out of the bag in your flat, would it?"

Igor chuckled. "No Captain; that would never do."

"That's the other thing. The General promised me promotion, so it's Major Rostow now. But you'd better call me Nikita from now on. More deception, eh?"

"Fine, sir. Nikita, I mean. Sorry. Won't happen again."

"Look, we'll walk around for a bit so no-one overhears us, then go back to the car and drive to a bar, the one you usually use. Just try to have a laugh there. Anybody asks, I'm your Uncle, your mother's very much younger brother, OK?"

"Very well, Uncle Nikita." They both chuckled.

By now they were on a path through a park. The sky was cloudy with occasional bursts of sun, and it was warm. Several people were about, walking dogs, flirting, cuddling under the trees, reading papers on benches, but no-one was in earshot.

The Major put his arm around Igor's shoulders, as a close and friendly Uncle might. "I've been told your boss will get a letter telling him about your six-month instruction tour of all the other CBRN places. He'll get it in about two weeks. In the middle of August, you'll be off to the Academy. Before those six months are up, he'll get another letter saying your tour has been extended as you are making good progress, and you may never return to Pochep. Explains away your disappearance to the UK." He fished in his inside pocket and brought out an envelope. He handed it to Igor. "This is a list of the first couple of places you'll allegedly be going to with dates. When the boss calls for you, you can tell him this is all you know, and will be told the rest of it later, and he must keep it top secret. Just memorise this, then tear it into small pieces and flush it down the bog."

"OK. How do I get to the Academy?"

"On the day there'll be a travel warrant waiting for you at Pochep station. When you get off in Moscow I'll be waiting for you and drive you there." He stopped and gave Igor a serious glance from those staring eyes. "I'll not pull the wool over your eyes. The course is bloody hard work, mentally and physically. What do you know about our Prime Minister?"

"That he was President last year, Medvedev was his PM, and now they've swapped roles. I know he's about fifty-seven, born in Leningrad." Igor thought a moment. "Not much else."

"He got a degree in Law at Leningrad too, joined the FSB, and eventually became its director. Went into politics and joined Yeltsin's government and became Prime Minister a little later. Did you know he went to the Academy?"

Igor shook his head. "Why no, I didn't."

"We were there together, part of the time. Believe me, he's a hard bastard, and not just politically. Martial arts were his thing, you know. Still are, I believe."

Igor smiled. "Well, I keep fit, so let's hope I survive this course. At least I haven't got to do the whole five years."

"Don't forget. Tell no-one in Britain you've been there. You were on a tour of our installations."

"Then you'd better get me some info on them to study. Include some secret – or pretend secret – nuggets for them. I'll never convince MI5 or 6 I'm genuine if I know nothing about them."

"We'll do that. At least you know all the jargon already. From time to time, we'll give you some stuff to write to your boss or a colleague at Pochep so you can say what you're supposed to have done and seen at the other defence places." They strolled on in silence for a while. Then Rostow said, "There's something else. You suggested that General Dennisov and his colleagues should think about setting up a restaurant for your contact to get information back here, and for us to let you have the stuff you can pass on to Porton Down to find its way to the Secret Intelligence Service. They liked it."

"They did? Good. What will they do about it?"

"Not 'will'. It's what are they doing. As you know, Putin is pretty pally with Assad of Syria and had his assent to find a suitable restaurateur. Dennisov told Putin what it's all about, and Putin liked it too. He simply told Assad he wanted to invest secretly in a UK business and Assad came on board. Sent a few names of great chefs with clean records to us. The man, Ismail Salamani, is as clean as a whistle, an excellent chef, and has no trouble going to the UK as he has relatives in Scotland. Been going there every couple of years for twenty years. Runs his own successful restaurant in Damascus. Knows the restaurant trade in Britain, too. Says a Middle Eastern theme will be very popular, the UK being so cosmopolitan these days."

"Is he prepared to go?"

"Delighted to. Apart from the fact he's had an offer he can't refuse - you know about Assad's methods, I dare say - he's being given the money to buy a place plus fit it out, and he's bank-rolled for the first two years. If he makes it pay in the first year he keeps the bank-roll. On top of all that, he gets to keep his Damascus place, so he can sell it or lease it out, whatever he wants. And he gets five hundred pounds cash every time he sends one of your packages to the Embassy." Rostow changed tack. "He speaks a bit of Russian and English with a Scottish accent."

Igor laughed. "Well, I hope it's not Glasgow. I wouldn't understand a word. I met some Glaswegians at Cambridge."

"Ismail's been over, got an agent to find him a suitable site, and he's buying it."

"So it won't look like a coincidence when I start going there. It'll have been open for about a year when I first go in."

"Yes. He's even chosen a name: "The Caspian Gourmet." Rostow clapped Igor on the shoulder. "OK. Where's the bar. I need that beer. And dinner."

Chapter 14

London, Wednesday, 27th April, 2016

After the lunch with Colonel Webster, Lacey and Shuttleworth walked down Pall Mall to return to Victoria via St James's Palace and the Mall. They hadn't gone far when the Sergeant put his hand on the Inspector's arm and they halted. "I've been thinking, sir."

Lacey smiled. "Careful, Peter. Don't want you getting exhausted."

Peter smiled back. "It's just that, well, that butler or whatever he is at that Club - Barton - might have seen something. Should we go ...."

"Back and ask? At once. Good thinking, Sergeant. This is your idea, so you ask the questions."

Five minutes later they were back inside the Club. They asked a passing club staff member if they could speak to Mr Barton. "Certainly sir. I'll fetch him."

Another minute passed. Barton came down the stairs to them. "Gentlemen, what can I do for you?" As a look of recognition passed over his face, he held up the palm of his left hand before they could reply. "Excuse me, but weren't you here a little while ago to see Colonel Webster?"

Lacey spoke: "Yes, Mr Barton, we were. I'm Detective Inspector Lacey. My colleague Detective Sergeant Shuttleworth wants to ask you a few questions."

The steward turned quite pale and put a hand over this heart. "Is the Colonel in some sort of trouble, sir? Or is it me?"

Lacey nodded at Peter who was chuckling. "Neither of you, Mr Barton. We came to see the Colonel about something which happened at the Club, or rather just outside it, some years ago. 1995. Were you here then?"

"I've been here man and boy, as you might say. I was assistant steward then. What happened?"

"It was in December. The Colonel was supposed to meet a Russian gentleman here for lunch. His name was Gordanov."

"Let's go to my office, if you please. I keep all the old diaries and restaurant booking calendars there. I can check to see if it helps me recall this. We get foreign visitors all the time. This way please, gentlemen." He turned and led them up the stairs to an office along a corridor and asked them to sit. He went to a bookshelf and wandered along it touching the spines of ledgers and large diaries, mumbling the years as he went. "Ah, here we are; restaurant bookings 1995. December, you say?"

Shuttleworth nodded as he took out his mobile. "Yes. Do you mind if I record this?"

"Not at all." Opening the book at the back Barton flicked over several pages. He stopped and scanned one, running an index finger down the entries. "This is it." He placed the book on his desk and waved them over. "See? It's my writing, my entry, done down in reception. 'Colonel

Webster to meet Mr Gordanov. Lunch 1.00 pm. Wait for guest in reception.' Very unusual for the Colonel."

Peter asked if he could photograph the entry with his phone, and Barton agreed. Then Peter asked him what was unusual.

"You remember he came down to greet you in the hall? Well, that's what he always did - does. But not that day. I remember it now. He told me the day he booked the table. 'I can't come down to meet him. Please bring him up to me at the table.'"

"Did he say why?"

"No sir. I was only a Club servant. You don't ask men like the Colonel what their business is."

Peter laughed. "Blimey! Do people still get called servants?"

"Well, not usually sir. One of those politically incorrect words now, isn't it? But I was taken on as a Club Servant forty years ago, and that's what I call myself and the others. It's what I am. We are here to serve members and guests, so we are servants." Barton stopped, looking puzzled. "Sorry, but you sent me off at a tangent. You were asking about the Colonel and his guest."

"That's my fault. What else do you recall about it?"

Barton took a moment to think. "Well, about 12.45 that day I made sure I was in the reception area near the doors so I'd see Mr Gordanov arrive. Straight away I noticed three men standing near the front steps, talking. Two of them were pretty big, fit looking. Didn't seem to be interested in the Club though. A few minutes later I saw a very smart military looking chap crossing the road towards the Club. I thought: 'This looks like the Colonel's guest'. As he got closer, he raised a hand as if he were giving a little wave to the third man outside; not the big fellows. Then he spoke to him. They obviously knew each other, and the third chap said something back. I couldn't hear anything though. Not through the glass doors and all the traffic noise."

Barton paused, thinking. Peter asked, "What happened then?"

"I'm just trying to get this straight in my head. I haven't thought about it for years." He hesitated again for a few seconds. "Yes, that's it. The man I took for Gordanov was carrying a briefcase. Something must have been said because he handed it to the smallest of the three men. I could see this one turn aside a bit, but I couldn't see what he was doing. Then he turned back and Gordanov - I assume that's who it was - put his hand in the case and took out some papers. He looked at them and this horrified expression flashed across his face. He was saying something and one of the big fellows seemed to sort of punch him in the upper left arm. Gordanov looked shocked and then quickly began to look like he was passing out."

Lacey said, "What had happened?"

"I can't say for sure, but I thought maybe they'd drugged him. You know, like they did to Gene Hackman in 'The French Connection'? You remember the film from the seventies?"

Peter laughed: "Bit before my time."

Lacey patted his shoulder. "Your education is incomplete, then." He turned back to Barton. "Anything else?"

"Definitely. A car drew up at the kerb while all this was going on, and the two big men picked up the one I thought was Gordanov, lifted him under the armpits and shoved him in the car. He'd gone limp, and his head was lolling all over the place. The car shot off in the direction of Trafalgar Square. I ran out through the door and saw it turn and disappear. It'd have gone into the Mall from there. The smaller man was walking off in the other direction." Barton stopped and took a deep breath. "Something else; struck me as odd at the time. Just down the road were two uniformed cops. They were looking at the car; then they looked back at me, turned away and walked off."

"Why was that odd?"

"Well, you know, I thought they might have taken an interest in someone being bundled into a car like that. Of course, they might not have seen that happen, but it still seemed funny to me."

Peter asked, "What did you do then?"

"I went back inside the club. I noticed it was just gone five past by then, so I waited down there for another ten minutes or so in case I was wrong and the Gordanov person was just late. He never turned up, so I went up to the Colonel in the restaurant. When I told him his guest hadn't come he didn't seem surprised. When I went on about what I'd seen, he seemed surprised – no, more angry – as if he … oh, I don't know, but he was furious."

"Would you recognise the smaller fellow who was at this kidnapping?"

"I doubt it. It was a long time ago. I only saw him for a few minutes."

Shuttleworth took a photo from his pocket. "What about this, sir?"

Barton shook his head. "It could be, but I can't be certain. Who is he, anyway?"

Shuttleworth put back the photo. "Have you heard about the Russian who died after a poisoning in Chichester a few days ago? Well, that's him."

Lacey held out his hand. Barton shook it. "Here's my card, Mr Barton. You've been most helpful. When you're off duty please come to the office so the Sergeant here can take your statement to confirm what he recorded just now."

"Do you mean Scotland Yard, sir?"

"I'm afraid not. This investigation is being conducted in Chichester where the man was murdered. We'll refund your train fare."

Barton agreed to go. The officers walked out of the Club. "Well done, Peter. Good thinking."

Peter smiled. "Thank you, sir. Do you think the bloke at MI6, er, Sawyer, knew about the drugs used on Gordanov, and the Police being nearby?"

"That's what I'm wondering. Maybe we'll have to have another chat with him."

"I'm not sure I trust him now."

"Then you may become a very good cop indeed, Peter."

Shuttleworth's mobile rang. "Shuttleworth." He listened intently for about half-a-minute. "Thanks; I'll tell him."

"Tell me what, Peter?"

"It's Sergeant Charcko, sir. Scotland Yard just took an anonymous call that two Russians posing as tourists were staying in a hotel in Brighton. Their room contained a couple of bottles of what might be Novichok."

"Hang on! Why 'posing as tourists', I wonder? Did she get the address?"

"Yes, sir."

"Tell her to get someone over there pronto. Tell them to report to me as soon as possible. And if any of the hotel staff have been feeling strange they should go to the nearest hospital, tell the doctor what happened, and to get in touch with me, and Captain Jordan."

"She said she heard that, and will do it at once, sir."

Chapter 15

August 2012. Igor at the Academy

Igor got off the train from Pochep in Moscow; an anonymous car - the same old filthy Lada 1500 he'd been in before - picked him up and Rostow drove him in unremarkable style to the Chelebityevo branch of the FSB Academy. Neither Igor nor anyone else in the know wanted outsiders not in on it to guess where he was heading.

On arrival Rostow showed his ID to the guards at the gate, and was greeted with: "Welcome, Major. Colonel Jastrovny is waiting for you. Please proceed."

Having trained there himself twenty years before, Rostow needed no directions to the Colonel's office building. Jastrovny was a burly bruiser an inch short of six feet, immensely powerful looking, but with a bit of a belly bulging over the belt of his trousers. After introductions he said, "So you've come to the Red Banner for a short course, Schaplinov. It's hard work, so I hope you're up to it. You're older than almost anyone we've ever had come to train here."

"I shall do my best, sir. I've read what I can about it."

"And what did you learn from your reading?"

"That the traitor Gordievsky was here, and so was our Prime Minister, Mr Putin."

"We're proud of Putin, of course, but ..." His expression hardened dramatically: "We prefer not to talk about the traitor." Jastrovny relaxed and smiled. "Anything else?"

"Yes sir, but it's not exactly relevant, just something I'm interested in."

"Well, go ahead. Try me."

"Thank you, sir. You agreed the traitor Gordievsky was here. There was another one called Pedchenko, and I wondered whether you ever found out anything about what happened to these men after they were sent to Britain on those prisoner swaps."

"I suppose you would worry about that when you're going there on a special operation, as one might say. We never did find out much about Gordievsky for a long time, and then someone made an attempt to kill him. But Pedchenko? We learned that he was given an alias – Boris Mamontov – but we never found out where he lived, or lives." Boris Mamontov was a name Igor was very unlikely to forget.

"Did you read George Orwell's 1984, sir?" Igor felt bold enough to ask with an impish grin.

The Colonel did not grin back. "Of course I bloody didn't! It was a banned book when I was young; even now it's almost impossible to get hold of. Even if you get one it's most likely in English and I don't read or speak it." He looked very stern as he asked, "So how did you get to read it, then?"

"A friend I was lodging with when I was studying in England lent it to me."

"OK. Why do you ask?"

"This Academy's nickname is School 101, isn't it?"

"So what?"

"In 1984 Orwell calls the torture dungeon Room 101. It's where Big Brother 're-educates' the victim's mind by exposing him to his worst fear. The hero, if that is what Winston is, is broken down by having his head put into a box with a wire mesh partition in it. The other side of the barrier is a large rat. He is terrified of them, and he sees that the partition can be removed. After that he will do or believe anything he is told."

Laughing nastily Jastrovny said, "Well, that's how people leave here, but we don't have to terrify them first. We just teach them to terrify others." He shook hands with Rostow, thanked him for delivering Schaplinov, and told him to leave.

The Colonel then summoned a junior officer to show Igor to his quarters and deposit his baggage, following which he returned to the Colonel's office. He was told of the things he would be learning, and of those which his short course would not include. The latter was a much longer list than the former, Jastrovny explained. "As I understand it, your role abroad is limited in scope, so you do not need to know much about gathering general intelligence, nor counter-intelligence; you won't be running or recruiting agents, spies, or double agents.

"You don't need to set up dead letter drops, create signal spots where chalk or other marks warn or tell others about things which are to happen, such as finding a message or cash somewhere else, or fixing or aborting a meeting." The Colonel's tone turned sceptical. "I've been told what is believed to be a fool-proof system has been set up for you to leave or receive messages and information, but I have no details."

"It is a system I devised myself. It is very simple, and there is no reason why anyone should discover it."

Jastrovny laughed. "I hope you're right."

"So do I. So what do I need to know?"

"You need to be fit, since anything can happen to a spy, which is what you will be. I know you keep fit to some extent with running and so on, but by our standards you're not what we call fit. I realise you're well over forty, so we do not expect you to get as hard and full of endurance as our newly qualified twenty-five to thirty year olds, but we can do a lot with you." He paused: "The skill you definitely need is recognising when you are being kept under surveillance and being able to shake it off. That is *'proverka'*, or what western intelligence calls 'dry-cleaning'."

"Thank you, Colonel. The one danger I'm sure I face is being followed to the contact point so often the other side work out that it may be the contact point, though I hope they would, even then, be unable to work out how or when, or even if, messages are being passed."

Jastrovny picked up a sheet of paper, looked at it briefly, ticked off some items with a pen, and then looked at Igor. "No-one else here knows who you are, so to make it harder for them to find out, if they are so minded, you will have a code name. It is a bit like yours, so it's easy to recall. It's Schaliapin: Maxim Schaliapin. Next, I know you're going to the United Kingdom and speak excellent English. To make sure you're still fluent, you will spend a couple of hours after dinner every night except weekends talking to one or more

English tutors and lecturers. There are three of them, one of whom is truly an English woman who comes and goes between Russia and the UK masquerading as a clothes buyer. She actually does some business too. It means she's always right up to date with colloquialisms, slang and the latest fashions. She tells us one of the recent ones is saying 'like' and 'you know' every few words."

"Well, I hope I don't need to adulterate the language that much! There's not much point in telling people something if they already know it."

Jastrovny laughed. "You'll need a lot of luck."

Igor acknowledged that with a nod.

****

Every morning at 6.30am a training officer took Igor for what started off as a half-hour jog, and over two weeks developed into a half hour run at faster and faster speeds. Sometimes a sort of steeple-chase or obstacle course was tacked on to the run. After a break for a short rest and a drink of water, an hour of circuit training followed including press-ups, sit-ups, toe-touching, and weight training which made Igor appreciate that he had not really been fit at all. He found muscles he had not felt for years, and a few he did not realise he had. Halfway between lunch and dinner every other day he was given karate and judo instruction, at first for thirty minutes, and after a month, for an hour.

The rest of the mornings and afternoons on those days he was lectured on spotting surveillance and how to avoid it, and shown video recordings of how, and how not, to do it. One of the most important things was never to try to lose a tail on his mission abroad unless it was truly necessary, as that would just raise suspicion.

After two or three weeks of these instruction sessions, he was set routes to walk trying to spot and then avoid any tail that might be following him. On completion of the exercise, he had to write up a report in his room, and it would be compared prior to dinner with that of the officer or officers who had been trailing him. The officers had been shown his photo, but knew nothing about him or his mission, he was told. These surveillance exercises took place on the intervening days between lectures. He was taken into surrounding towns, villages, and even into Moscow for them. The first time he was given a place to get to and a message to drop. He tried to be vigilant without making it obvious, but did not spot anyone suspicious. He made the drop unobserved, he thought. He'd now been on the course almost three months. During these exercises it was vital he lost the tail, if he could, every time.

He was told that despite his efforts at doubling back on himself, looking in shop windows, and other tricks, he was too crude and obvious. The 'tail' had picked up the message and photographed Igor dropping it off. Over the next few weeks there was little change even though he succeeded in shaking his tail off once or twice for a little while, but not sufficiently skilfully for the officer to be unable to pick him up again.

At the start of month five, he shook the tails off completely and completed his set task without being observed. The following week the tactics changed. School 101 used two women instead of one man, and they changed places so unobtrusively, each wearing different items of clothing every time they swapped, that Igor was properly fooled. Their reports and his matched exactly as to where he had been and what he had had to achieve. That went on for three weeks. After that, it might be two men, or a man and a woman, and their ages might differ widely. Middle aged or even slightly elderly women seemed particularly unlikely pawns in a spying game, and at first, he was bad at noticing them, but worked hard at it, and equally so at seeming to be casual about whatever he was doing.

All the time he improved, and his increasing fitness meant he could move faster when he turned a corner before the tail got there or vanish over a wall. On three occasions he managed to take a photo of one or more of the followers on his mobile phone.

In the fifth week before the end of the course he was unobserved by a team of four for good after first giving them the slip. He repeated that the following week, and the third week he evaded them twice to complete his target unnoticed. The penultimate week, he lost them four times. In the last week in the complex streets of an ancient Moscow suburb, he managed it every day, and took photos of three of his tails once and four of them another time. On the last day he was very casual. He soon spotted a female follower. He noticed that if he stopped to look in a shop window she stopped too and watched him in the window opposite. He took a street map out of his jacket pocket, and crossed the road. "Excuse me, Ma'am," he said in his best English accent. "I am lost." He waved the map. "Do you speak English? Can you help me, please?"

She was very shocked. "Niet. No speak." Very quickly she hurried away in the direction they had come from.

Igor muttered to himself: "One down, three to go." He saw that there were several other people about, any one of whom could be part of the tailing team. Setting off in his original direction, he saw that one man in a short brown overcoat stayed a steady one hundred and fifty yards behind him. Igor went into a bar on a corner, ordered a small vodka, and stood at a table, waiting. After a few minutes he went back to the same door and glanced into the main street. He saw the man waiting at a bus-stop, pretending not to be keeping watch on the pub door. Igor took his photo, went back in, drank his vodka, and slipped out of a different door into the side street, and stood there. After a few minutes the door opened and the watcher came out, looking shocked at seeing Igor standing there.

Making the best of a bad job, the man turned left down the side street and disappeared. Igor went back into the bar, exited by the front door and turned right the way he had been going. Taking a left up the next street he realised he was being pursued about fifty yards back by a woman; her high heels were clack-clack-clacking on the pavement. He was pretty sure she was following him when he took another left and so did she. He took out his mobile and deliberately took his time with a photo of an old but elegant block of flats on the other side of the road, forcing her to walk past him. When the woman and her black heels were twenty yards past him, he took her picture.

He reversed his path back to the first street and turned right into it. Apart from an elderly couple far down the street behind him, going slowly the other way arm in arm, Igor could see no-one. He made his way back to the main road, turned left, and was on his way to his objective. After a few minutes of brisk walking, he noticed three men talking outside a shop, and one was on a mobile. Igor realised the watchers were likely to be in touch with each other by mobile, and this one was being put on his scent. Sure enough, when Igor had gone some little distance past the men the one on the phone detached himself from the group and began to follow. Igor knelt down to fasten his shoelace, and the man went on in front.

Igor was now the tail. As his quarry passed a turning on the right Igor was around seventy yards behind him. Getting to that street, Igor turned down it, stepped onto a two-foot-high telephone junction box and vaulted over a fence into a garden. Some seconds later he heard running feet approach the corner, start up the side street, stop, and then sprint up the street. Igor walked quietly to the garden gate and saw his tail disappearing in the distance. Turning right out of the gate he walked casually back to the main road. He was not followed again. He had lost them. He made it to a letter drop and collected it, moved on to a park and deposited an envelope of cash in a rubbish bin, and caught a bus back to the rendezvous with his driver.

None of the tails' reports said Igor was clearly taking evasive action; he seemed to have disappeared normally. The two women even wrote that they believed they were following the wrong man. He produced the photos on his mobile as proof of his having observed his trackers. He received a glowing testimonial. The following day he was driven to Sheremetyevo airport, given a ticket to fly to Lisbon via Amsterdam, and plenty of Portuguese currency.

Chapter 16

London. Wednesday, 27th April 2016

Lacey and his Sergeant took the same seats they had occupied the previous day in Charles Sawyer's office in MI6 HQ. It was 5.00pm and they had gone to the Wizard's Palace straight from seeing Barton. They caught Sawyer just before he left for the day. He offered them tea.

Lacey declined for himself and Shuttleworth, "I don't think we'll be here long, sir. Just a few questions."

"Very well."

Shuttleworth produced his mobile. Lacey pointed to it. "May we record this?"

"Don't be silly, Mr Lacey. This is MI6, not Inspector Frost or Eastenders."

The phone was pocketed again.

"We have a witness to the seizure of Gordanov," said Lacey.

Sawyer showed no reaction to that. "That's not a question, Inspector."

"No, but we wondered whether you might want to tell us anything else about the incident when he was apprehended in London."

"I believe I told you all I know last time you were here."

"Maybe; maybe not."

"Is your witness Colonel Webster?"

"No, sir, it is not. He told us he was disgusted to have been a part of the incident, which he did not see himself, but he made it plain, though not in these words, that he was the bait for the sting by which Gordanov could be taken off the street."

"Did he now? Well, as you may have gathered when we talked before, I was not proud of it either, when I learned of it." Sawyer paused. "So who is your witness?"

"I'll ask the questions, if you don't mind, sir. We were told that Gordanov was apparently injected or drugged somehow, collapsed almost at once, and bundled into a car which sped away. Did you know about the tranquiliser?"

"No comment."

"What about the car?"

"No comment."

"In the circumstances, where you could have denied it, I'll take that for a 'yes' to both questions for the moment."

"Take it any way you like. I am confirming nothing."

"We were also informed that nearby the Army Club where the seizure took place, two uniformed police officers were standing watching. It must have been obvious to them that a kidnap was in progress, yet they did nothing. You see, sir, it seems to me and Sergeant Shuttleworth here that they might have been standing there doing nothing on your orders."

"I was not in this office that long ago."

"Of course not. This office wasn't here that long ago, but I think you know what I mean. Were those officers part of the SIS sting?"

"I cannot comment on what happened here so long ago." Sawyer stood up, arms folded. "Is that it?"

The two officers stood too, and Lacey said, "Not quite, sir. Last time you said you thought we'd find evidence it was the Russians, but then we got information that two of them had stayed in a hotel in Brighton, and when the local police got there, they found two small bottles of the ingredients for making Novichok in the bedroom those men were said to have used. One bottle was under one of the single beds as though it had got there by accident. Seems a strange coincidence, you telling us we'd find evidence, and then we are told where we'd find it."

"Are you suggesting, Inspector, that I had these bottles planted?"

"Are you denying it, sir?" Sawyer did not reply. "You see, we do not know where we got the tip-off about the hotel. It was an anonymous phone call, we could not trace the number, and it was less than twenty-four hours after we had interviewed you. Most phone numbers can be traced, even if they are only throw-away mobiles, or 'burner' phones, but untraceable phones are very rare."

"Pure coincidence,"

"But do you deny it?"

"No comment."

"I thought you might say that, sir. Good afternoon. Please have us escorted off the premises. You wouldn't want us roaming at large round here, would you, sir?"

****

Lacey and Shuttleworth walked in silence from the building to Vauxhall Bridge, where they stood waiting for a taxi.

"What did you make of that, Peter?"

"Not a lot, sir. You?"

"Much the same, actually, but I'm not sure I believed Sawyer with his last couple of replies about the bottles and the coppers."

"Or the car and the injection. So what now, sir?"

"We should pay Pedchenko's nephew a visit."

A taxi drew up, and they got in. "Victoria Station, please."

Chapter 17

Easter 2013. Lisbon, Portugal

It was Palm Sunday morning when Igor left the British Airways plane that had flown him from Amsterdam to Lisbon. His false passport in the name of holidaymaker Max Schaliapin cleared him through Customs and Immigration into the hot sunshine. He took a taxi to a non-descript hotel in the equally non-descript Rua Azedo Greco.

He'd made the reservation from Amsterdam. Rostow's minions had researched the place, but it had not been booked from Moscow as he was meant to be fleeing Russia and seeking asylum. If his claim to sanctuary were investigated, as he was sure it would be, making a phone call or internet booking from Moscow would be a certain give-away.

The Hotel Azedo was rather shabby, as was his bedroom, but it was clean. The restaurant was passable, but he decided to go to a cafe for lunch, and then walked down to the shore and along the beach front for an hour or two. He spent the time thinking, as he strolled about, how he would deal with tomorrow. It was essential he got it right. It wasn't the thought of being 'caught' and sent back to Russia which worried him. He wasn't going to betray the Motherland. No prison in Northern Siberia for him! No; it was just that he wanted so badly to succeed with his missions; his own and the one for the FSB.

He returned to the hotel for an edible but not remarkably good dinner. After that he spent the evening in his room, reading the papers he had been given which he hoped would secure his acceptance into Britain, and eventually into Porton Down. He needed to be on top of it all so he could deal with any questions.

Having done all he could to master the information, he took a penknife out of his suitcase. It was a remarkably good case, leather, with a very fancy green lining of what looked like silk, but probably wasn't. He slit the lining inside the lid, and then picked undone the stitching which secured a second layer of leather, also inside the lid. From the exposed gap he removed a slim package, also leather, from which he took a passport: his own, in the name of Igor Schaplinov. He put the papers and this passport with his false one.

He was ready for the morrow.

****

The next day at 10.30 am, Igor presented himself in reception at the British Embassy in Rua de Sao Bernardo, just to the west of the Travessa de Sao Placido. The pleasing architecture of this diplomatic edifice with its white framed windows in the four storeys of burgundy wall was impressive. He had walked there from his humble hostel. Staying in a grand international hotel or one of the great and famous local ones would not have been appropriate and might have attracted unwelcome attention.

A dark-eyed, dark-haired, olive-skinned Portuguese beauty with a name badge proclaiming her to be Juliana welcomed him. "Can I help you, sir?" she said in Portuguese.

Igor pretended to look about him warily, as if anxious not to be spotted, before speaking: "I need to see the Ambassador urgently." He said it in Russian. Juliana obviously did not understand, so he repeated it in English.

If Juliana was shocked, no trace of emotion disturbed her smile. "She is out at present, sir, but you would need to see the Deputy Head of Mission first, or one of his assistants." She consulted a diary. "He could see you at two o'clock, sir. Could you come back then, please?"

"I can. Let me just show you these." He pulled the two passports from the inside pocket of his linen jacket, and laid them before her without relinquishing his grip on them. As she looked at them, he said, "This one for Igor Schaplinov is real and the other, for Maxim Schaliapin, is a Russian passport, but it is false, and so is the name. As you can see, I am Russian. I want to ...." He was interrupted by Juliana laughing. "Did I say something funny?"

"No, sir. I'm sorry. You sound like an English – what do you say? - public schoolboy. You have no accent of Russia. There are many Russians in Lisbon."

"How do you know how a public schoolboy speaks?"

"Because the Deputy Head of Mission went at one, and the Ambassador's son goes at one, and comes here on his holidays. I not mean to make you cross, sir. You were going to say ....?"

Igor smiled. "Never mind. Just tell the Deputy he'd do well to have someone senior from MI6 with him. I'll be back at 2.00." Igor pocketed the passports and turned to go. He turned again to say: "And I'm not cross."

****

He turned right out of the Embassy and after another turn or two walked into the Estrela Park. Slightly agitated, he strolled around for forty-five minutes, sat on the grass for another ten. He left the park and found his way to a small back street cafe where he had a plate of grilled sardines with a crusty roll. He'd have liked to wash it down with a beer or, having looked up Portuguese wines, preferably a vinho verde, but drank water instead and a small black coffee. Turning up at the Embassy with alcohol on his breath would send the wrong message.

At 2.00 pm he was at the reception desk again. "Hello, sir," Juliana said with another smile.

"What about the Deputy Head of Mission? Will he ...."

"I tell him now you are here. He will see you. Is Mr Montague. Please sit over there."

Igor took one of the seats she pointed to as she made an internal call. Within three minutes a tall slim man in a yellow summer jacket and pale grey slacks bounded down the stairs. "I'm afraid I wasn't given your name, but you are the Russian who called this morning?"

"I am Igor Schaplinov, yes."

They shook hands. "Follow me, please. I am Desmond Montague."

Montague's spacious first floor office furnished in elegant Portuguese style overlooked the small park-like area to the right of the front of the Embassy in the street outside. The French doors leading to a small balcony railing were wide open, Igor noticed as he reached the door to the office. He caught the diplomat by the elbow and moved back from sight of the window.

"Mr Montague, please close the windows, and leave the net curtains in position. I cannot afford to be seen here. Juliana, your receptionist, told me there are many Russians in town."

Montague did indeed have a very upper class public school accent. "My! You are a mystery, aren't you? All she could tell me was that you are Russian, have no foreign accent when you speak English, and had two passports in different names. You certainly sound remarkably English to me." He studied Igor closely for a moment. "Juliana told me you wanted me to have someone from MI6 here too."

"I did. I am defecting and want to go to Britain as an asylum seeker. MI6 will want to know. They will make it happen."

"You're very confident, Mr .... er?"

"Schaplinov, Igor Schaplinov." He took his two passports from his jacket and handed them to Montague. "This one, in the name of Schaliapin, is the one with which I fled Moscow. I paid bribes to Russian Mafia to get it. The other is my own, in my name."

"Schaliapin was a famous Russian musician."

"Of course. You must be a man of culture too. I adopted the name because it looks and sounds a little like mine, and the two can easily be confused, which can be useful." Igor did not dare say that the name was given him by Rostow and his associates, as it would make it patently obvious he was not really a defector. Igor hesitated. "Yes, I am confident about MI6 helping me. I can help them more. I have information they would wish to possess. I shall say nothing else until you ask the Head of Station to join us. That's what you call the chief of the intelligence section here, isn't it?"

"How do you know?"

"I carried out a lot of research before coming here. No-one in his right mind would do what I am doing if they did not know something about the other side."

Montague picked up the phone. "Yes, Jason, please ask Mr Elliot to come to my office immediately. Tell him it's rather important and urgent."

A couple of minutes later there was a loud knock at the door which opened before the diplomat could respond, and a tough-looking man in a shabby suit badly in need of cleaning and pressing, rather unnoticeable tie and slightly grubby brown shoes charged into the room. "OK Des, what's all this important urgent stu ...." He tailed off when he saw Igor. "Sorry, fellers. No idea anyone else was here." Igor recognised a south London accent; definitely not public school, this one.

Montague smiled. "No, Frank, I didn't mention it. This is Mr Igor Schaplinov from Moscow."

The intense scrutiny Elliot was giving the Russian became even more significant. "Hello. I'm Frank Elliot, MI6. Not my real name, of course, but it'll have to do. What can we do for you, and more to the point, why should we?"

"First, you can check me out and see if I am a genuine asylum seeker," said Igor. "Secondly, you can give me asylum in Britain. Thirdly, you can look at the papers I have brought you, and see if they are of interest to you, or more particularly to Porton Down. You can then see if there is anything else I can tell you that may be worth knowing. And finally, you can get me a job at Porton Down."

"Fuck me! You don't want much, do you, mate? Wha'd'you know about Porton, then?"

"I know it is the British Chemical and Biological Weapons Research Establishment. If I work there I can help them."

Disbelief covered Elliot's face as he looked at Montague, who smiled when Elliot laughed. "Now why the 'ell should we believe that, old son?"

"Because I have just fled from the Russian CBRN plant at Pochep. Heard of that, have you?"

The two Englishmen reacted as though their gobs had been smacked rather hard. Igor went on: "Of course, Mr Elliott, you'll have your sources and be able to verify that, but you will also find these papers instructive if you pass them onto someone who knows about these nasty things." Igor took a few pages from his jacket pocket. "I do not expect you to make a decision at once." He handed Montague a card. "This is the hotel I am using. You can keep a very unobtrusive eye on me there for my protection and to ensure I do not run away. I'm certain you can have me followed so I do not know it is happening. If that is all, I shall see you tomorrow at eleven o'clock. You may retain the passports for now to assist your investigations."

Whereupon Igor walked out.

Frank Elliot scratched his head with both hands, then ran all his fingers through his hair. "Bugger me if that isn't one of the most arrogant bastards I've ever come across."

"Indeed, Frank. Save time, will you?" Handing Elliot the hotel card, he said, "Use my phone. Get a couple of your people watching the hotel as quickly as possible. They might get there before he does if he's walking. Show them the photos in the passports."

****

Igor was pretty sure no-one followed him to his hotel, but confident they would have him under surveillance once he got there. He was right. A middle-aged man and a woman were standing on the pavement on his side of the road fifty yards from the Azedo, talking. He put his head down, strolling slowly as though deep in thought, hands clasped behind his back. As he passed them, they were talking in Portuguese. They looked and were dressed like locals. Twenty yards later he heard: "Ate breve!" and by the sound of it, the woman was following him. She was moving slowly too, but catching him up a little. After another minute he looked up, woken from his pretence of reverie, glanced back, turned round, walked past the woman, and said to her in his public-school accent: "Damn, just walked right past my hotel!"

"What a pity!" Perfect English and perfect accent.

Igor crossed the road to the hotel. The woman's voice carried to him as he stepped off the pavement. "Shit!"

'Well, they won't be able to use her to spy on me again', he thought, but now he knew he was already under surveillance.

****

Back at the Embassy Frank Elliott was flabbergasted. "This bloke could be dynamite, Des." He threw Igor's papers on the desk.

"I wish you'd stop calling me that, Frank. I've told you often enough. It's Desmond!"

"OK. Get off your high horse now, Desmond. A couple of these sheets are things we already know, but the rest are things we either didn't know about at all, or which we suspected, but had no proof, like some virus research, and possible bacterial weapons."

"Can you make use of it?"

"I dunno. That's up to Porton Down. I'll have to fax it through to their head honcho, bloke called Horne-Basset, and he'll give it to someone who really knows what it all means."

"Better make sure you use an encrypted or scrambled machine, then."

"Huh. Wasn't born yesterday, y'know."

****

At 11.00am next day, they told Igor Schaplinov he would be flown in an unmarked cargo plane to an RAF airfield in Suffolk that afternoon, and handed over to MI6.

Chapter 18

Chichester. Wednesday, 27ᵗʰ April 2016

Colin and Peter went straight from Chichester Railway Station to the Police Station. Sergeant Sean Davies was on late duty. "Sir, we've got a report in already from the hotel in Brighton. Detective Charcko sent Constable Sharon Jones and D.C.Morton. They got back about ten minutes ago. They're in the canteen."

"We'll see them now. Tell 'em to see me in the incident room." Lacey turned to go, but turned back. "Oh, and ask D.S. Charcko to join us."

"Yes, sir, I'll get Jones and Morton, but I'm pretty sure the sergeant is in the room already."

Sure enough, upstairs Lacey and Shuttleworth found Kiara studying videos from CCTV cameras from all over the city. They greeted one another. Lacey was about to ask her what she'd found, but within seconds the woman, Constable, Jones, entered with D.C. Morton who, in a creased blue suit, a somewhat rumpled tie with half of his shirt hanging out, looked like the proverbial brick shit-house. Jones, in uniform, was petite, blond, and freckled.

They sat opposite Lacey and Peter. Jones put a packet

on the table. "I drove Harry over to Brighton. I took these photos while he interviewed the hotel manager. I snapped the hotel, the bedroom, and the en suite." She pointed at the packet. "All there, sir. Hotel's a bit run down, but in one of those lovely Regency squares with one side open to the seafront."

"That was quick, Sharon, getting the photos done," Shuttleworth muttered.

"We found one of those machines in a chemist's where you can do the printing yourself. The SOCOs'll take better ones than these, but they're a start."

Charcko reversed her chair to listen and then asked, "What about the bottles?"

Morton sat forward. "A cleaner found the bottles yesterday morning. The men who'd occupied the room left on the 24th. The hotel wasn't too busy, so the room didn't get cleaned straight away. Not knowing what they were, she took the bottles down to the manager. He told her to put them in the safe in case the men came back for them."

"Did she clean the room?" Lacey asked.

"No, it wasn't cleaned. She was sent off to clean a bridal suite instead. So when we saw it, it was just the way the two men were supposed to have left it, apart from the bottles. I got on to Brighton nick and asked them to have some SOCOs go over it and take the bottles to forensic."

"Good thinking, Harry. Did you see the maid, the cleaner?"

"Yep. She was Polish but spoke pretty fair English."

Sounding troubled, Peter said, "I s'pose 'er finger-prints'll be on the bottles."

"No, Sarg. She told me she always wears rubber gloves to do her job. She had them on when she picked them up and took them down to the manager."

"Did he touch them?"

"Bit of luck that. He just opened the safe and asked her to put them in it. When I saw him, I took them out. I'd got my gloves on and dropped the bottles in that." Morton put an evidence bag on the table.

Lacey took up the questions again. "So, we have two bottles. From what Peter and I learned at Porton each contains a number of the different ingredients for Novichok, and they have to be mixed to fill some other container to be reliably fatal. They'd have to have some safety clothing. Was any found?"

Morton shook his head. "No, sir."

"That is extremely odd." After a few seconds contemplation, Lacey asked, "What about these men? Were they Russian?"

"Seems pretty definite, sir. The manager gave me the register, and he'd taken copies of their passports." Morton picked up the packet of photos. "They're in here."

Lacey put on rubber gloves, tipped out the contents, had a quick look at the photos of the hotel, and then studied the register and passports more carefully. "So we're looking for Nicholas Milukov and Dmitri Balkonsky. A motor mechanic and a builder. Both born in Russia." He handed the papers to Peter. "Get copies of these off to Sawyer. Ask if MI6 can trace them. They must have an archive of known KGB and FSB operatives."

"Neither of them looks old enough to have been KGB, sir. Milukov is only thirty, and Balkonsky's thirty-four."

"When you've done the copies and sent them off, call it a day. I'm going back to my hotel. I'll see you here in the morning. With luck we'll have results from the SOCOs' inspection of the hotel. Tomorrow you can tell me what's on the Chichester CCTV footage I asked for, Kiara. Phone me any time if anything crops up."

"On my way, sir." Shuttleworth left.

Lacey turned to Morton. "Did anyone go into the Russians' room after they left and before the cleaner went in yesterday?"

"Sorry sir, didn't think to ask that. I can phone him now if you want."

"Yes, do that. Then you can go home. Tell me what he says as soon as I get here in the morning. 8.00am sharp. Off you go too, Sharon."

She and Harry Morton left. Kiara said, "I haven't much to report, having read through all the statements, but apart from Mrs Mason there's nothing really useful, as far as I could see. I've watched the videos from around Priory Park, too. Apart from seeing the bloke dressed like a vicar, I found nothing new. I just hope the other videos turn up early tomorrow." Then she gave Colin a triumphant smile. "But there's more, and it's good."

Lacey eyed Charcko cautiously. "Someone came in and confessed?"

Kiara laughed. "Not that good, unfortunately." She took a breath. "Not quite as good as that, though you might think it's better." She laughed again. "What's happened is that St Richards phoned. Yevgeny's condition may be improving, so Captain Jordan came down. They want her to check him over because she knows as much as anyone in the country about this Novichok stuff and what it does to people. She's staying at The Ship again, so I thought I ought to tell you as soon as you got back."

"What's that word everyone says now? Awesome! That's it. It's certainly very welcome news. I'd better get over there pronto."

"But that's not all, sir. Before you went to London you asked me to phone Bangor Hospital."

"Yes. Colonel Webster told us about Gordanov breaking his leg in Wales and had bled a bit. I wanted you to check whether they had a blood sample or other stuff which could be used for a DNA test. I thought it might help identify, or at any rate confirm, a suspect if it really was a member of his family, or some relative."

"Well, I got onto the Bangor hospital."

"And?"

"They still had a blood sample."

"I must say that's promising. Well done. But it's what? Over thirty years old?"

"Yes, sir, so I asked about that. They said that properly kept, as in hospital conditions, it can be OK for analysis for thousands of years. A bit like DNA from Egyptian mummies. So I got the Police there to collect the sample from the hospital and send it here as fast as possible. They actually put it in their county force helicopter and rushed it to the pathology lab in London. I asked the lab to expedite the analysis. They confirmed they should be able to get a DNA result. We should get it in the next day or two, they said."

"That's brilliant. Just brilliant. Like I say, well done. Now all we need is to find a relative to do the other half of the test and compare the DNA! Maybe that will give us the villain. Always supposing, of course, that the assassin was a relative." Kiara's smiling face suddenly looked rather glum. "Anyway, I must get off to see if Captain Jordan has any news for me." Her smile returned and they both laughed.

Lacey did not find the Captain at the hotel. She had gone out.

****

At 7.45 the next morning Lacey was in the incident room again, looking at the photos from the hotel, and reading back into the file for anything he might have missed, or connections he'd not noticed previously. A pile of CCTV tapes was on Kiara Charcko's desk; she was already viewing them.

Morton breezed in promptly at eight o'clock. "Mornin', sir."

Lacey raised a hand in greeting. "So what did the manager say?"

"At first he couldn't recall anything, but then I heard the receptionist reminding him they'd had an unannounced visit from people from the Tourist Board. They went round the kitchen and all the bedrooms, including the one these Russian stayed in. The manager remembered it then, as he'd gone with them, but one of the inspectors took him to another bedroom leaving the other bloke still in the Russians' room for a couple of minutes. That was the morning before Scotland Yard heard about the Russians staying in the room."

"Which was Tuesday, the 26th, and we first saw Sawyer on Monday. That very day some Tourist Board people turn up unannounced! How terribly coincidental." Quite incredulous, Lacey shook his head, drummed his fingers on the desk, then looked up at Morton. "Get on to the Tourist Board office which covers Brighton. See what they say."

"Will do, sir. The hotel has a two-star rating from the Board, so they do know about it. Well, at any rate there are two stars on the Hotel sign in the street outside."

"Well, they should be able to tell you if they inspected it on the 26th."

Morton went to the phone on his desk, and Lacey went back to the file. After a few minutes a civilian admin assistant knocked on the door. "Morning sir. Here's the report from Brighton SOCOs – just came in by fax."

"Thanks. Give it here. And could someone rustle me up a coffee? Black, one sugar?" The assistant said she'd see to it straight away. Lacey thanked her.

Lacey started reading the report at once. It was obvious that there were hardly any fingerprints in the hotel room apart from those of whoever had just stayed there. They were in likely places such as the taps on the sink and shower, the shower door, the handle of the toilet cistern, the bedside cabinets, and the lamps on top of them. There were more on the wardrobe doors, and the drawers in the chest which doubled as a desk. Some of those appeared smudged as though brushed with rubber gloves, since no other prints were overlaid on them, and there was no trace of any DNA which did not match the majority of the prints. A few random prints on doors and one of the bed-heads could be those of the maid or other staff, or previous guests. He'd have to get Brighton to question the staff and take their fingerprints for elimination.

A woman from the canteen came in and put his coffee on the desk. He looked up and smiled his thanks.

If the main body of prints belonged to the Russians, he had no way of identifying them as such. It was odd that these suspects, if they were the murderers, had taken no steps to clean the room before they left. One of them had very black hair, since a few short stubs of black bristles left after shaving were in the sink, and two matching hairs from someone's head were in the shower tray. He doubted that the very careful, conscientious maid had left much of an occupant previous to the Russians in the room, and she hadn't finished cleaning the room after finding the Novichok. Lacey thought how much he hated finding other peoples' hair in the sink or bath. The photos showed the whole hotel generally seemed far too clean for that, even if it was a bit run down, as Sharon Jones had put it. Indeed, as he read on, Colin saw that these hair samples had been matched to the DNA in one of the two groups of prints forming the bulk of them.

Shuttleworth came in carrying coffee and a bacon sandwich. "Sergeant Davies caught me as I was coming up the stairs. He said the city centre CCTV stuff is ready to watch."

Colin said, "Yes, I know. Kiara's already looking at it." Then he rose, pointing to the report. "That's from Brighton. Read it, and tell me what you think when we're on our way to see Yevgeny." He addressed D.S.Charcko. "Tell me about the videos when I get back. Show me any I need to see."

"OK, sir, will do, if I'm still awake. This is so boring."

Peter Shuttleworth picked up the report from Brighton and sat down to read it. A few minutes later Colin Lacey's phone warbled. "Lacey."

Jodie Jordan said, "Yevgeny is awake, rather groggy, but you might be able to talk to him gently for fifteen minutes."

"Thanks. I'll be there."

"He might go to sleep again."

"I'll have to chance that. See you soon." Lacey and Shuttleworth left for the hospital.

On their way to the hospital Lacey asked, "So what did you think of the SOCO's report, Peter?"

"Well sir, they must have worked hard and fast to get all those DNA analyses done, but there was nothing to indicate that those Russian blokes were up to no good. Apart from the bottles with no fingerprints being found there, of course, which seems strange. I mean, if they had to mix the stuff before they used it, you'd think there might be splashes on the carpet, or the sink or something. Or any clothing left behind. And if they were trained FSB officers, why would they leave the bottles or anything else behind?"

"Quite. And why would they wipe the bottles, but leave their prints all over the room?" The unmarked BMW pulled up in the hospital car park outside the entrance in the spaces reserved for the disabled. "Better put the 'Police' sign on the dashboard, Peter."

Inside the building they made straight for the ICU. When they got close, Jordan came towards them down the corridor. "Good morning, gentlemen. We've put Yevgeny in this private room here. As you can see, there's still a police officer here, in case any further attempt is made to kill him.

He's been thoroughly washed every day since admission on Saturday, so there should be no danger of contamination, but I'd like you to wear these surgical gloves, just in case." She handed over two pairs; she was already wearing hers.

The uniformed copper rose from his chair and the three men greeted each other as Jodie led the detectives into the small single ward. Yevgeny Pedchenko had clearly dozed off again, but awoke at the sound of the door opening and footsteps entering his room.

Jodie went to the bed and took his hand. "Strasvitchye," she said.

"Hello, doctor," replied Pedchenko. He had a thick Russian accent.

"How are you feeling today, Yevgeny? Do you remember seeing me when you woke up a couple of hours ago?" She spoke slowly and very clearly.

"Da. Ustal – ver' tire."

"Yevgeny, these two gentlemen want to ask you some questions. They are Police, but you are not in any trouble."

The Captain walked over to Lacey, and whispered: "Colin, he's groggy, and his English is terrible at the moment. He's probably still half unconscious. And he doesn't know his Uncle's dead." She looked back at the man in the bed. He still had a tube attached to a drip-feed stuck in his arm and was linked to a monitor. "It might be better if you come back tomorrow with an interpreter."

"OK, but I don't think an interpreter is necessary. He teaches Russian at the University here, and at Portsmouth. I'm sure when he's a good bit better he'll do fine; his accent'll probably improve too. Will you tell him about his Uncle, or shall I?"

"If he's better, I can tell him, as I can answer any questions he has about himself and the Uncle. Give me a ring."

"Fine. I'll call you later."

Chapter 19

London, July, 2013

Igor had been at the safe house for three months. An anonymous black Jaguar driven by a woman dressed as a chauffeur had picked him up from Brize Norton airfield on 6th April and taken him straight to an unremarkable terraced house in a side street off Northcote Road, Battersea. In the front passenger seat had been a very tough looking man out of the same stable as the fellow known as Frank Elliot, but taller and more muscular. He was evidently a minder or bodyguard. The weapon in a shoulder-holster near his right breast was hardly concealed by his jacket, which bulged around it. The man in the back with Igor introduced himself as Charles Sawyer from MI6. He did not introduce the minder or the chauffeur.

The door of the house opened as Sawyer and Igor mounted the three steps up to it. There was a patch of mown grass – hardly a lawn – on each side of the crazy paved path and the steps. A woman of about fifty with grizzled grey hair tied in a small bun at the back of her head with an elastic band came out onto the top step. She wore a grey twinset of some vintage with a grey skirt. Igor thought she looked forbidding and severe. Sawyer introduced her as Mrs Henderson, the housekeeper.

Igor extended his hand, and to his surprise received a charming smile as he said, "Igor Schaplinov. Pleased to meet you, Mrs Henderson." The smile completely transformed the lady's appearance.

"I shall be delighted to look after you, Mr Shaplinov." Her Welsh accent was musical.

Sawyer smiled too, and suggested they go indoors. The minder followed them into the lounge. They sat on the very comfortable pale brown leather sofa and armchairs, and after a few minutes Mrs Henderson brought in coffee and a plate of biscuits, announcing that dinner would be at six-thirty.

When she departed Sawyer laid out the plan to test Igor's value and the validity of his claim to asylum. "You will live here for at least two months, maybe three, depending on what you tell us and what we find out about you. We've checked back on your records and know that you came here on an exchange from Novosibirsk ...."

"Yes, to Cambridge."

"We shall see all the people you tell us about, to check whatever you tell us. Every day except Sunday, one of three people will come here to interrogate you. If you hold back anything we need to know, or which you ought to tell us, we shall find out and send you back to Russia."

"I shall withhold nothing. Who will my interrogators be, if I may ask?"

"Two men and a woman. They are all very experienced." Indicating the minder, Sawyer said, "Lindsay Cronin here will sit in on the interviews when he is on duty. He will do four days and nights on and four off, when Craig

Wynter will take over. When it is their turn, they will be with you all the time, except at night, when you will have your own bedroom, and they will have one. All the windows and outer doors of this house are fitted with security devices, for your protection, and to prevent you from leaving except with Lindsay or Craig. All the interviews will be recorded on sound and video, and the interrogators will watch and listen to all of them. They will know if you make any mistakes or contradict yourself.

"Who are your examiners to be? Gordon Ussher is a recently retired QC, a very senior criminal lawyer; he prosecutes and defends. His skill is legendary in Court and outside it. Gillian Parsons is an academic and Professor of Psychology who has worked for us for thirty years. The third, Fred Robinson, is a former undercover agent who has worked in many countries for over twenty years and has been doing these examinations of spies and defectors for the last eight. He's about the same age as you. You will find they all have very different styles."

"Will I see you again? Will you be taking part?"

Sawyer waived the suggestion aside. "I shall visit from time to time, and you will see me then. I shall be monitoring your progress by studying the examiners' reports and listening to some of the recordings."

Nothing happened for the next two days, but Igor was permitted to walk or do exercises in the back garden, as long as Cronin was with him. The minder was quiet and rarely initiated a conversation, but he was polite and spoke at reasonable length when Igor addressed him. He had a fairly strong Scottish accent which the Russian found hard to understand to start with. The house had a small but very well stocked library of all sorts of books, so Igor spent most of those two days reading and resting.

On the third day just as he finished breakfast, Mrs Henderson came into the dining room and announced that Miss Parsons had arrived. "She will see you in the library in five minutes."

Miss Parsons was about five foot five, and on the rotund side, but not fat or out of shape. Perhaps fifty-five, she had a lively face and twinkling grey eyes. In a grey tweed suit and pale green blouse buttoned to the neck she looked like the wife of a country squire or prosperous farmer. She placed a small recording device on the coffee table and switched it on. Igor said, as he approached her: "Good morning, Miss Parsons. I am Igor Schaplinov."

She remained in the armchair but shook his hand. "I know. I'm here to find out all about you."

He smiled. "And I am here to answer all your questions so you can check everything Mr Sawyer has told you about me already. Truthfully." He looked around and saw CCTV cameras in each corner of the ceiling.

She nodded and smiled. "You would hardly say you are going to lie to me. But we shall see."

"Am I allowed to ask a question?"

"You may. Whether I answer is another matter."

"I was told you are an academic, so I thought you would be 'doctor' or 'professor'."

"I am both, but it's too pompous to keep on about such things. I'm a Doctor of Linguistics and a Professor of Psychology. You are a Master of Chemical Engineering, I believe."

"Indeed."

"Then we have started." She rose and moved to the chair behind the desk, on which she put the digital recorder. Microphones faced each of them on the desk. She gestured him to a chair on the other side. "Who are your parents?"

Crunch time! He waived the query aside with a gesture he hoped looked as casual as he intended. Remembering the opposing view that accomplished liars look their inquisitor straight in the eye, and the contrary view that looking away can appear natural, he did both. He glanced down at his hands, which he kept motionless. Then he looked up at Parsons. "I do not know who my father was, ma'am. I am illegitimate. I think from what my mother said that he may have been a soldier, but I know nothing more than that. My mother is a country girl from Belokurikha. Now she lives in Novosibirsk where she runs a restaurant. It is her own business. She is Irina Schaplinova."

"Is that her married name?"

"It is her maiden name, and her father's name. She has never married. She gave me her family name. I gave the embassy in Lisbon a copy of my birth certificate."

"Yes, it was passed on to me. Does she have a boyfriend or lover?"

"No ma'am. She did once but he has been dead some years." The truth. Time for another lie. This time he just looked at her and then looked away. "I did not know him. It was after I had left home and gone to work hundreds of miles away from her and home."

"And you. Are you married? Or have a girlfriend or mistress?"

"No, no, and no. I have known many girls and ladies, but my work is – was – secret, in places where coming and going was restricted. I never met a girl I liked so much as to marry her, and life in a town like Pochep would not be easy for her, ma'am. She would be unable to leave and return easily either. Pochep is in the Bryanskaya Oblast, four hundred miles west of Moscow."

"You can call me Gill. 'Ma'am' makes me sound like the Queen. I'm not quite that important." She laughed, and Igor smiled back. He asked her to call him Igor. *If she can lighten the tone, so can I,* he thought.

And on it went, from 9.00am to noon, when there was a two-hour break for lunch. Mrs Henderson brought in coffee at eleven and tea at three, but the interrogation did not stop for that. They got going again at two pm after lunch until five-thirty, when Parsons had another cup of tea with him, but before she left at six, she asked, "I'm puzzled about your two passports, one genuine Russian, one for you, and one forged for your alias, Maxim Schaliapin. How could you get another passport?"

Igor grimaced as if ashamed. "There are corrupt officials everywhere. They give blank passports to the Mafia. I paid a bribe to them."

The pressure was intense and exhausting, but Igor was happy with his answers, confident he had given nothing away. Everything he said was true except the parts about his father, and that could only be checked if MI6 talked to Irina. The story about the corrupt official and the Mafia was a lie too; Rostow had had the forgery made at the passport office. It could not be a genuine one, as if seriously checked, it would have given the game away that he was being helped by the FSB. His mother had kept her secret all these years; there was no chance she was going to talk to strangers about it now, and no-one in the passport office in Moscow would dare tell anyone how Maxim's passport was issued. Century after century of repressive Tsarist and Soviet control made ordinary Russians reluctant to discuss much that is serious with strangers. There had been a reprieve under Gorbachev and Yeltsin for a decade or so, but since then, when the wealthiest oligarchs could suddenly find themselves in prison or exiled or worse, no-one was secure. The former mistress of a senior officer who was executed for treason and spying for the enemy was not going to talk to anyone. Nor would the passport officer who had had orders from Rostow keep his trap shut.

After their evening meal, Igor suggested to Cronin that they could practise judo and karate together, which was agreed, and Lindsay found an old practice mat in a storeroom.

They put the mat in the garden when the weather allowed. Lindsay was evidently so accomplished at these 'sports' that Igor soon appreciated that when necessary, the minder could turn himself into a killing machine. Happily, he took it easy with Igor who was not up to his skill or fitness, despite the training at the FSB Academy, but was getting faster and stronger over the following weeks. They made time to do at least an hour immediately before breakfast most days. Lindsay was tolerant in a kind way about Igor's efforts and gave him tips to improve his technique.

****

The next morning Igor walked into the library but there was no-one there. As the sun shone through the windows, he took a book from a shelf at random. They were all hard

214

covers, often good editions. He sat in an armchair and opened H.E.Bates's "Flying Officer X" stories, but had only just done so when what looked like a gym instructor in a black tracksuit with a broad yellow stripe down the edge of the sleeves and legs bounced loudly into the room, slamming the door behind him. Igor began to stand but the man said in almost a shout: "Don't get up. Sit down. I'm Fred. Fred Robinson. You're Igor Schaplinov. I'm here to make your life a misery."

Igor was so surprised that he laughed. "Wonderful."

"You think I'm bloody joking? Well, I ain't. I've got a nose for bullshit, mate. I listened to Gill's tape of her talk with you yesterday, and it smells like a cattle-pen. OK?" As he spoke, he sat on a sofa, put a recording device on a bookshelf, and turned it on. "So you just tell me the truth, and we'll get on fine."

"I don't know about bullshit, but you must have had a dog turd up your nose when you listened to the tape then, because I told her nothing but the truth. I'll tell you the same. I'm ready when you are."

"Right-oh, sonny boy." Robinson asked all the same questions as Miss Parsons, but often using different words, and sometimes in a different order. Igor gave him the same answers, in almost the same words he'd used yesterday. Fred Robinson appeared to get angry, but Igor could not tell if it was genuine or an act.

Eventually the interrogator, in his aggressive fashion, and striding rapidly about the room, reached the identity of Igor's father. He clearly did not believe Igor knew nothing about him and added: "Gill didn't believe that bit either."

"I don't know how stupid you think Russians are, but

we get Police and court-room dramas in films and on TV. Some are even British. I know no-one can be expected to prove a negative, so I can't do the impossible. But you could get one of your agents to see my Mum. You got her name off the tape or from Miss Parsons. My mother lives in Novosibirsk. Give me a piece of paper and I'll write it down for you. See if she can tell you." He did that and went on. "Your people better be bloody careful. If the Security Forces learn she's been talking to someone from MI6, she'd end up in prison or worse, and they'll know I'm here."

Robinson took that in his stride. He changed tack, and asked about Igor's education, a topic on which Parsons had only touched lightly.

"How did you get from a small, not very good school in Belokurikha to a better one in Barnaul?"

"I was a clever boy. How else? Only the kids of powerful people could move to good schools under the Communists. I had no-one. Otherwise you had to have brains and work hard. I was lucky to be noticed"

"Bit of a clever dick, aren't we, sunshine? But your Mum got a flat in Barnaul 'n' all, didn't she?"

"Yes, she did. She's clever too. Not well educated, but very bright, and beautiful. She was a successful waitress in a good restaurant in Belokurikha. Then when I got a place at Novosibirsk University to study chemistry, she found a better job in a restaurant there."

In front of Igor's chair, Robinson stopped his marching and leaned right down into his face. "You told Gill she rented a very nice flat. How could she afford that? Earning her pay on her back, was she?"

"One more question like that, and I shall not speak to you again. I know the good cop-bad cop routine but you're wasting your time trying that on me." As Robinson straightened up, Igor rose to his feet and casually returned the Bates book to the shelf. He turned back to Robinson. "You can be as rude to me as you like, but one insult about my Mother is one too many. I'm going to phone Mr Sawyer and ask him to deal with you."

Fred backed off two paces and held both palms out in a gesture of appeasement. "OK sonny boy, I withdraw the question." He sat down at the table. Igor returned to his armchair.

"So how did she afford a good flat, Igor?"

"First you can apologise. Fred."

Robinson's mouth opened and the expression on his face indicated he was about to tell Igor to ......, but he changed his mind and said, "OK, Igor, no more rude suggestions about Mum, and I'm sorry." He swallowed. "What about the flat then?"

"She earned more in Novosibirsk than in Belokurikha or Barnaul and although tips weren't generous, she did better out of them. You also need to understand that back then all housing belonged to the State, and rents were low – no capitalist landlords to profiteer from the poor then. It can be different now. It seemed like a good flat to us, but to you it would probably have looked like a pokey council flat. I've seen some of those; hardly the way you'd expect a rich democracy to care for its citizens. If your agent goes to see her, he – or she – can see it. She's still there, but she owns her own restaurant now." Igor laughed "So she's a capitalist!"

"Are you admitting you're a communist?"

"Far from it. Capitalism works well, but doesn't care for the poor when it's very right wing. That's wrong."

It was Fred's turn to smile. "I think we can agree on that. My parents used to rent, and some of our homes were hovels until they got a Council House. They could save up a deposit, then, and bought it." He paused. "How d'you get to Uni, then?"

"I did very well at the secondary school and was accepted on the chemistry course with ease. You didn't have to pay, so there was no need for scholarships, but I think I'd have got one if I'd had to." He laughed. "You'd think the Communists would want to keep the 'proletariat' ignorant to keep them subdued, but they valued education, though subjects like history, literature and politics were heavily slanted to show Communists good, Capitalists bad. The subduing was done by putting the frighteners on people."

"Your English is very good and pretty colloquial."

"Thanks. You will have been told I was at Cambridge for a year and lived with what you would call a posh family. I read UK newspapers if I can, and books. I used to talk to any tourists I could find when I went to Moscow, and there are some who go to my Mother's restaurant, when I go there. I like the language. The chap I did an exchange with at Cambridge came to stay with us, and there was an English lecturer at the University in Novosibirsk with whom I became friendly. He gave me elocution lessons, I believe they're called."

"Blimey! Chap? Whom? That is pretty posh upper class talk, that is, and no mistake."

"Hardly surprising. I expect you've found out I had a couple of English girlfriends and one from Canada. Simon Grant, the lecturer, and Alan Carpenter, my friend from Cambridge, both went to public schools, and Simon undertook to teach me to 'talk proper', as you might say."

"Cheeky sod, aren't you? But he done a good job." Robinson paused for a couple of minutes. Igor sat motionless, saying nothing. "So tell me about your work."

Igor did so for the next two hours. It was all based on what the FSB had given him permission to say. He was also asked about the documents he had brought with him.

****

Bespoke, the suit announced. Saville Row: subtle it might be, but it shouted its quality and refined tailoring. Pale grey with a chalk stripe, and, unfashionably, a waistcoat adorned with a gold watch chain. Winchester Old Boy's tie. Elegant silver hair brushed straight back, with no parting.

The man so attired pulled out the chair opposite Igor's and sat down. "Sit, Mr Schaplinov. I am Gordon Ussher." He made no attempt to shake hands. He was polite, but very formal indeed. "You will call me Mr Ussher; I shall call you Mr Schaplinov. I am not the good cop, like Miss Parsons, nor the would-be bad cop, such as Mr Robinson."

"Fine. More like George Smiley then."

The lawyer just about smiled. "You flatter me. But let us waste no more time. I have listened to the tapes and watched the videos."

Ussher then went over Igor's work at the Pochep research establishment with very much more refined manners and subtly worded questions than Robinson had deployed. Igor soon realised that despite the formality of the man, his style was attractive and deserving of trust. Igor knew what Q.C. meant: Queen's Counsel; top of the legal profession outside the judiciary. He almost cast a spell. Igor could imagine how it drew a witness in, whichever side Ussher was on, until thoughts and facts which should not be voiced were unwittingly revealed. Igor realised Ussher was dangerous.

He turned to the documents Igor had handed over. "Tell me about these." He held up a thin bundle of papers.

"Yes; the Novichok stuff. Well, it's self-explanatory, isn't it?"

"Oh, I can understand them pretty well, and our chemists have helped where I was in doubt, but what made you think we might want them?"

"Look, I know you know about it, and you've probably got some, or made it. We know it was sold to some Germans and they gave it to the Swedes who analysed it. The Iranians have made some, so if they can do it, it's 100% certain you can do it too, but I thought you might not know how we latched onto it in the first place. That's what those sheets tell you. It should help your people understand how we think, and what we were and are trying to do."

Ussher put an index finger on another pile on the desk in front of him. "And these?"

"I assume you've read those too." Ussher gave one small movement of the head. "They are, as you've seen, all about biological weapons. We've been messing about ..."

Ussher looked up and stared. "What a curious expression."

"Not really. This is alarmingly dangerous research. No-one knows exactly where it will lead, or what the consequences will be. What happens if a deadly strain of influenza virus is released by accident? Or on purpose by a renegade member of staff, or taken and used by terrorists? The UK and the USSR have had disasters with anthrax escaping controls during or after experiments. If terrorists can get hold of nerve gases and use them in Japanese underground trains and stations, why can't someone do the same with biological weapons?"

"Tell me what you were 'messing about' with."

"First, let's be clear. That wasn't my work, but I knew about it. These papers were not under lock and key. As it happens, what others were experimenting with was the flu virus, and also developing a new variety of tuberculosis resistant to streptomycin." Igor pointed. "And other things mentioned in those papers. There's been some success with the flu, enough to make an outbreak of it very disabling to an enemy army. So far the tuberculosis experiments have produced no significant results. In any case we should have to find a vaccine for our own troops and people before we could use either of these things."

Igor knew that the British and their allies did not know about that yet. He had a pretty good idea they were working on the same theories. Many nations would welcome weapons which would debilitate the enemy without killing them all. In the modern world, apart from Adolf's desire to rid the planet of the Jews, only the Americans and Australians had had any idea of eliminating the conquered altogether. They just happened to be the indigenous inhabitants of those lands. The vanquished, robbed of their leaders, were usually needed as a workforce, as in Africa and India, but in America for several centuries, and in Australia

221

for two hundred years, all they were really good for most of the time was target practice.

Ussher smiled, and the effect was as if a velvet glove had been torn off a steel fist. "Thank you. Now tell me. I've heard what you told Miss Parsons and Robinson about your parents. Let me be frank. Your father was a senior officer in the Russian forces, as well as posing as a diplomat on posting abroad, wasn't he?"

Igor felt as though he had been punched in the stomach very hard, but had been taught to anticipate this sort of flank attack. He put his head back so his immediate expression would not be clear, and laughed. Then looking straight at Ussher, he laughed again, more quietly, and said, "That's just a wild guess, isn't it. Why on earth would you think that?"

"There is more to your relatively meteoric rise through education and into these research establishments than just your intelligence. You had help."

"I deny it. Show me the evidence."

"I'm afraid that's not possible. If I do that you may discover how we learn these things."

"Or that you have no evidence to show me or tell me about. You'll be in the same situation as me, then. You can't prove a positive, and I can't prove a negative, which is harder, as there's never any evidence of nothing, as you well know from your professional qualifications and experience."

"You are very quick on the up-take, Mr Schaplinov."

"Yes. That's how I got to university and into Pochep. My mother is very bright but poorly educated. Her father took her out of school early to go to work. I believe I owe my wits to her. Whether my father, whoever he was, was clever or stupid I have no idea." Igor paused, sighed, and took several prolonged breaths. "I do not have to trust or believe you or your colleagues, Mr Ussher. I am a traitor to Russia, and you can put me on the next plane home. That is a fairly terrifying prospect. You just have to decide whether you trust me. Am I a spy? Or a double agent of some sort?"

"Very clever. And amusing, particularly the expression 'a fairly terrifying prospect'. Quite a master of the English talent for understatement, aren't we? "

"I must thank my English friends and teachers for that."

"Thank you. That is my next point. Please tell me about these friends and teachers."

Igor told Ussher all about his Russian teachers of English at school in Barnaul and the English students he had met at Novosibirsk University. He went into considerable detail about Simon Grant who was a lecturer in Chemistry at Southampton and had given him elocution lessons. He said that Grant was now a Professor of Chemistry at Bristol University. Grant met Igor at Novosibirsk University when he was on an exchange with a Russian lecturer. He had been to Harrow and Cambridge and was a few years older than Igor. They had stayed in touch through very occasional letters and the odd Christmas card.

Igor went on: "Alan Carpenter is a former Repton pupil. I met him when I went on an exchange to Cambridge, where Carpenter was also studying chemistry, and stayed with his family during the vacations, and some weekends. As it was another cultural exchange, Alan came back to Novosibirsk to stay with me and my mother as part of it." Suddenly deep in thought, Igor was smiling and shaking his head. "It was a remarkable experience."

"What was?"

"I had always thought Mother and I were so lucky to have our flat which seemed so large and luxurious, but I saw it for what it was when I stayed with Alan's parents. Their home was in a village called Long Buckby ...."

"In Yorkshire."

Igor looked puzzled and responded: "No, Northamptonshire." He leaned forward. "Or were you trying to trap me?"

The old lawyer said nothing, maintaining an expression carved in stone; but could Igor see a very slight blush creep into the lined cheeks? He continued: "It was a former priest's house, a rectory built in about 1850. It was beautiful, red brick weathered to a brown colour, with a pale mauve flowering vine over the front called.... ah ... Wisteria. It had a large garden with its own grass tennis court, and a vegetable garden. Alan and I also wrote to each other sometimes. I should love to be able to see him and Simon again." Igor paused. "Before you ask, none of us had any State or Defence secrets to share when we were students. We talked about our studies, and since then I have shared with them, and they with me, harmless information about scientific developments worldwide, as all scientists do. I am pretty certain my letters to them would have been opened by Russian KGB or later FSB, and theirs to me were usually delayed long enough for me to be sure these agencies had read them. It may all have been perused by your people, too, for all I know."

Igor added: "Of course, if your people were opening our mail you would know about that already."

Ussher leaned back in his chair, steepled his fingers under his chin, and smiled. "Indeed. The truth is often stranger than fiction, Mr Schaplinov. You may be what you tell me you are, or you may be something entirely different."

"Of course. As I said, that is for you to decide."

"Let me tell you a little story told to me by a retired Detective I met on a court case, and with whom later I used to play chess. He was a pleasant chap, and a good opponent. A terrible gasbag but he did have some interesting stories. I remember clearly one he told me. When he was a 'new' detective he went haring off over a roof after a suspect, cornered him, and the bloke said 'OK, you've got me, guv', and reached into his jacket. 'Oh, Christ, he's got a shooter', my friend thought. He was regretting his enthusiasm in giving chase, when the burglar pulled out a handkerchief and mopped his brow." He leaned forward again. "Maybe you will give us an unlikely surprise too, but it may not turn out to be so pleasant."

Igor's smile was wry, and not genuinely amused. "The question is: 'For whom?'"

Chapter 20

Chichester, Thursday, 28th April, 2016

The attempt to interview Yevgeny having aborted, Lacey and Shuttleworth went back to the nick. In the car Shuttleworth was thoughtful. "I've been thinking about what you said, sir. You know, about the Russians wiping the poison bottles clean, but leaving fingerprints all over the room and bathroom."

"OK, Peter, let's have it."

"Well, they wouldn't need to wipe the bottles if they intended wearing rubber gloves to mix the poisons."

"Maybe, but wouldn't that mean they'd have had to be wearing rubber gloves any time they handled the bottles?" Lacey paused. "Still, it's a good thought we must bear in mind." He halted again. "Tell you what, get Harry to phone the hotel and ask if any gloves were found in the waste bin in the room."

****

Lacey sat beside Kiara. He did not get close. He was well aware of her extreme attractiveness, and that she got more than her fair share of macho showing off and stupid jokes, as well as more serious attempts to flirt. She seemed deliberately to dress neatly but down to deter verbal harassment, or even more offensive behaviour. He had no intention of offending her by any behaviour which could be interpreted as using his rank to procure her favours, not that he had any intention of trying it on.

She started the CCTV sequence. "I've looked at these, sir." She pointed to a small pile of tapes from around the city. "No trace of the vicar Mrs Mason saw, not anywhere, except the one from New Park Road." She wound the film forward a trifle. "On the Russian front, as it were, this bit shows two men leaving the train station on the westbound side, so they could have come from Brighton."

"Yes, from the hotel."

"You can see their faces quite clearly in the next bit. They're the same faces in the copy passports the hotel gave us. A few minutes later here they are, in Chichester, walking up South Street towards the Cross, and next we catch them just passing the Cross, and turning left into West Street. This one shows them walking past the statue of St Richard and making for the main door into the Cathedral. I'll skip the scenes inside as they were there for over two hours, having a good look round and taking quite lot of photos. They spoke to no-one but a guide."

Colin said, "Right. We'd better get a statement from him."

"It's a 'her' actually, sir."

A flash of annoyance with himself crossed Lacey's face. "Sorry, Kiara. Just a sexist beast, aren't I?" He shook his head. "Sign of my advancing years. So they get off the train at ten-fifteen, go into the cathedral at ten-twenty-five, and come out at ...."

Kiara pointed to the time on the screen shot: "At twelve-thirty-seven, sir."

"Are there any shots of them in the New Park Road area?"

"None, Inspector. You can see them here outside the Cathedral looking at a map. Then they go back and wander round the Cloisters, come out by the Vicar's Hall into South Street, look at their map again, see? Turn left, go past the Cross to North Street. Then we see them enter the Old Cross pub, here." She fast forwarded again, showing the two Russians exiting the pub at thirteen-forty-eight.

"What happens after that?"

Morton came into the room. "I spoke to the Tourist Board, sir, told 'em what you want. They'll ring you soon as they've checked their records."

"OK, Harry. D'you want to look at these with us?"

Harry Morton drew up a chair as Shuttleworth put down the phone. "Sir, no rubber or other gloves were found in the Russians' room or bin at the hotel." Lacey acknowledged this.

Kiara showed the men wandering up and back down North Street, taking photos of some of the notable structures, such as the Assembly Rooms. "Then they go down East Street, into North Pallant, here, and ...."

Lacey sat forward to point at the screen. "That's a nice house, there on the left. They're snapping that."

Morton nodded. "That's where Mr Spencer lives; the surgeon who found the victims on the bench." As Charcko ran the film forward Morton said, "Let's hope they're not planning to bump him off too." His mobile rang and he answered it.

Charcko continued: "And here they are back at the station." The Russians were shown standing fairly still on the eastbound platform; it was a quite clear picture, so their features could be seen well. Comparing the film with the photos in the passports, it was plain that the taller of the two was Balkonsky. The shorter one, Milukov, looked rather squat and powerful. Both had very dark hair, but Balkonsky's was shorter and close cut.

Charcko continued: "A Brighton train comes in a few minutes later, and they get on it." She pointed at the screen. "There. They don't get off it and come back out of the station either. They must have left it somewhere else, probably Brighton." Charcko turned off the film.

Lacey sat folding and unfolding his fingers for a minute. "I'd like you to do a few things for me, Kiara. First, get on to the railway station and confirm that the train they got off, and the one they got on, were Brighton trains. Secondly, phone Brighton Police. Ask if they could round up Brighton CCTV material for that day, the one before, and the one after. Particularly near the station and their hotel. We need to find out what happened to these chaps after they left Chichester. They could have got off anywhere."

"Yes, sir."

"I'd like you and DC Morton to go over there when they've got it all together. Have a look at it. If it's any good bring it back for me to watch. No, bring it back anyway."

"Anything else, sir?"

"Yes. Take Morton round to the hotel again and find out what happened to the two men the day before, if they know where they went, and what sort of times they left and returned both days. Away you go."

She left with Morton. Lacey's phone rang, and he picked up the call, listened and thanked the caller. He turned to his Sergeant. "Peter, I think we should let the media have a copy of the CCTV films of the Russians and the vicar. It maybe someone will have seen something and be able to tell us."

"Yes, sir. D'you think we should give copies to the airports to see if they have a match of them leaving the country? Or arriving, come to that."

"Good idea. Give them those names, too. What were they again?"

"Nicholas Milukov and Dmitri Balkonsky."

"You know, I still don't understand how the PM knew they were Russian."

Peter chortled. "Lucky guess, sir." Then he turned serious. "Unless the SIS has access to this CCTV stuff remotely somehow. Airports, railway stations etc. And main tourist attractions like the Cathedral."

"More good thinking, Peter. Of course, they'd know a couple of Russians had arrived from the passport checks at the airports." Lacey paused. "I bet that's something else Sawyer knows. Maybe we'll pay him another visit after we've seen Yevgeny Pedchenko."

"By the way, sir, what was that call you took?"

"That was a Mr John Smith – yes, really John Smith - from the Tourist Board. He normally checks the hotel and certifies it. Never had any trouble there. Random checks are only for dubious places, usually because of lots of guest complaints. He has no record of a recent check by any of his colleagues, they all deny it, and he last did one two months ago. He thinks it must have been a prank or a scam." Lacey paused. "Or it could be something more sinister. I tell you what. Get Morton to see this Smith fellow while they're in Brighton and get a statement from him. I want the interview on tape too. Let's go to the canteen, get a coffee, and you can finish reading the Scenes of Crime report."

****

The young uniformed constable walked into the cathedral office. A tubby man in his fifties in blazer and red cravat asked if he could be of assistance.

"Yes, sir. On the 23rd a couple of Russian men visited the cathedral and toured it. CCTV shows they talked to a guide, a lady. We need to interview her – well, not me but the DCI in charge. Can you tell me who was on duty from ten am to twelve-forty-five pm that day, please?"

"Certainly, Constable. It'll be in the roster book." The man got up and went to a filing cabinet, withdrew a blue A4 book with a stiff cover, and returned to his desk. He found the date, turning the book round so the officer could read it; he pointed at the entry. "There we are, 23rd April, ten am to one pm, two men and one woman, Shirley Glover." He looked up, concerned: "Shirl's not in any trouble, is she?"

The constable smiled: "No sir. We're trying to find out if the Russians were involved in something, so we need to find out what they said to her, in case it gives any clues. Do you have her address and phone number, please?"

The man sat to fetch a notebook from a drawer of his desk. "Here we are officer. It's an address in Funtington, and there's the phone number."

The officer entered the details in his notebook. "Thank you, sir. I'd better get back to the station." Just as he reached the door the man jumped up, saying: "Officer, you asked about the 23rd. Isn't that the day two men were poisoned near Priory Park? I read about it in the paper."

"Got it in one, sir. But they're not the two I've asked you about."

Outside the cathedral the constable took out his mobile. "Turner here. Is that you, Sarge?"

"Yes, Davies here."

"Can you tell DS Charcko the name of the guide at the cathedral is Shirley Glover? She lives in Funtington." He read out the address and phone number.

"OK Barry, will do."

****

DS Charcko fetched PC Hunter out of the canteen where he was having a break. She wanted a witness to whatever Shirley Glover might tell her. She stopped her police Volvo outside the charmingly renovated former Council House in the village. In answer to her ringing the bell a smartly dressed brown haired woman in her forties came to the door. "Yes?"

Charcko held up her warrant card. "I'm DS Charcko. This is PC Hunter."

"Heavens, not in the poo, am I?" she said with a smile as she held the door open and stepped back to allow them in. "What can I do for you? Would you like tea or coffee? Let's sit in the lounge." She took the officers into a long room, clearly where the central wall had been turned into an arch to the room behind, giving a view of a garden filled with rose and dahlia beds.

"No tea or coffee thank you," Charcko said as she sat down on a red velour sofa. Hunter kept quiet and took out his notebook. "This shouldn't take long. You're Shirley Glover and a guide at the cathedral?

"Yes to both questions. I just do the Cathedral one Sunday every fortnight. I love it. In the week I do four days as a secretary at one of the local solicitors. Thursday's my day off."

"Right, thank you. Now you were there from about ten in the morning on the 23rd of this month?"

"Yes, at the cathedral and I left for lunch back here at just after one o'clock."

Charcko held up photos of the two men. "Have you seen these two before?"

Shirley removed her rimless glasses to look at the pictures and looked at them very carefully. She replaced the spectacles and looked again. Suddenly she nodded and smiled. "Yes, they were two Russians who asked me some questions about the cathedral. Well, only one of them seemed to speak English, so he did most of the talking. They were very interested in the ancient stone tombs of old gentry. I remember it clearly because I did a bit of Russian at school, so I used it on him a little. My accent made him laugh. Anyway, he spoke very good English."

"Did they say much?"

"Well, apart from their questions – pretty normal tourist stuff – they told me they were staying in Brighton and were only here for a short visit. Very polite. Even tried to give me a tip, so I told them to put it in the donations box." She looked puzzled. "What's this about? Did I do .... oh! Are they the men who were found dying outside Priory Park later that day?"

"No, the two you met are OK, and may have flown back to Russia. The two in the park were in hospital, and one of them died. We're trying to find out if your two were involved, or eliminate them from our enquiries. Did they say what they would do after the cathedral?"

"Only that they were off to get some lunch, so I suggested they tried the Old Cross."

"Was there anything about them making you suspicious or thinking they were odd in any way?"

"No, nothing at all. They seemed very nice. Even asked me to have lunch with them!" Shirley laughed. "I said 'no', even though it's ages since a younger man asked me out, let alone two. What would my husband have said?" Looking more serious, she said, "I wish I could be of more help."

Charcko stood up. "Please could you come down to the station to make a statement in the next day or two?"

"Very well. Are you Indian?"

The Sergeant bridled at that. "No, I'm English, but my parents are from Hyderabad. Is that a problem?"

With a broad smile Mrs Glover waved aside the annoyance Charcko had shown. "Not at all. I was born in Mumbai. My father was a military adviser with the Indian Army. I've visited Hyderabad many times. We have so few police officers from other races round here, and I think it helps everyone if there's a mixed police force, don't you? Are you stationed in Chichester?"

Charcko relaxed. "No, I'm from London, just here for this case."

"Well, it would be good if you moved here. Good luck."

****

234

Colin Lacey was in his hotel room having a shower before going to the dining room. When he came out of the bathroom wrapped in a huge white bath towel, his internal phone rang. "Colin Lacey."

"It's Jodie, Jodie Jordan. I'm in my room. I'm just going down to dinner."

"Do you want me to eat elsewhere?"

"No; why?"

"Well, you seemed pretty annoyed with me last time I saw you."

"Not so much you. More your sergeant."

"I think he disliked your idea we were naughty boys and he's a bad driver. He's a very good driver, and proud of it."

"Fine. Look, I want to talk to you about Yevgeny. I'm going down to dinner, and you can join me if you wish. Or not. It's up to you."

"Very well. See you down there in ten minutes."

As soon as they sat down Jodie told Colin, "Yevgeny woke up again briefly about an hour after you left. He was slightly more with it and making a bit of sense."

"I must see him straight away."

"No use, I'm afraid. He went back to sleep after ten minutes, and it would be dangerous to wake him now. You've got one body on your hands; you don't want two, especially if the second one is your fault. And if he's dead he can't tell you anything."

"OK, Doc. When, then?"

"In the morning. If he's awake he'll have been washed and seen to by eight o'clock, so what about then."

"I'll be there on the dot. Will you be there?"

"Better keep an eye on him, and how you handle him, but I can wait outside if you prefer it."

"Well, I shan't get stroppy with him. It's not my style. I hope to get better results by being kind and sympathetic, even when I'm talking to the likely villain."

Jodie laughed. "Yevgeny can hardly be a suspect. He'd have had to spray his uncle first and then himself, assuming he wanted to make it look as though someone else had done it. He'd have no idea if he were committing suicide!"

"You know, in many cases, he could be the prime suspect as he was with the deceased, but you're right. I don't think he murdered his uncle, nor was he trying to commit suicide if he had. What sort of motive would he have had?"

When the waiter came, they were both too excited at the prospect of getting to the bottom of this odd case to study the menu, so they made a rapid choice from the 'table d'hote'. Jodie was pleased her patient was recovering and Colin because he could talk to the man who might have most information. He did not say so to Jodie, but a compartment in his mind was still open to the chance Yevgeny might have been the culprit. Maybe he could have been an accomplice who was given a small dose to disguise his part in the plot, if there were one, but there would have been one hell of a risk of his dying, bearing in mind how deadly Novichok was. As it was, it had been touch and go whether he would live. And again, there was the question of motive.

Jodie Jordan told Lacey about her education, and that her favourite sports had been netball and tennis. His were cross-country running and tennis, so they talked about playing a couple of sets one day when and if the case eased up.

They had a glass of wine with their meal, and a short in the bar after that, and he walked her to her room. It had been a very pleasant, even entertaining evening. Colin felt emboldened to give her a kiss; only a chaste one, but nevertheless a kiss. As he bent to kiss her cheek, she turned her face towards his and met his lips with hers, and the kiss became rather warmer than he anticipated. Tempted to try his luck, he decided with a struggle to cut it short, and not spoil anything. They said "Goodnight" softly at the same time. Colin strolled away without looking back.

****

At 8.00am on Friday Lacey was striding rather urgently up and down outside the ICU, whilst Shuttleworth sat more calmly watching him. When Captain Jordan slid out of the Unit a moment later in her medical gear, she invited Lacey to don the same sort of outfit.

"I want Peter here to come in too. He can take notes and record the interview on his phone. Is that a problem?"

"He'll have to be properly clothed too and mustn't make a noise or interfere. We need to keep Yevgeny as calm as possible, and if I say 'Stop' you both have to leave at once."

"Understood. Got that, Peter?"

Shuttleworth agreed and they got into their hospital garb. Jordan led them into the room to see Yevgeny. The headboard end of his bed had been elevated slightly so he was lying in a semi-sitting posture. Not that it had a proper headboard; it was an up-to-the-minute electronically controlled sort. He smiled weakly at the Captain; she told him Lacey was there to talk to him about what had happened to him and his Uncle.

The patient nodded to her and looked at Lacey. "I saw you yesterday. Hello, Inspector."

"Hello, Yevgeny. Feeling better than yesterday?" Lacey was relieved that the Russian had recovered his excellent English.

"I've even had a little breakfast, but I do not know what day it is."

"It's Friday, 29th April. You've been in here quite a while."

"How many days?"

Peter said, "Seven including today. You came in here on 23rd April, last Saturday."

"Have I been very ill?"

Jodie leaned forward. "You have. You'd been poisoned, but you are getting better."

Yevgeny clearly thought that was a joke, for he laughed; weakly, but a laugh all the same. "Who would want to poison me?"

Lacey sat on the edge of the bed. "That's what we're trying to find out." He took out his ID card. "I'm Detective Chief Inspector Colin Lacey. This is Detective Sergeant Shuttleworth. We're investigating what happened to you, and who did it."

"I remember I was with my Uncle. Vladimir. Have you spoken to him?"

Lacey looked up at Jodie, not sure whether he should break the news so soon. She stepped to the bed and took Yevgeny's hand. "They haven't been able to talk to him, I'm afraid."

"Why? Is he in hospital too?"

"Yevgeny, it's worse than that, you see." She covered his hand with both of hers. "He was poisoned as well, and he was given a much bigger dose. He died on Tuesday. I'm sorry. We did everything we could to save him. You were both poisoned with the same horrid stuff."

"What was it? And why was he murdered?"

"It was Novichok, a nerve agent; it shuts the nervous system down. He had much more of it than you; his system could not take it, and we could not rescue him."

The Russian was silent for a few seconds, his eyes closed. A tear drifted down his left cheek. Jodie took a tissue and wiped it away. He opened his eyes. "But why did they do that?"

Colin Lacey spoke. "We don't know. We don't know if it was 'they' – more than one person - or only one. You must know that your Uncle had been a spy for Britain against the USSR." Yevgeny nodded in agreement. Lacey continued: "It's possible he was assassinated as a reprisal. Or perhaps someone affected by his spying did it in revenge, but the likely option is it was the Russian Secret Service. We've been investigating a couple of Russians who were here in Chichester at the time."

"So what do you think?"

"I'm keeping an open mind until I have more evidence and made more enquiries."

"Yes, I understand. I wish very much to help."

"Well, that's the thing. You could tell me everything you remember about that day."

"It won't be very much, sir."

"You needn't call me 'sir'. Call me Colin if you like, and this is Peter," he said, indicating Shuttleworth. "He's got a phone so he can record what we say, but you are not a suspect as far as we know. It's just very important that we have a record of what you tell us. Is that OK?"

"Definitely. I want my Uncle's killer caught."

"Very well. What do you remember then?"

"I think I'll start with the day before. That's …"

"Friday 22nd", Peter put in.

Yevgeny Pedchenko was lost in thought for two or three minutes. "It was a pretty ordinary day to start with. We had some breakfast, and the sun was shining, so we went for a walk down to the canal, er, crossed the cattle bridge at Hunston, had a pint of beer and some lunch in The Spotted Cow. We often do that. Then we walked home."

"What time was that?"

"Not sure, really. Three? Half past when we got home?"

"And then?"

"This is hard."

Jordan laid her hand on Lacey's shoulder. "Yes, it is hard, and you're looking tired, Yevgeny. Can we leave this until tomorrow, Colin?"

Yevgeny raised his right arm, bringing it down with a bit of a slap on the bedclothes. "No. It's alright. I can answer a few more questions."

Colin was relieved. "Thanks. So you got back from the pub at about three or so. Then what happened?"

"I'm sure we just stayed in, reading or watching TV. Then we went to bed. Next morning I went outside to bring the milk in and saw a large envelope on the doorstep under the bottles. It must have come that morning, Saturday. It was addressed to Uncle Vlad. I took it off the doorstep and brought it in."

"Had it been posted?"

"Well, it had no stamps on the envelope. We thought it must have been delivered by hand. I picked it up and Uncle told me to open it. The envelope had one of those plastic insides. I took the newspaper out."

"What paper was it?"

"Novaya Gazeta. It's a ...."

Colin nodded: "Russian paper owned partly by a former KGB man, Alexander Lebedev. He also owns three UK papers, the 'Evening Standard', the 'Independent' and the 'Independent on Sunday'."

Captain Jordan asked, "How do you know all that?"

"Part of my job at Special Branch and now in Counter-Terrorism." Lacey grinned. "Anyway, you can find it on the internet." He turned back to Yevgeny. "Why the Novaya Gazeta?"

"I have no idea. I flicked over the pages, and looked at some a bit more than others. I don't think Uncle touched it much; perhaps just the corner of one or two."

"Was that all?"

Yevgeny looked out of the window, collecting his thoughts. "No. I got interested in an article about.... oh, I don't know. But I rested my hands on the pages and stood there reading some of it."

"That explains it. Our forensic people ...."

"Forensic? What is that?"

"They are the ones who examine all the physical evidence like fingerprints, blood stains, footmarks, hair, to see who touched things or held them."

Yevgeny smiled. "Ah yes, I forgot. Like in 'Inspector Frost' or 'Silent Witness'. I watch in Russia TV."

"Exactly. Well, they found this poison - Novichok - on your hands, quite a lot of it. There was a small quantity on Vladimir's hands, too. We think most of that may have come from the front door."

Yevgeny nodded. "I remember that Uncle complained there was something wet or sticky on the door as he pulled it shut when we went out." Left to think for a moment, he added, "Was that enough to kill him?"

"It seems not. But you both had enough to make you feel very ill by the time you reached the bench by the old Roman Wall. What happened then?"

Yevgeny raised a hand off the bedclothes, waving it slightly from side to side. "It's all getting rather vague now. Volodya went to sleep, and I must have done soon after."

"Volodya?"

"That is the diminutive – how do you say? Nick-name? For Vladimir."

"Did you see anybody come near you?"

"I really don't recall that. Sorry."

Again, Jodie Jordan spoke to Pedchenko. "You look very tired again, Yevgeny. Do you want to rest?"

Shuttleworth grunted disapproval, but Lacey said, "I only have a few more questions for now, Captain, but can leave them if you say I must."

Yevgeny yawned loudly, rubbed his eyes, but made another gesture: "I'll be alright for a few more minutes, Inspector. I want to help as much as I can."

"OK. You asked just now if Vladimir had enough poison on his hands to kill him. That wasn't it. It seems someone sprayed a lot more of it on him, and you, from behind. It looks as though your Uncle was the main target.

242

You just caught some of the spray on the back of your neck by accident, but his head and neck were covered in it. Definitely enough to kill him."

Yevgeny sighed. "He was murdered then."

Shuttleworth muttered: "Assassinated, I'd call it! And it could have killed you, too."

Lacey glanced disapprovingly at Peter, but asked, "And you didn't see anyone who might have done it?"

"No. If I remember later, I'll let you know." Lost in thought for a moment, Yevgeny then said, "We both felt a bit tired, perhaps unwell, which is why we sat down, so we might have dozed. Then we wouldn't see anyone."

"Thanks; the poison on your hands probably did that. Look, we'll leave you for a while and come back in an hour or two if that's OK with the Captain."

Jodie looked pleased. "Yes, that's fine with me. If he sleeps for an hour or two that'll be good, and I'll let you know when he's awake."

"Alright." He turned to the patient. "What I want you to think about is what your Uncle told you about being a spy for Britain."

****

At noon Lacey and Shuttleworth were strolling in Priory Park, discussing the evidence so far, having had another look at the bench and its surroundings in New Park Road. Lacey's mobile rang. It was Jodie Jordan "He's awake. Had a good sleep for almost three hours. Woke up about half an hour ago; managed to eat and drink something. He's fit to answer more questions, but try not to upset him. It could make him relapse."

"I'll be the soul of discretion as usual." Lacey thought Jodie laughed before she said, "Modest, aren't we?"

"As one of my friends used to say, 'Colin, you have much to be modest about'." And Jordan definitely laughed.

Fifteen minutes later the two detectives were in the hospital Intensive Care Unit with Jordan and Yevgeny, who looked a little healthier. "I've been thinking about what you asked me, Mr Lacey. I really know very little. Uncle Volodya hardly ever talked about his work to me. I know he was in the KGB, and worked abroad as a so-called diplomat, spying for the USSR, and then as a double agent and spy for Britain. That was why he went to prison in Russia, and then he was sent here on an exchange of spies a few years ago."

"Yes, we know those things, Yevgeny, but thank you. I was hoping you might know something about his contacts in MI5 or MI6."

Yevgeny rubbed his hands in a worried manner, frowning with concentration. "There is something." He was silent for a couple of minutes, and Lacey left him to think, conscious that upsetting him or putting him back in a coma would do no good at all. Suddenly the Russian's eyes flew open; he raised his head from the pillows. "I have it. He once said something about a man called Archie."

"Archie who?"

"I don't know. Uncle said he didn't know either. It was just the name of a man from the British Secret Service who told him what to do, what they wanted, and paid him. He also collected the information Volodya had if he didn't put it in drop-off places."

"What else did Uncle tell you about this man? Anything?"

"There is something; it'll come ..." Yevgeny put his hands to his temples and rubbed them. Jordan came closer, took his left hand and said, "Are you alright?"

"Yes, Doctor. I have a slight headache, but I want to help as much as I can." He turned to Colin Lacey. "I remember. When he told me about Archie, he showed me a photo in a small book he kept in a drawer in his desk."

"D'you mean a photo album?"

Yevgeny nodded. "My Uncle was in it, looking much younger, so it must have been taken years ago. He was with another man. They were on a seat in a park. He said it was in London. The man was young too. Uncle said, 'That's Archie'."

"Thanks, Yevgeny; that may be truly helpful. Can you tell me anything else?"

He shook his head. "If I think of anything else I'll tell the Doctor or one of the nurses to let you know."

After shaking Yevgeny's hand very gently, and thanking Jodie, Lacey left with Peter Shuttleworth. They retrieved their car from the hospital staff car park, which Angus Spencer had arranged for them to use. Peter drove to the Police Station by the Canal Basin while Colin made a call on his mobile.

"Sergeant Davies, please." A short interval followed. "Hello Sean. I want you to get hold of the bloke from SOCOS and see if they found a photo album at Pedchenko's house. If they've got it, get it to me ASAP. If they haven't got it, please get someone round there at once to find it. I'll be in the canteen."

A few minutes later Colin and Peter were at a table eating sandwiches and drinking coffee.

"Yevgeny's mentioning a photo of his Uncle and Archie reminded me," said Lacey. "I read about some photos in Wikipedia when I tried to find out about Vladimir at the start of this case, Peter."

"Yes. It was in what Carl found for you. Wikipedia said the photos were mentioned in a Daily Mail article. You told me to read it and then phone the newspaper and ask for the photos. It took them a few hours; they said they'd been told about them but had never seen them. They hadn't been able to verify the story either."

Sergeant Davies approached them. He put an evidence bag containing the album down on the table. "It was in store with all the stuff brought back from the house. It's been fingerprinted. At least, the cover has. Should be OK to look through it for what you want."

"Thanks, Sean."

Donning surgical gloves, and taking the book out of the plastic bag, Colin began looking for the photo. He knew what Vladimir looked like. He was after a picture of him which might be years old. He'd turned over a dozen or more pages of photos when he saw one of the deceased with another man, also much younger. Vladimir appeared to be at least twenty years younger. Colin peered at the other man carefully, then pushed the book across to Peter. "What do you make of that?"

Peter had gloves on, too. "Well, it's Vladimir on the left. Must be around twenty years ago, I reckon. Looks like it's spring by the look of the trees. Hang on. There's something familiar about the other bloke." Peter looked up, thinking hard, then looked back at the photo. "Maybe I'm going potty, but I think that's our pal Sawyer."

"Exactly. Let's make a copy of this and go up to Vauxhall again. Eat up. Finish your coffee. I'll get PC Jones to phone and make sure he's available."

"Should we check the photo with Yevgeny first, sir?"

"Good idea. Go back to the hospital, will you? See if he remembers if that's the one. Ask him who the other chap is. Better ask Captain Jordan first."

Chapter 21

MI6 HQ, London. July, 2013

It was a humid, sweaty, summer day, overcast with heavy, light-grey clouds, and drizzling. Parsons, Ussher and Robinson exited their First-Class compartment at Paddington and caught a cab to Vauxhall. They had to wait a few minutes to be shown into Sawyer's office by his secretary, and they were followed in to the sanctum by a young man carrying a tray with a good quality china coffee set with silver accessories.

Sawyer rose from his desk and shook hands with them all. He wasted no time after inviting them to sit and serve themselves; Robinson played 'Mum' and poured. "So how did you assess our friend Schaplinov?" he asked. "True or false?"

The three interrogators spoke simultaneously: Robinson said, "False," Parsons said, "True," Ussher said, "Probably true."

Sawyer smiled. "Interesting. Fred, explain, please."

"Well, we 'ad a meeting about this yesterday; talked it all through, but couldn't reach agreement, as you can see. Gill and Gord got closer but ...."

"I wish you wouldn't call me that, Fred; it's horrid and demeaning. I don't call you Robbo, to remind you of your communist past."

"OK, Gordon, keep yer 'air on." He gave a quiet contemptuous giggle. "So, they think much the same, but I don't. Let's be honest. I didn't catch him lying, and we've all listened to the tapes of each other's interviews. There's 'ardly anything different about any of them. Whenever we've asked him the same questions his answers may use a few different words or expressions, but the meaning's the same, far as I could see."

"You must have a more positive reason than that, surely?" Sawyer asked.

Gillian Parsons interjected. "When we discussed it, Fred, I got the distinct impression you simply didn't like him. Wasn't that it?"

Sawyer rose and went to look out of the window. "Why was that?"

Ussher was looking intently at Robinson and saw his face flush.

Robinson nodded at Parsons. "He was too clever by 'alf. Had an answer for everything. Never faltered or stumbled. It all made sense, but I just didn't trust him at all."

Sawyer turned back to face them. "I've read all the transcripts. Seems to me, Fred, and I don't mean to be unkind, that he was simply cleverer than you, and that's what you didn't like. I don't think we can reject him for his intelligence, can we?" He stopped, still looking at Fred, who remained silent, and then turned his attention to Ussher. "Your assessment please, Gordon."

"True or false? Many in my profession say they can tell when witnesses are lying or not, but I think it a very inexact science. Different races, different nationalities, have different approaches to demonstrate their honesty. Some Middle Eastern and Indian sub-continent peoples think staring straight at you when speaking to you is rude, so they look away. That does not mean they are not telling the truth. They may not be, but you cannot assume it from whether they are looking at you or not. Many people from repressed areas which had crushing dictatorships for decades, such as the USSR, or East Germany, or still have one, like North Korea or China, have spent years avoiding telling the truth for fear of what will happen to them if they do. The fact that they adopt a poker face and give no reaction is a symptom of that. You cannot deduce from it that they are lying if they do say something."

Robinson slapped the arm of his chair. "Get on with it, Gord ... er, Gordon!"

With the same deadly smile he had given Schaplinov, in an icy tone, Ussher responded: "I shall get to it when I am ready." He sighed, exasperated. "I have no reason to disbelieve what the Russian told me. I agree with you, Fred, that he is highly intelligent. If his information is as useful and his work of the same quality as his intellect, we should be foolish not to see what he can do and what he can tell us."

"Very well. Thank you, Gordon. Your turn, Gillian."

"My reasoning is similar to Gordon's, Charles. I adopt what he said about being able to detect liars and tellers of the truth, and I found nothing dubious in his answers to my questions. I felt he suffered a frisson of apprehension when he answered a few of my enquiries, but nothing more than might be expected of someone who knows he is a traitor and is at risk of being returned to his country to meet who knows what ghastly fate."

Fred interrupted. "We 'ave to differ over that. He didn't turn an 'air no matter what I asked him, and he got damned arrogant sometimes, threatening to report me to you, Charles. It was like, I dunno ...., like he weren't worried what would happen to 'im, no matter what 'e did. Never seen nothing like it, not with all the people I've interrogated over the years."

Sawyer nodded. "I picked up some of that from the transcripts. I suppose it's clearer on the tapes."

Ussher indicated his agreement, and Gillian said, "Yes, the tapes do make Igor's arrogance plain, but they also show how crude and insulting Fred was a lot of the time."

"It's just a technique I use sometimes with tricky customers like 'im."

Ussher bridled. "If you'd told me my mother was virtually a prostitute you'd have had rather more than arrogance to deal with."

Fred laughed, pointing at Gordon Ussher; "Is 'e threatening me, Charles?"

Gillian slapped the arm of her chair. "You need to grow up, Fred. Before you interrupted just now, I was about to say that I have one worry about my judgement in this matter. I like Schaplinov. He seems a decent person, and with me at least he was quite charming. It worries me that I may not be quite as objective as I normally am."

"Get off, Gill. You tellin' us you fancy our Igor, then?"

Gordon Ussher raised his eyes to the ceiling with disgust.

Sawyer said, "Please show just a little decorum, Fred." He paused. "However, I note what Fred said about Igor's not being worried no matter what, and the slight reservation Gillian just voiced. We must be sure to be more than usually vigilant. Perhaps the three of you should interview him again in the near future, and we'll revisit your conclusions at that time. I shall listen to the tapes before making a decision.

"However, there is something else I want to try before I decide whether Igor stays here and gets a job at Porton. I've been looking at our files, such as they are, on his English contacts. They, you will recall, are Simon Grant and Alan Carpenter. As you know from your interviews with Schaplinov, he owes his upper-class English accent and excellent command of the language, formal and colloquial, to those contacts.

"What I intend over the next few weeks, is to encourage Igor to contact these men, and make arrangements to see them if he can. He will be accompanied by one of his minders. That's for his protection, and ours, in case he tries to escape. The minders will report to me, and they will be very discreetly followed by my people, who will also report. I shall have the homes of Carpenter and Grant bugged to see what happens when the visits take place. After the visits I shall go to see these men myself, and try to glean their views and feelings about their old Russian friend."

Ussher intervened. "You might consider having Carpenter and Grant's landlines and mobile phones tapped."

"And cut off. That would give us entry to their homes for the bugging. First, though, we must let Schaplinov off the leash a trifle so he gets used to moving around in London and the countryside. We don't want him arriving at PD, if we get that far, looking as out of place as a tart in a convent."

Robinson said, "We could move 'im to that flat we have in Upper Richmond Road. Cronin and Wynter can take care of him there."

"We can do that. It's empty at present. We'll ask Mrs Henderson to go there too."

Chapter 22

Chichester, Friday, 29th April, 2016

Sharon Jones came into the incident room carrying a tray with coffees from the canteen for Lacey and Shuttleworth, and teas for herself and Morton. She addressed Kiara Charcko. "I'm just going back for your chai, Sergeant."

"Thanks. No sugar."

Lacey noticed that Peter was, as usual unable to take his eyes off this beautiful young Indian woman for more than a minute at a time. "Maybe I'll have to give Peter some direction over this," he thought. The last thing they needed in a sensitive investigation like this was a cloudburst of emotional and personal problems creeping into the team.

A couple of minutes later Sharon returned with the chai for DS Charcko, and said, "I couldn't get hold of Mr Sawyer last night, sir, but I got him this morning, and he could see you tomorrow."

"Not today?"

"He was adamant he was booked up all day, including a serious meeting with the PM and senior members of the

Cabinet. He was clearly annoyed at the idea of having to see you again at all."

Lacey shrugged. "Well, even I can't expect him to put the PM off for me. So what time tomorrow, Sharon?"

"Ten-thirty, sir. He said you can catch the early train which gets in about ten o'clock and be with him by half past." She imitated Sawyer's posher voice. "'Tell Lacey he can have an hour, tomorrow's Saturday, and I don't usually come to the office at weekends unless it's a security emergency. I could make him leave it until Monday'. That's what he told me to tell you."

"Bloody hell!"

Lacey smiled to hide his wrath. "Well, Peter, he is an important man and wants to throw his weight about." Characteristically, he drummed his fingers on the desk-top. "OK. So where are we? Kiara, tell us how you and Harry got on in Brighton yesterday."

"We went to the Police Station first, to look at the CCTV stuff." Her account of that was that most of it was a waste of time showing nothing, but they had brought back to Chichester a few tapes showing the two Russians going in and out of the hotel and railway station, and for a walk along the Promenade. Lacey and Shuttleworth could look at them if they wished but she was not confident they would spot anything she and Harry Morton had not noticed. She pointed to a small pile of four tapes on her desk.

"Very well. You can have a go at that, Peter."

Peter looked at Kiara. "Maybe you could take me through them." She said nothing.

Lacey thought: 'Oh, God, here we go!' but said to Peter: "No, Peter. You can manage that on your own." Then he gave his attention to Kiara once more. "What happened at the hotel?"

"The manager was as helpful as he could be, which wasn't much. I took a copy of the register with me and the copy passports to remind him who we were talking about. I showed them to him, and he remembered. He laughed actually, saying he 'didn't forget people the Police had only asked him about a few days before'. He had no idea where they went or what they did while they were in Brighton. They were out all day both days. They were quiet, polite, caused no trouble, and paid up with no bother when they left.

Peter smirked. "If they were here assassinating people, they'd hardly draw attention to themselves, would they?"

Kiara ignored him. "The manager – Mr Burrows – let us talk to all the staff who had dealt with the men. He gave us the address of one woman who'd seen them, so I went to see her, while Harry went to the Police Station to collect the videos, and to take a statement from Mr Smith at the Tourist Board."

"Yes, sir." Morton handed over a sheet of paper. "That's Smith's statement. He confirmed none of his people had been to inspect the hotel that day."

"Thanks, Harry. What did the woman say, Kiara?"

"Nothing much really. She worked in the kitchen. Thought they were just a couple of pretty run-of-the-mill tourists, no trouble, very polite. Saw nothing strange about them at all. Hadn't seen Russians at the hotel before. That was it." Sergeant Charcko paused. "Oh! She took them early morning coffee in their room, and they were pretty normal then. I took her statement just in case, but it's not much use."

Lacey turned to Shuttleworth. "Did you get back to the hospital to see Yevgeny?"

"Yep; showed him the photo, sir and he confirmed the other bloke with his uncle is the one Pedchenko called Archie. Told me some other useful stuff, too."

Chapter 23

Northamptonshire, late July, 2013

"Alan Carpenter speaking."

A voice at the other end said, "Is that Alan Carpenter, the lecturer at Cambridge?"

"It is. How can I help you?"

"Well, Professor Carpenter, I wanted to ask you if it ...."
The line was dead. It was a cordless phone, so Carpenter pressed the button to get a line and redial, but there was no dialling tone. He replaced the instrument in its holder, as if to recharge the battery, and picked it up again, but still no dialling tone.

"What the bloody hell ...." he said as he made for the kitchen where there was another phone. It was dead too. He ran up to the bedroom, where Lydia was running the Hoover round. He found that the bedroom phone was useless as well.

"The phones aren't working!"

"What?" she shouted over the noise of the vacuum as she switched it off.

"The phones aren't working."

"What a nuisance. Phone BT on your mobile. It's on the kitchen table." She switched the Hoover on again. Alan ran down the stairs and took his mobile from the breakfast table. He rang the BT fault line and asked for someone to check his landline. They confirmed that it was cut off, even though the bill was paid. They would have to come out to check it.

****

Two hours later a BT van pulled into the drive, and two men got out. The noise of a lawn-mower came from the back of the house. Lydia opened the door when the bell rang.

"Hear you've got a fault on the line Ma'am," one said. He was short, with a Midlands accent, a moustache, and brown hair thinning and scraped across his scalp to try to hide the bald areas. The other was slim, taller, and looked to Lydia like a Pakistani.

"My husband's out the back mowing the lawn. Would you like a cup of tea before you start?"

"No thanks love. We better get on. I'm Sid and that's Ramesh. Just show us where the phones are, can you?"

Lydia showed them the phones in the study and kitchen. The man from the Midlands asked her to take Ramesh up to the bedroom phone. As they ascended the stairs Sid quickly removed the back of the phone, inserted a listening device, reassembled it, went into the study, and repeated the procedure.

Upstairs, Ramesh asked Lydia in a London-bred accent if he could use the toilet in the en suite, so she left the room. When he came out of the loo he examined the phone, and put in a listening device. He took out his mobile and called the other man. "All OK up here, Sid."

Downstairs Sid rang a number on his mobile and said. "Job done." Within seconds the phone in the charger in the study pinged. He picked it up and heard the dialling tone. He crossed the hall and stuck a listening device under the dining table. As he came out Lydia was coming from the kitchen. Sid was quick. "Sorry, Ma'am forgot my way back to the kitchen. All done. Loose wire in the study phone stopped all of 'em, and that's the phone picks everything up."

"Thank you so much. You were quick."

Ramesh had reached the foot of the stairs. "BT's 'ere ter please, Ma'am."

****

At about the same time a similar event was taking place with the phones in Simon Grant's Southampton house.

****

Igor was surprised and pleased when Mrs Henderson told him that he was allowed to contact Alan Carpenter and Simon Grant if he wanted to. He decided to start with Alan. He phoned his college in Cambridge. A college servant told Igor that, being Friday afternoon, the Professor was on his way home to Long Buckby for the week; it was about seventy miles from the college to the village in Northamptonshire, and the Professor did not like to drive both ways every day. He normally stayed the week in his college rooms from Monday morning to Friday evening, the administrator said, but he was preparing at home for a seminar at St Andrews the week after next.

Alan's wife, Lydia, answered the phone on Saturday when Igor rang the number. She called Alan, who was amazed. "Igor Schaplinov? I can hardly believe it. How long is it? Decades. What on earth are you doing here?"

"I defected a few months ago. I'm cared for by certain people. They said I could phone you, and come to see you, if you have no objection."

"My dear chap, why on earth should I object? I'd love to see you. What an adventure! Defecting! I've just got to hear all your tales." Alan laughed. "Sounds very James Bond."

"No, not like that at all, Alan. Well, perhaps a little. I was worried, but it all went rather smoothly, surprisingly so, really."

"Listen, hang on a moment while I speak to Lydia – that's my wife – and see when you could come. Where are you, by the way?"

"In lodgings in London."

"That's good. Won't take you too long to get here then. Hang on."

A couple of minutes later Alan said, "Lydia asks if you can come Monday, stay till Thursday?"

"What about the seminar you're preparing for? In ten days, isn't it?"

"Oh, that's fine, Igor. I'm well ahead with it, and shall have tomorrow, Friday, and the weekend which should see it completed. If you want to take a look around the countryside you can, while I can do some more work on my talk. We can spend some time reminiscing and telling each other the latest career moves, though I reckon yours will be more exciting than mine. I leave for Scotland on Sunday afternoon."

"There's one small problem, Alan. A minder goes with me wherever I go, so he'll have to come too. He's a quiet sort; won't get in the way. Is that OK?"

"Certainly. Heavens, you're 'cared for by certain people', and have a minder. Gets more interesting with every passing minute! See you Monday."

****

Two days later, Craig Wynter drove Igor to the Carpenter's Old Rectory home in Long Buckby. Craig used his own car, a beautifully maintained red 1965 MGB with wire wheels. "Not the fastest piece of kit on the road," he told Igor, "but I love it."

"I can understand that. I can't even afford a bicycle at the moment. Still, one day...."

Igor remembered the way into the village and recognised the rectory when he saw it. Outwardly, it seemed to be much the same, with the white window frames gleaming, and the garden virtually manicured. Rose bushes thronged the flower beds, the edges of which were lined with lobelia and alyssum. The only obvious change was the extent to which the wisteria now practically covered the front of the house and arched over the porch, surrounding most of the windows.

Alan and Lydia came out onto the porch steps to greet them as the car drew up. Alan said, "Welcome, my old friend!" They shook hands and put their other arm around each other. As they separated Alan introduced Igor. "This is my wife of eighteen years, Lydia."

Very attractive with dark brown hair falling to her shoulders, vivacious tawny eyes, and a comfortable figure, neither slim nor overweight, Lydia offered her hand which Igor shook with both of his. He could see that they were a very happy couple.

During these exchanges Wynter stood back, but then Igor introduced him.

"So you're the minder, Mr Wynter," Alan Carpenter observed. "Is he a good boy?"

"Very good, so far." Polite laughter followed.

Lydia showed the two men their bedrooms on the first floor at the eastern end of the house, then took them to the lounge for an aperitif prior to dinner. Alan was already there nursing a scotch in a cut crystal glass. Lydia had a gin and French, Igor and Wynter asked for scotch too, with ice in Igor's case. Wynter's accent was ordinary London. After receiving his drink and saying "Cheers," he said little.

Conversation was very general, light-hearted, and stayed that way when they went in to dinner. Much of the talk was about various aspects of science, in particular the interest Alan had developed in genetic engineering and the use of chemicals in that field. A slightly more serious tone emerged.

"Will these experiments help or not? Will we do damage to ourselves or the environment altering the way things are apparently 'supposed' to be?" Alan stopped. "Here I go, lecturing again."

"But it is a very intriguing subject." Igor was animated. "After all, people have been doing it for hundreds if not thousands of years, but perhaps not so scientifically. Your Squire Coke of Holkham was experimenting with ways to improve crops and cattle almost three hundred years ago. Vineyards have tried grafting different types of grapes and orchards grow modified apples. No harm has resulted from that."

Lydia put her hand on Igor's arm. "Is that so? Aren't some types of banana in danger of dying out because experiments have led to disease? The seeds have been bred out so most bananas contain no seeds, making crop failure a terrible risk. Aren't seedless grapes and mandarin oranges in the same boat?"

Dinner continued in this vein, and afterwards Alan took Igor and Craig Wynter out to his three-car garage. It housed a black Volvo saloon, a small Suzuki run-about, and a beautiful Jaguar XK140 in British racing green of earlier decades. "The Volvo's mine and the Suzuki is Lydia's, but in practice we each drive both cars. The Jag is my pride and joy. There's a race for old cars at Silverstone tomorrow, and I've entered. Would you both like to come?"

"Yes, please," said Igor. Craig, owner of the more modest MGB, gladly agreed. He'd have had to go anyway to keep an eye on his client.

"One of you can come in the passenger seat if you like."

"It'll have to be Mr Schaplinov. I can't leave him sitting watching." Chagrin was writ large on Craig's face.

Carpenter smiled. "Don't worry. I shan't stop to let Igor out and run away!"

Craig Wynter did not smile back.

****

"That was very exciting, Alan." Igor pulled off his crash helmet.

"Yes, it was. We did well to come third out of sixteen. But then that Jag E type has a twelve-cylinder engine, and the Aston Martin DB5 is enormously powerful. James Bond had one in 'Goldfinger'."

"The speed the DB5 was doing, I thought the driver *was* Bond."

Alan Carpenter led the way from the parking area for the participating cars to the grandstand. Craig Wynter was waiting for them, and congratulated Alan on his driving.

As he sat next to Craig Alan said, "There are several more races, so we'll watch a couple, and then go home, if that's OK."

Igor said it was, and Craig nodded. A woman with two teenage boys was walking in their direction along the row in front of theirs. As she got closer, Alan stood up, holding out his hand in greeting. "Hello, Wendy. I didn't expect to see you here."

Smiling, the woman indicated one of the boys. "It's Guy's birthday, and he wanted to come here, so here we are. He's sixteen. Jason is fourteen. They're both car mad."

"How do you do, Guy, and Jason." Alan shook hands with the boys, and then introduced Igor and Craig to Wendy Slater. Everyone sat, the boys either side of Alan. Guy asked, "Was that you, driving the Jag XK140?"

Craig Wynter moved away a couple of seats, and Wendy sat next to Igor. "I thought Alan said your name was Igor."

"It is. I'm Russian. Alan is an old friend of mine from University."

"But your English is perfect. You must have been living here for years." She covered her mouth with a hand, uncovered it and said, "Forgive me. That is so personal and rude."

"Not at all. I was taught how to pronounce your words properly by Alan and another friend at University here and in Russia."

Wendy giggled. "Elocution lessons, then."

"Exactly."

While the boys and Alan talked about cars until the next race started with a completely different field of beautiful old vehicles, Wendy enquired lightly, conversationally, about Igor's background, and he about hers. Not a beautiful woman, nevertheless her bright blue eyes and curly honey blond hair cascading over the collar of her pale blue blouse fascinated Igor. He had not conversed so easily with a woman for some months, found her very attractive, and guessed she was about forty.

"How do you know Alan?" he asked.

"Known him for years. He was at school with Jonathan – my husband. We live in Long Buckby too."

"Is Jonathan here today?"

"I wish he were, but he died five years ago. He had an aneurism in the neck. We had no idea. It burst, and he dropped dead." She was silent and Igor said nothing, regarding her carefully. Wendy looked sad for a moment, and then smiled. Glancing over at the boys still grilling Alan about the cars and the races, she turned back to Igor. "I miss Jonathan, but I've got the boys, a good job, a nice house, so I'm just thankful that I had a good husband for almost twenty years. Many people never get any of it."

Igor told her a little more of his past, but nothing about his father, not even the lie that he did not know who his father had been. He left the impression his mother had struggled on her own but succeeded in the catering world. "What is this good job you have, and obviously enjoy?"

"I'm the accounts manager in a large firm of solicitors in Northampton."

"If I can get into the town tomorrow, would you let me take you to lunch?"

Wendy laughed; Igor was disappointed. Then she looked straight at him, smiled broadly, and said, "Sorry. That was a bit sudden. I haven't had a date for years, even if it's only lunch. Yes, please, that would be lovely."

"It's a bit of a surprise to me, too, but then I'm only here for a few days. I just know I'd like to see you again." Igor rubbed his cheek, pondering. "You'll have to tell me where you'd like to eat, as I've never been there before."

Wendy suggested the St James's Tavern, not far from where she worked in Cheyne Walk, and they agreed to meet there at one o'clock. She confirmed Alan had her phone number, and Igor said he'd have to make some arrangements to get into Northampton. He did not tell her about Craig Wynter, but now he knew where they were to eat, he could tell Craig who could keep a surreptitious eye on them.

****

At twelve fifty-five next day, Igor walked into the pub and found the dining area. The barman directed him to a window seat at a table for two.

Alan had raised no objection to Igor leaving the family for lunch, as he had decided to revise his notes for the Scottish seminar, and Lydia was meeting friends. Craig Wynter drove Igor into the town in his MGB. They left the car separately in the car park, and Igor walked off to the pub, Craig followed about fifty yards behind, wearing dark glasses, a cloth cap, and completely different clothes from those he had on at the racetrack, and appearing to be interested in everyone and everything but the man he was minding. He went into the pub in time to see Igor directed to the window seat. Craig ordered a beer, walked out round to the side of the building where Igor sat, found a bench, and leaned against the wall next to the window. He could keep watch on Igor, but could not be seen from the other chair at Igor's table.

Wearing an emerald green dress which set off her fair hair perfectly, Wendy entered the dining room a few minutes after Igor sat down. Igor immediately stood, they shook hands, and Igor held her chair as she sat. He ordered wine, a glass of white for her and a red for himself. She looked at the specials board on the wall and suggested the prawn salad. Igor agreed.

He told her of his work on chemical and other weapons, and the story about why he had defected. Not the true story about wanting to trace the man who had betrayed his father, but the inaccurate one about wishing to help the British learn more about the weapons the Russians were developing.

Like most people, Wendy was unaware of the poisonous warfare research carried on at Porton Down and in the USA. She found the experiment carried out on sheep on the island of Guinard a hundred years ago particularly revolting.

"We did a similar thing to reindeer in Eastern Siberia much more recently, you know."

Wendy bristled. "No, I don't know. Or didn't. These ghastly, deadly toys governments want are for use on people, aren't they? People like my two sons? Does it make it right if both sides do it? Can they be controlled? Can your government make sure it doesn't kill Russians? Can the UK government guarantee it won't kill me or the boys?"

Igor lowered his head and studied the backs of his hands lying on the table. When he looked up, he smiled. "I agree, it is all wicked, but the argument is the same as the one about nuclear bombs. No country will use one when the enemy has one."

Wendy returned the smile, disarmed. "Sorry. I sounded as though it's all your personal responsibility."

"It's the fault of all scientists. We keep asking: Can I do this? Can I make this do that? What happens if …? As a result, we unleash terror and destruction."

"And there are always people who want to buy it." She smiled again, putting her hand over his just as the barmaid brought their food.

After eating was finished, they had coffee, and then walked across Becket Park down to the river Nene. As they crossed the road, Igor took her hand to negotiate the traffic. She did not remove it. Igor felt happier than he had done in quite a while, despite knowing that Craig was not far behind them. By the water they stood in silence for a few moments, and then Wendy reached up a little to kiss him softly on the cheek. "I must go, or I'll be late back. I've got a mound of work to do."

"I'll walk with you,"

"No, your friend Craig is waiting for you. He's sitting on the seat under the tree over there." She walked away. Hopeful, Igor called after her: "I'll phone you next time I get to Northampton."

Wendy looked back, laughing. "Yes, do that. Come alone next time."

Igor wondered how long that would take, and how she'd recognised Craig Wynter. She was obviously very observant.

****

Craig and Igor drove back to The Upper Richmond Road flat in Putney on the Thursday. Craig said he was having some days off and Lindsay Cronin would take over.

On Friday Craig Wynter went to see Sawyer at the MI6 building. After very brief preliminaries about Long Buckby, Craig made his report.

"As far as I could tell, Schaplinov never varied from anything he told you, according to the briefing I had. Family history was identical, single Mum and all that, career the same. Over dinner the second night he had a long talk with the prof about their sciences and how they had progressed, jobs they'd had, where they thought they wanted to get to."

Sawyer jabbed a finger at his desk. "What about Porton?"

"Igor told him all about hoping to go to work there. Asked him to give him a reference if necessary."

"Nothing to make you suspicious, then."

"Not so far as I could tell, but you're going to deal with Carpenter yourself, aren't you?"

"I may do, or send one of the others."

Wynter took a moment, scratching his eyebrow. "There was one thing. He took a woman out to lunch on the Tuesday. I took him into Northampton and tried to make myself scarce whilst still keeping an eye on him. Carpenter had taken us both to a car thing at Silverstone and we'd met her there, but I'd kept myself to myself. She didn't know I was his minder."

"What was odd, then?"

"I knew where they were to eat, and I waited outside the pub where I could watch Igor, but not be seen by the woman. Wendy Slater was her name. They went for a walk when they left the pub, and I followed at a distance. They stood talking by the river, and I sat under a tree a good way away. I could not hear what they said, but it looked like he wanted to ask her out again. Later he told me she said, 'Yes, but come alone next time.'"

Sawyer looked furious. "What did you make of that? Surely Schaplinov told her about you?"

"He swore he didn't. Anyway, why would he? He wants to stay here. He's not going to mess things up for himself, is he? What I made of it was that this woman Wendy Slater must be very bright. She works for some solicitors. Attractive too."

"We don't pay you to be attracted, Wynter."

"I wasn't, but Igor was, and I'm telling you why. Just the facts."

Sawyer rose and strolled around the office for a few minutes. Eventually he sat again. "He's going to see another of his English friends soon, I hope. We'll send him alone, followed in another car by Cronin. He mustn't tell even his friend he's under surveillance, let alone anyone else he meets."

"Too late where the Prof is concerned. He had to tell him who I was, as I was staying with them too. They hadn't seen each other for years, so he could hardly just ask if he could 'bring a friend', could he?"

Sawyer snorted with exasperation, dismissed Craig, and then telephoned Gillian Parsons. "I'm going to Northants to see some friends of Schaplinov's. I want you to come too and talk to a woman called Wendy Slater."

****

The next day Sawyer's driver dropped Gillian off at the start of a cul-de-sac, part of an estate of 1960s houses. She walked up to the turning circle end and rang the bell of the four bedroom detached house with the green up-and-over garage door. A blue Volkswagen Golf stood in the driveway. The house, lawn and garden looked well cared for.

"Hello; you must be Jason. I'm Gillian Parsons. I have an appointment to see your mother."

"No and Yes. No, I'm not Jason; I'm Guy, Jason is my little brother," the teenager said as an equally tall boy appeared behind him, punched him lightly on the shoulder, and said, "And Yes, Mum is expecting you." He turned to Guy. "Not so much of the little, squirt."

The boys laughed at each other, making Gillian smile, as they politely stood back and invited her in. Jason disappeared up the stairs, while Guy led Parsons through to the lounge where Wendy Slater sat reading a book which she immediately put on the coffee table. She noticed Parsons appraising the furniture, puzzled by the curious mixture.

When the ladies had introduced themselves, Wendy offered tea or coffee. Upon Gillian accepting, Guy went to make tea for both of them.

"I saw you were mystified by the furniture," said Wendy. "The seventies and eighties stuff is what Jonathan and I bought in second-hand shops when we married and had no money. The year after he died - that was in 2005 – my Mum passed away. The antiques were part of my share of her estate. Dad died years and years ago. I gave some of my furniture to charity shops, but I've never found time to sort everything out properly."

Parsons said, "My father always told me it was bad manners to comment on people's choice of furniture."

"But you didn't say anything." Wendy smiled. She paused. "This is quite strange. I've only met Igor Schaplinov twice, once briefly at Silverstone three or four days ago, and we had lunch together two days ago, yet a Mr Sawyer rang to ask me to see you today to tell you what I thought about this Russian visitor."

Gillian Parsons nodded her agreement. "Mr Sawyer is more or less my boss. I'll be quite frank with you, or at least as frank as I am able. Schaplinov has recently defected and …"

"Yes, he told me. He certainly seemed to be very frank."

"The point is he wants to work at a very sensitive British establishment on very hush-hush projects."

"He told me that too. It's Porton Down, it's chemical and biological weapons, and we almost argued about the evil side of the world which appears to make that necessary."

Gillian hid her alarm, breathing in and out slowly for a minute or so. "By which he meant what?"

"No, not Igor. Me. He did not blame the Russians or this country. He tried to explain why nations feel they have to possess these awful things."

"So when you used the word 'side' just now, what do you think he meant?"

The door opened and Guy entered with the tea things and a plate of biscuits. "Do you want me to pour, Mum?"

"No thank you, dear. Just put the tray on the table, I'll see to it." Guy left, closing the door behind him.

"So, what do I think he meant by 'side'? Again you've misunderstood. It's my word, not his. He wasn't saying it's the fault of any particular side. Just that it's the way the world is – the human race, if you like."

This time Gillian hid her relief. "What else did he talk about?"

"Well, we talked together. He told me about his childhood, his single Mum, not knowing who his father was. He told me a bit about his career in chemistry, why he'd defected."

"Which was?"

"He wants Britain and her allies to know what the Russians have and what they are working on."

Parsons leaned forward, elbows on knees. "So what did you make of him?"

"He was kind, generous, charming, and, I thought, truthful. He'd like to see me again, he said. I hope he does. I haven't met as nice a man since my husband died."

The MI6 woman took a sip of her tea and put the cup down again. "What I need to know ..."

"Is whether I trust him, and whether you should." Wendy Slater hesitated for a few seconds. "I believed what he told me. But then I liked him, as I've made plain. I can't say my attitude is neutral or objective."

Gillian laughed gently, cynically. "In the end I doubt any of us are, truly." She did not add that she also had liked Igor. She relaxed or appeared to, asking many questions in a conversational manner, based on the things she, Robinson, and the QC, Ussher, had learned from their interrogation sessions.

****

Five minutes after leaving Parsons at the Slater house, Charles Sawyer got out of the black Jaguar in the driveway of the Old Rectory, and as he made to knock, the door opened. Lydia Carpenter stood there, classily attired in a one-piece burgundy trouser suit and a black jacket. She extended her hand and Sawyer shook it.

"I saw you drive up, Mr Sawyer. Do come in. My husband is expecting you. He's in the study."

"Well, actually, Mrs Carpenter, I want to see both of you. I mentioned that yesterday to the Professor on the telephone."

"Then I'll fetch him, and we'll sit in here. Please go and sit down." She opened a door and pointed to the armchairs.

The lounge was large with a view of the garden, which the spy master admired much as Schaplinov had done, especially the roses, in which Sawyer was something of a connoisseur. As the Carpenters joined him, he voiced his appreciation.

Alan Carpenter was somewhat prickly. "Thank you, but I am not happy about your visiting us, even though I agreed to your coming."

"Frankly, Professor, you had little choice. This is a matter of national security, and I could have had you brought to my office in London. As it happens, I have no desire to alienate you or Mrs Carpenter. Remaining on polite terms will be better for all of us."

Normally a speech such as that would have quelled the spirit of many, but the Professor was made of rather sterner stuff. "Then I should have been pleased to come, but you might have been less than overjoyed when I subsequently let all my academic friends know what had occurred, and suggested they should discuss it with their students, or write papers about it."

Sawyer saw no point in continuing in this vein. "I hazard a guess that what has annoyed you is the fact that I want to enquire about - you might prefer to say spy on – your old friend Igor Schaplinov."

"That is it precisely. He may be Russian, and that may, to you, be reprehensible, but to me he is and always has been an honest and very able scientist."

"You think we should trust him?"

"I trust him. Whether you can or should is a matter for you. For my part I have never had reason to doubt him, and I cannot imagine that he intends the UK any harm."

"I agree." Lydia was firm. "In the four days he was here he never gave me the slightest concern."

"What did the three of you talk about?"

Alan shrugged. "The things that might interest you and your organisation were his work on chemical weapons, his education, his career, the absence of a father in his life."

Lydia added, "He described life at the Pochep installation, and quite a bit about what he does - did - there. But I daresay he told you all that." She twisted her wedding ring around, and then looked up at Sawyer again. "I found it remarkable that with no father, and a single mother working hard to support him, he managed to get from one low level of education to some of the highest that the Soviet Union had to offer."

"I agree," Alan said. "He is every bit as clever as I, but had none of the advantages. It explains a lot about our friendship."

A sceptical expression passed over Sawyer's face. "Yes, it's remarkable, the one aspect of him we have no way of checking." He crossed his legs, letting the quiet hang for a moment. "We've had our people at the Embassy in Moscow, and our illegals, checking on him at the Schools, Universities, and the Institute. All they come up with is that he was very clever, worked hard, and did it all on his own."

Lydia was enthused. "But unlike so many clever people, he isn't out to impress, and thus be a bore. I know 'nice' is a tired word, but he's just very nice."

A grunt seemed to emerge from Sawyer. Then he asked them in great detail about everything that had transpired during Igor's visit.

****

While Sawyer was engaged with the Carpenters, Igor Schaplinov was walking back from Richmond Park with Lindsay Cronin along the Upper Richmond Road in the sunshine. Traffic was noisy, and heavy, but he needed some exercise, and a variation from the judo they practised together when they had the opportunity.

When they had entered the flat, Igor made them both a cup of tea, black, Russian style. He then phoned Simon Grant in Bristol and arranged to see him the following weekend. Grant was as surprised and pleased as Alan Carpenter had been. Again, he was invited to stay.

****

The following day Sawyer called Ussher, Parsons and Robinson to his office. On the way back to London the day before, he had discussed with Parsons what, if anything, they had learned from talking to Wendy Slater and the Carpenters. As Parsons succinctly put it, "Not much."

Charles Sawyer wanted to go through it again with Ussher and Robinson, hence the meeting. On reaching their homes the night before, Sawyer and Parsons had dictated comprehensive accounts of their interviews, using voice recognition software, and printed out the results. Copies were given to Ussher and Robinson.

Fred Robinson was, in his usual fashion, blunt with a rapid conclusion. "Don't think you learnt anything at all, did you? Apart from the fact that he fancied this Wendy, and it looks like that was mutual."

The elderly lawyer was more thoughtful before saying: "I agree. All three of those interviewed had been told the same stories by Schaplinov, not necessarily in the same words, or in the same order, but sufficiently similar to each other to have, as it seems to me, the ring of truth. Probably." He took two or three slow breaths. "And we have heard the recordings from the devices planted in their phones and elsewhere. None of us have found anything worrying from that either. Of course, one might say that it was all very carefully prepared and rehearsed and could therefore be an act. Unfortunately, we did not have the advantage of seeing the story-teller in action, so we cannot take inflection, emphasis, body language, or expression into account." After a pause he continued. "On balance I continue to think we can trust him, but we need still to be very cautious. Possibly we should consider that sending him to Long Buckby with

278

Wynter was a mistake. He may have been inhibited by the minder's presence from relaying more personal information, or feeling sufficiently relaxed to be somewhat indiscreet when ...."

"Come off it, Gord. He ...." Robinson suffered a look from Ussher such as a tiger might give its prey. "OK, OK, Gordon. Sorry. But don't forget he was alone with the Slater woman in the pub, so Wynter could hear nothing of what he said."

"Very well, perhaps so, but I should certainly find such a presence, even outside, something of a hindrance or embarrassment, even if you might not, Fred."

Sawyer held up a hand towards Robinson cautioning him to keep quiet. "It is a useful thought, Gordon."

"What do you suggest?"

"If Schaplinov intends to do something untoward we should give him a chance. Let's tell him he can go to see his friend Grant by train unaccompanied. We put someone he doesn't know on the train in the same carriage to see if he does anything. We contact Grant and tell him he has to wear a wire and have it on all the time our Russian is with him and his family and see what we collect that way."

That strategy was agreed, and Robinson suggested they try to get CCTV somewhere in the house so other interpretive skills could be brought to bear. That was also accepted. The next night, the Grants' satellite dish was disconnected by an operative with cat-burglar talents, the local business which had supplied it was contacted first and told that they would be provided with an engineer to check and repair it, and that anyone relating those facts would be prosecuted for endangering national security. The proprietor was reminded of his membership of the Communist Party when he was young, and that securing a conviction would be easier than falling off the proverbial log. When Mrs Grant called them to ask for the TV to be checked, the engineer from MI6 soon arrived, checked the TV and the wiring, installed minute battery powered CCTV cameras in the lounge and dining room where the TV sets were, announced it must be the satellite dish, and went on the roof to reconnect it.

He was very quick. Mrs Grant was delighted with the small bill when it arrived. The boss was equally thrilled to be paid for a job costing him nothing and said nothing to anyone.

Chapter 24

MI6 HQ, London. Saturday, 30th April, 2016

Once again Lacey and Shuttleworth were kept waiting, despite the fact that they were on time, and Charles Sawyer had stipulated that they could only have an hour. They were ushered into his presence at ten fifteen. There was no offer of refreshments on this occasion. Sawyer was sitting behind his desk, did not rise, did not shake hands, and did not invite them to sit, but they did so anyway.

"Well, Mr Lacey, what can I help you with this time?"

Lacey restrained himself from saying that Sawyer had been of precious little help to them hitherto. "I'd like you to look at a photo, if you would be so kind, and tell us what you know about it."

Peter put the photo album on the desk and opened it at the picture of Pedchenko and 'Archie' sitting on the park bench. He turned it round for Sawyer to look at. As Sawyer leant forward to do so, Lacey saw a tiny and very brief, momentary crack in the spy chief's poker face.

"What makes you think I know anything about this?"

Lacey smiled. "I fancy you cannot pretend you do not know the man on the left."

Sawyer said, "That is Pedchenko."

Lacey continued. "The most famous defector of the last couple of decades. He's the one lying dead in the morgue at Chichester, the reason we are here."

Looking once more at the photo, Sawyer said, "Yes, I see that now. It's an old picture. So what?"

"Who is the chap on the right?"

"Where did you get this?"

Lacey pointed at the photo. "Please answer my question first. Who is that man?"

Sawyer looked away. "I really have no idea."

Shuttleworth laughed, looked at Lacey, who nodded his assent, so the sergeant told the ex-spy: "You see, Mr Sawyer, the dead man's nephew, Yevgeny, is awake now; 'e told us about the photo; 'e told us about this little album. The Scenes of Crime people had recovered it from Pedchenko's home. Yevgeny told us that the other man is Archie."

Sawyer's face adopted a paler shade. He stayed silent.

"He also said Archie was 'is uncle's contact at SIS, gave 'im instructions, collected 'is information, and paid 'im for the Soviet secrets 'e handed over."

"What has that got to do with me?"

Lacey leaned forward and put his palms on the desk. "That man is you, isn't it?"

"Don't be ridiculous!"

"Mr Sawyer, we both recognised you from the photo, old as it is, and Peter here checked it out. We found a photo of you at your graduation from University, not that long – maybe five years - before this photo was taken. We had part of it blown up." Colin removed a photo from his jacket pocket, putting it on the desk next to the Pedchenko picture.

"It came from a local Nottingham newspaper. The headline was "Local Boy Honoured at Oxford.""

Fury covered Sawyer's visage. "Are you telling me you've been investigating me?"

Lacey responded icily. "No, sir, we are investigating a murder, and to do so we need as much information about the victim as we can get. You just happen to be part of it."

"Why - how - did Pedchenko have this picture?"

Shuttleworth replied. "He told Yevgeny you gave it to Uncle Vladimir and told him that a copy would go to the Embassy if he did not do what SIS wanted. In other words, it was blackmail."

"How dare you!"

Lacey smiled again. "Oh, we dare alright! You met your spy in the park, and you had the photo taken. Now he is dead, no wonder you do not want us to find out why, or who killed him."

"I shall speak to the Home Secretary and have this investigation shut down. Making any of this public would breach national security. You could well end up in prison for a very long time."

Lacey stood. "You may recall, sir, that I was threatened with that sort of tactic over the missing plane, SEA439. If we have a press conference about this matter, I shall go public. Perhaps my interest in truth and justice is greater than yours. When governments create a situation where the dregs can rise to a position to exploit the vulnerable and conceal the truth, it will happen."

"Get out!"

"We're going. Thank you for your time. Good morning." Shuttleworth picked up the photos. As they walked down the corridor he quoted, mimicking Lacey; "'Create a situation where the dregs can rise to a position to exploit the vulnerable and conceal the truth, it will happen'. You ought to get that published, sir, or carved on a few notable gravestones."

"What is more important is that Sawyer denied nothing. He even forgot to say 'No comment' this time."

"Yeah. He just wants us to accept the Russians did it. Too easy."

Lacey put a finger to his lips. "Let's talk about this on the train. We need a compartment to ourselves."

Forty-five minutes later they were on the Chichester train from Victoria. They had a compartment to themselves, though at one point Lacey had to tell two women who tried to enter that his colleague seemed to have flu. The ladies beat a hasty retreat.

When they'd gone, Lacey said, "What you said as we left Sawyer was very interesting, Peter. Why is Sawyer so keen to make us think Putin is behind the murder of Pedchenko? I don't get it. Putin is not stupid. If he wanted Pedchenko murdered, why would he let his people use a Russian poison? It's like that other Malaysian plane, the one which was shot down over the Ukraine."

Peter said, "You mean MH17."

"Putin is said to have supplied the Ukrainian rebels with an old Russian ground-to-air missile to shoot it out of the sky. Doesn't that strike you as daft? It brings him, Russia, and the rebels into disrepute, and creates sympathy for the Ukraine government, at least in the West. If I'd been Putin, I'd have acquired a US missile on the black market - arms dealers will sell anything to anyone - and given that to the rebels. If I were the CIA and wanted to damage the rebels and Putin, I'd have given them an old Soviet missile."

A moment later Peter sounded puzzled: "Do governments ever tell us the truth about anything? Maybe it wasn't Putin."

"Precisely." After a few moments of thought Lacey added, "Talking of telling the truth, when we came to see Sawyer a few days ago, he told us he regretted what had happened to this spy Oleg Gordanov. He said that 'we' used Pedchenko to lure Gordanov into a trap, which resulted in his being abducted back to Russia."

"Yep, outside the Army and Navy Club when 'e went there to meet Colonel Webster."

"But doesn't it follow that if Sawyer was Archie, and Archie was Pedchenko's liaison, and used Pedchenko to set up Gordanov, Sawyer was the person responsible for what happened to Gordanov?"

"Blimey, sir, I think you're right! So did 'e – you know, Gordanov – 'ave any family who might want revenge on Pedchenko?"

Chapter 25

Bristol, Somerset. Early August, 2013

On Sunday mornings the Grant family went to Church. Igor had no religious faith, but went anyway for the experience. He found the post-service coffee session in the Church Hall very interesting and pleasant. Several members of the congregation engaged him in conversation, and one couple, the Mannings, talked with him in Russian. They were colleagues of Simon's at Bristol University. Simon joined them with his wife Valerie, and the Mannings invited the three of them to dinner the following evening.

During Igor's stay in Bristol conversation ranged over the same general subjects as with Alan and Lydia Carpenter, save for the scientific exchanges, in which neither Simon nor Valerie had a great interest. However, Simon expressed some trenchant views about the political implications of weapons research.

Dinner with the Mannings on the Monday was entertaining; they talked about their numerous visits to Russia, their love of the Russian people, and most things Russian. They had visited the obvious places such as Moscow and St Petersburg, but also many towns, cities and parts of the countryside even Igor had not seen, such as Omsk, Archangel, Lake Baikal, and Vladivostok.

Igor asked Simon how he came to be at Bristol University, as the last he heard, Simon was still lecturing at Southampton.

"I was headhunted to be a professor there. I now hold the English Literature Chair," replied Simon. Igor congratulated him. "But I am still as keen on literature from almost anywhere as I was when we were young. Remember the talks we used to have in Novosibirsk, Igor?"

Literature was a subject all five found fascinating. Discussion ranged over Pasternak, Tolstoy, Dostoyevsky, Solzhenitsyn, as well as British and American authors, such as Gore Vidal, Herman Wouk, Ken Follett, and Geraldine Brooks from Australia. All were captivated by fiction with a clear political slant. On a slightly lighter note, they also revisited Ian Rankin and Scott Turow.

On the Tuesday morning Simon went to the college to deliver a lecture, and Valerie ran Igor to the station. Before he left, Simon took Igor into his study, took a sheet of paper from his printer, and after putting a finger across his lips, and then mouthing "Say nothing!" he wrote: "I've had to wear a wire. Sawyer told me to."

Igor picked up the pencil. "Not surprised, not worried either. Nothing to hide." After showing it to Simon, he picked up the box of matches lying by Simon's rarely smoked pipe, went into the loo, set light to the paper, and flushed the ashes down the toilet.

Within the hour after Valerie Grant returned home from dropping Igor at the train, one of Sawyer's men collected the discs from the recording device.

****

Late that afternoon Sawyer and his three gurus sat in his office listening to the Grant/Schaplinov tapes.

"Don't tell us nothin' we didn't know already," was Fred Robinson's comment.

Gillian Parsons was more detailed. "What he told the Grants and their dinner guests was very much what he told us, and what he said to the Carpenters. However, he did not talk as though his stories were learned by heart or rote, like an actor or highly practised preacher. I find there is always a strong element of spontaneity, not exactly as if he were telling the tale for the first time, but as though it is real, true, even if he has told others the same thing in the past."

Robinson leapt in. "Well, he's said all this stuff lots a' times, ain't he? Doesn't make it true, does it? I'm still not buying it. It's daft to bring a foreigner from what's a more or less enemy country into a secret establishment."

"Perhaps, but it all adds to what I said last time. I think we should trust him, but be careful," said Gillian.

Sawyer thanked Gillian for that. "Let's not forget Werner von Braun. The Americans trusted him when they took him from building V2s in Nazi Germany to designing space rockets in the USA, including the Saturn rockets and the Apollo missions." He looked at Ussher. "Gordon?"

Ussher contemplated his signet ring. "I have sympathy with Fred's point of view. On the other hand, I also agree with Gillian, but would enter a minor caveat."

"A what?" Robinson chuckled.

Ussher shook his head at the man's ignorance. "A caveat. A warning, as in 'caveat emptor', or 'buyer beware'." He paused, glaring at Robinson. "We have come this far with our defector. We had found no reason to distrust him, and now we've tested him by allowing him to travel on his own, visiting friends unaccompanied. Mrs Welch, our spy on the train, said he did nothing odd, going to Bristol, and old Roberts reported nothing suspicious as he returned from there. He made no attempt to escape or contact anyone. We've listened to the recordings, and at no stage did Schaplinov tell or ask his friend Simon, or Valerie Grant, or their guests the Mannings, anything untoward or which might cast doubt on his bona fides." Leaving his ring alone, Ussher looked up at Sawyer, glanced at Robinson and back to Sawyer. "We still have nothing against him apart from Fred's intuition. On balance I favour letting him go to Porton and see what he can do to help there."

Fred said, "I'm not too 'appy, but even I can't raise any serious objection."

"I agree with Gordon," said Gillian.

"Thank you, Gillian." Sawyer stood and walked a few paces behind his desk. "Yes, so do I, but I think we'll give Igor a week of freedom, to see what he might get up to, and if he's still clean at the end of that, we send him to Porton, if they'll have him. We withdraw the minders, and just have him tailed and under surveillance."

Gordon Ussher tapped the table with the end of his fountain pen. "What about the follow-up interviews we were supposed to have with Schaplinov? Should we have those this week, and compare notes before we make a final decision?"

They all indicated their agreement, and Sawyer said he would make the arrangements.

Chapter 26

Long Buckby. August, 2013

Wendy Slater collected Igor from Northampton Station on the Saturday morning. On three counts he was very happy to have been told he had a week of freedom. He'd had a visit from Parsons at the flat in Putney. She told Igor she and her colleagues had seen his friends, as she had previously informed him they would. Secondly, she took him to Porton Down where he was interviewed by a pompous fellow called Horne-Bassett and a couple of scientists, and would be notified of the result of that after his week of liberty. He felt that the Spymaster must trust him, at any rate to some extent.

Thirdly, he could arrange to see Wendy again, with a bit of luck. He phoned her immediately, before the minders had even had a chance to remove their belongings from their bedroom. "If I've nothing to hide," he asked himself, "why not do everything as openly as possible?"

"But are you coming alone this time?" Wendy sounded amused.

"Definitely, because the minders have been withdrawn."

"Minders? You mean the man who was with you at the racetrack, and then following you about when we had lunch that time?"

"Correct. I was a marked man. But better than that, I have a week off before I start work."

"Work? So you got the job you wanted?"

"Perhaps. I'm probably going to Porton Down, but I don't know for definite until next week. Then I shall be on what they call probate for six months."

"No, Igor, they call it probation," she said with a laugh. "Probate is for dead people."

Igor laughed as well. "Alan and Simon may have taught me to speak with a good accent, but clearly I don't know everything yet! Then he added: "I'll be on the train that gets in at nine thirty tomorrow morning, if that's OK, and then I can catch the late train back to London."

"You can stay the weekend or longer if you want. It's the holidays, and the boys are away at Scout camp in Wales for two weeks. They don't get home until next Saturday."

"Wonderful. I can't stay till then, though. I've got to move to a flat that's been found for me in Salisbury, only a few miles from Porton."

As Igor walked out of the station he saw Wendy, dressed in a pale yellow broderie anglaise blouse with a dark tartan skirt and leather strappy sandals, leaning on the roof of her blue Golf. To his surprise she ran towards him, and kissed him, took his hand, and led him back to the car.

"Throw your bag on the back seat," she said.

In the car, seatbelts fastened, and the engine running, Wend turned to Igor. "Fancy a pub lunch, then?"

291

"I certainly do. I haven't been in a pub since I came over to Cambridge all those years ago."

She drove south out of Northampton and stopped at the pub in Stoke Bruerne overlooking the canal. They ate sandwiches and drank half pints of bitter in the sundrenched garden by the water. Igor paid. The gaily painted canal barges, some festooned with flower boxes, were a source of wonder and delight to Igor. As they talked of this and that, relaxed and only slightly inhibited by what this meeting might lead to, Wendy frequently placed her hand over Igor's as it rested on the table top.

Igor felt it was a long time since he had been so content, if that was the right word. 'Content' did not suggest the excitement gripping him. Had he but known it, Wendy was in a similar state. After another half pint and a coffee each, she proposed they go home to Long Buckby. She took Igor's hand and led him rapidly to her car, then drove rather fast through Alderton and out onto the A5, through Towcester, and the crossroads at Weedon. She laughed: "Years ago, this is where the TV based a programme about a Motel and called it 'Crossroads'. I was only a kid then."

"You're not exactly ancient now." Igor became serious, gazing at her. "You're a very attractive woman, Wendy."

She said nothing, turning off the old Roman Road towards her village. "Here we are," she said as she pulled into her drive. Igor retrieved his bag from the car as Wendy unlocked the front door. "I'll show you where you sleep."

He followed her up the stairs to the front of the house, and into a pale green room with a dark green carpet, a king-sized bed covered in a saffron velvet throw, a Victorian button-back armchair upholstered in the same material, and matching curtains.

Igor put his bag down on a low chest of drawers, and as he turned back, he saw Wendy pulling the curtains closed. She gestured to the dressing table on which were several bottles of perfume and other feminine weapons of war.

"This is my room too." She smiled almost shyly, stepped forward, took Igor's hand. "I'm not making a mistake about what we want out of this visit, am I?"

By way of answer, Igor enfolded her in his arms and kissed her nose. "No, no mistake." Then he did the kissing properly. He felt her hands creep between his chest and her breasts as she started to undo the buttons on her blouse.

****

The week rushed past in a blur of sun, ripe cornfields, fine rural scenery, quaint villages, lunches and dinners in old pubs, stunning historic buildings, and a trip along the canal in a rowing boat hired in Stoke Bruerne. They visited Castle Ashby, walked in the countryside, and took in the monument at the scene of the Battle of Naseby, the downfall of Charles I.

Days started and ended with physical activity of a particularly pleasant kind, and the day was often interrupted by this type of encounter. Very late on the fourth evening, after three strenuous rounds, they were talking, as usual about their lives, relationships, careers, and backgrounds. Wendy had told Igor about her parents, and was asking him about his. Igor was yawning as she asked, "What did your father do?"

As he drifted off to sleep, relaxed, very happy, and completely off-guard, he replied to that last innocent question. "He was an army officer." Then Wendy fell asleep too. In the morning, neither of them remembered the conversation.

****

By the time Wendy left Igor at the railway station at the end of the week, both of them wondered whether this was to be an enduring relationship, or just a summer romance.

They dismissed that. It was too soon, too juvenile, and too mixed up with some very serious bedroom passion, both demanding and gentle, frequently exhausting, but always deeply satisfying. For Igor, tempting as remaining in England might be, his plans meant he had to go back to Russia eventually. Before the automatic carriage doors closed, Igor leant out of them. "I'll be back as soon as I can." Wendy shouted: "Yes, do!" as the train pulled out.

****

Once again Sawyer met his three interrogators in his office over coffee, and this time cake. "Schaplinov was a very good boy. As Wynter and Cronin reported, as soon as he was given a week off, he phoned this Wendy Slater and arranged to visit her. We had some very unnoticeable people follow him on the train to Northampton, and keep an eye on him all the time he was with the woman in Long Buckby, and wherever they went."

Ussher coughed. "Did they learn anything?"

Sawyer shrugged. "Only that Schaplinov and this woman appeared to become very fond of each other. As you know, we had her phone tapped. She received no phone calls of any significance to us, and our Russian friend made and received no calls at all."

"We know; we've 'eard the tapes too." Robinson was surly, as usual.

"So what's the verdict? Gordon?"

"Same as last time. We send him to Porton."

"Gillian?"

"Agreed."

"Fred?"

"I s'pose I'll go along with that."

Sawyer picked up the phone to Igor. "We have decided to let you go to Porton Down for a trial period. A driver will pick you up on Monday and move you to the new flat. You start work on Wednesday."

****

College Street proved to be a mainly residential road lined on both sides with terraced houses. Igor's flat was on the second floor of a three-storey building, and had a large sitting room with a kitchenette, a modest sized bedroom with a double bed, wardrobe, a chest of drawers with a mirror on it, and a bedside table with a reading lamp. The sitting room was furnished with a two-seat sofa, an armchair, a small dining table with two chairs, and a TV and DVD player on a side table. The upholstery was brown, the walls beige, and the carpet pale green, as were the curtains. The top twenty or thirty feet of the spire of Salisbury Cathedral could be seen from the window.

The driver who brought him in a powerful Audi from Putney was a tough looking fellow out of the same mould as the minders, Wynter and Cronin. His name was Trevor. He explained:

"This road goes down there to the A30. You turn left out of it onto the A36, and after a couple of miles it becomes the A338. That takes you straight up to Porton Down." He beckoned to Igor with a wave of the hand to come to the window. "See that blue car down there? It's a Ford Focus. Nothing posh, but it's yours."

"I've got a Russian driving licence, Trevor, but I have never driven in England."

"Yeah, they told me. Told me to give you some driving lessons, an'all. You ain't got to do a driving test. That's all taken care of, mate. We'll go out somewhere quiet after lunch and I'll show you a bit, and we'll do some more tomorrer. Just don't want you killing yerself, they don't."

"You drive on the wrong side of the road here in England. I've got to get used to that."

"You got a bleedin' nerve, you have. Free bloody flat, free car, good job at Porton, gets a driving licence without a test, and you want us to drive like this was Russia!"

"I apologise. I was tactless."

Trevor laughed, clapping him on the shoulder. "It's alright mate, Just pullin' yer leg, ain't I? D'you fancy a pint an' a sandwich?"

"Thanks, but you go." Igor pointed to his bag and a suitcase. "I think I'll stay here and unpack. There should be some food in the fridge and kitchen cupboards. I'll get myself something."

Trevor moved to the front door, looking at his watch. "OK, mate. I'll be back 'ere for you at two to see how you 'andle the car."

After a few hours on the road and giving Igor a few hints and tips Trevor was satisfied that the Ford Focus was in a safe pair of hands, and that the Russian was not out to wipe the British from the face of the Earth with it.

Chapter 27

Porton Down. August 2013

After the driving lesson, Igor spent the rest of the day unpacking his few possessions and stowing them in cupboards, drawers and the wardrobe. Trevor had dropped him at a convenience store not far from his flat. There he bought some coffee, tea, sugar, biscuits, cheese, some tins of fish, backed beans and other easy things. He intended to go into town for more serious shopping another day, probably on Saturday. He made eggs and bacon for his evening meal, with an orange and an apple afterwards. Was he becoming too English? Of course not; he had to show that he was adapting, integrating, making himself fit in.

He needed to find a gym; he enjoyed feeling fit; it made him alert. He missed the workouts with Craig Wynter. On the Tuesday, Igor went for a long walk around the city, found a gym, and went in to join. He found a good shopping area with major stores such as Waitrose and Tesco's, so he did some shopping there and then. Carrying the heavy bags home, he wished he'd taken the car there. It had been a hot sunny day, it was a warm evening with the sun still shining, so he took went into a pub, put the bags down, had a beer, and then had the landlord's 'Tuesday Night Special' dinner.

By the time he reached home he was tired, finished his last bits of unpacking and tidying up, sat down in front of the TV to watch but fell asleep after a few minutes. He awoke and got into bed at midnight. He set his alarm for six thirty am as he had to be at Porton Down for work at eight thirty.

On Wednesday morning he reported to the Research establishment at eight twenty. He was taken to see Horne-Bassett who introduced him to the woman who would supervise him until he was settled in, as he put it. Igor knew that was a coded expression for keeping an eye on him until they were sure he was not up to spying or another equally security-threatening activity.

This lady was Amanda Richardson, sturdy, fiftyish or thereabouts, with a short thick halo of grey hair which stood up all round her head. She greeted Igor pleasantly, and shook hands with him. She then took him to look round the poisons research department where he would be based and showed him to a desk in a large room. She introduced him to Barry Turner and Jennifer Ingram and told him the other two would be there shortly. A large folder of protocols and procedures was given to him, and he was left to study it before any work would be assigned to him.

While he was reading it, two more workers entered and sat at the other two desks in the office. They did not speak to Igor, but looked him over, so he went to each desk and introduced himself. They were Ken Nixon and Angela Groome. Ken was reasonably friendly, but Angela Groome's welcome could only be described as icy.

He had to ask Amanda where the toilets were, and later she took him to the canteen where he could get tea, coffee, and lunch.

The third day when he went to the canteen and took his lunch back to a table, Ken came and sat opposite him. They made idle conversation for a while, and then went back to their desks.

"Well, that's a start of sorts," Igor thought.

****

After almost another year, Igor felt settled and secure enough in his job, and pretty well everything else about living in Salisbury, and working at PD to get to grips with tracking down his target. Many of his evenings and weekends were then spent on his laptop. He was trying to find any reference to Pedchenko or his alias, Mamontov, which might give a clue to his whereabouts. At first, he wondered about the Electoral Roll, but discovered that as the former spy was not a British citizen, nor a citizen of one of the other countries who could vote in the UK if they were permitted to live there, searching into that would be a waste of time.

His second idea was that if there were anything it would be in the archives of the major newspapers for 2011 when the exchange of Russian and NATO prisoners had taken place. He started with 'The Times'. The exchange had received wide coverage for several days, but nothing positively identified the man he was looking for, nor where he might have been taken. Igor moved on to the other serious British media outlets, the 'Telegraph', 'Guardian', 'Independent', the Sunday papers, but continued to draw a blank. He tried the 'New York Times' and 'Washington

Post', reasoning that as a number of the NATO spies had gone to the USA there might well be useful information there, but again, he found nothing. He had tried entering the two Russian names of the ex-spy into the search engine, which threw up all the articles and news pieces in which those names appeared, but few related to the swap of spy prisoners in 2011, none used both names together, none told him the current whereabouts of this man, and many just related to other people with the same names.

The process was laborious and tiring, because he had to read all the newsprint which might possibly contain the nugget he sought. He could ignore the sports and finance pages, but the front eight to ten pages of British, international, or even social news might contain what he was looking for. Studying these could take the free part of his leisure time for a whole evening, and much of a weekend when he was not engaged on something else.

Chapter 28

Chichester, Saturday, 30th April, 2016

"Did he have any family who might want revenge on Pedchenko?" Lacey repeated. He was looking out of the window at the scenery of the North Downs around Dorking as the train sped towards Sussex. Silence prevailed for a few moments. "How can we find that out, Peter?"

"Don't ask me, sir, I don't know Russia, or Russian, or even any Russians. Well, apart from Yevgeny. Read Dr Zhivago once, though. In English, o' course"

"No. I'm talking to myself really, I suppose." Another few miles rattled past the windows as the train sped through the countryside before Colin spoke again. "What was the name of the old colonel we saw at the Army and Navy Club?"

"D'you mean Ramsey Webster, sir?"

"Indeed I do! I have his number back at the station. I'll phone him as soon as we get back."

****

"Webster."

"Colonel, or should I say Ramsey?"

"Who's calling?"

"This is Detective Chief Inspector Lacey from …"

"Counter-terrorism! How could I forget! You came to the Club about my Russian friend Gordanov. Colin, isn't it? How can I help you this time?"

"It's the same investigation. The death of the ex-spy Pedchenko."

"I thought the newspapers were saying two Russians did him in for Putin."

"Correct. That's what's being said, but it's not true, as far as we can make out so far. The media jump to conclusions to sell copies, but we've got an open mind until we have some evidence to connect someone to the murder."

"Don't see how I can help with that."

"You may well be right, Ramsey, but we've got to start somewhere, and you knew Gordanov. So, we're wondering whether there was anyone in Gordanov's family, or maybe a friend, who would want to take revenge on Pedchenko."

"For betraying Oleg Gordanov, you mean?"

"Yes; did he have a wife or a child? Did he ever talk about anyone special?"

Webster cleared his throat, and hesitated. "This is all so long ago, Colin. I'll have to give it some thought. The old memory's not what it was. I'll give you a buzz when I've got anything for you, old chap."

He asked for Colin Lacey's number and took it down.

Lacey replaced the phone in its cradle and looked up at Shuttleworth. "He says he'll ring when he's remembered anything. Doesn't sound too promising."

"We don't have a statement from 'im yet, sir. Maybe we should get 'im in."

"Good idea. Has the Club butler, er, Barton, come in yet?"

"No sir."

"Look, Peter, I think we should borrow an office for a few hours at Scotland Yard, and get Barton and the Colonel in there to take statements and videos. Barton might have remembered something else, too."

"OK. I'll phone the Yard and ask, or maybe Paddington. I'll fix something. D'you want me to go and see the witnesses, or an officer who's there anyway?"

"No. You go. You know all about it and may see a question someone else would miss. If it looks as though either of them might tell you something else really important I ought to come too. Difficult." Lacey sighed. "I suppose I'd better stay here to keep tabs on everything and everybody."

As Shuttleworth rose from his chair to make the calls from his desk, Lacey's phone rang.

"Lacey speaking."

"Colin, it's Ramsey Webster again. I've already thought of something. I'm fairly certain Oleg told me he had never married, but you asked if there was 'anyone special'."

"Yes, I did."

"You remember I told you and your sergeant about a walking trip in Snowdonia when Oleg hurt his leg? Well, it was then. We did a lot of talking as we strolled along. I told him about my wife and the two children – a boy and girl – and asked him if he had a family. He said he had no siblings, and his parents were dead. He was not married, and never had been."

"That's rather disappointing."

"But the point is, he spoke of a girl who was 'special'. He wanted to marry her, but did not think he should be married, as his career was potentially dangerous. Trips abroad at unpredictable times would prevent him from being a good husband, and, if it came to it, a good father. In any case, he was a bit of a ladies' man. He didn't boast about it, but he'd obviously had quite a few conquests, and I saw for myself that the women found him attractive when we were both abroad."

Colin thought about that as he was making notes. "But none of his liaisons produced any off-spring?"

"Not as far as I know, but who can say? He was very discreet. Some diplomats and military advisers are really stupid and get themselves into situations in foreign countries where the risk of being blackmailed into spying or becoming double agents is huge. As I told you, he never tried to get any information from me, if he was a spy, and he kept his nose very clean. I remember one function we were at - in Nigeria, I think it was - where we were both approached. A couple of really gorgeous women propositioned us, offered to have a foursome there and then in the hotel."

"What happened?"

"Nothing. I wasn't into adultery, let alone orgies. My lovely Georgina is quite enough for me, No, nothing happened. Oleg dealt with it. He was very polite, didn't give them the brush off. Just told them we were already suited with some ladies." The Colonel stopped. "But I've gone off at a tangent, haven't I?"

"Yes. I was hoping you could tell us about the girl he wanted to marry."

"Sorry. That's the problem with getting long in the tooth. Yes, Irina."

"You remember her name?"

"Couldn't forget it. My mother's name was Irene. Irina was so similar it stuck. He even told me her surname, but I can't remember it. I know it reminded me of some Russian classical composer, but can't remember it for the life of me."

"OK, Ramsey. I'll get Peter to research Russian music and get back to you with some suggestions. Did Gordanov tell you anything else?"

"Just that she came from a holiday village down towards the Altai province, south of Novosibirsk, I think he said it was. Bekoluka? Something like that?" Webster was silent for a few seconds. "No. I've got it. Belokurikha is what it was called. Ring me about the composer."

"Thanks Ramsey, we shall, but we need to get a statement from you, and we have someone else to interview, so we'll fix up an interview room at a central London police station, and you can come there, and we'll get all this down."

The call ended. Colin turned to Peter, handing him his notes. "This may be good, or it may be nothing. Get onto the Yard or anywhere else not far away so it's easy for the Colonel and Mr Barton to get to. Then get on the internet and search for all the Russian composers you can find and make a list. When you've got an interview room and a date to use it, phone Webster and Barton and make appointments for us to see them there."

"Yes sir."

"And tell the chap you speak to about the interview room we want one where the tape machine and CCTV actually work."

"Might not be a chap, sir. Lot of women in the force these days," Peter said with a smile, leaving the room in haste.

Lacey laughed. "Don't start getting cheeky with me, Shuttleworth!" Then he recalled Charcko making the same point, and told himself: 'I've really got to get used to that. But I can't bring myself to say 'they' when I'm only talking about one person. Maybe I'm just a politically incorrect dinosaur'.

Chapter 29

Salisbury. August, 2015

Two years had elapsed since Igor Schaplinov had started at Porton Down.

Igor realised from the start that he was regarded with some suspicion by other members of staff. Maintaining a cheerful demeanour, never rising to any bait in the way of criticism of or jokes about Russia, and being perfectly happy to lend a hand to any task, no matter how trivial or menial, he had won a large measure of trust.

The only part of the establishment which was now closed to him was the store where dangerous products and ingredients were tightly secured. He had never been inside. If he needed any of these materials, or was sent to fetch any for another scientist, he had to wait outside the door to the store office, which was always closed in his face. He had to ask over an intercom for what he wanted, and produce his pass. One of the store employees used to bring out what Igor wanted, and Igor then carried it back to the laboratories where it was in demand.

During these visits he could not see where the storeman went. He had no idea what type of security device might prevent access to the storeroom itself, but from his work in Pochep he knew there was bound to be something. It was obvious that anyone wanting to enter this potentially dangerous area would have to have whatever sort of digital or electronic entry gadget would get him through the door without triggering a host of alarm systems. Or it could be a finger or palm-print recognition apparatus. Igor had no alternative but to wait and see whether he would ever be authorised to go into the store. If he asked anyone about it, he would make his colleagues even more suspicious.

In the labs he had been shown how the British scientists worked, and many of the things they were working on. In turn, he showed them the methods used for many things at Pochep. He took part in discussions about the work; his contributions from his experiences in Russia were treated with respect. During these talks he found that one of his colleagues, Ken Nixon, a chemistry graduate born in Hull, who had studied at Manchester and in Berlin, had similar interests. Both were intrigued by the possible genetic modification of viruses for health care purposes, even though the main reason for studying this field at Porton was in how to kill large numbers of an enemy, and finding antidotes to protect their own troops. They also liked classical music, the theatre, and country walks.

During these walks they told each other about themselves, their educational backgrounds, and family.

"I've never been married, Ken. Had a few girlfriends, but nothing serious, No children either."

"Well, I got married when I was quite young; twenty-five, actually. The wedding was fifteen years ago last month."

"So you're forty?"

"Yep. I'll be forty-one next month, Igor. And we've got three kids: two girls, fourteen and twelve, and a boy of eight. Marion's age is a secret."

"Marion?"

"My wife." Ken paused a moment. "You must come to dinner sometime."

"Only if you ask Marion first."

"How daft do you think I am?"

They both laughed.

****

Most of the time Igor went alone from the Weapons Establishment back to his flat, cooked for himself, watched TV or read, or went out for a stroll around the city, or to the gym. Despite his lack of any serious religious feelings, he liked to wander round the cathedral precinct, or to sit in silence in the peace of that huge ancient monument to the worship of the Almighty. Often he listened to the choir rehearsing the hymns for the next service. He really enjoyed the practices and performances of great musical works of the masters of composition, their Masses and Cantatas, or to the organists practising with enormous swellings of sound, or soothing passages such as 'Jesu, Joy of Man's desiring', or 'Oh for the Wings of a Dove'. Once he walked in and heard the choir singing a chorus from Rimsky-Korsakov's "Alexei the Man of God." He was delighted to hear one of his favourite pieces of Russian music. Even so, he was disappointed that the English basses simply did not possess the depth and richness of their Russian counterparts.

Every two or three weeks he drove up to Northamptonshire to stay with Wendy, or she drove to

Salisbury to his flat. They walked in the historic parts of the city, and in the countryside. He took her to dinner at the Caspian Gourmet during some of her visits.

"Tell me, Igor," she said, "which country round the Caspian does all this represent?" Igor looked around as though seeing the place for the first time. "I've not been to all those countries, Wendy, so I can't be sure, but it looks to me like decoration of the restaurant isn't clearly identifiable with any particular west Asian country; nor is the cuisine."

As the sea which gave the restaurant its name was surrounded to East, West and South by the mainly Moslem and Arabic nations of Turkmenistan, Azerbaijan, and Iran, that was only to be expected.

Strict Islamic customs were not observed, and of course, alcohol was served. In fact, the wine list was first class, including some excellent vintages, rarely seen in Britain, from Russian and other former Soviet era satellite countries. There were waitresses as well as waiters, all attired in baggy pantaloons with shirts or blouses with leg-of-mutton sleeves, denoting an Ali Baba atmosphere, but the women each wore a see-through veil secured from their foreheads by a brass hair band as a gesture toward the Koran. Much brass was also in evidence with ornate tops for the smaller tables, brass coffee jugs with long spouts, and a hookah on a shelf above the counter. The ceiling was a midnight blue sprinkled with silver stars, and the walls hung with a diaphanous crimson material, creating the impression of a desert tent. The ambience, the quality of the food and its variety, and the style of the wines had made the Caspian very popular.

Igor had been going there about once every fortnight or three weeks, but not on the same evening, and occasionally to lunch. He had become acquainted with the Syrian owner, Ismail Salamani, who had been instructed in his duties, and told to expect Igor. He had a chance to make a fortune in this restaurant. Apart from that, he had every incentive to look after Igor, for betraying Putin and Assad was not a healthy option. Both men strove to deal with each other on a purely host and customer basis; the last thing they needed was for someone to suspect there might be more to their relationship than that.

Over the next few months Igor introduced Ken Nixon to the restaurant, and from time to time went there with Wendy, Ken, and Ken's wife, Marion. As expected, when he had discussed the acquisition of the restaurant with the Army Officers in Moscow, he knew he would be followed there by Sawyer's people, and often to other places. He took no steps to indicate he was aware of them, or to evade them. His objective was to establish an irregular pattern of behaviour with his eating there to allay suspicion. He also suspected he was followed when he went on his own or with Wendy to dinner at the Nixon's house.

Up to this point he had given or taken little spying material, either to or from the proprietor, apart from odd snippets of information he was picking up as he gathered more responsibility in the Establishment. When on his own, he always used menu drops and had left and collected nothing from behind the toilet cisterns. They were exactly the old Victorian type he had suggested. As he had told the generals, the cistern was only used when he was with another person – Wendy or Ken, or any other friend he had made. When he dined there as a party with Wendy, Ken, and Marion, there was no drop or collection of any kind.

It was to be expected that other people from Porton would frequent the Caspian Gourmet, but he rarely knew who they were. However, a couple of times he saw a woman he knew by sight dining there, usually at lunch, once alone, and once with another woman. On both occasions she was clad in an Army Uniform, and from the insignia on her shoulders, was obviously an officer. He recalled she had given one or two of the talks he had attended, so, to ensure she had no reason to suspect him, he introduced himself the first time, and said hello, exchanging brief, innocuous remarks with her and the friend the second time.

He now felt that he could make more serious progress with his career as a spy – a double agent, in fact. His first venture, a few months later, was aided by a stroke of luck. By coincidence, it was his icy colleague at work who accidentally provided the means.

Chapter 30

Chichester. Sunday 1st May, 2016

"How did you get on, Peter?"

"Very well, I think sir. Considering I only asked yesterday, they give me a very well-equipped interview room at Charing Cross nick. It's a very beautiful old building."

"I know, I've seen it. Used to be Charing Cross Hospital." Lacey made a hand gesture cutting off that subject. "You mean the tape machine and video camera worked?"

"They did, sir, an' I 'ave copies of the tape and the video with me; they cover Barton and Webster."

"They both turned up, then."

"Yep. I got 'old of them last night and they were pleased because it's not a long walk from the Army and Navy Club. I saw the Colonel at ten and Barton at noon this mornin'." Shuttleworth rubbed his chin, and smiling, said, "You can see Webster would've been popular with his troops. He waited for Barton so they could walk back together, more like friends than master and servant, but Barton clearly showed 'is respect."

"I can imagine. We'll play the tape and video later, but give me a rundown, will you?" Lacey waved him to a chair. Peter had travelled by early train to Victoria, and returned on the early afternoon one, having a snack lunch from the buffet car.

"Well, sir, Barton confirmed everything what 'e'd told us before at the Club, an' I took it all down."

"Nothing new to add?"

"No sir. That was it. But Webster came up with the goods. First off, I took down 'is statement about the kidnapping of Gordanov, and what led up to it, and what 'e tried to do about it afterwards. He had no more details to add, but when I showed 'im the list of Russian composers, he read it, muttering, 'No', or shaking his head until 'e was almost at the end. Then he said pretty loudly, 'Schaliapin; that's the name'. Made me jump, 'e did. He went quiet for a minute; then 'e 'eld the list towards me and pointed to that name and said, 'No, that's wrong. It wasn't Schaliapin. It was Schaplinov'.

"I said, 'Schaplinov?' And he said, 'Yes, Schaplinov. You remember; you and the inspector wanted Irina's surname. In fact, the Russian way, with a girl they put an 'a' on the end, so she was Irina Schaplinova.' So I wrote that up too, and he signed it all."

Lacey smiled, took a deep breath, sighed loudly, and said, "Well done, Peter."

The Sergeant was quiet for a few seconds. "But?"

"What?"

"There's a 'but' there somewhere, ain't there, sir? As in "Well done, Peter, but …."

Lacey chuckled slightly, and sighed again before saying: "Well, you're right, of course. Finding her name is a breakthrough, but now we have the headache of trying to find one Russian woman called Irina Schaplinova amongst a population of one hundred and forty-five million. We know she knew a Russian KGB man called Gordanov in a town called Belokurikha. We know Gordanov was executed in 1995, so they must have known each other some good time before that, because he'd been kidnapped in London and taken back to Russia eighteen months earlier." He was quiet. "That's it, isn't it?"

"I guess so, sir. But we can make inquiries, can't we? I mean, loads of Russians live 'ere now, and they're not all friends of Putin's, are they."

"Quite right. And there are Russian societies and Churches, and there will be teachers and lecturers in Russian, and people who do business there." He laughed sceptically. "All we've got to do is find someone who knows or knew Irina."

"I'll get onto it, then, sir." Peter made to leave the room, but turned back. "Shall I get Sharon and Harry to …. er …. I mean, shall I ask D.C. Morton and P.C. Jones to help? There'll be a lot of phoning and visiting to do."

"Yes, Peter. Good idea. Get Jones onto Russian churches, and Morton onto their clubs and societies, and when they've done some of that, they can both look into businesses and educators who go to Russia or have been. You do the same and follow up on anything else or any of their stuff as you see fit."

315

When Peter left the room, Lacey picked up the phone, dialled MI6 and asked for Charles Sawyer.

"He's away for the day, sir. It's...." was the response.

"Sunday. I know that." Colin could hear the exasperation in his voice. "This is Detective Inspector Lacey from Counter Terrorism. I've been to see him three times about the murder of Boris Pedchenko, the ex-spy, and ...."

"I remember that, sir. Mr Sawyer told me he has no desire to hear from you again."

"If I were in his shoes, I wouldn't want to speak to me either. You phone him, then. You must have a phone number for him. Please tell him to ring me at once." Colin dictated the number. "I'm about to call a press conference, and if he doesn't want his name brought into it, he'll ring me immediately."

Lacey cut the call and then rang the hospital. "May I speak to Captain Jodie Jordan, please?"

"Who's calling?"

"Detective Chief Inspector Lacey. Captain Jordan is caring for the Russian, Mr Yevgeny Pedchenko.

"Please hold a moment, and I'll try to put you through to the ICU."

After a few seconds a nurse answered. Colin repeated his question. "Yes, sir, she was here, but she's gone back to Porton Down now, as Mr Pedchenko is doing well. He's been moved to an ordinary single room. Do you have the number?"

"Thanks, I do." It was six thirty pm. Colin had hoped to meet Jodie for dinner. He'd have to try another time. He hadn't seen her for a few days. His phone rang. It was Sawyer. "What do you want?"

"We've got a bit more information; someone who might have wanted to do away with Boris Pedchenko."

"I've already told you, it was the two Russians."

"Maybe, but we've no evidence linking it to them, so we have to keep an open mind. We've come across a name, and I wonder whether it means anything to you."

"Try me."

Putting Sawyer on trial would have suited Colin very well, but what he said was: "We may be looking for someone called Schaplinov." He could have sworn he heard a sudden intake of breath or a gasp, then silence for a moment. "Are you still there?"

"Yes, of course I'm here. I was trying to recall if it meant anything, but it doesn't. Anything else?"

"Just that the name seems to have come from Belokurikha in Siberia."

"No, sorry, it means nothing." The phone went dead.

****

Early on Monday morning Lacey phoned Porton Down and was put through to the Captain. "What can I do for you, Colin?"

"Come back to Chichester and let me take you to dinner."

Jodie said nothing, and then, "Mr Pedchenko is doing well. The doctors and staff at St Richards are quite capable of looking after him now. I'll only be back if he deteriorates, or there's some other problem." She paused. "Off course, there's nothing to stop you driving up here, is there?"

Getting what definitely seemed like an invitation surprised Colin. "When?"

"How about today? It's Labour Day today, but I've got to work, so I've got tomorrow and Wednesday off."

"Jodie, that's fantastic. What's your address?" He wrote it down. "I've got to do a press conference about the murder in a couple of hours. I'll see you about four; we can go for a walk. You tell me your favourite dining place, and we'll go there. I'll check into a hotel."

"Perhaps we'll have a think about the hotel, Colin." He was puzzled. Did she mean the choice of hotel, or was it ....? He decided not to get too excited. Jodie asked, "How's the case going?"

"Oh, I don't know. That's what the press conference is about - the two Russians, see if anyone knows where they are, and another name has cropped up. Seems we might be looking for a son or daughter of another Russian spy called Gordanov who was executed in Moscow. It's possible, if he had a child, his son or daughter might have murdered Boris in revenge for the death of their father, though the weird thing is, if they weren't Russian, where did whoever it was get the Novichok?" They ended the call.

He checked through the files again looking for anything he'd missed, or any lines of investigation they still needed to pursue. He posted more items on the whiteboard, including the details of Irina Schaplinova, and went for a short stroll by the canal to clear his thoughts so that he could start afresh for the media.

He was back in the station by nine thirty am, and a few moments later Peter came in with Harry Morton and Sharon Jones. "Have you found her, then?"

Peter said, "Not exactly, sir, But it seems we may 'ave a lead. 'Arry found it."

"Yes, sir," Harry said. "I found there's a lot of Russian schools and education places round London, and I got onto one in Dulwich. They didn't know of this Irina, but they said they'd ask around the staff and parents of their students, and get onto some of the other places and ask them. With luck someone will get back to us with something."

Jones spoke up. "I didn't have as much luck as that, but one Orthodox priest in London said he'd ask around and contact some of the other priests and clergy for me."

"You did tell all these people we're looking for a woman who used to live near Belokurikha? And whether she had any offspring?"

"Yes sir," all three said simultaneously. Peter added, "I was doing some clubs but they turned out to be mostly drinking holes. I 'ad no luck with Churches or businesses, but someone might still phone us if they come across anything."

"OK, then," Lacey said. "We'd better wait and see what comes up. And there are still Universities with Russian degree courses to look at, so you'd better divide them up and get on with it. I'm going away now for a couple of days, after the press conference, but you all have my mobile number so if there's anything worth reporting, don't hesitate to let me know. Any of you able to keep on with this search now or over the Bank Holiday if necessary?"

All three said yes, but Harry Morton had to be with his family on Sunday afternoon. His son had a big match with his football team.

"Right then. I want you three to come in to help handle the reporters, hand out photos of the two Russians, and Sharon, you find Charcko so she can play them some of the videos." Lacey was not looking forward to this. He knew that frequently some in the media wanted to denigrate police efforts, and were bound to go on the attack about why they had not already arrested someone. However, if they published the photos of Milukov and Balkonsky, that might produce a result. The CCTV shots of the 'vicar' could also be fruitful. What he would not do was mention Schaplinov, as it was too vague. If the killer was a child of Irina and Gordanov, and he or she were still in Britain, they'd do their best to vanish, and he didn't even know which sex they were or what they might look like.

****

Just before noon, Lacey headed for Salisbury. Most of the way traffic was fairly light, but it was raining until he got to Alderbury, when the sky cleared, the sun came out and shone on the river. He had arranged to meet Jodie Jordan at the main entrance to the Cathedral. Dressed in blue jeans with a yellow scarf knotted in front and tucked into the open neck of a red blouse, she was waiting there when he arrived. She wore black strap sandals over bare feet. Her hair was combed into a French pleat again.

'Lacey, you are paying too much attention. Just how smitten are you?' he asked himself. "Lovely to see you, Jodie," was what he actually said, as he took her hand, and she offered her cheek for a kiss. He was far from reluctant to oblige.

"It's good to see you, too, Colin." Then she reached up for a proper kiss. "Shall we look around the cathedral?"

"Yes, but can we get a coffee first? I'm parched after driving. Is there a café here?"

"They do food and drinks in the Refectory. It's off the Cloisters."

"Sounds good. Except in Constable's painting I haven't seen this cathedral before; at least not all of it. I'm looking forward to exploring it. I sat in here listening to music once. I just love old historic buildings like this, castles, stately homes. Is that a bore?"

"Well, if it is, that makes two of us. And I wondered if you would like to go to Wilton House while you're here. Or would you prefer a walk somewhere?"

By now they were sitting at a Refectory table in the Cloisters. "I won't mess about, Jodie. I just want to have your company. You choose; walk or Wilton House."

"If you're not playing hard to get, I shan't either. Let's walk. There are some glorious riverside walks near here, and we can let our hair down chatting."

"I'd rather you didn't let yours down. It looks so elegant. So do you."

"Even in jeans?"

"Even in jeans." Lacey reached across the table for her hand. As he did so she turned hers palm up so that she could hold his. "In fact Jodie, in everything, except the uniform, perhaps; no, even in the uniform, that hair-do makes you look all brisk business and a high degree of discipline, but in your civvies you look, as they say, a million dollars, though why not quid I've no idea."

Jodie smiled with a hint of making slight fun of him mixed with a great deal of sheer joy. "I think you're glad to see me, which is good, because I wanted to see you again too."

"I haven't seen you for what? Three days? Four days? It feels like a month."

After lunch and coffee, they spent a couple of hours giving the cathedral a close examination, talking about much of it, and about many things of no importance whatsoever. They held hands a lot, and when leaning close to read inscriptions on tombstones or details about stained glass and all the other notable objects, Colin often put his arm around Jodie.

Later she took him to her car and drove to the River Avon, and they walked along the riverbank footpath for a couple more hours. There were quite a number of halts for kissing and cuddling, and Lacey felt like a teenager. As far as he could tell, Jodie felt the same.

She took Colin back to her flat where they had both changed and she cooked. She lit candles, and the dinner was romantic in atmosphere. Later Colin said, "I forgot to book in at a hotel," but she showed him into the spare room, and told him she'd booked a table at the Allium in Ox Street for seven o'clock for Tuesday evening.

Colin hated what he had to say next. "Sorry Jodie, but we had a bit of a breakthrough with the Pedchenko case this morning, and I doubt I'll be able to stay tomorrow, let alone till Wednesday. I'm sure I'll get a phone call from Shuttleworth or someone saying I've got to get back fast."

Looking somewhat hurt, and very disappointed, Jodie simply said, "Well, that's a shame. Will you be able to come back by Saturday?"

Feeling every bit as disappointed himself, Lacey replied: "I don't know, but I shall do my damndest."

Jodie said, "I'll just have to wait until then, won't I?" She took his face in her hands and kissed him "Good night."

Lacey went to bed feeling thoroughly miserable, and doubting he would sleep a wink, worrying that he had ruined everything, or at any rate his job had,

They spent the next morning in similar fashion, but with rather more kissing and cuddling than before, even in quiet moments touring Wilton House and its grounds. After lunch they were exploring old parts of the city when their peace was interrupted after little more than an hour by Colin's mobile ringing in his jacket pocket. He answered the call. It was Shuttleworth.

"Sorry, sir, but I think you'd better get back here as soon as you can. There's some new information about Irina Schaplinova. And the press conference has produced a couple of results about Milukov and Balkonsky, and a bit about the vicar."

"Bloody hell, that's good! What is the news, then?"

"Well sir, first up, some Russians in Dulwich say they came from Belokurikha and knew a Schaplinov family. Next, a ticket office woman from Brighton Station says she sold tickets to Milukov and Balkonsky on the 24th to go to Penrith in Cumberland by train. Then a lady in Keswick rang to say she had two Russians staying at her hotel. Both women thought they were the men in the passport photos and videos we showed the reporters yesterday."

"That's fantastic, Peter, but shit! I was hoping to stay here in Salisbury tonight." He made an apologetic gesture to Jodie and whispered "Sorry." Back to the mobile he addressed Shuttleworth again. "I'm going to leave here as soon as I can, so I want you and Sharon to get hold of these

Russians straight away, and go up to Dulwich and take their statements. In the morning I'm going to go up to Keswick with Sergeant Charcko to see this hotelier. Meanwhile I want her to go to the station and see the ticket woman. See you tomorrow." He finished the call and turned to Jodie.

Before he could speak she shook her head and said, "Look, it's the job, isn't it? I realise you took a chance coming here at all. Same sort of thing has happened to me several times with Army and Defence business. So if you've got to go, you've got to go, haven't you?"

"What can I say, Jodie? Last night and today have meant so much to me. I'll do everything I can think of to be here Saturday."

"Don't worry. I'm going nowhere unless a war breaks out, or I'm needed back in Chichester for Yevgeny. We'd better get back to the flat and you must skedaddle as fast as your car will go - within the law, of course." She hugged and kissed him and they walked quickly back to her car.

Chapter 31

Porton Down. August, 2015

Igor had been using his computer keyboard at his desk in the laboratory office, typing some rather mundane information summarising the work done on smallpox in different countries reported in scientific magazines. That was the sort of work he was frequently allocated. It was about five thirty pm, people were leaving for the day, and Angela Groome, the fairly chilly woman who worked at a nearby desk which faced his, said goodnight. Igor looked up as she passed rapidly by, wishing her a pleasant evening. As he turned back to the screen, he noticed a couple of sheets of paper under her desk, but by the time he looked round to call her attention to them, she had disappeared.

He left his seat. Only one other man facing away in a corner was in the room now. Igor retrieved the pages, which were typed on one side. The heading was 'Genetic Manipulation of Viruses'. This was certainly not taken from a scientific journal.

Igor was excited. The contents would be of great interest in Moscow, since Pochep had its own virus modification programme. He took two sheets of clean paper from his desk and put the two he had found between them to keep them clean. Then he went to the toilets and put the papers flat inside his shirt on top of his vest. He was thankful he wore no deodorant or male 'smelly' which might transfer odour to the document, arousing suspicion. After tidying his desk, he left.

On the way home he kept a very wary eye out for anyone following him. When he parked outside his flat, he nipped indoors, wore a pair of thin rubber gloves to wipe the genetics papers carefully with a clean tissue to smudge any fingerprints he might have left on them when he picked them up, put the sheets in an A4 envelope, and went for an apparently casual stroll as though refreshing his mind after the day's work. He doubled back a couple of times and walked round the same block twice in opposite directions, on the face of it admiring the design of some of the houses and other buildings, and employed other evasion tactics. Seeing no-one interested in him, after half-an hour he slipped into a corner convenience store some distance from his home. He knew there was a photocopier there, and he used it to copy the document. He donned the gloves again for this, as he did not want to risk his fingerprints being discovered on the copies if they were intercepted.

Back in the flat, putting the gloves on again, he wrote on the back of the copies. What he wrote was: 'Do we have anything to give?' Then he hid them between two sheets of clean cooking foil beneath the carpet where it ran under his chest of drawers. Before doing so, he checked the room for hidden CCTV cameras, as he had been trained to do at the FSB camp; He could never be sure to what extent Sawyer and his colleagues really trusted him. There were none. The originals went into the document case he took to work most days. He cooked a chop and vegetables, watched TV for a while, and went to bed early.

Rising early the next morning, Igor arrived at Porton Down at eight am, knowing it was unlikely the woman opposite his desk would be there so early. He removed the original documents with other papers from his case, put them neatly down, and then slid the virus papers into his in-tray with another sheet on top of it. He was not now concerned about a few of his fingerprints being on the original; the fact that he had found it in the office and picked it up would explain that. Fifteen minutes later his colleague walked in. When she had divested herself of her handbag and coat, Igor took the paper from his tray and walked round his desk to hers. "Hello Angela."

She looked up with her usual frigid expression. "Good morning, Igor. You OK?"

"Fine, thank you. Look, I tried to call you back about this last night, but you were out of here like a scared rabbit …."

"Yes, I'd got to get to my mother's to take her out to dinner and a theatre. It was her birthday."

"What did you see?"

"'The Constant Wife', at the theatre in Salisbury. It's an old play, but very well done. You should go. Sorry, what did you want?"

"Oh! Just to show you these. I found them under your desk last night. I saw them as you were leaving but you'd gone so I picked them up and put them in my tray to give you today - if it's yours, of course."

A deep frown creased Angela's forehead as she glanced over the two pages. "Oh shit!"

"Is it important?"

"All I'll say is thank God you found it. I owe you big time." She gave him a proper smile for the first time in the two years he'd been working there.

Igor waived the acknowledgement away. "It was nothing." Should any questions arise, Angela would be able to explain why his prints, as well as hers, were on the papers.

The next evening Igor took his document case, going alone for dinner to the Caspian, sat at his usual table, and was greeted by the proprietor, Ismail Salamani, who handed him the menu and wine list, both of which were generously printed on parchment-like A4 paper inside dark red gold-embossed leather covers. When Ismail returned, Igor ordered the *sebzi govourma plov.*

Ismail kissed the finger-tips of his left hand. "Most excellent choice. Azerbaijani dish. Meat tonight is goat, strong flavour, freshest vegetables from special market garden. You will enjoy much."

Igor handed him back the wine list and the menu in which he had inserted the copy virus papers in an envelope addressed to a woman he had never met, at Imperial College, London. There was no such woman. 'She' was a fictitious front in case the paper fell into the wrong hands. The envelope would never get to the College but be handed to a contact of Ismail's who would deliver it to the Russian Embassy. From there it would make its way by diplomatic bag to Pochep.

From the wine list Igor ordered a half bottle of a red from the Don Valley.

****

At the weekend a few days later, back at the Caspian for lunch, Igor collected an envelope from the menu folder, which was handed to him, as always, by Ismail. He put it in his breast pocket, paid his bill, and left. When he reached his flat after walking there casually by a roundabout route, so as not to attract any attention or appear to be anxious or in a hurry, he opened the envelope. He had written on the back of the copy virus paper he'd found under Angela's desk in English. He did not write in Russian Cyrillic script, as it would be obvious where his message was meant to go had it been intercepted. The envelope contained a short note telling him that Russian agents had reported that China was experimenting with a flu type virus in a town called Wuhan.

The next day at work he approached Angela in the canteen. He carried a coffee to her table. "Mind if I join you?"

"Not at all, Igor." She gestured to the chair next to hers, then swept a curtain of blonde hair back and away from her left eye. She had quite a pretty face with dark blue eyes, but was painfully thin, as if she were anorexic. Despite that, she was tucking into a plate of sausages and mash with a cup of tea. "We've been working in that room together for what, two years now, and have never had what you could call a real conversation before, have we?"

"I think that's my fault, Angela. For a long time I felt like a very new boy, and as I'm Russian, it took some people quite a while to feel like talking at all. In any case, I tend to keep myself to myself."

"You're not the only one. I'm the same. I think working in this place stops anyone feeling like sharing personal stuff, let alone private thoughts and feelings. The women don't even talk about clothes, hair-dos or domestic problems, and the men don't even seem to chat about last night's football."

"I've noticed, but I'm quite friendly with Ken Nixon. We go walking or to concerts occasionally, and we go out in a foursome to dinner with his wife Marion, and my friend Wendy."

"Anyway, I come here to work, and I like my work."

Igor laughed. "That's two of us again, then. Actually, I came to your table because there's something about work I wanted to mention to you. I think it may be of interest."

"Fire away, then."

Igor took a deep breath and held it a while as he ordered his thoughts, before expelling it rather loudly. "OK. Here it is. You remember those papers I found and gave you back a few days ago?" Angela Groome nodded, and Igor continued. "I saw it was about "Genetic Manipulation of Viruses." I woke up this morning thinking about that and remembered that a section at Pochep – not my section – was doing that sort of thing before I left."

Angela shrugged. "I dare say they were."

"The thing is, one of those people, someone I was friendly with, told me they had heard from a Chinese informer that the equivalent Chinese research group was looking into some new version of a kind of flu in a city called Wuhan. If your section or bosses don't know about it, it might be worthwhile their looking into it."

"Blimey, Igor, if they don't know, they'll be very, very interested, and even if they know already, it will confirm what they believe to be the case. If it's true, it can be very dangerous. They may intend to use it as a battlefield weapon to disable or kill troops, but if the virus escapes by accident or from negligent storage, or even deliberately for sabotage or other reasons, it can be even more deadly amongst civilians too. They have no defence equipment to handle it."

"I know about the use of anthrax on Guinard in Scotland, and we had that sort of accident in Siberia."

"I already owe you one, Igor. If my superiors do not know about this, it'll do me some good and do a lot for you; I'll tell them how I found out. You'll get the credit."

"Well, thanks, but you needn't tell them about the papers I found. I shall not mention it." Igor paused for a heart-beat or two. "I wish I'd thought of this before, but it wasn't my kind of work. It just popped into my head as I got out of bed."

Angela smiled: "I'm very glad it did. I'll let you know what happens. Can I get you a coffee?"

****

By the end of August Igor knew for definite that the deadly poison store was secured by iris recognition technology. After Angela told him she 'owed him one', he plucked up the courage to ask her about access to the stores in a general conversation in the canteen one lunchtime. She made no bones about telling him.

As far as anyone knows, there are no two identical pairs of irises on the planet. The chances of a false match are billions to one. The scanner, which looks at the eye, stores a picture of the iris of everyone working at Porton Down. When members of staff want access to the store, they have to stand a specific very short distance from the scanner. This distance is marked by a line on the floor. The scanner takes a photo of the eye, which is then compared in milliseconds, by the computer system to which the scanner is connected, with the stored picture, and if there is a match, the door can be opened.

At one time the PD Establishment's Security Team had considered using retinal imaging for the identification of staff. It had discovered that various eye problems, such as glaucoma and macular degeneration, could change the appearance of the retina without the person in question being aware of it until their eyesight was beginning to worsen. If the appearance of the retina changed sufficiently the recognition equipment would, in the end, fail to recognise the eye. When that occurred there would be no match, and access to the facility would be denied. By contrast, with iris recognition, that problem was less likely to an infinitesimal degree. The iris is a very stable organ, which does not change for decades, if at all. One of the very few causes of such alteration is eye surgery, such as cataract removal. Obviously, the person operated on would be able to report the likelihood of change to their iris and its photo, and a new image could be stored by the scanner.

How was Igor to overcome this problem? Even if he had that level of security clearance and his iris was stored on the scanner, he could not go into the store to get Novichok ingredients because, by presenting his eye to the scanner, it would record the fact that he had entered it. Then it would be easy for Security to find out who had stolen the poison if any were found to be missing. He must carry out some research into the way the system worked, and whether there were any methods by which it could be fooled. He found some websites on the internet dealing with the subject, but wasn't satisfied. He made enquiries for the best ophthalmologists and opticians in Salisbury, and made an appointment to have his eye-sight checked. He used a false name and address. He used the name Francis Chambers.

He hardly needed spectacles, but in the middle of September ordered some reading glasses from Mr Collard, the expert he chose, so he would have a legitimate reason for going back when he could ask about the iris photo technique. He had not wanted to raise that question at their first meeting.

The glasses were ready a couple of weeks later. He raised the iris question then.

"Yes, I do know about this," Mr Collard said. "It was a subject which was of growing interest when I was at University, and a few years later I was called in to help with the best way of taking the photos and comparing them with the eyes to see how detailed and accurate the pictures might be."

Igor nodded. "So you can't fake it then?"

"How do you mean, Mr Chambers?"

"Well, I work in a place where there is a lot of security, and part of it is this eye recognition stuff. If someone had a photo of my eye, a good close-up photo, could they get a contact lens like it? And deceive the machine into letting them through the door, as it would think it was me?"

"I really don't think so. It's like fingerprints. For all we know, there are no sets of prints or irises identical to any other set on the planet. But the iris is the safer bet because it is much more complex with millions of tiny particles which make it and its colour. Compared with that fingerprints are fairly simple. Not only that, but soft plastic copies of prints have been made from those left on glass. The false ones can then be used to leave prints which create the impression someone else did the burglary or whatever the crime was." Mr Collard laughed. "In one of the early James Bond films they did that. Nowadays the real identity of the person can be ascertained by testing the fingerprint for DNA, so if the false print and the DNA of the person whose print it is supposed to be do not match, the suspect'll walk away free."

"That's interesting."

"But why do you ask?" Collard said.

"Oh, just that it bothers me that someone might get into our place by fooling the security scanner, steal some of our commercial secrets and cost us millions."

"You're very conscientious."

"Thanks. I suppose I am. And how much do I owe you for the glasses?"

"Go out through reception, Mr Chambers, and the young lady will deal with that, thank you."

Igor smiled and shook hands with the optician with a cheerful smile, which was only on the surface. Inside, as he walked away, he was seriously depressed. *'How on earth am I going to get hold of the Novichok now?'* he asked himself. He didn't want to use a gun or stab the man who betrayed his father. That was much too risky. Some kind of deadly poison was the only way to proceed. He began to wonder if the whole idea of coming to England was a mistake and a waste of time. For him it definitely might be, but at least he was spying for his Motherland.

He had another serious problem. No matter what he did or looked into or searched, he had so far been unable to find out for definite where Pedchenko might be living. He had been investigating that for months. Without that simple fact, he was stymied.

Chapter 32

Chichester. Monday, 2nd May, 2016

At 8.00am Lacey was sitting at his desk, hands linked behind his sandy-haired head, cogitating the fact that they might be getting closer to the Schaplinovs, and now the two Russians who had stayed in Brighton and visited Chichester the day of the murder might be in his sights. If it were not them in Keswick, had they flown back to Moscow or somewhere else in the world's largest country? Or gone to another country? All he knew was that they'd left the hotel in Brighton.

He went out to find Shuttleworth or Charcko and found the woman. He could have used the internal phone, but he disliked sitting still for long periods. Walking about the office a bit was healthier than physical idleness; it kept his blood and joints moving, and he could still think. He took her back to his office.

"Kiara, please get hold of Customs or Passport Control and find out whether the two Russians who were at the hotel in Brighton have gone home, gone elsewhere, or are still here. I realise we are looking into the Schaplinov connection, but we can't assume those two …."

"Nicholas Milukov and Dmitri Balkonsky, sir. I've already been on to Customs and passport control. I did it after you asked that I should see the woman at the railway station. I'm waiting to hear back from them. They've got over two weeks' data to search, and lots of airports all over the country. Even with computers it takes time, they said, and they've got thousands of flights a day to monitor at the same time. The people monitoring domestic flights are doing the same. I told them to start with the 24th, but we can't be sure they went anywhere much, let alone home to Russia or abroad to some other place."

"Shame, but good thinking, Kiara. We can't assume they're nothing to do with it just because we couldn't see them near Priory Park on CCTV. If they've gone home, basically we've had it. The best we could hope for is a video from Moscow saying they came but did nothing naughty; that would prove nothing either way, but we haven't even any evidence linking them to the bottles in their room."

"I had a real slice of luck with the trains. I phoned Brighton Station, as we'd had the phone call from the woman in the booking office. She remembered two Russians, as they'd been there more than once. Seemed to me she'd taken a shine to one of them."

Lacey smiled. "Never mind that. Just tell me what this stroke of luck was."

"Well, sir, I shot her an email with a photo from the clearest CCTV film, she said it was definitely them, and was able to look it up at once because they'd paid with a debit card from Gazprombank or GAZP, a Russian Bank. They bought tickets right through the rail network. They said they wanted to go to Keswick."

"The Lake District."

"Right. They booked to Penrith, the nearest station."

"And?"

"I phoned Penrith and the bloke in the ticket office there remembered them asking about the bus because he'd done some Russian at school. He said they were going to Keswick. Then I got onto the hotelier lady in Keswick who rang after the press conference. She owns and runs the Keswick Park Hotel. Guess what? They'd got two Russian blokes staying there. They had their names in the register, and it was them: Nicholas Milukov and Dmitri Balkonsky!"

"Well, how fantastic is that."

"It gets better, sir. I emailed her the same CCTV picture, and the receptionist phoned back five minutes ago to say that it's definitely our two; they're still there, not leaving for another week. So if we go there we won't be wasting our time on a coincidence in a million."

"Did you tell her to say nothing to them? Last thing we need is to warn them off."

Kiara shook her head and smiled. "She asked me if she should keep it to herself or tell them we might come. I told her to keep quiet, not to tell anyone, even her husband." She smiled again. "She was OK with that."

"Brilliant. You're coming with me. We're off to Keswick ASAP. You go and get your kit and tell Peter and the others we're off for a day or two on an enquiry, but don't tell them where. We can't risk anyone saying anything to anybody. Next thing you know some leaky cop'll be selling the story to the paper or TV. I've just got to make a call."

"Before you do, sir, there was something very odd. Although the ticket lady at Brighton station identified

Milukov and Balkonsky from the picture, she told me that the debit card was in the name of Boris Dologhov."

"What?"

"That's what I said, sir."

"Bloody hell! Sorry, I try not to swear, but this is serious. It puts them right back in the frame. But wasn't the name on the card in Russian script?"

"Yes, but she was bright, that lady. She got him to write it on the merchant copy bank slip. Here's the copy she faxed to me."

"Weird! And he wrote it in our alphabet, not Cyrillic. Why would he agree to that if he'd just bumped someone off?" Colin asked rhetorically.

Kiara said, "I went to the station and saw the woman. She was happy to make a statement confirming she'd sold the tickets to the Russians, and about the credit card."

Charcko left Lacey's office and shut the door. Looking at his watch and seeing it was almost noon, he picked up the phone. "Jodie? It's Colin. Look, I may not be able to phone you later."

"Why? Do you need to?"

"I want - need – to talk to or see you every day."

"Sorry, Colin. Is that your idea of a joke? Where are you going?"

"No, it's not a joke. If you haven't worked it out already, I like you a lot, OK? And now I'm sorry that where I'm going is a secret for two, maybe three days, but we've had a real breakthrough. Either we've found the villains, or we're going to be able to eliminate them from our enquiries."

"Fair's fair, I suppose. There's stuff I'm not able to tell you, as you know." She hesitated a second. "And oh, by the way, I'm glad you like me."

That knocked Lacey back a good bit, but he managed to utter: "That's OK." When he got his breathing under control he said, "Don't tell anyone about the villains. I'll be back as soon as I can. Bye."

Just then Shuttleworth knocked and entered.

"Mornin', sir. Sharon 'n' I saw the Ruskies in Dulwich yesterday.

"You found them, then, Peter."

Peter nodded; "They were very keen to make statements and talk about old times in Belokurikha. They've been 'ere a long time, so their English is good. And they say they knew a family called Schaplinov."

"They did? Better let me read the statement, then." Lacey held out his hand, and Peter handed it to him. "But there's something else, Peter. Didn't you say on the phone there's some news about the vicar who was at Priory Park?"

"Yes, sir there is. The caretaker from Priory Park come into the nick with a pale linen jacket and a Panama hat. 'e said 'e'd had to go over to the Northgate Car Park toilets the day of the murder as there'd been a complaint one was leakin', and he found these things on a peg in a cubicle. 'e kept them as lost property, but when 'e saw the CCTV clips on TV, 'e thought they might be the vicar's, so 'e brought 'em in. Trouble is they'll have a bit of 'is DNA and other stuff on 'em, but they should also have some of the killer's if they were 'is, so I thought I'd send 'em off to the lab to test. The park keeper let us take a saliva swab from 'im so we can eliminate 'im."

"Great thinking, Peter. If we get our hands on a real suspect we can test him against any traces on the hat or jacket. That won't prove he did it, of course, but it may be another circumstantial evidence link."

When Peter left the room, Lacey picked up the statement from the Russian and began to read.

Mily Destrov of 36A Sutton Road, Dulwich will say:

I used to live in Belokurikha, in Southern Siberia, Russia. It was a holiday town, with lovely country for the summer and hills, snow and skiing for the winter. I worked as a head waiter in a good restaurant. I knew a man called Schaplinov. He was a farmworker from a village a few kilometres from Belokurikha, and used to bring fresh vegetables to the hotel kitchen to sell. I knew him because of the amount of time I spent going in and out of the kitchens as part of my duties.

His produce was always very good quality, so I used to buy from him to take home to my mother for the family table. His daughter was a very pretty girl with dark hair. She was called Irina Schaplinova. She worked under me as a waitress. Because she was good looking she was very popular with the men customers, some of whom were important and well-paid. She was a very good moral girl, and as far as I know did not do 'business' with them, though many of my waitresses made money on the side doing this.

When she was about twenty or so she suddenly left Belokurikha and the village and went to Barnaul. There were rumours that she had had a baby, but I do not know if they were true. When I saw her father, he would not discuss it or tell anyone anything.

Mr Schaplinov was Russian, but his wife was more Asiatic, which is why Irina was so dark of hair and complexion. Strangely, she had very striking blue eyes where you might expect brown eyes.

I came to England from Russia in 1991 after the Berlin Wall was demolished. My wife came too, and our two children. Our daughter lives in Coventry, and our son lives with his wife in Dulwich, near us. Their three children go to school there. I was born on 3rd September 1960. I teach Russian at Dulwich College. I went to London University and got a degree in Education.

Dated 2nd May 2016.
Signed Mily Destrov.

Mrs Destrov's statement was to a similar effect, but shorter as she had had much less contact with Irina or her father.

Lacey sat back, and again linked his fingers behind his head, his characteristic contemplative position, staring unseeing at the ceiling. So Colonel Webster's memory was on target. There was a family called Shaplinov with a daughter named Irina, and they came from Belokurikha – well, near it, anyway. There were rumours Irina had a child. Pieces of the jigsaw were suddenly falling into place more often and faster. 'How are we to find a man called Schaplinov who might be our murderer?' he asked himself.

Two minutes later Charcko and Lacey were in a police BMW on route to Keswick as fast as safety and speed limits allowed. Lacey hated the sound of sirens. They had around 580 miles and over six hours driving ahead of them. They stopped for a sandwich and coffee at a service centre near Newbury, and reached the Keswick Park Hotel just after seven o'clock. Traffic had been heavy and slow around Birmingham and the other large Midlands conurbations.

It was a fine-looking Victorian building almost in the town centre, in Station Road, but there was no station now. Lacey went to the desk and rang the bell, looking at the Three Star sign from the tourist board. A very smart lady appeared. Lacey proffered his warrant card and spoke quietly. "I think you spoke earlier to my Sergeant here. As you can see, I'm Detective Inspector Lacey and this is Detective Sergeant Charcko."

The woman said, equally softly: "Yes, I did. The two Russians are in the dining room."

"Do you have a couple of single rooms for us?"

"We have no single rooms, Mr Lacey, and only one double room left, but the bed's a king size, so it splits into two singles. But I could get one of you into the Bed and Breakfast down the road, or ...."

Kiara interrupted, addressing Lacey: "That's OK, sir. We can manage, and if we're in this hotel we can keep an eye on the Russians much more easily." She turned to the receptionist. "Would you split the bed up please?"

"Are you sure about this, Kiara? We didn't even stop to get a toothbrush, let alone pyjamas."

"That's OK Mr Lacey. We keep spare toiletries, and even pyjamas and nighties people leave behind. We launder those, of course. I'm sure we'll find something suitable."

Lacey was embarrassed, but raised his hands in surrender. "Very well." He paused. "Yes, we'll take the room. Now, can we have a table in the restaurant? Near the Russian guests, if possible, please."

The lady led them to the dining room, and as they entered, a couple were leaving a table two places away from the one the Russians were occupying. She summoned a waitress and asked her to clear and wipe the table at once. While waiting, Lacey spoke softly to the Sergeant. "You were quite right about keeping our eyes open, Kiara, but either or both of us could be in trouble if it gets out about us sharing a room."

Kiara laughed. "I can take care of that. I'll go out and phone Sharon Jones's mobile in a minute, tell her what's going down, and ask her to tell the rest of the team tomorrow and to keep shtum until then. I trust you, and even Shuttleworth won't be suspicious. He thinks you're sweet on the Army Captain."

Now it was Colin's turn to laugh. "You could say that." Charcko smiled and walked off to make her phone call. She was back quickly and gave a thumbs up.

Within five minutes Lacey and Charcko were sitting at the table, beautifully clean and precisely laid with cutlery, glasses, and linen napkins. After hors d'oeuvres, the people at the intervening table got up and left. Lacey went over to the table at which Milukov and Balkonsky were sitting. "Hello, I couldn't help overhearing you, and noticed your accents. I hope you don't mind me talking to you."

"Not at all," Milukov said in passable English. "We are from Moscow."

"Ah, the lady at the desk said there were some Russians here. Would you like to have a drink with us in the bar when we've all finished eating?"

"My friend speaks little English, but yes, happy we would be to drink with you."

"But your English is very good."

"Not so good. My mother is English. I tell you in bar."

Forty minutes later all four rose from their tables and made their way to the bar. The taller of the two, Balkonsky, led the way. The shorter one, Milukov followed and Lacey and Charcko brought up the rear. In the flesh Milukov looked even more powerful than on the CCTV. He looked dangerous, but seemed very pleasant.

Milukov asked for a lager. Balkonsky pointed to a vodka bottle and held up two fingers, saying, "Pliz." Lacey ordered him a double, a Glenmorangie for himself, the lager, and the orange juice Kiara asked for. Lacey decided to come straight to the point. He produced his ID and indicated Kiara should do the same. He told the Russians who they were: "We're here because we need to know what you were doing in Brighton and Chichester a few days ago."

Balkonsky looked puzzled, clearly not understanding what was going on, but Milukov smiled. "We got off the plane on – in? – Gatwick Airport, and I want see some history places in England. We stay in Brighton where beautiful buildings and squares by sea, and go Chichester for Cathedral. We stay three days, then come here."

"How long are you staying?"

"One more week."

"Why Keswick?"

"See grandparents."

"Your grandparents live here?"

"Why? Is problem? They is English."

Colin glanced at Charcko, thinking this was getting stranger and stranger. "But you are Russian."

"Long story. My father Russian, in merchant navy. Come to Liverpool many times. My mother's parents have seaman's hostel in Liverpool. Managers. Father stay there, meet mother. Very young. Fall – er – how you say? at - no, in - love? Mother get on ship, go Russia with father, get married in Petrograd."

"So you came to Keswick to see your grandparents, your mother's parents?"

"Is so. When they leave hostel, they live here, Keswick. Ver' small house. No room me and friend." He put his hand on Balkonsky's shoulder and seemed to be telling him what was being said. He then muttered in Russian to Milukov, who nodded "Ya!" He turned to Lacey: "He say, why you ask all this? We just on holiday see mine grandparents."

"In a moment I'll tell you, but first another question. Do you have bank card?"

"What is?"

Lacey took his NatWest card from his jacket pocket. "A bank card like this?"

Milukov smiled: "Ya! Yes! I have." He fished a card from his leather jacket and handed it to Lacey. "For to pay hotels, train, you know." As Lacey studied the card Milukov asked, "Is trouble?" He looked concerned.

The detective told Kiara to give him the copy bank debit ticket from the railway station and handed it to the Russian. "The trouble is that the name on the card is not the name on your passport. Why is that?"

Milukov turned at once to Balkonsky and spoke very fast in Russian. Their conversation lasted a couple of minutes. Charcko plainly thought they should be interrupted, but Lacey waived the idea, thinking it better to let them continue to be as relaxed as possible. The last thing he wanted was to provoke some sort of international incident by appearing heavy handed or arresting them. He still had no evidence linking them to the crime.

Both Russians were looking somewhat angry or disturbed now. Milukov came back to Lacey with; "We do nothing wrong. You tell us why we be questioned, or we get lawyer, get Consul or Embassy now."

Lacey spoke to Charcko. "Come with me." To the Russians he said, "Excuse me."

They stepped out into the hallway and round into the dining room, which was deserted. "What do you think?"

"Me, sir? That's your job."

"I know that, Kiara, but I just want to know what you think first. If you don't want to say, then don't."

She shook her head. "OK sir. Well, we can't arrest them on what we have, and if they call a solicitor or their ambassador, we won't get anything. I don't think we have a choice but to tell them and see what they say, if anything."

"You'll be pleased to know that is exactly my analysis, and we don't want a gang from the Russian Embassy round our necks. This case is hard enough as it is. Let's go."

Back in the lounge Lacey saw the Russians had new drinks before them. He and Charcko sat down.

"Very well, Mr Milukov, I'll tell you why we are questioning you. We are investigating a murder. A Russian living in Chichester was killed there a couple of weeks ago when you were there looking around and visiting the

Cathedral. He was killed with Novichok, a Russian chemical weapon."

Both Russians looked stunned, and Milukov said, "We know this Novichok. Russian state uses. But many countries have it now. We did not bring this. Could be found on us at airport, and we not allowed in. Not need poison to see my grandparents, to tell them my mother, their daughter dead last month."

That shook Lacey and Charcko a bit. "The trouble is two bottles of mixture for Novichok were found in your room at the hotel in Brighton, and it looks bad that your passport and bank card do not match," said Lacey.

Again Milukov spoke rapid Russian to Balkonsky. It was obvious that Balkonsky was denying any knowledge of the bottles and the other was agreeing. They looked more worried than angry now. Milukov switched his attention back to Lacey. "Is complex, but we telling truth. We take you tomorrow to see old people. You find we tell truth. Also, card and passport different." He scratched his head. "Is more hard in English. My mother, she try to teach me when ...." He put out a hand at the height of the head of a small child. "But I not good, not work hard." He looked sad, just as a man who had lost his mother a month ago would look when made to speak of it.

Kiara was thinking if he wasn't telling the truth he was one hell of a good actor.

After a deep breath or two to regain his composure, the Russian continued: "Truth. We are FSB." Lacey coughed and Charcko gasped, but Milukov went on. "Our – er – boss – he not want us to come under real names, be found out.

Not here to spy or do bad thing. Just to see dyedushka and babushka. Ah! Sorry. I say Grandfather and Grandmother."

"Are the passports forgeries?" Charcko asked.

"Yes, but FSB make. Create records, background. CIA do it, MI6 and Mossad do it. All country do it."

Lacey had to choke back a laugh at that; after years in Special Branch and SO15 he knew exactly how accurate that was. Milukov addressed Balkonsky again in Russian, and he nodded and said, "Ya!"

"We not run away. No reason why we do that. Do nothing wrong." He paused again. "Tomorrow after eating," (he gestured towards the dining room), "you come to see grandparents. You see I tell truth. We wait for you."

"Thank you. We are very sorry about your mother, but we have to check."

"Sure. Russian Police do same thing."

"Final thing before you ask. My real name, Boris Dologhov." He put his hand on the other Russian's arm. "He Mikhail Semyenvago."

Charcko was almost too dumbfounded to say: "And you're both with FSB in Moscow?"

"Ya! Yes."

Lacey stood. "You have admitted to entering the United Kingdom with false passports. That is a criminal offence for which you could be arrested and sent to prison or deported. It won't help my murder investigation to have you sent back to Russia. I'd rather test your truthfulness and if appropriate, eliminate you from our enquiries."

Milukov, as Lacey thought of him, still looked mystified. Lacey apologised and did his utmost to explain it all in simpler terms. Milukov grasped the reference to prison and being sent back to Russia. "But we tell you all things because we tell truth. Want you to believe us."

"Have you killed anyone?"

Milukov translated for his sidekick's ears, and he smirked. Milukov bit back a chuckle, and held out his hands palms up, as if making an offering. "No kill anyone – in England."

****

First thing in the morning Lacey phoned Sawyer. He had been talking to Charcko who said they shouldn't just let the Russians go without finding out what the Secret Service people thought, as it might endanger national security, and they would lose their jobs or worse. However, as he had predicted, Sawyer's reaction was: "Look, if all you've got on them is false passports, for Christ's sake leave them alone. If you think they're your assassins, that's different. I need a row with Russian about a trivial couple of passports like a hole in the head."

It struck Lacey as very odd that Sawyer was no longer so obsessed with pinning the assassination on the two Russians.

By noon the next day the detectives were on the road back to Chichester. Lacey was at the wheel. "Well, Kiara, what did you make of all that?"

"I dunno. Strange, the lot of it, if you ask me." A pause and Lacey thought *'Well, I did ask you,'* but he kept that to himself. Charcko continued: "Talking with them in the bar, I was pretty sceptical, even when they admitted they were KGB and told us their real names. I mean, we never heard back from Sawyer whether he knew their false names, did we? You know, Milukov and Balkonsky."

"Right, but I bet MI6 has a note of Dologhov and Semyenvago."

'But this morning, at the old grandparents' home, I began to believe them. When the old girl got out the Russian Death Certificate and the official translation into English, and she started weeping and wailing about her daughter's death, what else could you do but believe her?"

"What about when the two men arrived in Keswick?"

"I'll come to that, but she had all these photos of the daughter, when she was young and still at home in Liverpool. And Milukov aka Dologhov had a photo of the same woman in his wallet. I mean to say, how could they fix all that up? So, back to your question. They left Brighton the day after the murder, got on a train, and came straight up here. It's now what – the third of May today, so they've been here, staying in the hotel, and spending nearly all the time with Grandma and Grandpa for over two weeks."

"And hardly any murderer, let alone an assassin sent by Putin's old firm, would hang around any time at all. They took a good walk every two or three days to keep in trim, round Derwentwater, up Skiddaw, places like that, but I don't think we can arrest them for that."

Charcko laughed. "The prisons round here would be full of tourists. This is one of the most beautiful and popular holiday areas in the world."

Lacey glanced across at her. "You know, Kiara, your reasoning just now was spot on. You're good and getting better. You're going to be a great detective and go places in the force."

He looked back again from watching the traffic and could have sworn she was blushing beneath her beautiful Indian skin.

Then he felt her looking back at him. "I just want to thank you – about last night, I mean. Letting me use the en suite and taking yourself off to get changed in the shared bathroom for the single rooms, and coming back in the room once I was in bed with the light out avoided any sort of embarrassment. And then you did the same sort of thing this morning, so I was fully dressed when you came back, dressed completely yourself. Such perfect manners."

"Well, goodness, Kiara, you make me sound like a gentleman; I've always hoped someone might mistake me for one."

****

The rain was torrential from then until they turned east to get onto the M42, the M40, and then the A34 and back to Chichester. It was a slow journey. They did not get back to the nick until seven thirty pm. Lacey left Charcko there, went back to his hotel, and phoned Jodie.

Chapter 33

Salisbury. October, 2015

Ten o'clock on a Saturday evening, warm for October, Igor and Wendy were holding hands walking back to his car from the beautifully maintained white painted 14th Century pub restaurant where they had eaten. The car was in the car park at the other end of the road, Catherine Street. Igor had just asked her when it would be convenient for him to visit her in Long Buckby next, and as she turned to look at him and reply, someone on the other side of the road caught her eye.

"Just a minute, Igor." She pointed across the road. "Isn't that Ken Nixon?"

Igor glanced across. "You're right, it is." He continued to stare.

"Should we go over and say hello?"

Igor shook his head. "I don't think so. Have you seen who he's with?" He was taking in quite a sight: black patent high heels – five inches at least – decorated with what appeared to be sparkling sequins on the toes; fine black fishnets; a short black skirt barely covering the area at the top of the tights; a bright yellow silk blouse stretched over an exaggerated bust; and a bouffant hairdo reminiscent of the 1960s.

"Oh my God! I see what you mean. It's another woman, and it's not Marion. It could be embarrassing."

Igor chuckled and said, "It could be more than embarrassing. It's certainly not Marion, but it's not another woman either. It is not even an ordinary man." Arm in arm, the couple turned a corner. Holding Wendy's hand, he almost dragged her across the road to the opposite corner of that turning in time to see Nixon and his friend stop at a door. Igor whispered: "The person wearing those sexy female clothes is a gay transvestite who is quite notorious here. I've seen him in a pub or two touting for business. I had no idea Ken went with him, or that he might be bisexual."

"Surely not. Ken and Marion are happily married, aren't they?"

"They certainly appear to be, but I've always thought there seemed to be something odd, a bit strained, about their relationship. They always ..." Igor broke off and took his turn at pointing across the road. "See that? They just knocked on that green door, waiting for someone to open it. What does the little sign above the door say?"

Wendy peered across at the name, which was not easy to read by the light of the street lamps. "It looks like 'The Gaylord.'"

"That's right. It's a club." At that moment the club door opened. A bouncer in black from head to foot looked Ken and his 'friend' over, nodded, and they went in. The door shut behind them. Igor added: "Does the name tell you anything? Of course it does. It's not very subtle, is it?"

"I doubt that it's meant to be."

"Dead right, They have rooms there you can hire for the hour or night. Come on Wendy, let's get home."

"Yes, let's. I don't even want to think about what goes on in the rooms in that place. Besides, I've got a much better idea of what I want going on in my bedroom." She put an arm round his neck and drew him close for a searching kiss. "Tell me: how do you know it's a club?"

"It's listed on the internet. I was looking at the list when I moved here. It says 'Members Only'. I didn't realise for sure what sort of club it is until tonight. And before you ask, I haven't been there and have no intention of going."

They both laughed and Wendy kissed him again.

The following Saturday Igor had dinner at The Bell and Crown pub with Ken and Marion. During the course of very general and genial chatter, Igor asked what they had done last weekend. Marion responded at once with: "Nothing much. Ken had to go away."

Without any hesitation or embarrassment Ken agreed, adding: "Yes, I had to go to Birmingham University for a conference on recent developments in Nuclear Fusion. Got there late Friday and home Sunday afternoon." Igor was sure this came out pat because it would have been what Ken had told Marion. A short silence. "And you? Did you see Wendy? How's she?"

"She's fine thanks. No, she came to my place. Just some quiet walks and dinner in a pub." Igor looked at Ken. "This one, actually."

Marion said, "Well, it is an old beauty, isn't it? Spotless. Look at the shine on these floorboards! And the food is lovely for the price."

Keeping an eye on Ken, Igor said, "Yes, it is." Ken had blinked, looking stone-faced, appearing to study the beamed ceiling of the old pub; it had not escaped his notice that The Bell and Crown was only three hundred yards round the corner from 'The Gaylord'. The rest of the evening passed very pleasantly, and Ken was soon his normal talkative self. They parted at ten pm and made their respective ways home.

****

On Monday, thanking God and his lucky education for his perfect English accent, Igor took an early lunch break, went for a walk and phoned the Physics Faculty at Birmingham on his mobile. He was put through to the department which had run the fusion conference.

"This is Dr Ivor Chaplin from Exeter," said Igor. "It's about the nuclear fusion conference the weekend before last."

"Yes, Doctor. We had the conference here."

"I was expecting to see my friend Ken Nixon at the conference, but I couldn't make it and haven't been able to get hold of him. Did he turn up? If so, I owe him an apology."

"One moment, Dr Chaplin, and I'll look at the guest list." After a few clack-clacks on a keyboard the woman's voice came back. "Sorry to keep you waiting, sir. There's no Nixon on the list, and no-one of that name signed in either. I've got the register here."

"Thanks for your help. I'll just have to keep trying to phone him."

Igor thought it was a stupid lie for Nixon to have given him, let alone Marion: unless, of course, she was used to this sort of behaviour. He found it hard to understand what some spouses would, like Marion, put up with for the sake of keeping a marriage together. Perhaps they thought it was better for the children. Or maybe she really didn't know what was going on. He hoped that was the case.

The next day Igor went to a camera and photography shop. He bought a digital camera. He wanted to be able to print on the printing machine in the shop the photos he proposed to take. He did not want anyone else to see the pictures or films he took. He told the proprietor he was preparing a book on the habits of nocturnal birds and animals and needed a night vision appliance which needed no flash or other light. Several were shown and demonstrated. Igor decided he must buy a more expensive type in the hope of getting the best results. He bought an ORDRO HDV-V12 HD 1080P Video Camera Recorder Infrared Night Vision Camcorder. It was extremely light and easy to carry in a large pocket. He could film whatever he saw, and did not need to develop pictures.

****

On a rather cold November night, dark in the gaps between the streetlamps, the weather was very damp. The drizzle had stopped an hour ago, but the pavements were still wet. Igor Schaplinov could feel the moisture building up in the soles of his leather shoes. He wished he had a pair of what the English called wellingtons, or even some cheaper shoes with rubber soles. His overcoat was sodden and dribbles of rain were still running off his cap into the neck of his shirt. Miserable was how he felt, very miserable.

He was hidden in the setback doorway of a building almost opposite 'The Gaylord', in a part of the street where rays from the street lights barely penetrated the deep gloom.

To avoid the risk of obvious suspicion, he left his lair every half-hour or so and sauntered up the road in one or other direction but not out of sight of the club. When satisfied no-one was observing him, or that no-one was about, he returned to the doorway for another interval.

Misery wasn't all of it. He was fed up. Since he'd bought the camera six weeks ago, he had kept his watch here, like a policeman on surveillance duty, every Friday and Saturday except one, when he had gone to Wendy's for the weekend. Remembering her warmth and that of her bed did nothing to cheer him at this point. Two weeks ago, he had even asked Ken Nixon in a light and inconsequential fashion what he had planned for the weekend, and the casual answer had led him to believe that the man might be visiting this haunt. He did not show up.

Igor was thinking this was a waste of time, he'd have to find another tactic and was about to slink away when he heard a voice, a laugh, and then a snatch of conversation as footsteps increased a little in volume. He recognised Ken's voice before he could see him. A moment later Ken came into view with his companion of the previous occasion. They held hands; the 'woman' was dressed in different but equally sexy garments, with a raincoat cast over her shoulders. Igor set the camera to work silently and videoed the couple as they walked towards the club, when they stopped at the club door, knocked, and were admitted.

Igor went straight home after retrieving his car from the car park at the other end of Catherine Street. He was frozen so he played the filmed encounter standing against a radiator as soon as he had shed his damp clothes and shoes. The result was very satisfactory; he had what he needed. He sent the film to his mobile phone, and also copied it onto two USBs.

He decided not to confront Ken on Monday, but to leave it to the following day, to allow more time for the man to feel that he was secure, and that no-one knew about his 'lady' friend or the club.

On Tuesday morning Igor went to Ken's desk. "Hello, Ken. Fancy lunch at the pub today? We haven't had a chat for a while?"

"Great idea, my boy, but I've got a meeting in the lab at one, but I could do tomorrow. That do?"

"Very nicely. We can go in my car."

****

Wednesday lunchtime found Nixon and Schaplinov sitting at a small oblong table in the pub. Igor had driven them there. The Royal Oak was old, and so was the furniture, but everything was clean and spotless. They both ordered a pint of bitter, Ken the steak pie and two veg, Igor scampi and chips. Igor paid.

"I'll get the bill next time. Cheers!" Ken raised his glass. Igor did the same.

"Did you have a good weekend?"

Igor shook his head. "Not really. Too wet. Spent most of it indoors, reading the papers. Watched a bit of TV. Bought a book in a Charity Shop Saturday morning and read a lot of it."

"Yes? What was it?"

"Alison Weir's 'The Lady Elizabeth'. I like historical novels. This one's about Elizabeth I's childhood and life up to becoming Queen. She must've been a very clever woman to have survived."

"Many people reckon she was the greatest monarch England ever had. Didn't see Wendy, then?"

"No. Next weekend probably." The landlord called out that their meals were on the bar, so they went over to collect them. As they tucked in, Igor asked, "What about you? Did you and Marion go anywhere?"

"It was quite nice Saturday morning, so drove out to Broadway for a look round and lunch." In between mouthfuls of food, they continued to chat.

"It's a pretty place. I've been there with Wendy."

"But it started to rain in the afternoon, so we went home, and after dinner we went to the flicks and saw ..."

"Flicks? Now that's an English word I don't know."

Ken snorted a short chuckle. "It's old slang – colloquialism – for cinema, like movies, films. I think it's really old, from the early days when the pictures flickered on the screen because the technology and the reels weren't so good. We saw the late screening and got home about midnight."

"Flicks. I'll have to remember that. Was the film any good?"

"Very. Michael Fassbender in Macbeth. Only came out last month. If you like historical stuff you should go. Take Wendy." Ken put down his knife and fork. Igor finished his last bite, and pushed his plate aside, and said, "Very nice."

"Yeah, the grub here's not bad, is it?"

"Not the food, Ken. The stuff you make up."

Nixon sat up straight, and his smile vanished. "What does that mean?"

Igor leaned forward with his elbows on the table. He was about to speak when the barmaid came over to take away their plates. He gestured for her to clear the beer glasses too, ordered two black coffees, and gave her the money.

"I said what does that mean?"

"I'll tell you when the coffees come and the waitress has gone." When the coffees arrived Igor said, "You remember when I had dinner with you and Marion three weeks ago?"

"Of course."

"And you told me and Marion you'd been to a conference in Birmingham the weekend before."

Agitated and in a louder voice, Ken replied: "Well, what's wrong with that?"

Igor put a finger across his lips. "Sshh. You certainly don't want everyone hearing this. What's wrong with it is that you weren't in Birmingham. It was a lie. You were in Salisbury, and you went to 'The Gaylord Club' on the Saturday evening with a friend."

"Rubbish! How dare you." Nixon was getting angrier by the second, red in the face, but he struggled to keep his voice low.

"Oh! I dare, Ken, since Wendy and I were walking back from the pub down the road and saw you two go in there. I have to say, he does look pretty convincing in his girlie costumes."

"You're out of your mind. I'm a married man with three kids!"

Igor smiled and reached down into the pocket of his coat on the back of his chair. He took out his phone and the two USBs. He plugged one into the phone and held it up for Ken to see. "I didn't imagine this or make it up, Ken, though I admit I invented the bit about staying in on Saturday. This is you and that fellow going into the club on Saturday. This is the two of you holding hands as you walk down the street."

"You fucking bastard. What's all this about? What have I done to you?"

"Nothing, Ken. You've done nothing. But does Marion know about this? Won't you be a security risk at PD if this gets out? How about the press?"

"You're a cunt. You think you're going to get money for a story out of this? Is that what you want? You'll finish my marriage, alienate my kids?"

Igor raised his hands in a pacifying gesture. "Right now, you think I'm your enemy. I'm not. We've been friends, but I want you to do something for me. If you do, nothing will happen. So Marion doesn't know?"

"Of course not! What makes you think she might?"

"I'm not sure. Sometimes when we're with her something seems to be not quite right."

"Well, you're right about that, but it's not what you think. Marion likes sex, and so do I, but I'm bisexual, so when I get home from a night or a weekend with Jackie …."

"That's his name?"

"That's the name he uses. He was baptised Jack, so he calls 'herself' Jackie. So, as I was saying, after a spell with him, I can't always get it up for Marion for a day or so. Then she's cranky until I've given her one or three."

"Right; she doesn't know, and you've also got the job at PD to worry about."

"You're blackmailing me. I could go to the Police."

"You could, and I might get prosecuted, but if you do that, this story will come out and you'll be finished anyway: job, Marion, kids, front page of the Sun and Daily Mirror, everything. Do what I want, and nothing will happen, as I just told you."

Nixon slumped in his chair and buried his face in his hands. His shoulders shook, and he appeared to be crying. He put a handkerchief over his face and made for the toilet. After a minute or three he came back, blowing his nose into the hankie. "What do you want me to do then?"

"We must get back to work. I'll tell you in the car."

On the drive back to the labs, Igor laid it out for Ken. "If you want this to go away, and no-one but me ever to know about your peccadillo, you have to get me some Novichok."

Disbelief and shock were writ large over Ken's face. "You've gone fucking bonkers, mate. Novichok? It's fucking lethal."

"You've started swearing an awful lot, Ken. I don't care for it. You've never done it before."

"I've never been blackmailed before or threatened with my life being laid waste, either, that's why." Nixon took a deep breath and calmed down fractionally. "What is this, some sort of Russian spying thing?"

"Don't you worry about that! Russians don't need to be told about Novichok. We invented it." Igor paused. "What I want it for is my business and the less you know, the less trouble you can get into, let alone tell anyone about all of it, since you won't know it all."

"But I can't just go into the store and steal it. It's dangerous, and we could both die."

"So you're ready to do it?"

"Do I have a choice?"

"Frankly, no. We've been friends and while you may not think so, I'm still your friend. I really don't want to hurt you, but if I have to I shall. If that all sounds like what an American would call hypocritical bullshit, I can't help that."

"Too right. But the poison doesn't last all that long if it's ready to use."

"I know that, Ken. So I want you to get me a couple of small bottles of the two mixtures that make the dangerous liquid when they're put together."

"Well, pardon my French, but you are fucking mad. You could kill yourself mixing them."

"I know that too. I've worked with it in Russia, remember."

"So why don't you go in the store and get it yourself?"

"You know why. I'm only allowed in the entrance to the store office, and the storeman fetches things for me. I'm not cleared for the dangerous materials store, but you are, and your eye is keyed into the security system."

"You've really worked this out, haven't you? If anyone gets found out it'll be me, won't it? Like I said before, you really are a cunt."

"I can't help that, Ken. In any case, what you have to do is go in there soon, and get a bottle of one mixture, and go back two or three weeks later and get the other one. I shan't be using them for a little while, and by the time I do, it'll be some time before they link the two visits to you, if they manage to do it at all. If I kill myself with it, it'll be by accident, and only you will know that. The Police would look at it as suicide. They may wonder how I got the stuff, but when they know where I worked, they won't bother to look any further. If you get me a set of safety gear as well, there will be nothing for the Police to investigate."

The car had pulled up in the PD car park, and they sat silent for a moment. Ken Nixon said, "I'll think about it."

"Sorry to be mean, Ken, but you don't have time for that. I want the first bottle soon. I'm not waiting for ever. And here's a copy of that USB for you, so you don't forget."

Ken opened the car door, got out, and slammed it as hard as he could. Igor felt guilty about this business, as he liked Ken, but he saw no other way of getting the poison. Life could be tough. The end of it had been tougher for Oleg, his father.

****

A week later Nixon came out to the car park and gave Schaplinov the first sample. It was in a small, strong glass bottle, and securely wrapped in a plastic bag. Sixteen days later he gave him the second bottle, similarly wrapped. "I'll get you some safety gear tomorrow."

"Thanks, Ken. If you do, I promise no-one will ever hear a word about this from me."

"Jesus, Igor. You're a criminal, and God knows what else you're planning, so how do I know what a promise from you is worth?"

"Sorry, Ken, but you've just got to suck it and see."

It was the weekend before Christmas.

Chapter 34

Long Buckley, December, 2015

The weekend before Igor received the second bottle and the safety clothes, he visited Wendy. Rising late after an energetic late night and a fairly early morning, they went for a walk in the cold frosty air to The Old King's Head for lunch.

"Who was the old King, then?" Igor asked.

"Nobody's really sure, but it was probably Charles II. Local historians are sure it's late 17th Century, and so far that's their best guess based on the research. No surviving licensing records back then. That's if the law required licences before 1685 when Charles died."

"James was the next King, wasn't he?"

"And then William and Mary." A short silence. "The pub still has a thatched roof."

"I've seen it. I've been there in the past with a friend who lives here. When we came for a drink in 2014, it was closed. Alan thought it was – what do you say? A gonner?"

Wendy laughed. "A gonner! I haven't heard that for yonks. Your knowledge of English idioms is incredible."

She stopped walking and talking. "You have a friend here? You haven't told me that before. Alan, did you say?"

"Yes, Alan Carpenter. You know him. He lives at the …."

"The Old Rectory. I know him slightly. I know his wife Lydia better. And you were with them at Silverstone when he raced his XK140. You're a very naughty boy if you've forgotten that!" They both laughed, and Igor said, "Wow, what a clot!"

Wendy and Igor had reached the pub, and Igor pushed the door open for her. They went to the bar, ordered two pints of Tiger, and studied the chalkboard specials. Wendy said quietly: "That's the landlady behind the bar." Then more loudly she called across the beer pumps: "Hello, Katie. Matt not working today?"

"How are you, Wendy? Yes, he's slaving away, but not in here. He's in our study – well, part of our bedroom really – he's got a desk and his computer and stuff in there."

"Matt's really an IT wizard, Igor. He works in here for fun when he's not pounding the keys and scouring the internet. Katie, this is my friend Igor."

Katie held out her hand across the bar and Igor shook it firmly but briefly. "Very nice to meet you, Katie. How do you do?"

"Goodness. I always thought you had to be Russian to be called Igor."

"He is Russian, from Southern Siberia," Wendy said.

"But your English is better than mine!" Katie was speaking to Igor.

"I studied English at home in Barnaul, and at Novosibirsk University with an English lecturer, came here on an exchange with Alan Carpenter, and he came to stay with me and my mother. They both went to public schools and taught me to talk 'proper'. And I've been living and working here for a few years now."

Katie turned to Wendy. "Does he mean our Alan Carpenter, then?"

"Yes, the Old Rectory."

"Well, I'll be blowed! I expect Alan and Lydia'll look in here soon; they usually pop in for a drink on Saturdays."

Igor placed their food order and they retreated to a table near the fire, and out of the draught from the door every time a customer came or went.

"So what's the story with the pub? It's no wonder it closed. It was really dingy when I came with Alan years ago."

"There are quite lot of people here in Long Buckby – about 6,000, I think. Wasn't much of a pub then, but at least it was ours. Then in 2014, Everards the brewers bought it, renovated it as you see, brought in Katie and Matt to manage it, and it's been humming like a good old country pub ever since."

"No loud rock to stop conversation."

"Thank God. And the food's good."

At that moment Katie placed their plates before them. "So our grub's good, is it Wendy?"

"Definitely. Looks good, doesn't it, Igor?"

"Certainly does. So let's stop talking and tuck in. I'm starving."

Katie laughed. "Let me know what you think when you've eaten it all, and I'll tell Dominic." She went back to the bar.

"He's their brilliant chef," Wendy added.

Having finished eating and talking, Igor went to the bar to pay. Wendy joined him to saying goodbye to Katie and some of the customers she knew. As they left the pub Igor opened the door for her, and Alan Carpenter and Lydia walked in. Alan had been pushing the door simultaneously. "Good Lord, Lydia, look who's here! Igor, where did you spring from?"

"Hello Alan. Hello Lydia, long time no see." He put his hand on Wendy's shoulder. "You know Wendy Slater, of course."

"Oh we know Wendy, don't we? Not well, but we've all lived here a long while," Lydia politely offered as Alan ushered her in and closed the door. He laughed and said, "Not just a long time in my case; it's been forever! Look, we could have them to dinner tomorrow night, couldn't we, darling?"

Lydia gave a mock grimace and said, "Why Alan, will you be cooking?" Then she laughed. "No, that would be lovely."

"I'm afraid I can't, Lydia. I have to leave tomorrow after lunch as I have to prepare for a busy day at Porton on Monday."

"Why is that?"

Igor smiled and laid an index finger at the side of his nose. "Hush-hush stuff."

Alan said, "Yes, of course. But you must both come next time you're up here. Where are you staying, Igor?"

Wendy blushed a little, and Igor replied: "With Wendy. We've been good friends ever since that race meeting you took me to at Silverstone. Look, I'll give you a ring next time

I'm coming up, but it may be a while as Wendy's coming to me quite a bit for the next couple of months."

Wendy looked at Igor with some surprise, Lydia and Alan noticed nothing, and Alan said, "OK, then give us a ring as soon as you can, and we'll arrange something." He invited them to stay for a drink, which they did. After that they all said goodbye, shook hands or exchanged embraces and kisses, and Igor and Wendy departed.

A few minutes later Wendy stopped and held Igor's arm. "I didn't know you had to leave after lunch tomorrow, and what was that about me coming to you all the time for a while?"

"Sorry Wendy, I forgot to tell you about tomorrow, and as for the other bit, I've really got a lot going on, so I can't get away as easily. If you can't come to me very often, I'll just have to grin and bear it. Well, on second thoughts, I shan't do much grinning." He also realised he wouldn't get to do much baring either.

Wendy remained subdued for quite a period, but recovered by the evening, during which, and some of the night, they spent themselves much as they usually did. However, both felt that some sort of milestone had been passed, and Igor could not tell her that he daren't be away and miss getting the second Novichok ingredient from Ken Nixon, nor that his plans would probably speed up once he had it.

****

Igor spent Christmas with Wendy and her sons at Long Buckby. It had been a happy time, and everyone had good presents for the others. The boys were sufficiently adult to understand that their Mum was young enough to need fulfilment and had voiced no objection to her sleeping with Igor, even if they felt any resentment, and they showed none either.

For Wendy and Igor, the sex was as good as always, but the affectionate aspect of it seemed to have departed, leaving a purely physical release and relief. The emotional side of their relationship was slowly fading, and towards the end of the holiday they found the courage to talk about it. Both felt that they should just let it go, and if something better came along for either of them, that would finish it. It seemed very civilised and grown up, but of course, Igor had other plans.

As soon as he returned to Porton Down from Wendy's, Ken Nixon made an excuse to meet him in the grounds of the Establishment and handed him the second bottle of Novichok ingredients. They exchanged what appeared to be tidily wrapped but belated Christmas presents. Igor gave Ken a John Grisham novel. Ken's gift to Igor was what appeared to be a book about Catherine the Great. It was in fact completely and cunningly hollowed out, and the hole contained the bottle.

It was now mid-January, and Igor spent much of his time making his plans, checking them over and over, doing all in his power to make sure they would work without a hitch. He needed to ask at Porton Down if he could take a holiday, and if it mattered if he went abroad. It was important that everything should appear as normal as possible and be approved at work. He could not take the risk that someone might stumble on something and become suspicious. He knew the English saying, 'hidden in plain sight'. He calculated that if he had as much of his plan in sight as he could contrive, the risks were less.

Unfortunately, he could do little, and certainly not plan his 'holiday' until he knew where to find Pedchenko.

****

Time seemed to be flying by at the speed of light, and Igor still needed to find the exact whereabouts of Pedchenko, aka Mamontov. His searches of all the leading internationally known English and American newspapers had yielded nothing, and he was fed up with it, having been doing it for about eighteen months.

He had even tried the French papers, Le Figaro, Le Monde, and even Le Canard Enchaine, and some German and Italian media publications. He had to use the 'translate' facility to read them, which took even more time, but his luck was out. Going through one of them that way took even more time, and perusing scores of them seemed like a life sentence.

It was when he turned to the English tabloids that he had more luck. He'd combed through many issues of the Sun and was working his way into the past issues of the Daily Mirror, when he found it. It was only a short news item, tucked into the bottom right-hand corner on page four, just a follow up piece several weeks after the exchange in 2011 had ceased to be of front page, block-buster headline significance.

Immigration Unrest Down South.

A growing number of people along the south coast from Dover to Weymouth are voicing concern at the influx of foreign refugees, asylum seekers, and others coming to live in their counties. Many of the newcomers hail from Eastern European countries, are prepared to work for lower wages and salaries than locals, are taking their jobs, and that pushes down rates of pay. They are also concerned about the disappearance of traditional English shops and businesses, and the speed with which the names of foreign businesses replace them. Particularly prominent are Polish shops. A rumour which it has been impossible to verify says that amongst these immigrants is a spy released from Russia in a spy swap in 2011, who may be living in West Sussex.

Igor made a copy and marked the last sentence in green highlight. Chichester was the county town of West Sussex, he knew. That was the place to start. If you wanted to hide and stay hidden, a reasonably large town where the Police were not constantly on the alert for serious crime in prospect, as they were in London, Birmingham, Glasgow or the other cities, was ideal.

Chapter 35

Chichester, Monday, 2nd May, 2016

"Hello, Jodie speaking."

"It's me, Colin."

"I thought it would be." She laughed briefly. "Let's rephrase that: I hoped it would be. How did your day go? Your secret trip?"

"Well, it needn't be a secret any longer, not between us, anyway. I went to Keswick, and to allay any suspicions which might arise if I don't tell you this bit, I went with Sergeant Charcko, and we ..."

"You mean that gorgeous Indian girl?"

"Indeed. And we had to share a bedroom for the night. All very innocent. She said I behaved like a perfect gentleman."

"I believe you, Colin. I know what you are like. Can't help remembering the old Chinese saying, though: woman with skirt up run faster than man with trousers down."

"There was none of that, or of anything else of that nature." They both laughed. "No; it was a necessity. We'd found out after the press conference that the two suspect Russians were staying in a hotel in Keswick, so we went up there, booked ourselves in, and had to share a room with two single beds so we could keep close to these fellows. There were no other empty rooms. Anyhow, we interviewed them, and they admitted being here on false passports, and being FSB personnel."

"Crikey, Colin, you should have arrested them for that."

"I could have, I know, but we, Charcko and I, both believed they were genuinely there to visit the maternal grandmother of the one called Milukov, who's really Boris Dologhov. She lives in Keswick; he came over to tell her his Mum, her daughter, had died last month. We had no evidence at all to link them to the murder, and the last thing I need right now is to get involved in a relatively unimportant passport case with huge diplomatic overtones. It'd just muck up the murder investigation completely. At least we have eliminated them as suspects. In any case, I checked with the head of MI6, and he said exactly the same, that he needed a diplomatic row with the Russian government like a hole in the head."

"So where does that leave you?"

"Damn it all! I'm really going to break our rule about what we tell each other because this is a pretty important secret at present, but I know you won't tell anyone." After a moment he said, "We're now looking for a Russian called Schaplinov who ....?"

"Who? Schaplinov, did you say?"

"Yes, he ….."

Jodie burst in again. "You're not going to believe this, but there's a chap called Schaplinov who works at PD. I've met him briefly, but he's got such a public school and Oxbridge accent I thought he was probably a descendant of

Russian refugees living in Britain since 1917. Could he be the one?"

"I've no idea, but anything's possible. I'll have to look into it at once. I'd better get hold of Horne-Bassett right this minute."

"But it's late. He won't be there now. I'll give you his home phone and mobile numbers. I have them for emergencies." A few seconds later Jodie dictated them and Colin took them down.

"I've got to go."

"OK, but if you're here all day, can we have dinner together? I could change the booking at the Allium."

"That would be great, but you're at Porton and I'm in Chichester. I don't know if I'll be coming up to Porton. Sorry. I must get on. Bye."

Next, he phoned down to the reception desk, and Sergeant Davies answered.

"Yes, sir?"

"Sean, I need to get a search warrant pronto, Can you get hold of a magistrate who can see me tonight? I've got to make a phone call, but I should be with the beak in twenty or thirty minutes."

Davies assented, and Lacey called the home number Jodie had given him for the head of PD.

"Hello. Who's calling?"

"Detective Chief Inspector Lacey. Sorry to bother you out of …."

"Hours? No problem for a man who told me I run a good organisation." He chuckled. "To what do I owe the pleasure?"

"I won't beat about the bush. I'm in a hurry. Do you have someone called Schaplinov working at Porton Down?"

"We do. He's a Russian. MI6 – you know – Sawyer and his minions? – vetted him and said he could work here. I had to interview him. He's given us improvements in some of our research methods from the chemical weapons place he worked at in the USSR and then under the Federation. He defected and came over hoping to work here. He brought us secret stuff, and he's provided more since he arrived at PD. What's this all about?"

"He may be the murderer of the ex-spy Pedchenko we're looking for. I need his full name and address. We need to find him as soon as possible."

"Unfortunately, you're going to have to wait, or fly to Milan. He went off on holiday almost a week ago."

"Are you sure of that?"

"Absolutely positive. Very unusual. He actually came to see me to ask if he could go. Most personnel just ask their head of department, but he was worried that as he was Russian, it might look bad unless he had my consent. So I gave it. Even told him where he might enjoy himself."

"Bugger."

"Look, give me a few minutes, I'll find him on the staff list on my laptop and phone you back."

"No, please do it now. I'll hang on."

After a few minutes silence apart from the sound of tapping on a keyboard, Horne-Bassett gave the address in College Street, and the new suspect's full name: Igor Vasilyevich Schaplinov.

Lacey thanked him. "One last question. Do you have a DNA analysis lab at PD?"

"No, Chief Inspector, we do not. The closest one I'm aware of is Cellmark at Abingdon, over in Oxfordshire."

More thanks, and Lacey put the phone down. A second later Sean Davies rang. "I got hold of Mr Herniman, sir. Been on the bench for years. Very thorough, wastes no time. Wanted to know what it was all about, and said he'd come to you at once when I told him it was about the murder. He lives in Whyke Road, so he'll be here …. Hang on. It's him now. I'll bring him up."

Herniman was just as Davies described him, grasped the facts and the evidence fast after a few questions, declared himself satisfied there was reasonable cause, and signed a warrant to search Schaplinov's Salisbury flat.

Lacey then called Salisbury Police Station and asked to speak to the senior officer present. He explained the situation, asked for and got a team of SOCOs to meet him at the flat at eight am next day. Having done that, he collected the DNA report on the blood of Oleg Gordanov, alerted Peter Shuttleworth to get the BMW ready for a drive to Salisbury at six in the morning, and picked up a set of skeleton keys. Finally, he sought out D.C. Morton. "Harry, get hold of Passport Control and flight information at Heathrow. Find out if there was a flight for Milan last week with a passenger called Igor Schaplinov. I'll be off to Salisbury really early tomorrow, so leave a message for me at the nick there, or get me on my mobile."

Lacey and Shuttleworth were outside the building in which Shaplinov's flat was located by eight am, and a SOCO team was waiting for them. After knocking loudly at the door and yelling 'Police', Lacey opened it with the skeleton key. A local bobby armed with a battering ram was disappointed not to be able to deploy its destructive power, and returned to the police station.

The SOCOs were already dressed in complete Novichok-proof non-contamination crime scene gear, and gave Lacey and Shuttleworth sets to don. Then they entered. Very quickly the map on which the Russian had marked the area of Chichester where Alexandra Road had been highlighted, and a spectacle case with a label for Boris Mamontov were found and placed in evidence bags. No laptop, iPad or other device could be seen. However, out of the kitchen waste bin, a female officer picked up two small bottles which looked unlike any ordinary culinary containers. She showed them to Lacey, who directed her to wrap them carefully in cling-film, place them in evidence bags, and label the bags.

Next, he phoned Jodie Jordan and asked her if any remaining contents of the bottles could be analysed if he had them sent to the Research Establishment.

"Send them over to me and I'll prioritise it," she replied. "It should be done by this afternoon. Can you wait? Or will you have to get back to Chichester?"

"Not sure yet. I'm hoping for info on whether our Russian friend got on a plane to Milan, and I can't do much else until I know if that's Novichok in the bottles or not." Colin hesitated, then said, "Maybe dinner tonight will be OK. You could chance your arm and book a table."

"OK, Send the bottles over." Jodie cut the phone.

Still dressed in safety gear, Colin took the two bottles in their evidence bags out to a police motor-cyclist and told him to get to Porton Down as fast as possible and deliver the bags to Captain Jordan as a priority. The rider put the evidence bags in a secure pannier. The bike roared away.

Back in the flat, a SOCO told Colin that there was a set of protective chemical-proof clothing in the dustbin outside. It looked as though Schaplinov had contrived to mix the two bottles into another container himself. "Not only that sir, but there are some marks on the carpet which might be where he did the mixing and spilt a little."

"Right. No-one is to go near that or touch the safety gear in the bin unless they still have their own equipment on."

The officer chuckled. "None of us are contemplating suicide sir, but I'll tell 'em."

Colin then rang Jodie again and asked her to send someone to check the carpet for Novichok. He added that their dinner date was safe, as he was still waiting here in Salisbury for information, from Passport Control and Airlines, and the results from the bottles. She had had no idea that Schaplinov was supposed to have gone on holiday, nor where he might have gone instead, she speculated, apart from Moscow.

Lacey and Shuttleworth left the SOCOs to it after the Inspector asked the senior officer there to bag as evidence anything which looked as if it might have DNA – spit, urine, saliva, dirty handkerchief - on it, and get it to the Cellmark lab in Abingdon ASAP for analysis and comparison with the Gordanov report which he gave him.

At Salisbury Police Station, Lacey asked the duty Sergeant if there was a message for him. 'No' was the answer. He and Shuttleworth were shown to an interview room and given report sheets so they could start at least making notes for full reports of the activities yesterday and that morning. Around eleven, as a constable brought in two cups of coffee, Lacey's mobile rang. It was Harry Morton.

"Just got off the blower with Heathrow, sir," he said. "I managed to get hold of them last night, and they say they've been working on it right through since then. Good news and bad, sir."

"Do your worst, Harry."

"The good bit is they found the flight to Milan. It was in the afternoon on the 28th of April. Schaplinov was booked on it, but 'e never showed up. They called him three times over the tannoy or whatever it's called, but nobody came, so the plane went without 'im. So are we up the creek without a paddle, sir?"

"Looks very much like it, but I need to make another call. I doubt I'll be back till tomorrow, and I'll bring you, Kiara and Sharon up-to-date then."

Colin dialled Sawyer's number, and the spy chief answered. "What can I do for you this time, Lacey?"

"Last time we spoke, Mr Sawyer, you told me that the name Schaplinov meant nothing to you."

"I did and it doesn't. So what?"

"Just this. Yesterday I spoke to Mr Horne-Bassett at Porton."

"Again, so what?"

"I'd been told there was a chap called Schaplinov working at PD, a Russian called Igor Vasilyevich Schaplinov."

"How was I supposed to know that?"

"Two reasons. First, you and MI5 keep an eye on foreign nationals from suspect countries. Secondly, and more significantly, Horne-Bassett told me you had vetted the man for security clearance and told him to give Schaplinov a job."

Sawyer said nothing, there was a very brief period of silence and then Colin said, "Unfortunately, he seems to have disappeared, leaving a false trail suggesting he flew to Milan for a holiday. Bearing in mind that you could be in deep shit, if you'll pardon the expression, is there anything you can tell me that might help us find him?"

"If we're pardoning expressions, Lacey, fuck you. But he came here in 2011 posing as Maxim Schaliapin. He may have disappeared using the same alias." He terminated the call.

Colin phoned Harry Morton again. "Harry, now you've got the Passport contacts, I want you to get on to them again. Our suspect may have left the country under the name Maxim Schaliapin. Ask them to get a search going to see if anyone using that name has left the country in the last week or so. 28th of April is a good bet, and he probably boarded a plane that left some time before the one to Milan you asked them about before."

"OK, sir. I'll get onto it immediately. Take 'em a while, I guess."

"And another thing. Please phone the lab to which the vicar's garb from the Car Park toilet went. When they have tested anything for DNA, please ask them to send their report to me, and a copy to a Mr Joseph Adamson at the Cellmark lab in Abingdon, to be put with the stuff about Schaplinov and Gordanov. I want to know if any samples from the hat or jacket match the Schaplinov material."

****

Having finished writing their notes, the two detectives went out for lunch, and then for a walk. There was nothing else for them to do. About four o'clock Lacey's mobile vibrated.

"Lacey."

"Joseph Adamson at Cellmark, Chief Inspector. We have a result. The DNA from the items we received from the flat in Salisbury match with the report results you sent with them to this extent. The two sets of DNA are from related people. Both are clearly male, and if they are not father and son, I'm from Mars."

Colin did not wish to make any mistake by indicating what he wished to hear, so he asked, "Could you tell which is which?"

"Certainly we could. The one in the report you sent over was the father, and the one from the Salisbury flat was the son. I'll have a written report ready for you in the morning, about nine, I'd say."

"What about the report from the lab in London about some clothes? Did you get it? I've had their report; I asked them to send you a copy."

"Yes, Inspector, I was just coming to that. We got it, and the data is very interesting. It matches the data from the stuff in the Schaplinov flat."

"Well done, Mr Adamson. Boy-oh-boy. I think that cracks the case for us."

When the call ended, Colin told Peter they would be staying over-night, and to find himself a B & B or hotel, but not to bother about him, as he was suited. As soon as they returned to the station Peter left, but not before jesting,

"Doesn't Captain Jordan live here, sir?" Then he roared with laughter and walked away very quickly.

Lacey smiled, shook his head at the impertinence, and then phoned Jodie. "I've got to stay here tonight so our dinner is on."

"Good. I booked a table."

"I'd better find a hotel, then."

"Don't worry about that now, Colin."

"I'm not worrying, but I'm stuck at Salisbury nick. Peter's taken the car to find somewhere to stay."

"Stay there then, and I'll pick you up in about an hour. Can you get a cuppa?"

"You can always get a cuppa in a nick, Jodie. See you later, then."

****

When they got back to her home, she dressed in garments better suited to what Lacey hoped would be a romantic dinner in a good restaurant. He had brought a change of shirt and underpants in case he had had to stay in a hotel, so he had a wash and changed into them. They took a taxi. The Allium was almost full and excellent.

As the head waiter led them to the table Jodie had booked, Colin thought she looked stunning in her blue ankle length dress, with a citrine pendant on a gold chain, and the black shoes he'd first seen at the hotel in Chichester. Her long hair hung in waves level with her shoulder blades. He hoped he didn't look too bad himself in the pale linen suit, brown brogues, and a red tie he'd warn all day. She did not say what she thought when he told her: "You are beautiful, Jodie," but she smiled radiantly at him, and often took his hand at the table.

She asked him what use the tip had been that she had given him regarding the Russian.

"It was invaluable. He was definitely the man who attacked the Pedchenkos with Novichok. I got a warrant to search his flat, found stuff which would have his DNA on it and the lab gave me the result this afternoon. It even tied in with DNA on some clothes he had worn to commit the murder. Schaplinov and Oleg Gordanov were very close relatives and the analysts are as certain as they can be Oleg was Igor Schaplinov's father."

"That's brilliant. Just brilliant. I'm so pleased for you Colin. You and your team, you've all worked so hard and pretty fast for such a strange case."

"Trouble is, he's probably left the country, and we have no idea where he's gone. We're very unlikely ever to be able to charge him with the murder, or bring him before a Court."

Jodie confirmed that the two bottles from the flat had contained Novichok ingredients. Apart from those serious but celebratory subjects, over a leisurely dinner and a bottle of wine they chatted inconsequentially as though every word was as important as the Sermon on the Mount, and could hardly take their eyes off each other. They finished with a Remy Martin each, and coffee. The alcohol was not a problem. They'd called another taxi.

"Look, Jodie, maybe I'm hopelessly lost and out of order, but I've got to speak now or forever hold my peace."

"How do you spell 'piece', Colin?"

They both laughed briefly and a trifle nervously; the atmosphere was tense. "I think you know. This is serious. I'm forty, and you're mid-thirties, I imagine, so without wishing to be crude, Jodie, I expect we've both been round the block a few times, and know what we want."

"No, it's not crude. It's realistic." Jodie was quiet and thoughtful for a few seconds. "And you wish to say that you want our relationship to be more than casual friendship, don't you?"

"That's it exactly. It's all rather sudden, as I've only known you just over a week, and some of that we've been rather tense with each other, but I can honestly say I've never felt like this before. I've thought I did, but now, with you, all the other times are just a burning candle compared with the biggest sun in the universe."

"Wow, Colin, do you write for Mills and Boone?"

Colin's face registered real hurt. Jodie immediately took his hand. "I'm so sorry, Colin, that was a wicked thing to say. I have a horrid sense of humour, and at a time like this it's unforgivable. Can I make up for it by asking you to ask me to marry you?"

"Are you sure?"

"I have only one slight reservation."

"Jesus, help me! You're treating my emotions like a dangerous roller-coaster." He sighed. "OK, so spit it out."

"Just that we mustn't let our work get between us, as we did with this Novichok case to start with."

Colin leaned back, smoothing his hair down as he contemplated what to say next. "You mean if I keep asking you for information, or you keep telling me it's a secret. Or vice versa."

"Something like that."

"I think we can handle that. If I ask for information, and you say 'No', I don't push it, and if I ask and you cannot answer, you don't get cross just because I asked."

"Yes, we can both do that." Jodie paused. "Now ask me the other question."

"The other quest…. oh, yes." Colin rose from his chair, went round to Jodie's side of the table and knelt before her. Smiling broadly, he raised his voice. "Jodie Jordan, will you please marry me?"

A hush settled over all the surrounding tables. Jodie blushed furiously but announced fairly audibly: "There's nothing I should like better."

All the other diners applauded. Lacey bought drinks or coffees for everyone who wanted one.

****

As they left the restaurant Colin said, "I haven't even got a ring for you."

"We can look for a ring another time. And I never intended that you should go to a hotel." Jodie kissed him with passion and said, "Right now we're going home to my place, going to bed, and staying awake all night if I have anything to do with it. I can't wait until after the wedding even if you can!"

'*Must be the way getting to be a Captain in the Army makes you; straight to the point, and no mucking around,*' Lacey thought, but did not say. Why should he? He was delighted with her enthusiasm.

****

Tuesday morning, and spring sunshine poured through the windows onto the bed. The evening before, in their desperation to get into bed and to grips with each other all they thought of was pulling their clothes off. Pulling the curtains would have delayed the moment. Lacey and Jordan lay wrapped in each other's arms and perspiring somewhat after exerting themselves for mutual pleasure and satisfaction.

Jodie sighed with happiness and contentment. "How many times was that, then?"

"Don't ask me, darling. I lost count about four o'clock." He nuzzled a nipple. "Tell me something."

"Anything. Ask away." Colin nuzzled again.

"If you keep on doing that, I shan't be able to tell you anything."

"OK, I'll stop for a minute or two. What I want to know is, I was falling for you almost from the start, but it was clear to me that there was little chance of my feelings being reciprocated. I thought you were beautiful and very, very, intelligent. You just didn't seem to like me, though; you were abrupt, rude, making fun of me. And then last night, you agree to marry me. Before that we'd just had some interesting kisses and some cuddling. What happened?"

Jodie smiled and stroked Colin's hair. "Simple really. I'd never met anyone like you, apart from my Dad. You were polite, behaved like a gentleman all the time. You treated me as an equal, when many of the men I deal with look down on a woman, even if she is a Captain. Whether they're looking down or not, you can see they're sizing you up for sex, and many try their luck." Jodie rolled onto her back pushing her hair out of her eyes. "But you didn't try anything on at all." She hesitated again. "I know I can be all those horrid things you mentioned. It's a defence mechanism most of the time. But when I kissed you at the hotel, I hadn't been able to stop thinking about you, even though it was a really short time since we first met. And then, when you came up here on Sunday and Monday, I fell in love with you."

She turned her face to him once more, and said, "So when you were working up to ask me the vital question, and my stupid joke nearly put you off, I knew I had to get you to ask me to marry you. And I did, and then you did, and here we are." A few seconds later: "Are you alright with that?"

"Yes, very."

"Good, because you can go back to nuzzling these again."

****

After half-an-hour of rather gentler, slower exertion, they both fell asleep, but not for long. Colin's phone rang on the bedside cabinet. "Lacey."

"Mornin', sir. Harry Morton here."

"What time is it?"

"Half nine sir. You OK? You sound a bit groggy."

"Never been better Harry. I got engaged last night."

"Let me guess. To the Captain, sir?"

"Got it in one, Harry. Now, what's up?"

"Well, it's good and bad, I suppose. The Passport Control and airports etc really pulled their fingers out. A Maxim Schaliapin boarded a flight to Vienna at Gatwick early mornin' on the 28th, just like you thought. I'd given them his real name too, and they went further. They found he'd flown out of Vienna on an Aeroflot plane to Moscow within an hour of getting off the plane from here." Morton left a gap. "We're not going to get him now, are we sir?"

"Very unlikely, Harry. And I can't see him getting into hot water in Russia for killing a man who was to them a traitor. It causes them a little diplomatic embarrassment, that's all. But Putin never worries about that."

Lacey rolled over and got out of bed. "I'll be on my way back soon. Should be with you by noon. I'll come back with Peter as soon as I can. You get Kiara and Sharon in the incident room when we arrive so we can have a conflab."

He turned the phone off, called Peter Shuttleworth's mobile, knelt on the bed, kissed Jodie awake, told her in between kisses he'd got to go, had a shower, a piece of toast and a cup of tea she made him, and, after more hugs and kisses, was on the road with him in thirty minutes.

****

Peter Shuttleworth drove back to Chichester as fast as was legal, and they arrived at Chichester nick at twelve thirty pm. Morton, Charcko and Jones had gathered in the incident room. Sitting themselves around the room with Lacey's chair back to the whiteboard, the team brought each other up to date on what had happened during their various duties, and Sharon Jones entered it all on the board.

Kiara recalled from her study of the files the story about Schaplinov's visits to the Carpenters and the Grants in Long Buckby and Bristol. Colin asked her to phone these two families to find out if they had had any suspicion the Russian was about to flee the country. Both families were extremely shocked, but neither could cast any light on that. Alan Carpenter told her that Igor had a friend who had seen much more of him over the last two or three years, and gave Charcko Wendy Slater's address and phone number. Kiara phoned.

"Hello. Wendy Slater speaking. Who's calling please?"

Kiara introduced herself with her rank.

"What is this about?"

"Mrs Slater, I believe you know an Igor Vasilyevich Schaplinov."

"Why? Is he in trouble?"

"Do you know him?"

"Yes, I do, quite well. Or I should say I did. I haven't seen him for a couple of months."

"Why is that?"

"Oh, you know, we were what the papers call 'good friends' with all the implications, but he just seemed to be changing, so we sort of lost interest in each other. He said some odd things, and it put me off." She stopped for a few seconds. "So is he in trouble or not?"

"He's left the country, Mrs Slater. We think he's on his way back to Moscow after laying a false trail. I wondered whether you could shed any light on that."

After half-a-minute's silence, and a sigh, Wendy said, "Well, that probably explains a lot. If he was planning that, his enthusiasm for me must have been on the wane."

"That's not all he was planning, ma'am. You know of the Novichok poisoning in Chichester, I expect. Well, we have very strong evidence that Igor was the assassin."

"Why on earth would he do that, officer?"

"Our information is that he murdered a former Russian spy who sold secrets to Britain, and betrayed Schaplinov's father to the Russian secret service, so he was executed."

Again, Wendy Slater was silent for a few moments. Then she said, "That's very hard to take seriously, because he was such a nice man. But who can say? I'll tell you what though; it reminds me of something Igor said to me one night quite a while ago. He told me his father was a senior KGB officer. I'd completely forgotten that."

"Thank you, Mrs Slater. That may be useful. We may get a copper from Northampton to see you to take a statement. It may be there will be diplomatic moves to try to have the Russian Government send him back here for trial."

Wendy laughed. 'Well, I'm happy to make a statement, but I cannot see much chance of Igor being sent here."

"You may be right, but it's not my decision. It's probably not even my boss's decision; he's the Chief Inspector heading the investigation."

Kiara thanked Mrs Slater for her help and finished the call. She went back to the incident room and related her talk with Wendy. Lacey thanked her and said he was heading a discussion of what action to take with Sawyer and MI6. Shuttleworth said they obviously had to tell MI6 and the government what had happened. Morton and Charcko agreed.

Sharon Jones surprised everyone. "Well, we can tell them, or at least you can, sir, but I can't see much happening, can you?"

Charcko said, "Why not, Sharon? We've had a Russian here posing as someone come here to help us, murdering a spy we rescued from Russia in a swap, and gone back to Moscow free as a bird. Someone's got to do something. How d'you work that out: no-one will do anything?"

"Yeah, sounds strange, doesn't it? He wasn't just posing though, was he? The boffins at PD say he gave them lots of useful info. But look at what happened when you and the guv'nor here let Mamontov and Balkonsky go. He asked

Sawyer, and Sawyer didn't want any sort of row with the Russian government, all diplomats and stuff, did he? He agreed they should walk away."

"Quite right Sharon," Lacey joined in. "He pretended he didn't know much about Pedchenko, yet he'd been Archie decades ago, controlling his activities. He more or less denied, certainly would not admit, he was Archie. He admitted MI6 had set up Gordanov for betrayal by Pedchenko. And finally, he and his interrogators had let Schaplinov work at Porton, where our killer almost certainly acquired the Novichok he used for the murder."

"So 'e's not going to want to put 'is own neck on the block by pursuing this case any further and provokin' a Parliament inquiry. These VIPs never catch it really, do they?" Peter added.

Lacey laughed. "I cannot imagine the Prime Minister making a fuss about it either, having told everyone it was the two Russians."

Harry Morton's contribution was: "It was probably Sawyer who told the PM about the Russians, and we reckon we know it was Sawyer who got the Novichok bottles planted in the Brighton hotel."

Everybody laughed, and Lacey wound up with, "OK then. I'll tell the head of Counter Terrorism, he'll talk to Sawyer, and perhaps the PM, and no-one will ever hear anything much more about it. It'll be a nine days wonder in the media, and that will be the end of it." After a few seconds he added: "Unless I write a book about it, of course.

Epilogue

28th April, 2016. Wien-Schwechat Airport, Vienna

As Igor Schaplinov walked through the arrivals hall, he was thinking how painless his 'escape' from England had been. He'd boarded the British Airways flight at Gatwick not long after nine in the morning, and here he was, not as much as three hours later, about to be picked up by Major Rostov and a couple of other Russians from the Federal Security Service and flown back to Moscow. He had had his last day at work at Porton Down the day before, and been wished a good holiday by his colleagues, including Ken Nixon, who had been looking extremely worried and rather pale. Many made pleasant remarks about Italy, the lakes, the food, and the friendly people. If only they knew, but then they would soon enough, when the press were all over it.

On the plane from England, Igor had once or twice imagined the repeated public announcements that would soon be ringing out at LHR calling Mr Igor Schaplinov to board the EasyJet flight to Milan. He had come to Vienna under his alias of Schaliapin.

What he thought about now was how he had spent his last few weeks in England.

****

In Chichester, Saturday, 20th February Igor parked in the Northgate Carpark just after nine in the morning. Before he left Salisbury at seven, he had looked out the reading glasses he had bought from Mr Collard, the optician; he did not need them. Amongst his small collection of stationary items he had a box containing a roll of peel-off sticky labels. He had stripped one from the roll, and written Boris Mamontov, Chichester on it. Opening the spectacle case, he stuck the label on to the lining of the lid. It was all he needed to take.

Igor walked into the centre of town, and close by the Old Cross at the junction of the four main streets named after the four points of the compass, he asked for directions to the library. He was told to go along West Street past the cathedral, take the second turning on the right, and he would find the library about one hundred yards down on his left. This confirmed what he had found on the internet maps.

In another few minutes he was outside the library in Tower Street, and observed from the notice that it did not open until nine thirty. His plan would misfire if he waited in the street; he needed to go in after a few members had been in and out, so he walked away, and made his way back to the Old Cross. He wandered about for a while, bought 'The Times' in a newsagent's, found The Buttery Café in South Street, and went in. He had to descend the steps into what appeared to have been a crypt or other mediaeval underground chamber, with stone pillars supporting the stone ceiling. He ordered a black coffee and pretended to be reading the paper.

An hour later he finished his drink, paid and made his way back to the library. Outside, he knelt down, ostensibly to retie his shoelaces, and, having checked the coast was clear, placed the spectacle case on the ground and pushed it away a few feet as he stood up. He started to step away, appeared to notice the case, and walked over to it and picked it up. Having opened it and read the label, he entered the library and went to speak to a member of staff sitting at a small desk further inside the building. The dark-haired young woman took off her glasses, looked up from the computer screen, and said, "How can I help you, sir?"

"Good morning. I was just passing the library and saw this spectacle case near the door here. It's got a label in it. Look,"

Igor opened the case and showed the lady the label. "See, it says Boris Mamontov, and I wondered whether you might have a customer of that name."

"Well, I can look, sir, but I'm not sure I should tell you anything. It's his privacy." She turned back to the computer keyboard and was clearly typing in the name after searching for the members' directory.

"Have you got it?"

"Yes, but I can't share it with you. You can leave it here and we can ask him to come and collect it."

"Well, I suppose that would be OK, but it's a bit rough on him, don't you think? I mean, I could take them to him today."

"I'm sorry sir, but ...."

"OK, forget it, but you wear glasses yourself. Supposing you lost them and found out you could have had them back straight away, but someone hung on to them over a whole weekend or longer? How would you feel?"

"Yes, I see what you mean." She took out a post-it pad and wrote the address in Alexandra Road, and handed it to Igor. "I just hope I don't get into trouble."

"Don't worry. I'm not going to tell anyone, apart from Mr Mamontov. I'll just say that a very kind person helped me."

She wished him luck, and he left. Unbelievable luck was what he called it. He intended to ask in the centre of the city for directions to Alexandra Road, but as he passed the Cathedral, he noticed a large scale map on a notice board, and studied it for half a minute. It took him just over ten minutes to walk there, identify the house by its number, and another ten to get back to his car. He was back in Salisbury just after two, having stopped for lunch at a pub in Alton.

Now he knew exactly where to find Pedchenko he could finalise his plans.

Regarding the holiday (or rather, his escape), he decided to go straight to the top, and asked for a meeting with Horne-Bassett, which he had in the middle of the following week. He was surprised how easy it was. The three-piece suit was thick grey tweed for the winter, and the gold watch chain was as noticeable as it had been previously.

Horne-Bassett asked, "But you've taken holidays before, haven't you?"

"I have, sir, but not abroad, and because I'm Russian, I wanted to make sure I don't do anything wrong and lose my job here, or get into some worse kind of trouble."

The big man leaned his elbows onto the desk and laughed. "Well I'm damned, Shaplinov. You've been here a few years now, I've never heard anything but good reports about you, and you brought us some good secret stuff about Russia and Pochep, and what goes on there. The top brass in London were very pleased." He broke off, smiling. "Where do you want to go?"

"I thought I'd like to take a look at the lakes in Northern Italy."

"Good choice. Try Petenasco on Lake Orta. One of the smaller lakes, but some lovely small hotels and a charming village. Lovely walks and boat trips too. Not too far from Lake Maggiore, where Stresa and the Boromeo Islands are well worth a visit. Mrs Horne-Bassett and I have had a couple of really wonderful holidays in that part of Italy. When will you go?"

"Perhaps some time in April? Maybe the end of the month? I don't fancy going in the winter."

"That's good. There might not be too many tourists there then. Tell your superiors I said permission is granted, and it gives them time to arrange for your work to be covered by other personnel. Good luck."

"Thank you, sir," Igor said, thinking that Horne-Bassett always used a big word and as many as possible. *'He's rather pompous, but he's given me what I wanted, so I shouldn't complain,'* he thought.

The following Saturday morning, Igor drove to Shaftesbury, and was sitting in Hays Travel by nine thirty. He booked an afternoon flight to Milan from London Heathrow for 28th of April in the name of Schaplinov. Then he explored the lovely old town, and had lunch in an old pub, The Ship Inn. He was very glad of a pint of bitter after his walk; Gold Hill was rather taxing, fit though he thought himself.

He also found a charity shop and bought a suitcase, clean and presentable but not fancy or likely to attract attention. When he got back to his flat, he affixed the new labels he had picked up at the travel agents, having written the name and other details on them.

The following Saturday he drove to Winchester, found a travel agent, and booked another airline ticket to Vienna, a very early flight for the same date as his LHR flight, but leaving from Gatwick. This one was in his alias, Maxim Schaliapin. He booked neither flight on the internet; if anything went wrong, or his computer were hacked, it would be too easy for the Police to find out what he had done.

The next day at work, to keep up the charade that he and Ken were still friends – as important for Nixon as for Igor – he arranged to have a Saturday dinner with him, Marion, and Wendy, who was to visit him in a couple of weeks' time, though with waning enthusiasm. He really could not see the relationship lasting much longer.

The dinner went well for the four of them; Marion was pleased to see him and Wendy, all appeared to be normal, though Ken was rather quieter than usual. It was now the middle of March.

The following week, Igor went to the Caspian and inserted an envelope into the menu folder which he handed to Ismail as he ordered, for onward transmission to the Russian Embassy. The note inside gave full details of his flight to Vienna and sought confirmation he would be collected for a connecting flight to Moscow, which the Embassy would organise. He also asked them to send him a new passport and visas in his own name and that of his alias. As both were the names of Russian citizens, he needed visas for both Italy and Austria.

A week later, on a day off, Igor went to London by train, and visited Watts & Co in Tufton Street, Westminster. He could have got what he wanted at a costume hire shop, but he wanted to be absolutely sure that what he bought was genuine and would stand up to the closest scrutiny if necessary. At this renowned and long-established clerical clothing company he could be certain of all that. He told a very pleasant tailoring consultant that he lived in Salisbury and wanted a new outfit for his day-to-day functions at the cathedral. Whilst being served he swept many a glance around the premises and was astounded by the variety of designs and extraordinary truly bright, magnificent capes and other regalia for bishops, priests and deacons.

"May I suggest made to measure, sir?"

"Thanks, but I'm only here for the day, and want to buy off the peg, please."

He bought black trousers, a matching black jacket, a black shirt with slots for a white clerical collar, and a collar to fit it. They even offered some cufflinks in the shape of a cross or a fish, so he chose the cross. Finally, he tried on a fawn linen summer jacket which the tailor assured him was what would be most suitable when the weather warmed up. He acquired that, too.

Two months later, on Friday, 22nd April, 2024, back in Chichester, Igor parked his car in The Woolstaplers Car Park, walked into the Travel Lodge in Chapel Street, and asked for the room he had booked several days before from a public call box. It had a king size bed, and although the room was basic, the bed looked good. He wished he had someone to share it with, but the last thing he needed was someone knowing where he was and what he was doing.

After locking the door, he spread a thick black plastic bag over the sink, put a newspaper he had bought on the plastic, donned the complete suit of safety protection gear Ken Nixon had given him, including a special facemask. Then he used the perfume bottle to spray the paper with a large dose of Novichok and put it in a plastic lined A4 envelope he had brought for the purpose. He washed the bottle, the mask and the plastic bag very carefully in water he boiled in the kettle. He boiled the kettle four more times and, still wearing the gear, used the hot water to clean the sink as best as he could. He showered himself thoroughly for fifteen minutes. As far as he knew he had not come into contact with the poison. Finally, he put all the contaminated clothes, gloves and mask in another plastic bag.

At ten pm, he took the bottle and the envelope, went out, and walked rapidly to Alexandra Road. He saw that the lights were on in Pedchenko's house. He put on a clean pair of long rubber gloves, walked as silently as possible up the short front path and put the envelope, which he had addressed to Boris Mamontov, on the doorstep under two empty milk bottles he saw there. Having done that, he sprayed more Novichok around the lock and door handle and walked away equally rapidly.

Igor went back to his hotel, put the gloves he had just used in the bag, showered thoroughly again, dined in a pub in the Hornet, watched a little TV, and went to bed.

In the morning, early, he ate the basic breakfast of cereal, toast and tea left in his room, paid his bill in cash, and left. He was wearing his vicar's get-up, but without the white collar, which was in his jacket pocket. The top shirt button was undone so he looked quite casual. It was a fine day. He had the Panama hat on, but with the centre crease pushed out so it looked less like a homburg and almost like a bowler hat. He carried the linen jacket, folded inside out to show a white silk lining, over his arm. He took the black plastic bag with his other clothes, and the bag of contaminated gear, to his car. He hoped that the poisoned newspaper and door would be enough to do away with his Dad's murderer, but he had a default plan. Igor carried a black leather handbag, on a strap over his shoulder. That bag contained the Novichok 'perfume' bottle, a pair of pinkish, almost flesh coloured rubber gloves, a red cravat, a pair of large lensed, dark sunglasses, and green baseball cap, and the plastic bag the gloves came in.

He walked to the toilets in Priory Park, where he inserted the clerical collar into the black shirt, and put on the linen jacket. He walked into the park and up onto the path round the old Roman Wall. From there he could see across the football field to Pedchenko's front door.

He saw a youngish man come out, take in some full milk bottles and the envelope, and go back inside. Igor strolled up and down the length of wall opposite the house, apparently meditating, but never taking his eyes off the house for more than a few seconds. Soon after ten o'clock he saw the young man and Pedchenko come out. The ex-spy turned back to the door to close it and appeared to be locking it. *With luck*, Igor thought, *he will have touched the poison on the door and handle.*

He watched as the two Russians came straight across the pitch towards him, noticing that by the time they reached New Park Road they seemed to be staggering a bit. They made it across the road and more or less collapsed onto a park bench almost directly below where he stood. The only precaution Igor could take for his own protection was to put on the pair of pinkish rubber gloves, which he hoped would not be easy to spot. He was still up at the wall at that point. He hurried out of the park, his hat with its centre crease restored pulled well over his forehead. As he went round the corner into New Park Road, he passed an elderly lady walking the other way.

The two men were still on the bench. They seemed to have fallen asleep. As he approached them, he took the bottle from the bag. He slowed his pace, and pretending to be studying and admiring the shrubs and the plants in the flowerbeds, he stepped off the footpath, made his way behind the bench, and gave the back of the older man's head and neck a massive blast of Novichok from the perfume bottle as he passed behind them.

He continued to stroll along the garden area for another hundred yards or so, then returned to the footpath, turned left at the roundabout, and walked quickly along Franklin Place, crossed the road by the pedestrian underpass, and went into the toilets in Northgate Carpark. There he put the gloves into their bag, took out the collar, opened the top three buttons of the shirt, and left the jacket and hat on the peg in the cubicle. He tied the red cravat round his neck, put on the sunglasses, picked up the leather bag. He also put the gloves and their bag into the leather one. Igor urinated and flushed the toilet, and then walked casually back to his car in Woolstaplers.

Igor drove in strict obedience to all speed limits and other rules of the road back to Salisbury, listening to Radio Four. He was very confident no-one had any reason yet to connect him with the likely certain death of Pedchenko, who was already being reported on the radio in a storm of publicity to be very seriously, and probably fatally ill in hospital. Further on, he halted in Petersfield, took a rowing boat out on the lake for an hour, enjoying the sun and the exercise, and dropped the perfume bottle into what looked like the deepest water. The black leather bag he deposited in a waste bin as he left the boat with its owner.

On Monday he returned to work, where there was a great deal of chatter about the assassination, in which he took a small part. He could not afford to keep away from it, for fear of arousing suspicion, but on the other hand he had to avoid saying too much for the same reason. Wednesday, he said goodbye to his colleagues and gave them two good bottles of wine to share, cleared out of his flat, leaving it looking as though he still lived there and would be back there from holiday, and drove to Gatwick, booked into a hotel, got up early the next day, and, as Maxim Schaliapin, boarded his plane to Vienna.

He was not without some slight concern that Rostov might have been ordered to arrest him for the murder of Pedchenko, as the Russian government was bound to have picked up news of his death from the British and other Western Press and TV. His worry was only low level because he was happy that when he came to explain why he had done it, he would actually be regarded as a hero on two counts. First, for having liquidated a traitor who should have been executed if Yeltsin hadn't abolished the death penalty, Secondly, for exacting revenge on the Judas who had betrayed his father, a man who had always served the Motherland faithfully and honourably, and who had met a dishonourable death because of that treachery. He could prove the treachery with the trial transcript.

His mother, Irena, would be so happy to see him again, and he her. His cup was running over. Maybe he'd even find a good, intelligent Russian woman to share his life, and perhaps bear him a child or two. After all, his four-year loving and affectionate relationship with Wendy had changed him; something stable was infinitely preferable to the occasional temporary affairs and one night stands to which he'd been accustomed. He had it on his conscience that he might be said to have taken advantage of her but reflected that she had made the first very overt offer of sex, not him, happy about that as he had been.

Advantage had also been taken of Ken Nixon. Igor had a conscience about that too, but it was Ken's own fault, he thought. He had been stupid to foul his own doorstep by having that sort of liaison with a man in Salisbury. If they'd taken themselves off to London or Newcastle or somewhere else miles from Porton Down, no-one would have been any the wiser. In this day and age Ken would have been in the clear if he had come out of the closet, but his marriage and his relationship with his children would probably have collapsed.

Igor had had enough of being a spy and of lethal poisons and weapons of war. He'd look for a civilian job. There was money to be made in Russia now.

Acknowledgements

It is impossible to write a novel like this one without being able to get a lot of information. I read newspapers, watch what I hope are serious news programmes on TV and listen to them on the radio. I'm not very interested in what journalists and pundits think is going on. I prefer to get what I hope are the facts and then make up my own mind.

If you get your information from something like Sky News you are almost certainly being led by the nose up a distorted blind alley. I avoid all commercial media if I can. The Australian Broadcasting Corporation has a reputation of being rather left wing, but I do not agree. It has that slur because it is not suffused with greed, and does not kowtow to big business, as it does not have to court advertisers. To a very large extent, the Australian SBS broadcasts are similar. The BBC is best of all.

Much of the information included in here comes from Wikipedia, but the parts about Belokurikha and Barnaul come from a holiday my wife, Christine, and I had in that part of Siberia in 2003, as guests of a truly wonderful family. Christine had been their guest in 1994 when she was a mature student doing Russian at college in Chichester. Their son came and stayed with us as part of an exchange.

The book by Robert Harris and Jeremy Paxman, "A Higher Form of Killing", surely a sarcastic title, is a must read for anyone who thinks governments of any colour are capable of telling the truth.

Unlike my other efforts at novels, my wife was its only proof-reader, and did a grand job. However, no-one, no matter how clever, is likely to detect every mistake I make.

My friend Michael Davies put this to publication for me with Ingram Spark. He has helped many writers in this way, as well as publishing an enormous number of his own books. My favourites are *"The Jason Conspiracy"* and *"The Nightmares of God",* and several of his crime stories.

I dedicate this book to Christine, my rod and staff.

Terry Stanton.
Port Macquarie, NSW.
October, 2024.

www.ingramcontent.com/pod-product-compliance
Lightning Source LLC
Chambersburg PA
CBHW070158120726
47909CB00001B/164

* 9 7 8 0 6 4 5 9 6 7 2 9 6 *